TRUTH
IN *wildflowers*

KIMBERLY ROSE

For our communion with our friends & foes.

EBooks are not transferable. They cannot be sold, shared, or given away. The unauthorized reproduction or distribution of this copyrighted work is a crime punishable by law. No part of this book may be scanned, uploaded to or downloaded from file sharing sites, or distributed in any other way via the Internet or any other means, electronic or print, without the publisher's permission. Criminal copyright infringement, including infringement without monetary gain, is investigated by the FBI and is punishable by up to 5 years in federal prison and a fine of $250,000 (http://www.fbi.gov/ipr/).

This book is a work of fiction. The names, characters, places, and incidents are fictitious or have been used fictitiously, and are not to be construed as real in any way. Any resemblance to persons, living or dead, actual events, locales, or organizations is entirely coincidental.

All Rights Are Reserved. No part of this book may be used or reproduced in any manner whatsoever without written permission, except in the case of brief quotations embodied in critical articles and reviews.

Copyright © October 2014 by Kimberly Rose
Ebook ISBN: 978-0-9909103-0-5
Print ISBN: 978-0-9909103-1-2

To Vickie, the rocky to my road, and the vodka to my tonic.

PROLOGUE

August

Blurred. Black, and grey, maybe some white, but mostly black. There's a lot of black. My converse blur below me set amidst a pile of bottles on the dry dirt. I should have never come here. I'm not blind to the power of this place. I didn't flee here to find any peace in my hell. I came here to add to the flames. I didn't care much for improving my mood. How could I? My mom told me to stay present. Whatever that means. She encouraged me to take the time I need to grieve, but that people needed me. I call bullshit. The one whom truly ever needed me isn't here. No one needs me. I don't even need myself. What good is a guy who can't save the people he loves? I failed her.

"Dude." Wes's shoes crunched up the path behind me. "The dirt field and that six hundred and seventy two pack treating you alright?" He sat down beside me on the bench and patted my shoulder causing my limp body to sway.

"No." I shrugged my shoulders at him. Getting drunk sounded like a fantastic idea when the service ended, now not so much. I still remembered it all. I still felt it all. Only now my singed soul blurred a little to the left.

I held my shit together since the night of the accident trying to be the strong one. Spouting words of consolation and promising some sick divine plan in this hell. The moment the casket descended into the ground and disappeared in the grass that façade crumbled. My lungs collapsed with my heart folding in on itself. I suffocated on my grief. Thick dark hands enveloped my throat and squeezed tight until my eyes watered. The bastard choked any purpose of living out of me.

"I'm not sure what to say here." Wes held out a pack of gummy bears, but I declined.

"Nothing." I preferred the silence. I liked being wrapped in the isolation more than token words of sympathy. *Sorry*? The word and the lowered eyes accompanying it made my stomach churn. I'm not deserving of compassion or hope to heal. What I deserve, is to feel the bone crushing pain to remind me of how I fucked up.

The weather at the service was abnormally windy. The scent of freshly cut grass mixed with cheap cologne assaulted me with blow after blow. Life. I fled. Familiar voices rapped in the wind at my back, but I didn't stop. I ran until I reached the stagnant space of my car where the wind couldn't pummel me and the grass couldn't nauseate me. I yearned to be roused from my nightmare. I needed to wake up to the hillside covered in color and life, but when I got here I received a sucker punch in the form of dirt, miles and miles of dirt. No color, and no life.

We sat in uncomfortable silence when Wes leaned down to the rocky soil below us. Out of the corner of my eye I caught him twirling a dandelion in his fingers. I chanced a glance at the flower and followed its fluttered decent to the ground as his fingers let go.

"Come on." Wes stood up and dusted off his black pants. He looked ridiculous in them. He shouldn't have dressed up. I didn't. "I'm going to go find a trash can for all these." He kicked a glass bottle. The empty vessel rolled across the dirt until it was stopped abruptly by a rock. "Then I'm taking you home."

"I can't go home." I couldn't face any reminders of my life being taken away. My entire life gone, but I was still living. The twisted world cursed me.

"Alright dude," Wes said. "You can crash with me as long as you need too, but we need to get out of here. We are taking this day by day, and this day is about done." He cocked his head towards the sun beginning its decent below the hill.

I nodded and stood up on swaying legs, but only because I had to piss. Days, the beginnings, the ends, the in-betweens, they didn't mean anything to me anymore. The days were just heartless bastards.

CHAPTER 1

Kensie

I wondered if I could catch the breeze. If possible, I'd catch one and bottle up the ease in which it blows. I flopped my hand out the window, and only the wind forced it to move. The streams of fresh air wove themselves between my fingers and clasped tightly around my palm. Trading places with my arm, I slid my head out of the window. The caress of the fresh air brushing across my face intoxicated me. It stroked its fingers through my hair, and with a tender touch, it pulled out all my worrisome thoughts.

"What the hell are you doing? Get your head back in the vehicle." Lennon's shriek yanked me from my Zen.

"Clearing my head." I pulled my head back into the stillness of the bug.

"More like losing your head to a semi!"

I rolled my eyes at Lennon and tossed my cell phone back into my bag. "You're so dramatic sometimes." "Never." She grinned at me and focused back on the road. "What'd your dad say?"

I deleted the voicemail my dad's wife left me. He and I seldom spoke, but when we did, our conversations resembled nails on a chalkboard. I don't remember when our relationship morphed into one of obligation, but it was somewhere between the pain and numbness.

His wife was cordial enough, but she was always making excuses for him. His stepdaughter succeeds on both social and academic scales. She was what Lennon called a Facebook whore, collecting friends like baseball cards. Of course, his stepson was an athlete, unlike me. Dance doesn't qualify as a sport.

My dad left my mom. Said he wasn't happy anymore, hadn't been in years. I couldn't pinpoint the exact moment it all fell apart, though I tried to in my young mind. I noticed the tension steadily increase the older I got. When he'd encourage me to try a sport instead of dance, they fought over how to support my interests. When I brought home C's instead of A's, they fought over who was supposed to help me with my homework. I ev en remember them fighting over how late to let me stay up on a school night.

"He said nothing because, that was Jodie." Always Jodie. "They want to see me for Thanksgiving." I couldn't help but roll my eyes as I climbed out of the passenger side of Lennon's old bug and gave the door a couple of good slams before it latched shut.

"He can't even call his own daughter himself? Daddy Douche needs to man up."

Lennon knew all about my absent father

and his impeccable, shiny new family. I don't often gripe outwardly about the situation, but she's lived with me long enough to catch on.

I sighed to myself, holding the door open for her as we walked into the tattoo shop, causing a jingle from the bells tied around the handle. "If you go, you should wear that Halloween costume from last year. That'll shock the self-righteous shit right out of that family." Lennon strutted past me.

"The naughty Pocahontas one? I still can't believe I let you talk me into that." Lennon had somehow convinced me to be her date to one of the frat parties. She went as a "Tantric Turkey." I didn't ask any questions, but it turned out amazing with a splattering of brightly colored feathers in just the right places.

"You rocked it. Especially the pigtails." Oh the pigtails. Frat boys liked tiny pieces of cloth mixed with those beauties. By the end of the night, Lennon became known as my roommate with benefits. I had said what I needed in order to keep them away. "This place seems legit." Lennon sauntered around the waiting space.

The shop exceeded my expectations thus far, resembling more of a lounge than the concrete abyss I'd imagined. The light was brighter in here, and it took my eyes a beat to adjust. I blinked several times, letting the cream walls come into focus. Pictures of tattoos and artwork that resemble tattoos, cover every surface of the walls. Thick, burgundy curtains over the front windows block out most of the natural light.

"Be with you fine ladies in a sec!" A voice

hollered above the hum of a tattoo needle and a soundtrack of instrumental rock. Lennon raised her studded eyebrow and sauntered to the wall of example pieces. She fit in perfectly here with her spunky red hair and pixie cut. She had donned one of her trademark band shirts and plaid skirts that only seemed to highlight her personality.

"I don't know... a butterfly or something?" I suggested, shrugging my shoulders and tracing my eyes casually across the artwork. I admit this wasn't a well-executed plan. One look at my dad's new family pictures posted on Facebook courtesy of his "daughter", and I was pulling Lennon out of the door and down to the shop. I needed something to permanently set me apart from the explosion of khaki and polo smiling back at me.

"Seriously." She stared at me. "A butterfly?" I didn't know what was wrong with a butterfly. I'd seen a lot of girls on campus with them.

"Okay... a rose?" I suggested with a toss of my hand in the air. Lennon's stare stabbed the side of my face.

"Oh Jesus... my individuality is curling up in a fetal position. You know you could always do something less drastic. A little nose ring would look spicy on you."

"Nope, it's got to be a tattoo, Len." My dad despised tattoos, and his perfect little family was pretty clean-cut, so I doubted any of them had one. How cool would it be, though, if my sweet stepsister, Bethany, had a tramp stamp? Dad would probably lose faith in humanity, or at least in clean-shaven, suit-wearing humanity.

I'd always tried to keep myself looking just like their family. I guess that was how I feigned inclusion. From the outside, I blended in flawlessly sitting at the dinner table with them every Sunday night. On the inside, however, I never fit in. A weed in their otherwise manicured garden.

"Well, let's do this." Lennon hopped her elbows up on the front counter causing her little feet to dangle off the ground. "Hello? Earth to tattoo man. I'm gonna need a walker here soon." Oh no, my little friend wasn't dramatic at all. I hip checked her, or intended too.

A low chuckle vibrated through the floor, shocking my senses and rendering me motionless. I felt the tremors pulse up through my feet, then legs, right up to the ridges of my hips. The clanking of the tattoo gun echoed in the empty space.

"What can I get ya, little lady?" A tall and extensively tatted guy walked up to the counter, wiping his hands on a paper towel and laughing. The chuckle didn't belong to him—shame because he was one hunk of a man, though a little furry on the face for me.

"Well, cowboy," Lennon clicked her tongue against the roof of her mouth, "my girl here wants a generic tattoo lacking any sense of imagination or identity." She rolled her eyes at me and pointed a tiny finger to the artist. "But make sure it is aesthetically pleasing."

The artist popped his lips and opened his arms wide.

"Lucky for you, I specialize in pleasing and

have been known to look good doing it."

Lennon and I shared a look of shocked horror and she narrowed her eyes at him. "You keep your hands on your gun, cowboy. She can please herself fine on her own." My face heated. I should have never told her about my rabbit.

Cowboy wasn't fazed. "Noted. Let me finish up this ugly fool back here and I'll be with you in a minute." He smiled a dimpled smile and winked at me as he headed back to the customer he was finishing up. "For the record," he shouted back at us, "I can do better than fine."

I slapped my palm to my face, but I laughed. I couldn't pretend his overinflated ego wasn't a bit charming.

"And so can he." He winked directly at me and tossed his head toward the customer in the tattoo chair.

"Thanks, dude." The customer spoke, and holy vibrations. It was *him*. I feared looking in his direction, but the way my skin prickled suggested he had been watching me before I noticed him. I faced Lennon but chanced a quick glance at the ugly fool out of the corner of my eye.

"Shit," I murmured under my breath. He was anything but ugly. He was quite the opposite of ugly. He was handsome, gorgeous, masculine, fucking hot, but nope, not ugly at all. I had to repeat the word ugly in my head to keep myself from doing the very thing I was doing now. My traitorous body had drifted to face him without my permission and left me in prime gawking range, drooling, gaping, call it what you will. I called it appreciating. I was appreciating his resistance to ugly and mentally raising my arm in support.

"Shades of blue or plum?" Lennon's snarky voice broke my stare.

"Blue or plum what?" Seriously, now was not the time to discuss colors. I was knee-deep in a personal revelation.

"For the wedding." I widened my eyes in embarrassment over being caught. "Maybe you should date him first." She patted my shoulder and walked through the saloon door, leaving it to swing between the two front counters. My breathing matched the nervous rhythm. I hadn't been on a date in three years.

"Check it out, little lady." The tattoo artist waved Lennon over. "See if this is up to your expectations." His eyes bypassed Lennon and winked directly at me again.

"It's Lennon, cowboy, and my friend you keep winking at is Kensie." Her eyes urged me to meet her at the chair where the vibrating stranger sat.

"Stop winking at her, Wes." His voice tickled my insides, but I forced myself to walk. I came up on the three of them, growing self-conscious with the stranger's eyes following me. I sensed them daring me to make contact, but I ignored the pull. Instead, I peeked around him and looked at the tattoo on his back.

It rendered me speechless. From what I noticed in my hungry assessment of his large frame, this guy didn't have any other tattoos. This one, though, this one covered most his solid back. The tattoo mimicked a series open wounds on his skin, an artistic juxtaposition of grotesque and beauty. Each wound held bold script work between the lash marks. Wes (I assumed was the artist's name) wiped a fresh red scar he had just completed.

"What does it say?" I asked in a soft voice that didn't sound like my own. If I had moved closer, I'd be able to read it, but the distance I now stood from the stranger was a safe one.

"It's from this song called 'Sweet and Low' by this band Augustana," he answered, turning around and locking his dark eyes on mine. They held my own reflecting relief at finally making a connection. They also resembled chocolate. I loved chocolate. What a coincidence that his eyes were the exact shade of chocolate I loved, and why was I comparing his eyes to food? I mentally put his chocolate eyes back in their velvet box, where I could devour them later.

"I know that band." Thank God I sounded more certain of myself this time. "They're one of my favorites. I think in this song he's asking, or begging really for an honest love?" I asked as if the song wasn't familiar, when I'd actually spent hours in my room with it on repeat.

His eyes narrowed at me. "Or asking for her to save him from his fear of love?" He posed his own interpretation as a question too, but not because he didn't know the song. No, he had to be well acquainted with the lyrics to have them inked into his skin.

"Fear," I muttered, once again losing the strength in my voice. I knew fear well, but that didn't mean I wanted it permanently etched on my body. Having fear etched on my heart was plenty.

"See? That's a tattoo worth having," Lennon said from behind me, breaking my stare. "A butterfly you picked off the wall isn't something you'll want forever." She had a valid point. I felt more connected to this stranger's tattoo than I did to the one I chose five minutes ago.

I disregarded Lennon, wanting to know more about the stranger. "Why all the scars with the lyrics?" I found myself curious about his tattoo, but more than that, I was curious about him. This piece of art across his back reflected a piece of his soul back onto the world. It fascinated me.

His eyes flickered around the room. Crap, I made him uncomfortable. "I mean if you don't mind me asking. You don't have to answer. I was just curious. It's just that it's really gorgeous and seems like it may hold meaning..."

"It's okay." He cut off of my nervous ramble with a reassuring smile that did things to me, wonderful, tingly things. "You're right. It means a lot to me." He adjusted himself in the chair to get more comfortable, but I doubt he sought physical comfort. No, my question clearly caused an amount of irritation in him, or annoyance. Oh god, I hope I'm not annoying him. "It represents my past, things I need to remember." His answer was vague, but it wasn't my place to pry any further.

"My past choices don't need a permanent place on my skin." The thought made me sick. What would I even get? A shadow? That was what I had become, after all, a reflection of myself without any definition.

"You're not immortalizing the poor choices you may have made." He worried his bottom lip between his teeth, choosing his words carefully. "Think of it as representing your survival of those choices that made you who you are today."

"What if I don't like where I am today?" He stared at me then. The kind of stare that strips you bare, but I was cloaked in warmth.

"Then I suppose you keep moving." He watched me until I broke eye contact. He'd made it sound so simple. I'd been trying to move for three years only to find myself in the same place I'd started.

"Hmph." I'd forgotten Lennon was here with me. For a moment, only my stranger and I existed, but there was Lennon now smirking at me along with Wes. I shook myself from our moment.

Sensing my unease, my stranger gave me an out. "When you do decide what you want, Wes here is the perfect guy to do it." Wes puffed up his chest at the compliment and smirked, about to say something when my stranger cut in. "Shut it, Wes. I meant you're a talented artist. " He quickly caught himself before Wes had a chance to respond. "And he'll be completely respectful and appropriate the entire time." He glared over at his friend and reached into his pocket grabbing a handful of gummy bears. He tossed them into his mouth and chewed, moving his puckered lips in a circular motion.

"Dude, it's like you don't even know me,"

Wes said with a slow shake of his head and snapped me from my thoughts of what life like a red gummy was like right now—lucky little bitch.

"Oh I know you," my stranger said, "too well." I didn't miss the warning glare he gave his friend.

Wes put his arms up in front of himself defensively and winked at me again.

"You're pushin' it." My stranger mumbled lowly, but my ears were so in tune with his voice I heard it clearly. My heart rate picked up, creating a pulse in the walls around me. Time to go.

I forced a smile at the two of them, but it got stuck on my stranger and widened. "Okay, thanks, guys. Your work really is amazing, Wes, and thank you..." My good-bye trailed off, not knowing his name.

"August." He offered his hand and I couldn't believe it happened. I mean, I've read it in my romance novels, but stuff like this didn't happen. I got the chills when I placed my hand in his. They must keep the air pretty cool in places like this. I'd have to remember to bring a sweater when I come back.

"Uh-hum... Staring... Uh-hum." Lennon coughed behind me, pointing out the obvious. He had a perfect smile. The corners of his eyes wrinkled, making his chocolate eyes sparkle. His teeth, straight and white, but not Ross on *Friends* white, and his lips glistened from where he had just licked them. I bet they tasted like spearmint or maybe peppermint. Crap, I did it again. I mentally put his lips back in their wrapper.

"Kensie. I'm Kensie." My body had warmed, leaving me hot and flustered. I needed air. They must keep it pretty warm in here for some reason. I'd have to remember to wear a tank top when I come back.

"Nice to meet you, Kensie." He licked his lips again. Damn him and his bubble gum lips. "Maybe I'll see you two in here again soon." He nodded toward Lennon, who had a shit-eating grin directed right at me.

"Yep, will do. We'll let you guys get back to it. I'll be in touch, Wes." I grabbed Lennon's hand and dragged her out of the shop while rambling on about coming in sometime after the semester was over. I almost made my way out unscathed until the vibrations of his laughter buzzed through my body, arousing the dormant curiosity in me.

***

"Seriously, Kensie, I don't think I've ever seen you get so flustered over a guy." Lennon kicked off her black converse sending them to thump against her closet door. "I wasn't flustered Len. The thermostat was all messed up and it was making me uncomfortable." She harped on me the entire drive back to our dorm and wouldn't let up. Becoming flustered wasn't typical behavior for me, and Lennon wasn't about to pretend she didn't notice.

For three years I'd avoided dating. My dry spell started after the night that scared me into celibacy, but I couldn't have explained why it continued, until now. No one man had captured my attention in those three years the way August did today in just a few minutes. Maybe it was purely a physical attraction, but even that hadn't happened in three years. I should be ecstatic to find my lady bits haven't grown dependent on size C batteries, but instead it terrified the ever-loving shit out of me.

"Thermostat my ass. You two were licking each other in your minds. I saw it." Lennon continued to set up her computer and pull out her English Lit book.

"Licking? Really Lennon?" I stared at her, even though I should have been used to what comes out of her mouth. "Telepathic tonguing I call it." She waggled her eyebrows making it difficult to hide my smile.

"Hi, girls." Capri waltzed in and interrupted the beginning of Lennon's recollection of my humiliation. Capri is in her English Literature class here at SDSU. We met when she started coming over to study with Lennon in the beginning of the semester and bonded immediately. Capri placed her books on Lennon's bed and sat herself next to them with one long slender leg crossed over the other.

"Lennon won't stop nagging me about some guy from the tattoo shop today."

"I heard. She texted me and said he gave you an eyegasm." Capri giggled.

"Ugh, Len! Really?" I groaned and smothered myself with my own pillow. She wasn't too far off.

"Stop fighting it, Kensie." I heard Lennon and Capri giggling and peered up above my pillow to see Lennon biting on her lip and shimmying her shoulders. I laughed and threw my pillow at her.

Lennon side stepped my pillow and plopped herself down on the bed next to Capri. She tapped her pencil against her notebook. "See, and right here, this is you."

Capri looked over to Lennon's notes and nodded in approval. "Yeah that is you, Kensie."

"Who, Kim K? Megan Fox? Oh I know, Gail?" I asked.

"I'm sorry, who?" Lennon put her hand up to stop me.

"Oprah's friend, the one who got to go all over the country and eat?" Capri said and looked at me for confirmation.

"Yeah, Gail King. She got to eat pizza and burgers all over the place." Seriously, she had the best job.

Lennon shook her head at me, "No, no, just...no." She tapped her paper again, "You my friend are Elizabeth Bennett."

"Omigod I *love* Elizabeth." If I could go back in time and have dinner with anyone it wouldn't be Elizabeth. No, I'd *be* Elizabeth. There's nothing better than a strong and intelligent woman, and she's a prime example of what I had been trying to accomplish for myself. It doesn't help she landed the Regency Era hottie.

"Yeah, I know you do," Lennon scoffed at me. "Now I get why. You're oblivious to what's right in front of you." For the record, I am not oblivious to how ridiculous I looked ogling August today. I am very much aware.

"I always liked Georgiana," Capri piped up scribbling away in her notes. Lennon huffed and thumped her head against the wall behind her. I could see why Capri favored that character though. She was a lot like the shy and beautiful sister of Darcy. "What?" Capri glared at Lennon. "She's sweet. I wish Austen wrote a follow up book so we could see Georgiana fall in love too."

Lennon flopped to her side across a pile of textbooks. Her hysterics had Capri and I both laughing. "Okay," Capri swatted Lennon's rear end, "who should we like oh, wise literature major?"

Lennon pulled herself upright and smiled broadly. "Katniss. That chick is badass. She even has a suit that lights on fire." Call me Katniss then because I'm positive I've been on fire since about three o'clock today. "You know what Kens?" Uh oh, she squinted at me. "We need to light you on fire."

"Excuse me?" I asked at the same time Capri dropped her pen on her notebook. "You want to set me on fire?"

"Not literally, figuratively. Whether you admit it or not, a revelation took place today. Change is acomin.'" Lennon threw her head back and shook her arms in the air. "A spark has been ignited-a. I am vowing right here, right now, in this place of educational worship, to help you feed the flame-a." She was standing now and patting her forehead with a plaid stocking. Capri joined in on the antics and waved herself with a folded up piece of paper *mmhmm-ing* along.

"Stop." I said in between my laughing fit. "Get to the point."

Lennon tossed her stocking at me and I swat at away, "I think....youshoulddateagain." She cringed away from me.

"Oh, not this again." I rolled my eyes and flopped back onto my bed. Lennon spent her fair share of time trying to convince me to date again. I swore to her I would once I found someone worth dating. The truth? I was terrified.

"You should Kensie," Capri encouraged me. "You might meet your very own Darcy." She went for the jugular. How could I say no to that? In all honesty, they might be right. I had experienced an interest in a guy today that I hadn't had in years, or ever.

"I've told you," I sat up and pulled a pillow onto my lap, "If I find someone who peaks my interest I'll date." August more than peaked my interest, but I'd never see him again. The thought disappointed me a bit.

Our conversation decreased as Lennon and Capri gave up on their lost cause and honed in on their Lit homework. I couldn't stop thinking about August from the tattoo shop, and the phone call to Jodie I had to return at some point. I lay back onto my bed and sunk into a pile of pillows. I allowed myself a moment to relax with the assurance I'd call Jodie later.

My iPod had served as a good distraction in the past. Here's to hoping it would distract me from August thoughts. What were the chances I'd ever see him again anyway? Below the calming hum on the song that started, I heard

Capri's phone ring.

I closed my eyes listening to the rhythmic sound of my latest playlist and sunk deep into my Zen. Somewhere within the lyrics and my fully relaxed limbs flashes of August entered my mind. Flash. Deep chuckle. Flash. Heated Chocolate eyes. Flash. Wetted lips. Flash. Strong arms around me.Flash. Laid out on the tattoo table.

My eyes flew open and stared at the florescent light above my bed. That escalated quickly. A pen crossed the path of the bright light and plunked onto my nose. I sat up and turned the iPod down and sought out Lennon. "That was Capri's brother. Put on your sexy panties. We are going out to Tommy's tonight."

CHAPTER 2

The busiest I'd witnessed Tommy's get was on open mic nights, and on the nights it hosted a D.J. Music and college kids mixed well. Tonight was no exception with the bar already full of coeds. The cold air brushed a shiver up my spine. I was thankful I had on my skinny jeans and loose tank rather than the mini skirt, aka tube top, Lennon had been trying to talk me into wearing. She had no problem wearing her usual plaid skirt paired with a tight tank tonight, and Capri took the attention for us all in a short, white Tee shirt dress with her super sexy cheetah print heels. Heads and eyes followed while Capri strolled by oblivious to the wanting stares. Lennon proceeded towards our usual table at the back end of the bar, but I was too tempted by the music filling the hazy air.

"I'm going to hit the dance floor first." I yelled above the music to Lennon. She nodded and pointed to the bar where I knew I would be able to find her and Capri once I got this out of my system. I worked my way into the middle of the crowd and let the beat take over my consciousness.

Nothing had ever come close to igniting the deliverance in me that dancing did. The creaking of the old wood floor under my feet prompted the immediate loosening of the ties in my mind. I swayed my hips to the rhythm of the song, seeing only the subdued hue of the lights through my closed eyes. I brought my arms up around my head and moved my shoulders from side to side. The worry from my day began chipping away until my conscious thoughts took a step back while my euphoria set in.

Only the occasional brush from a nearby stranger caused a break in my daze, but I kept dancing. My hips began a more aggressive thump as the beat of the song changed and my consciousness returned. Strong hands took hold and a warm body closed in behind me. I turned around in his grasp to see an attractive blond with a cute smile, but that's not what I was here for. I shook my head and mouthed sorry to the handsome stranger while scooting away towards the outer edge of the floor.

After the first two songs, my throat became uncomfortably dry. I searched my friends out by the bar while dancing my way out of the crowd. Not to my surprise, I spotted them in the corner chatting up a couple of guys. With Lennon's spitfire personality, and Capri's undeniable beauty we always attracted a couple of grazers when we went out. As I sidestepped a gyrating couple, I felt a tingling in my spine. I shook my shoulders to release the sensation, and looked back up to see the group staring straight at me.

Standing next to a grinning Lennon was the source of my tingle. An unforgettable man with chocolate eyes and bubble gum lips leaning up against the bar. August. My breath and my legs stopped working in the middle of the dance floor. I was jostled by a nearby couple grinding voraciously against one another and put back into motion.

The stretch between the dance floor and the bar became too close, and yet too far. My eyes traced back and forth between the group; Lennon waving like an idiot, August staring at me with his lips tugged up at the corners, Capri inspecting the glances between August and I, Wes flirting with the girls next to him, and back to August's curious stare.

"Kensie, you remember August and Wes right, from the tattoo shop? Capri's brother?" At the exact moment I paled from the realization of who August was, Capri had a look of recognition on her face. "My brother is *the guy* from the tattoo shop. The guy?" Kill me now. My euphoria from the dance floor was nun chucked by mortification. Who knew Capri possessed ninja skills?

"I'm the guy." August smirked at me clearly amused at the fact that he had been talked about after we met him today. "You dance." He stated as a fact and let his eyes roam over my flushed body.

"I dance." *Nice one Kensie.* I put one arm up to casually brush my hair off my neck to release the heat engulfing my body. Dancing plus August equaled inferno. The move didn't happen as suave as I'd intended, and my arm reached a bit too far out. In one swift motion, I swatted at a tray of shots being carried by a waitress and sent them crashing to the ground all over Capri's heels. "Omigod, I'm so sorry

Capri," I said dropping to the floor.

"It's no big deal, Kensie." Capri swiped at her shoe with a napkin and stood back up leaving me scrambling on the ground. Handing remnants of shot glasses to the waitress above. My blunder was humiliating enough without seeing August's amusement.

I reached for a piece of glass, but another hand grabbed it first. I was too slow in my reaction time and grasped the hand rather than the glass I'd aimed for. "Sorry," I said out of instinct.

"Stand up Kensie," August stood with my hand still grasping his and guided me up along with him; my movement muddled to his chivalry. I watched him until a soft smile swept across his face, and then I realized my hand was still in his. I knew I should pull away, but the way his palm engulfed mine felt so safe, so protected. A gentle squeeze came from him followed by the brush of his thumb over the back of my hand. The movement was sweet and gentle, so much so that I nearly overlooked the intimacy in the physical connection. I pulled my hand back quickly and apologized again. I couldn't believe I let his touch linger on me. I barely knew him.

"Holy shit, Augustus!" Wes said turning away from his admirers. "That's the girl." He grabbed Capri's arm to force the attention she was already giving him.

"The girl?" I couldn't help myself. "Seems that way." August said studying me.

"He nearly beat the shit out of me because I

winked at her." Wes continued to tell Capri, "Of course I had to keep doing it. Augustus never gets that upset over a chick." Never? What a coincidence because I never get this roused over a dude.

Lennon laughed and elbowed me in the ribs. "Enough of the introductions, or re-introductions." Lennon crossed her arms and eyed August. "How could we have never known you were Capri's brother?"

With a slow shake of his head August took a long sip of beer. "Don't know, but I'm ready for that to change."

"You're just saying that cause you wanna see Kensie more." Her sweet smile came back when she teased him and poked him in the side causing him to squirm. My eyes caught the way his muscles rippled beneath his thin white shirt.

I wanted August to agree with Capri. I *really* wanted him to agree with her, and the constricting in my chest prompted a fight or flight response in me. I chose flight. "Let's go grab a seat." I said already a few steps away from the group in my escape.

"You know the more you run, the more obvious it is that you're interested in him." Lennon said catching up to me at the table. She knew me better than anyone so lying to her would be pointless.

"I admit. I'm interested." I fought the urge to see if August was behind me. Then I added an extra swivel to my hips for good measure, "That doesn't mean much of anything though." I sat down at a table towards the back that would fit our new larger group and spotted August still at the bar talking with Capri and Wes.

"Don't worry, he saw it." Lennon patted my arm taking the seat next to me.

"Saw what?"

"Your attempt at getting him to watch your ass. He saw it, and he watched." Again, she knows me well.

"Did he like it? Could you tell?" Wait, no it doesn't matter if he liked it. "Wait, I don't want to know." I put my hand up to stop her reply.

"Yes, you do," She smirked at me, "and based on his awkward shift in stance I'd say there's a pretty good chance he liked it."

I smirked right back at her, "I do have a pretty good ass."

"You do. You have that whole dancer's ass thing goin' for you." She said before taking a sip of her drink making me laugh. She always had something to say about my apple bottom. "Hey Kens," She said losing the amusement from her tone. "Have fun tonight." I could pretend not to know what she was getting at, but I knew. "Have fun getting to know him, and let him get to know you. Don't overthink it."

I nodded, but didn't respond. Talk about a tall order. I overthink. It's what I do. I have a difficult time allowing myself to get to know someone without thinking about how I'd fit in their life, or how long they'd be in mine before moving on. For me there are two kinds of people. The people I am acquainted with, and the people I have a relationship with. I trust the relationship people. I'd like to trust August.

***

"Is he always such a flirt?" I asked August nodding towards Wes who had surrounded himself with a gaggle of giggling women. Capri and Lennon left to use the restroom leaving me alone with August; so sly those two.

"Yep." August laughed taking a sip of his beer.

"He's a charmer."

"It seems you're missing out. There are plenty to go around." I kept my eyes on Wes while he showed off his tattoos.

"Huh." August regarded me with narrowed eyes.

"What, you don't like to share?"

"No, I don't," he said, "but I'm trying to figure out why you keep trying to pawn me off on other girls."

"What are you talking about?" I feigned shock, though not well. I'd never make it as an actress.

"Well first, you pointed out the red head checking me out." He nodded towards her beer bottle in hand.

"She gave you fuck me eyes."

He smirked, "Then you said the waitress was giving me special attention."

"She kept coming over here sticking her boobs in your face."

"I think she was just clearing the empty glasses." He said still smirking.

"With her boobs in your face? She sicced them on you." I was not amused.

His smirk rippled into a steady chuckle. I found myself smiling along with him. "So tell me Kensie, do you want me to leave you here at the table and indulge my admirers, or is it okay with you that I'd rather indulge myself right here with you?"

The smile fell off my face and landed somewhere around the sticky residue on the floor. *Indulge* would never sound the same again. Visions, inappropriate, yet oh-so-right visions of August and chocolate swirled in my brain. I had to set him straight before he got the wrong idea.

"Look, I get what this is." I started and he cocked his head to the side studying me while taking another sip of beer.

"What exactly is this?" He asked leaning forward placing arms on the table.

"You chat me up." I leaned forward too placing my arms directly across from his. So close, in fact the hair on his arms tickled my own.

"Oh, you're British now?" His breath stroked my cheek. He smelled like beer and a hint of mint. His tongue slipped out from between his lips and swept across the bottom one leaving a glisten in its wake.

"No, let me finish." I said softly tearing my eyes away from his mouth. "You chat me up, you feign interest, and you...you take me home." I tripped over the last words.

August sucked in a sharp breath and jolted back choking on a sip of beer.

"You okay?" I asked sitting back myself trying to shake off the absence of his close proximity. How did that even happen? One minute I was sitting in my own space, and the next I was practically crawling across the table towards him. If he hadn't choked I wouldn't have been surprised to find myself straddling his lap.

He cleared his throat. "Yeah, um, wow." Wow exactly. "It's how it is August, I get it." I said regaining my composure, and I did. I undoubtedly got it. "But I'm not going home with you, so you can move on." I waved my hand around the room towards all those damn girls who were fixated on him. Hussies.

He smiled at me, but didn't speak right away. I chewed the inside of my cheek wondering what he was thinking when he finally spoke up. "Well, that's good then I guess. 'Cause I don't want to take you home."

My jaw dropped and my face warmed. I thought he was interested in me, but I'd misread him. Oh god, he was being cordial because I'm his little sister's friend. I groaned and put my head in my hands staying burrowed in my palms when he spoke again. "The taking home kind leaves an hour later, never to hear from me again. I'd like you around a lot longer than that." I peered through my fingers at him. He did? "So, can I chat you up some more?" He asked and I lowered my hands laughing.

"Only if you talk British to me."

Lennon and Capri joined us again giving me noticeable winks and nods of encouragement towards August. He pretended not to notice but smiled and winked with them when they weren't aware. He had me laughing.

Laughing was good.

Wes paraded to our table a short time later with a round of shots. "No thanks," I slid the shot back towards him, "not tonight." With a history like mine, one learns to drink cautiously. My growing regard for August didn't need a veil of alcohol to inhibit my heedfulness.

"Well, I guess you need to make sure you play fair. Then, you won't have to take your shot." Wes said sliding it back towards me.

"What are we playing?" Capri asked Wes and sniffed her shot followed by the scrunch of her nose.

"Truth or Dare." He said eliciting a round of groans, except for Lennon who pumped her fist and yelled, "Yes!"

The rules seemed simple. Each person went around the table choosing a truth or dare. If you chose not to answer your truth or perform your dare, you had to take a shot. Of course, Wes wanted to go first and he was obliged.

"Okay little lady," He turned to Lennon, "truth or dare?"

"Dare." That didn't surprise me at all. Lennon's ferocity is just one of the many qualities I love about her.

"I dare you to give one of us a lap dance." He said with squinted eyes for added affect.

Lennon didn't hesitate. She stood up and pulled her chair away from the table giving herself enough space. As if the stars aligned in Wes's favor, Brittany Spears' "I'm a Slave 4 U" began to play through the speakers. He rubbed his palms together and bounced up and down in his chair. Lennon executed her slow, seductive strut in Wes's direction with perfection.

With each exaggerated sway of her hips she ran her hand delicately across her collarbone. She teased her hand across her body until she stood just inches from Wes's legs. Then she smirked grabbing Capri's hand from next to him and pulled her towards the chair. "What?" Wes ran his hands roughly down his face. "You tease! That's not fair."

Lennon glanced a sexy smirk over her should and pushed a giggling Capri into the chair.

"She's too sweet for a lap dance." Wes slumped into his chair, "You're wasting your time." Someone was a sore loser. Capri's eyes cracked in the dim light, but she covered it well with determination pulling Lennon down on her lap.

August and I watched the girls tease Wes with their dancing. They playfully touched each other and made kissy face looks at him. The poor guy looked so distressed pulling his eyebrows together and huffing his arms across his chest. I think I even heard a whimper from him a time or two. How traumatic.

"I think I deserve a re-do." Wes pouted when the girls sat back down in their seats.

"How did you not enjoy that?" I asked him from across the table. "Two smoking hot girls groped each other for your pleasure." His chest puffed up and peered back and forth between Capri and Lennon.

"You're absolutely right." He said, "I'm a lucky bastard." He grinned at the girls, "August your sister is fuckin' hot, and you're not so bad yourself little lady." He winked at Lennon deserving the wadded up napkins she and August threw at him. Capri scanned the crowd around the bar and seemed to not notice, but I saw the blush staining her cheeks. Interesting.

I'd somehow been volunteered into going next. By somehow, I mean Lennon kicked my chair on her way back to her own seat and told me I was up.

I scanned the group running my finger around the rim of the shot glass considering my options. Lennon performed her dare, and fantastically so. I had no doubt Wes would choose a dare. Capri would choose truth although; she might surprise me tonight and choose Dare to prove Wes wrong again. Oh, whom am I kidding? I'm picking August.

I squashed down the tremor in my stomach when my eyes met his, "August." He smirked and sat up placing his elbows on the table. "Truth or dare?"

"Truth," he said without reserve. I could work with that. I'd kind of hoped he'd pick a dare so I could integrate some creative clothing removal, but truth might work out in my favor.

I contemplated everything I could ever want to know about August. What inspired his tattoo for one? His biggest turn offs, biggest turn on, his....shoe size? As much as I wanted to let go of my insecurities for the night, though, I couldn't. So instead of asking him a question that would likely make me swoon more, I chose a question to help me keep him at arm's length.

"What is your biggest weakness?" I made

sure not to look in Lennon's direction because I'm sure she knew exactly what I was scheming.

"Weakness, difficult question for a man of strength." His eyebrow cocked at me accompanied by a cheesy grin. Wes encouraged with a pound of his fist.

August sat a minute and seemed to contemplate my question seriously this time. "I guess I'm too loyal." He said staring at the beer between his hands. "Yes, you are." Capri jumped in.

"C." Wes warned her in a whispering tone, more affectionate than I think he intended. He shifted back in his chair further away from her, and Capri did the same.

"Too loyal?" I asked August. "That's your answer?"

This is freaking ridiculous. I didn't need to look at Lennon to know she was smiling. I sensed her toothy grin mocking me.

"Too loyal." He focused on his hands gripping the beer.

"Take a shot!" I said throwing my hand up.

Ridiculous. Loyalty? How about *I bone random chicks*, or *I get bored easily*, or even *I chew with my mouth open*.

He jumped and widened his eyes. "What?"

"Take a shot. Your answer is ridiculous." It also doesn't make him any less appealing. In fact the opposite, he might a well have told me he owned Pemberley and answered to the name Fitzwilliam.

"What are you, the truth police?" He laughed, but I kept my poker face.

"How is loyalty a weakness? Girls love loyalty. Every girl within earshot dropped her panties for you with that admission." His eyebrow lifted. "Except me." I finished. Panties were firm in place.

"I have to agree with Kensie on this August." Lennon smiled smugly at me. "Loyalty is pretty hot, right Kens? Take your shot."

"No." August pushed his shot away. "It's my truth. Deal with it and drop your panties." He sat back in his seat and folded his arms over his chest. Damn if the flex in his forearm didn't momentarily distract me. In that moment, I found a new love for forearms. "What's your weakness then, officer Truth Ruiner?"

"Does this count as my truth?" I asked him buying myself some time to choose a weakness. I had a healthy list to consider, but thought to go with one he'd find unattractive since it was clearly impossible for him to be.

"If you want it to be? Or you could go with a dare?" He shrugged.

"Truth it is, then." I said, "I'm a floater." Lennon sighed next to me. She'd heard enough about this over the last three years. Too much, I guess.

"That's disgusting, Kensie." Wes said looking repulsed. "I mean, really, you were pretty hot two seconds ago. Now?" He shivered and waved his hands in front of his face. Wow, I hadn't expected Wes to be the person most horrified by my fault.

"I don't think I understand. What do you mean you float?" August asked paying close attention to me.

"I float through life. I'm not headed in any particular direction. I just float, hoping I'll drift towards a purpose." I surprised myself with my honesty.

"Oh, thank fuck." Wes said making us all sit up straighter, "I thought you meant you were a floater, like ya know, you drop giant shits." What?

"Oh, Wes," August shook his head and squinted his eyes in pain. He threw another bunched up napkin nailing Wes in the forehead. Capri scrunched her little nose at him and shifted away again. Lennon, of course, laughed her ass off.

"That's disgusting." I said to Wes still taken aback at what he thought I had meant. "I just meant that I don't know what I'm doing with my life. I float through it." Giant shits? How is it possible woman are charmed by this man? It must be the tattoos.

"I don't know Kens, I'm having a hard time here."

August said and spun his beer around in his hands on the table. "Are you sinking?" He worried his bottom lip between his teeth. By all appearances I succeeded in deterring him from me, but instead of feeling relived I felt the churn of disappointment. Twice now, in a matter of twelve hours, I'd admitted to him what a deadbeat I was. I guess the apple doesn't fall far from the tree.

Ouch.

"Not anymore." I answered honestly. I'd already sunk. I drowned.

"Well that's something then isn't it?" He

stopped spinning his bottle and studied me. "Now, you swim."

Time froze. The bar patrons silenced, music evaporated, walls and lights faded into the background. All I saw was August. All I heard were his words. Swim.

What was it with this guy making life sound so simple? Keep moving. Swim. I suppose they could be simple suggestions had I been able to trust the direction I'd go in.

"Take your shot, Kensie." August's firm voice tore me from my isolation.

"What?"

"I said take a shot." I stared at him still unsure of why I had too. "Just because you haven't made it to where you want to be doesn't mean floating it a weakness. Especially not when you've pulled yourself up from wherever you were before." I scrunched my nose in confusion over the way he flipped my weakness on me. He smiled and nodded down at my glass. Before I could pick it up, Lennon swiped it from my hands and tossed the shot back. I mouthed a silent "thank you" to her.

"Moving on." She said and pointed over to Capri. "You're up." Capri squinted around table at us while Wes hummed the Jeopardy theme song. Her eyes stopped on him, and a pleading grin spread across his face.

"Wes."

"Yesss." Wes clenched his fists.

"Truth or..."

"Dare!" He shouted before she finished asking.

"See those girls you were talking to earlier? Showing off your tattoos?" Capri nodded toward the bar. "Yeah?" Wes furrowed his brow.

"I dare you to show them one last tattoo." His face fell and Capri nodded her head silently smirking.

"Shit." August mumbled to himself and covered his face in his hands.

"You!" Wes shouted and pointed across the table at August.

"Oh, this has got to be good." Lennon whispered next to me.

"You told her? I can't believe you told her. You were sworn to secrecy!" Wes stood up and leaned over the table gripping the edge with white knuckles. August shrugged at him sheepishly.

"It was too epic not to tell someone, Wes. Capri's a safe tell. She's a vault." Capri never told a secret. I guess that loyalty "weakness" ran in the family.

"Until now, you fucker." Lennon and I laughed while Wes straightened out his clothes and stood up a little taller. Atta boy. You look confidant, you feel confidant.

"You could always take your shot." I suggested snickering.

"Shots are for pussies." He said before sauntering over to the group of girls who had already had their predatory eyes fixed on him.

"What is this tattoo of anyway?" I asked my friend as Wes approach the gaggle. They immediately surrounded him in a ring of batting eyelashes and flipping hair.

"It's a portrait of Siegfried and Roy, right August?" Capri asked her brother who laughed into his fist.

"When he finished his apprenticeship, the guys took him out to celebrate and ended the night with a free tat of his choice."

"That's what he chose?" Lennon was doubled over in a fit of giggles.

"Yeah," August chuckled along, "but the best part is the text under it says, *I can be your tiger, bitch.*" I couldn't believe it, but I could. I really could. We all laughed hysterically, the room barely visible through my teary eyes.

Wes disappeared in the sea of silicone, but the moment when they saw his tattoo was clear. They gasped. They cringed. They twirled ends of hair in confusion. Then they slowly parted and walked away leaving Wes alone and glaring daggers at the table. He stomped over pointing at August before he even got back to us. "You. You secret teller, are going down. For that, you get a dare."

August shrugged his shoulder and took a sip of his beer. "Name it. Your dares don't scare me."

"Alright Augustus, right here, right now, you have to get up on that piece of crap stage and sing to the crowd."

Capri groaned. "Wes, you know August can't sing worth shit. This is supposed to torture him not us." I looked over at August's pale skin and shaking his head at Wes. "Uh,uh dude. You know I hate karaoke. I'd need a bottle of Jack to get up there and you know I don't drink the hard stuff."

"Torture." Wes grinned at Capri. She shook her head and for the first time all night gave Wes a small smile.

"Alright! This is going to be fun! Let's go Augie. I can't wait to see this." Lennon cheered him on, though August remained frozen.

"You can do this. Imagine we are all naked." I smiled at him and took a sip of my drink that was now a mixture of melted ice, cranberry, and vodka. Did I flirt? I don't know where that came from.

"Well, if that's the case I hope you are ready for my full attention." He beamed across the table at me with sweat already building on his forehead. Poor guy, he really didn't want to do this. "Aren't you going to wish me luck?" He asked me before chugging the rest of his beer.

"Who needs luck," I asked him, "when you will have all of your fan girls throwing their panties at you regardless of your talents?"

He quirked up his eyebrow at that. "I don't suppose your panties will be flying at me?" I shook my head and tried to hide my smile when he sauntered away from the table obviously very proud of himself.

***

With the exception of August who sulked up to the DJ, we all took seats around one of the bar tables. I'd be lying if I said I wasn't looking forward to this. I could stare at him unabashedly. "I couldn't help but notice the twinkle in your eye." Lennon leaned over and whispered to me.

"No twinkling here." *Deny. Deny. Deny.*

"Bullshit. I've only seen you twinkle for three reasons. Dance, chocolate, and ... well, okay two reasons. I've gotta assume the third is for August."

"His very own twinkle, huh?"

"Appears so, and if he crushes your twinkle, I crush him." She pounded her fist into her palm. Bless her feisty heart. She believed she was intimidating. "And don't think I didn't catch onto your little stunt you pulled back there. Stop looking for reasons to stay away from him."

My eyes followed August who was taking his place on the small make shift stage. Capri caught me admiring her brother and gave me a reassuring smile. I knew what that meant. She was giving me her blessing. Within twenty-four short hours I found myself immersed in twinkles and blessings. Not a bad place to be, scary, but not bad. Maybe I should try some optimism and look for reasons to be around him.

With August fidgeting on the stage I sensed a steady beat start to pulse through my chair. Others around me still remained engaged in their conversations unaware of the music starting. A familiar song poured through the speakers sending a hush rippling across the tiny bar.

"Oh no, he didn't." Lennon giggled and bounced her head to the music. "That's your man."

"Not my man." *My man.* The words nestled themselves onto my lips.

August started as the chorus of The Humpty Dance came on; or talk, was this even singing? Whatever it was, it was ludicrous, but entertaining. We cheered and hollered for August as he wobbled his head up and down to the beat and sloppily rapped the song. He stepped down from the stage and plodded toward us thrusting his hips every half beat. I'm not sure what words could describe his moves. A good dancer he was not, but endearing, yes. My eyes were blurry with tears as he came up to our table. The playful glint in his eyes stole the laugh from my throat. I put my hands up at him and shook my head.

As the chorus blared to life again he grabbed my hand and pulled me from my chair. I indulged in the feel of his rough palm against mine once again, and followed him up. I think I'd follow him off a bridge if he were holding my hand. In this case, I let him thrust and grind himself around me before he left to return the microphone to the D.J.

It wasn't long before nearly the entire crowd was on their feet. The D.J. went with the momentum and continued to play a string of hip hop and dance hits from the 90's. Capri and I danced suggestively with each other trying to get Lennon up from the table. She laughed at us, but sat firmly in her chair.

I caught sight of Wes to our left dancing with one of his many girls, and I was shocked at what a skilled dancer he was. He moved with an undeniable amount of swagger and intimately connected with his partner. I turned my attention towards Capri and saw she was watching the same thing, but where I was impressed her face was shrouded in annoyance. I nudged her with my hip breaking her icy stare when a grin graced her face.

I smelled him before I felt him. He smelled like a hunky man covered in soap. Delicious. I resisted the urge to turn around and nibble into him, instead dancing as if I hadn't noticed his presence. Instead I focused on the crowd moving in a steading rolling motion. The lights had been turned down adding a glow to the dance floor.

Ignoring August became impossible the moment his hands gripped my waist. I froze stumbling back into him. My breath was paralyzed in my lungs. I hadn't been this physically close to a man in three years. The thought made me want to flee.

"Relax." He whispered into my neck sending an immediate tremble down my body leaving a trail of heat that begged for the tickle of his breath. He slid one hand from its welcome place on my hip along the front of my stomach and pulled me further into him. I went willingly relishing the feel of his solid arm draped across me. The urge to move away faded into the beat of the music.

August gently moved me along with him keeping us pressed close. Watching him move on his own during his performance was nothing compared to being held in his arms. I thought he was uncoordinated and stiff, but now it was clear he knew what he was doing.

My solid and jagged movements softened allowing my body to meld into his. He swayed us together closely and intimately. Allowing me to forget where I was. The space around us dimmed further until it was just he and I. August's fingers pulsed with the music kneading into my skin. I sunk further into his large shielding frame welcoming the safety of his touch.

Surrendering to the music and waving my white flag to August, I dropped my head back onto his shoulder. He took the invitation and nuzzled his nose into the crook of my neck. My warming skin welcomed his nearness, and my stomach fluttered at his touch. I tilted my head to the side allowing him more access. I wanted to feel his lips against the sensitive space. I wanted the wetness of his tongue against the heat of my skin. When he didn't comply, I ground myself back into him stealing a growl from his throat. His nose brushed across my neck sending my stomach into a welcome spasm, but still I needed more.

I turned to face him and draped my arms over his shoulders. August followed my lead and wrapped his arm around my waist letting his hands rest on my backside. I kept my eyes averted from his and I straddled my legs around one of his. He took this invitation and hauled me in so that I was practically sitting on his thigh. The jolt of the closeness shook me to my core. The lyrics of the music had vanished, and all that remained was the steady beat thrumming where our bodies connected.

I couldn't control the quiet moan that left my lips at the moment of contact. He responded with a grip of his hands and I smirked at the knowledge that he enjoyed my response. We continued to move together. Every roll of my hips and every lunge of his leg built a steady need within me. I began subconsciously pulling at his firm, rounded shoulders within my hands.

I leaned into August and brushed my nose up his solid chest and made my way up along his neck. He tilted his head to the side in a groan and I continued my path tracing his jawline up to his chin inhaling his clean scent.

He dipped his head into me aligning our parted lips, and bringing them close, so damn close. I inhaled his breath and he gripped me tighter in his hands. I felt the tips of his nails dig into me and sucked in a shaky breath at the feel of his need against me. Suddenly, the faintest trace of his lips brushed against mine. In the softest and slowest movement, August's tongue met my bottom lip in a wet and sweeping motion. My mind followed its glide from corner to corner.

I looked up at August for the first time since our dance began and connected with his lowered eyes. They screamed in lust and want begging for me to return the action. I sucked in a sharp breath and fell away from his embrace. What was I doing?

I stumbled back another step almost falling into the couple behind me, but August reached out and caught my arms.

"What's wrong?" He asked voice gruff and so damn sexy.

"I just, I..." I couldn't find my voice. I wanted to say I got carried away, and I had. I wanted to tell him to move away, but I only wanted him close again. I wanted to run for the door, but I felt the need to reattach myself to him and sink my lips into his. Completely caught up in confusion I shook my head and stumbled my way back to the safety of our table.

"Holy hump dance, what was that?" Lennon asked sliding a glass of water across the table at me. I took it without response and drank half of it in a few gulps. I shook my head at her still lost for words.

"It was hot. I'll tell you that much. I need a cold shower and I wasn't even the one dancing." She fanned herself off.

"I got carried away." I said pulling my hair up off my neck.

"And what's wrong with that?" Lennon asked.

"A lot. A lot is wrong with that." I said thinking about how quickly I could have given myself over to him, and how easily we both could have regretted it. We barely knew each other.

"For as long as I've known you, you have maintained control in everything you can. That," she nodded her head towards the dance floor, "is the first time I have witnessed you lost in a moment. If you were able to get carried away in August, then dammit Kensie, let him take you."

I huffed out a frustrated grunt. Lennon was right. No guy had swept me up so quickly, but that was exactly what I needed to be wary of. If I couldn't control myself around August, then I needed to keep my distance.

Not even a few minutes later August took

his seat across the table from me. He didn't look up at me, but I could feel the heat roll off of him. Heat we created only moments ago. I blushed and looked down at my glass of water.

I felt Capri take her seat next to me and glanced at her. Her eyes were practically bugging out of her head at me. I shook my head at her advising her not to ask. The table was awkwardly silent with knowing when Wes found his way back to us.

"Whew, it was getting' sexified out there." He said and every head snapped to him. "What?" he asked innocently. Still silent, the gentle vibration of our table had all of us checking our cell phones. I saw it wasn't me getting a call and placed mine back into my pocket. I looked up at saw August staring at his phone with furrowed brows.

"I gotta take this." He mumbled and stood up from the table quickly retreating to the door.

Capri eyed him warily from across the table. She and Wes whispered heatedly with each other while August was gone. Capri would gesture towards the door and Wes would nod seeming to try and calm her down.

"What do you suppose this is all about?" I asked Lennon who had been watching the exchange with me.

"Not sure. She seems upset with August's phone call."

"My thoughts exactly. I wonder who it is?"

"Let's find out." Lennon waved to Capri to get her attention, "Should Kensie be worried?"

"What the hell?" I smacked Lennon on the

arm. "I'm not worried." *Lie.*

Capri shook her head reassuringly. "Nope, just family stuff." That explained it. I certainly could relate.

When August came back in, he took his seat on his own side of the table, but still hadn't looked at me. I couldn't blame him. I was the one who ran away.

Sensing the shift of atmosphere Lennon stood up from the table. "Time to head out." She said stretching her arms above her head. "Capri and I have an early study date tomorrow."

I nodded and stood up to join her, but not before looking one last time towards August. My eyes collided with his. I was surprised to see, not disgust or disappointment in his eyes, but something else. Curiosity maybe. Like he couldn't figure me out. *Good luck buddy. I'm still working on that myself,* I thought and gave him a soft downturned smile. He returned the same exact smile to me before I turned away and headed with my girls for the door.

CHAPTER 3

One thing I've always been certain of is the strength of my friendships. I've always chosen quality over quantity preferring a few close friends I know I can trust to a truckload of acquaintances I can sometimes count on. Since coming to college I met a lot of really great people, but only two have stuck. Lennon and Capri were the best kind of friends. If they fell, I'd pick them up and help them fly. Right now, I'd let those bitches fall.

"Can you guys keep it down?" I mumbled from somewhere under my pillow. I knew they had a study date, but what I didn't know is that it would be in my room at the butt ass crack of dawn.

"Wait, did you hear something? Was that Sleeping Beauty? Guess you can call your brother and tell him we won't need him to come by after all." Lennon told Capri making her laugh.

"Ha." I said shoving my pillow aside and glaring at them through one squinted eye. "Why are you studying here anyway? Isn't there a coffee house or a library you can be at?" I asked them pulling the pillow back over my head. Why is the sun so bright in the morning?

"Yeah," Lennon said, "but then I'd have to get dressed. This way we can study in our pajamas."

"I brought you a coffee." Capri's voice twinkled through the air, God love her.

I stuck my hand out from under my blanket and pulsed my fingers open and closed before a warm cup was placed into them.

"I love you. You're my favorite." I said sitting up and letting the pillow fall to the ground.

"You're my favorite too." She said smiling while Lennon flipped us both off.

I took a slow steady sip of the delicious brown goodness when Capri's phone chimed. "You even have people call you at this hour? What's wrong with you people?" I grumbled taking another sip.

"Right now?" Capri said to the person on the other line. "It's eight a.m. Why can't you get them later?"

"See. We only grace you with our presence this early. Others have to wait." Lennon said flashing me a charming smile that didn't belong anywhere on her petite face.

Capri hung up the phone with a huff and tossed it back into her purse. "Who was it?" I asked cradling my coffee in my hands.

"My brother." She said casually. See that's the thing. Capri has always mentioned *her brother*, but has never called him by name. Had she done that I may have been able to connect the dots on who he was. Then, I could have avoided Tommy's last night and our entire awkward dance floor exchange that left me both mortified and completely turned on like a damn light. Then, I could have avoided the searing pain from the burn of the coffee I just spilled on my leg at the mention of Capri's brother.

"Shit." I cursed blotting off the scalding liquid with my bed sheet.

"Is he looking for Kensie?" Lennon asked.

Capri tapped her pen against her chin and pursed her lips. "Probably, actually. He said he needed to come get his jumper cables from my car for Wes. I guess his car died at some hussy's house. I personally think August should let him perform the walk of shame all the way home."

"I'd pay to see that." Lennon laughed. "So what did August say?"

"He said he would be here in five minutes." Capri said casually with a gleam in her eye escalating Lennon's laugh.

"What?" I shouted and jumped up from my bed spilling more coffee onto my toe this time. "Shit. Hot. Hot." I put the cup down on my nightstand and ran my fingers through my matted hair. I hurried to my closet and pulled out my shower caddy slamming the doors closed. I turned in a circle looking for my sandals when I caught sight of two smirking bitches on Lennon's bed.

"What?" I said teetering on my feet trying to appear as calm as possible. Neither of them spoke, so I turned on my heel and headed out the door. I turned to yank it shut, and spun around towards the hallway. My efforts were thwarted when I ran smack dab into the middle of a solid clean smelling, delicious man. *Crap.*

"Good morning." His chest rumbled against

my hand that was splayed across it. I yanked it back quickly and placed it stiffly at my side.

"Good morning." I said keeping my voice as even and unaffected as possible. I was completely affected though. At this point, I wanted to scale him like a tree and reenact the whole his tongue on my lip thing from last night.

"Nice jammies." He said smirking. His eyes lazily traced their way down my body widening and appraising with each sweep of his gaze. I followed his heated stare tilting my head down and gasped when I saw what I was wearing.

I stared down at my tank and boy short underwear combo. How could I forget I slept in my underwear? I had two choices right now. I could cower back into my room and put some real pajamas on, or I could proudly strut myself down to the restrooms without a care in the world.

I straightened my shoulders and looked up at August. "Thanks." I said confidently and moved to make my way around him. His arm shot out towards the wall and blocked off my way. "Excuse me." I said as pleasantly as possible, though my heart was hammering in my head.

"What happened last night?" He asked leaning towards me much closer than he was a second ago. I took a step towards the wall and away from him.

"What do you mean?" Ugh, why did I just say that? Of course I knew what he meant. I was buying myself time though. Time to figure out what on earth I was going to say next.

"When we were dancing. I thought we were having a good time, well" he stopped himself, "I was having a good time. A damn good time, and then you...you-"

"Freaked out." I finished his sentence for him. "And I was um, enjoying myself." God this was so awkward.

"You were?" He asked taking another step towards me and placing his other arm on the wall boxing me in. His scent assaulted me in the most perfect way. With arms propped up on either side of me he took another step closer to me. I could feel the warmth of our bodies twirling together in the tiny space between us. I wanted to close the distance, but stood my ground, against the wall.

"Is this okay?" He asked bending his head down toward me and brushing the tip of his nose along my cheek.

"Yes." I whispered losing sight as my eyes closed. I leaned my head into him. My pulse pounded through my veins and my breathing became ragged in anticipation. I wanted so badly to have his lips on mine, to have his body press against me. His breath brushed down my face and stopped suddenly. What was he going to do? Kiss me? Turn away? I held my breath waiting for his decision. I just wanted him to grab me and throw me up against the wall already. Then, his lips pressed gently onto my skin and wrapped themselves around my jawline. I inhaled quickly losing all sense of myself in a haze of want, no need. My shower caddy tumbled from my fingertips in a loud clatter on the ground.

Still immobile I felt the heat of August pull away from me and bend down to the floor below me. I stood fixed against the wall and tried to reel in my heaving breaths. With August placing my things back into the caddy, I heard my dorm room door open. My head whipped around and was met by Lennon's laughing eyes.

"Everything alright out here?" She asked, and I could hear Capri laughing in the room.

"Fine." I said and at the same time August responded.

"Good. Kensie dropped her shower caddy. Just helping her clean up." He said sounding utterly unaffected by what had taken place. He stood up in front of me and held out the caddy.

"Thanks." I mumbled still staring at Lennon and took the caddy from August's hands. His thumb intentionally brushed against the top of my hand the in the pass off, and I snapped my attention back to him wide eyed and thoroughly overwhelmed. I yanked the caddy away from him and turned speeding my way down the hallway toward the bathroom. I could hear Lennon say something to August, but I was too focused on a really freakin' cold shower to care.

It only took a second of the ice cold water to drench me before I decided that method of cooling off was overrated. I turned the shower to my usual temperature of scalding hot and continued to wash away all frustrations over August.

What I couldn't understand was how he had the ability to reduce me to someone I didn't even know. All it took was a brief moment of having him close for me to lose all control. He consumed me and left me both wanting and running. How? What was it about him? All I wanted was to keep him at a safe distance, one where he is simply Capri's brother and I am simply her friend. When he came around my wants were smothered by my desires. This was not healthy.

What I needed to do was learn to stay far away from him when he came around. Physical proximity proved to be disastrous. If I could keep him at a safe distance, then I could regain my self-control when it came to him.

***

I had no idea my self-control would be tempted again so soon. The girls and I weren't huge football fans, but we went to a few games a year. I personally loved getting caught up in the atmosphere. The hum of excitement, the people painted in head to toe black and red, blow horns, shouting, and nachos, can't forget the nachos.

Capri called me to inform me that August and Wes would be joining us at the game tonight. I found it odd that just a few days ago Capri's brother was just that, her brother. Now he was August, and for some reason August was around a lot more than when he was just her brother.

I banished my initial worries over seeing him again and spent the majority of my day pumping myself up. Tonight my will would be tested. I'd either fail and succumb to my mystical attraction to August, or I'd prevail and maintain a safe friendly distance. I planned on a victory.

"I want the end seat." Lennon stated as the three of us shuffled into our row. The guys were meeting up with us as soon as August got off work for the night.

"How come you always get the end seat?" I complained ducking and sidestepping the guy behind us who was leaning over into our row.

"I like to have the option of tripping unsuspecting drunken patrons as they pass." She said sitting down into her seat. She was joking of course. I think.

I placed myself strategically in the seat between Capri and Lennon, that way August would be at least one person away from me.

The game hadn't started yet, but the stadium was alive. Everywhere was a smearing of red and black. The row of guys behind us stood with their arms wrapped around each other and swayed back and forth in a chant. The group of people below us danced half-hazard to the pre-game music blaring the sound system. The sloshing of beer from one of the girl's hands back onto my jeans explained the sloppy movements. I'm glad I went with a more casual choice of jeans and an Aztec hoodie.

The family to my right sat in their seats and skimmed the crowd warily. I guess they missed the memo about student section seats. I heard the sound of a deep voice barking from behind us and shook my head. College games, always entertaining.

"Trade me places, Kensie. I'm not sitting next to him." Capri said standing and pulling her designer bag onto her shoulder. She never went casual, but she never complained when she'd end the night with beer and nacho cheese on her pea coat.

"Sitting next to who?" I asked standing in confusion.

"Wes." She hissed, and put her hand on my shoulder guiding me in front of her to trade seats. The man in question stood on the stairs next to our row and barked into the crowd. Lovely, he was the barker, and I was now going to be sitting next to him.

He shuffled passed Lennon who stuck her foot out making him stumble. Completely unphased he righted himself and cupped his hands around his mouth for another round of barking.

"We're Indians you know. Not bulldogs." Capri told him and he sidestepped her. His reply was to turn around and bark directly into her face making Capri jump back into her chair.

I turned my legs so Wes could scoot by and sit in his seat, but he surprised me when he kept moving and sat in the next seat over leaving the one directly next to me open. Oh no.

"One more bark dude, and you're walking your ass home." His voice rumbled next to me sending a blanket of chills across my skin. I stared at the field paralyzed in fear. One sentence and I was already losing in my quest for control. This was not good.

Then, one long denim clad leg stepped into my way followed closely by another, and oh dear God, his ass. His ass was directly in my face.

The vintage wash of his jeans hugged and highlighted the rugged and perfect curve to it. I was face to face with the best ass I had ever seen. Then it was gone.

"Hey." He said placing that perfect ass in the seat next to me.

"Hey." I said still looking down at the field. Then, silence. That was it. He and Wes talked with each other and I stared fixated on the empty field waiting for kick-off. A knot of disappointment formed in my chest at his obvious disinterest in me, but I swallowed it down. Maybe keeping my distance wasn't going to be so difficult after all.

The sound of the drums rolled through the stadium bringing sections of the crowd to their feet along with it. I stood up at the same time August did and fell into him when I lost my footing. His arm caught me and brushed across my back when I righted myself. "Sorry." I said focused solely on the searing space of my back where his hand was.

"You good?" He asked giving the spot a gentle rub before pulling his hand away. Was that a friendly rub?

Like an *atta kid* kind of a thing? Or was it a caring rub, like an *I'd be willing to rub more than your back* kind of thing? *Why do I even care, why am I thinking about this?*

"Yeah, good." I said breathing deeply. *Relax Kensie.*

We took our seats just after kick off, and August continued to chat with Wes. Trying to pretend that didn't disappoint me, I decided to go stock up on my game snacks. "Snack bar, girls. Want anything?" I asked rising from my seat intentionally keeping my back to August. *See, I don't care either.*

"Chardonnay." Capri said and I smiled. I used to wonder who on earth drank the tiny bottles of wine at a game. Then I met Capri.

"Cotton candy and beer." Lennon piped up. "Want me to come with?" She asked.

"Nah, I got it." I said shuffling past them and making my way up the stairs to the concessions.

I returned thirty minutes later with a handful of snacks and a carton of drinks. I handed Lennon her beer and cotton candy on my way passed her, then Capri her tiny bottle of wine. I sat down in my seat and put my soda in the holder before settling back with my nachos on my lap.

"Where's my snack?" He muttered right next to my ear. A shiver raked through me all the way to the tray of nachos in my hands.

"You didn't say you wanted anything." I replied nonchalantly as if the nearness of him wasn't threatening my sensibilities. The sound of his voice in the low intimate rumble he used sucked me in so easily. If I let my eyes shut for a fraction of a second I could see him using the same tone with me lying under him and his face nestled into my neck. Yeah. Snap out of it Kensie.

"You didn't ask." He said exiting my space, and sitting back into his own. I breathed a silent sigh of relief, but missed the clean scent that drifted from his skin and beckoned me towards him.

That's when he did the unimaginable. He reached across the armrest separating us and grabbed a chip from my bowl of nachos. It wasn't just any chip. It was one that was covered and oozed with cheese. The best kind. My jaw dropped and I watched helplessly as he popped this chip into his mouth and chewed.

If shock hadn't grabbed hold of my wits, I would have taken notice of the way his jaw flexed with each chew of that chip. The muscles, *I had no idea there were even muscles there*, rippled and pulsed chew after chew. It was obnoxiously hot.

Focused on the field below us his hand darted for my paper bowl again. Having regained my senses I yanked the bowl out of his reach making him turn to seek it out.

"Back off." I seethed.

His eyes widened and a smile pulled up on one corner of his mouth. Even only half smiling his eyes glistened. So irritating. "A little protective over your food?" He asked still smiling, though this time the other corner turned up creating a full on heart stopping beautiful grin. If he were mine I'd lean in right at this moment and kiss him. I had no choice but to smile back.

"A little." I said taking a bite of a dripping chip.

He watched me smiling, and appearing somewhat amused. Then, it all happened in slow motion. He reached out and swiped his finger under my lip. I watched his eyes when they lowered to my mouth and the glisten that was there initially crackled. I continued to stare at his eyes and focused on the rough pad of his fingertip scaling across the softest part of my lip. With a mind of its own, my tongue slipped out of the corner of my mouth. August sucked in a sharp breath and his eyes snapped to mine. My stare held his when he slowly pulled his hand back. "Cheese." He said so quietly only the vibration of his voice through my body alerted me to his speaking.

"Thanks." I said and looked back towards the field with the sound of my heavy heart drowning out the crowd. I took in another deep breath and leveled myself. "Yeah, so anyway. I'm a little protective of my food. I think I must have been in the Great Depression in a past life."

August tossed his head back and chuckled aloud. "You don't say?" He asked looking back at me with the glisten in his eyes again. "So what? You had to fight for your food?"

I shrugged licking cheese from my fingers. "I suppose. It would explain my deep attachment to food, and my unwillingness to share."

He laughed again warming me in a new way. I liked the sound of it. It pulsed through me like a star in the night seeking a moment of attention.

"So, this past life thing, do you have others or is that your only one?" He asked, amusement lacing his voice.

I pondered his question before answering. "I most likely lived during the 1800's too." I said taking another bite of my nachos.

"The 1800's?" He questioned me.

"Life was so romantic then." I said, the

cheesy chip froze in my hand halfway towards my mouth. Why did I say that to him? I must have sounded ridiculous. Sure I'd openly admit that to Lennon or Capri, but why did I just say that to August?

"Yes, because women's oppression and smallpox are so romantic." He said with a smile on his face.

"Err. Okay, that's not romantic at all." I said cringing. "What about you? Where do you think you were in a past life?" I asked him. Cheers erupted around us and the crowd bound to their feet. August sat steady though, turned toward me with his lips pursed in thought.

"Hmmm, well, I was most likely Hercules." He said with a completely straight face. An uncontrollable laugh burst from my gut, and I was glad the noise from the crowd was loud enough to cover it. August's eyes squinted closed and he laughed along with me. So there we were. Laughing together. TOGETHER.

I don't know when it happened, but my fears seemed to fade away the more we just talked. It was as if the words deconstructed every worry and plucked them off on by one leaving an opening wide enough for him to slip in. We continued to talk about everything and nothing.

We covered topics from superstitions to hidden talents, and we laughed the entire time. I had no clue what the score was when he excused himself to get a beer, but not before asking me if I wanted any more nachos.

"Having a good time?" Capri nudged me with her shoulder.

I shrugged, "Yeah." I couldn't lie. I was having a lot of fun. August and I got along so easily and so seamlessly. Where he finished discussing a topic, I picked up discussing another. Even when we quieted down and sat together in silence it wasn't awkward or nerve racking, but comfortable, and it wasn't long before one of us picked up a new topic of conversation.

"Dude, I hope he got me a beer too." Wes' voice spoke loudly from two seats over. "Yo, Augustus!" He shouted down the crowd. I lifted my chin up to see over and through the people in front of me and sought out August. It would have helped had I stood on my tiptoes, but I didn't want to look that obvious.

As if the football God's recognized my dilemma the crowd parted giving me a direct visual on August's whereabouts. In that moment, I chastised the God's for granting me the view. A few rows down August stood amongst a group of obvious sorority girls decked out in the specially made football shirts and red ribbons in their hair.

He laughed with them, but it didn't look as honest as his laugh was with me, or maybe I was just seeking a reason to not feel disappointed. A brunette reached toward his should and gave him a little pat, pat, squeeze. For a brief second, not even that long really, my heart tightened in my chest, but then I let it go. This is what I wanted him to do. Keep his distance. With him down there flirting, I could be up here and not feel suffocated with whatever buzzed in the air around us.

When he finally took his seat next to me he

nudged my knee with his own. "Hey." He said.

"Hey." I said back.

He turned and looked at me, closely, and quietly.

"What's up?" He asked eyebrows lowered over his eyes.

"Nothing." I said with a shrug and pretended to be enthralled in the game I knew nothing about.

"Oh hell, you gave me the *nothing*. That means it's something." He said taking a sip of his beer before placing it in the cup holder. "All was good and then I left to get a beer, and now I'm met with an ice queen." He said the words and I snapped my icy stare to him.

"You got a beer, you said hi to some friends, and now I'm watching the game. No big deal." I said raising my eyebrow at him. I knew I was being a bitch, but whatever. I didn't need him to like me.

He chuckled softly to himself, "I see." He said doing a lousy job of holding back his smile. "You're jealous." He released that grin from ear to ear.

"Psh. Am not." I said sounding much too juvenile, so I cleared my throat and tried again. "I'm not jealous. It really doesn't bother me. We're just acquaintances through Capri, two people hanging out. There is no reason for me to be jealous."

"Hmmm, acquaintances." He said more to himself than me and turned his head back towards the game. "Okay." He said with a shrug and grabbed his beer again before resting back into his seat. That was that. We didn't say another word to each other the rest of the night besides polite goodbyes at the end of the game. It was exactly how I wanted the night to end, but I felt completely let down on the walk back to the dorms. I'd accomplished my victory, but rather than sweet it tasted incredibly sour.

CHAPTER 4

"Go away sun." I muttered into my pillow. I dislike mornings, no I abhor mornings. As my roommate for the last three years, Lennon has caught on to my vampiristic tendencies towards the sun. It's likely why she opened all the blinds and windows in the room before she left for her early study session this morning. I'm going with, she was trying to be helpful in getting me out of bed, rather than she was trying to blind me and reduce me to sparkly dust. I mean seriously, my eyes are still closed and I have the urge to squint.

I cracked open one eye and sought out my alarm clock. I groaned when I saw I still had a few hours before my interview. My current job at the campus pool hall wasn't, shall I say, working out for me anymore. It's not my fault. I couldn't handle anymore underclassman asking me if I could rack their balls. When I asked one of them if his balls had even dropped yet, my supervisor suggested I start looking for a new job elsewhere.

Finding a new job had to be a top priority. While I earned enough financial aid to pay for tuition and board, it still didn't cover my coffee fixation. My dad would insist on helping me if he found out my financial aid didn't cover everything, but I don't want anything from him anymore. Nothing. Nada.

He did buy me a car when I turned sixteen. At the time, I was still optimistic about winning his attention, so I accepted it. Now, I've come to realize all he wants to share with me is his money, a business transaction of sorts.

I forced my feet to swing over the side of the bed and sat up rubbing my eyes with the palms of my hands. I questioned why I still agreed to live with Lennon when I spotted a glorious cup of coffee on my nightstand from her. God bless her. I'd have to make sure I thanked her when I got back later.

After showering, and drying my hair I still had another two hours before my interview. I tried to eat, but the coiled nerves in my stomach weren't having any of it. To say I was lacking confidence would be an understatement. Any time I ran through interview questions in my head, the image of my father correcting me popped in my head.

Pop. When will you be done with your little dancing hobby?

Pop. Bethany can help you study.

Pop. You don't need me to go with you, practice more independence.

I scrunched my eyes together and banished my dad's negativity. Lying back on my bed, I pulled out my cell to call my mom.

We didn't talk as often as I'm sure she would like us to, but I made sure to call her every weekend and check in on how things were going. Being that it had just been she and I for so long, we have developed a strong bond. Even in my teen years when I quietly rebelled, she and I maintained a healthy relationship. She is everything someone could want in a mother. She celebrated when I succeeded, guided me when I faltered, and supported me when I fell. It's clear now why she and my dad never worked out. They are complete opposites, and not in a good way. "Baby Girl!" My mom chirped into the phone.

"Hi, Mom. What's going on?"

"Oh the usual, sweetie. Working and missing you."

From the outside looking in some might think our relationship to be a bit codependent. That couldn't be farther from the truth. My mom is insanely strong on her own. She's devoted the last couple of years to helping me adjust to her divorce, and then to helping me grow up. Now that I'm gone, I think she has to remember how to live for herself again.

"Did you sign up for the online dating thing I suggested, Mom? "

"No, that stuff is not for me, and my daughter certainly doesn't need to worry about it." She scoffed through the phone.

"Mom, I'm not worried. I think you should start having some fun again. Meet someone you can go out to dinner with or see a movie with. Try to meet some people you want to spend time with outside of work." I tried to not sound pushy.

"Well, look who's being schooled by their daughter."

"Don't say schooled, Mom."

She laughed, "I know, and you're right. I don't want you worrying about me though. Make sure you are having fun and getting the most out of college. Oh! You have that interview today right?" She asked cutting herself off.

"Yep, I'm leaving here in about an hour."

"Good luck, sweetie. I'm sure you will do great. Are you nervous?"

"Not really. I'm just curious about what the job entails. I'm ready for something new, and who knows, maybe it will help me figure out what to do with myself in the long run." I started to sound exasperated.

"Oh Kensie, we've talked about this. You'll find your direction. Sometimes it's not so much about looking for it, but about patiently waiting for it. Just keep working hard like you've always done and you will get there." She reassured me. She's always been great at that. Making me feel like what I do is enough.

"Thanks Mom, I love you. I'll let you know how the interview goes." I hung up from my conversation from my mom feeling motivated and ready for this interview. I dressed in a casual black pencil skirt with red flats and a white tee shirt. I threw on my yellow floral scarf to dress the whole thing up. It wasn't a job at a law firm, after all. One quick touch up of my straightened hair and I was out the door.

***

My text alert dinged at me as I parked my Accord behind the youth building. I pulled out my phone and sucked in a breath at the name shining on the screen along with a snapshot of his gorgeous face.

August put his number in my phone last night as "Humpty" when I had gone to the concession stand. I didn't notice until he texted me when Lennon and I had gotten in for the night. He merely texted "Goodnight, Kensie." After the way we had left each other at the game, the text was a welcome surprise. I lied in bed awake for another two hours after looking into those chocolate eyes on my phone. I may or may not have pulled up my phone list a few more times just to admire him before I fell asleep. A battle between head and heart was being waged. Heart rooted for me to let go of the past and give into August, head rooting for me to walk away.

Humpty: Truth or Dare?

Me: Isn't a dare negligible since you can't see if I'll actually perform it?

Humpty: I knew you'd pick truth. :)

How'd he know? Of course I was going to pick truth. Truths are only as honest as the person telling them. I hadn't decide how honest I wanted to be with August yet, so I'd hide behind half-truths and omissions if need be. I answered him quickly as I walked around the corner to the front of the San Diego Youth Center, or S.Y.C.

Me: Truth

Humpty: Favorite flower?

Me: Rose

Unoriginal, I know, but they're my favorite. Especially Mr. Lincoln's. They smell heavenly. I turned off my phone and pulled down my skirt before walking into the tall brick building. I didn't want to show too much leg. Or maybe I did. Does leg get you a job? I bet some thigh does with the right interviewer. What the hell am I thinking? This is a youth center. I pulled the neck of my shirt up a bit for good measure.

I checked in for the interview at the front desk and took a seat off to the side. The room was small with only a few plastic chairs along one wall. The room wreaked of old stuff. Old teacher desk, old carpet, old woman picking at her blue hair behind the old desk. I doubt she knew she was fluffing her hair with an Afro pick.

As I waited, I peeked through the window behind me into the gym. On one side, kids played basketball with one of the leaders. The other half of the court had a group of teens sprawled out on yoga mats stretching their legs.

"Kensington, John is ready for you." Ick. I cringed at the pretentious family name my dad chose for me.

The receptionist slowly, slowly, slowly, led me to a tiny and musty office down the hall. Holy shit. I'd be fluffing my own blue hair with an Afro pick by the time we get there. I did get a chance to take in closed door after closed door on the way. Perhaps one was the door to my classroom.

I nearly ran into the puff of blue hair when she stopped abruptly and pointed to the only open door without saying a word. I briefly wondered if working here with a bunch of teens had sucked the life right out of her. Yikes.

I peered around the doorframe before

walking in and was greeted by tall gentlemen. John, I assumed.

"Kensington, pleasure to meet you. I'm the Youth Director, John." Nailed it.

He was quite handsome for an older man. I guessed close to my mom's age with his deep smile lines and salt and pepper hair. He had warm eyes that soothed my pacing heart.

"You can call me Kensie, and thank you for calling me for the interview."

I managed to survive the basic interview questions. I answered them all honestly, and John seemed pleased. When he asked me about my hobbies outside of work and school, I shoved my father's condescending voice aside.

"I like to dance. I've been dancing since I was four." I answered holding my breath for his reply.

"Hmmm," John said tapping his pen against his chin while looking at this clipboard. Here it comes, my moment of rejection. "Might work." The breath of air escaped my lips in a whoosh. "We're looking for a dance instructor for our fourteen to sixteen year old girl class. A lot of young women in the class come from some tough backgrounds. They are great kids, but it sometimes takes a lot of patience when dealing with them. Might be a good fit for you if you are up to the challenge?" He cocked one eyebrow at me in question.

"That sounds great, actually." I answered straight away unable to hide my grin. "I have a lot of experience in leadership when it comes to dance. I was the captain of my high school dance team. I even taught the tiny tot class at the studio I went too. I know they weren't teenagers, but I'm sure it takes about the same amount of patience. I'd love to give it a shot." Belonging murmured through my veins, fracturing the walls forged within them.

John smiled standing up from his seat and I followed, "Brilliant. We're glad to have you as a part of our team. I think you'll be a fine mentor for these girls. From what I've seen in this interview, you are a very responsible young woman." I smiled at him and shook his hand. Responsible? I wasn't sure about that, but I wouldn't let him down.

Before I left the youth center John gave me all of my new employee paperwork and wrote me in on the schedule to start immediately. I'd be teaching my first class at the center tomorrow. I withheld myself from doing a little jig in celebration.

Powering my phone back on during the walk back to my car, it pinged relentlessly with messages.

Humpty: Roses.

Humpty: Okay. Favorite Song?

Humpty: No? First kiss?

Humpy: Too much too soon?

I giggled and texted August back immediately, still buzzing from my interview.

Me: Sorry, was at a meeting. Song Dave Matthews, Crush. First kiss, Jake Turner-eighth grade, horribly sloppy and awkward.

Humpty: Oh, poor Jake. It was probably one of the best moments of his life.

Me: I doubt it. I head butted him on the

way in.

Humpty: Rookie mistake. I'm sure you've improved since then.

Hot. Hot in here. I turned up the AC full blast. For me, kissing always had been a means to an end. It was the necessary step towards getting through the emptiness. When I thought about kissing August, my mind went numb in an entirely different way. All my thoughts, my worries, were obliterated the moment I found his lips near mine. Maybe it was because we'd come so close to it, but hadn't kissed yet, or maybe it was just him. Either way there was something about August, and about the magnetic pull between us that turned my mind down enough to feel.

Me: Wouldn't you like to find out?

Okay, too brave. I needed to take it back a step.

Me: I mean, maybe you wouldn't.

Me: That's okay. It doesn't matter.

Shit. I need to shut up now.

Me: Let's not talk about my kissing habits anymore.

Oh god. I scared him off with my rapid-fire texts.

Humpty: You're cute when you ramble, but you're right. I'm dying to find out. Shit, I can't think about anything else.

I dropped my head against my horn releasing a honk and making the receptionist who was now walking by, jump. Her blue hair didn't move an inch with the motion. I waved and apology at her and watched her lift two wrinkly fingers up to her mouth and waggle her tongue in between them. I did a double take to make sure I saw that right, and sure enough that tongue flicked back and forth between the split digits. I was both impressed and horrified. Those teens hadn't sucked the life out of her after all. They made her a Granny gone wild.

Maybe it was the high from scoring the job, or maybe I fed off energy of porn granny, but I had a bout of bravery thundering in my heart.

Me: Me either.

I stamped my feet on the floorboard. I'm going for it. I'm going to put myself out there and see where this thing with August, whatever it is, goes. What's the worst that can happen in a text message anyway? If he doesn't respond favorably, then I can play it off without having him see the humiliation splayed across my face.

On the way back to my dorm I couldn't stop thinking about August. His eyes, his tall body, his humor, and the effortless way he consumed my mind. As hard as I tried last night to find a reason to not be interested in him, it became clear to me that there was something there between us. The chemistry was undeniably there, but if I wanted to explore something more, something deeper, then I had to give it a chance.

Squeezing my way into a parking spot I heard a text come up. I mean really, can they draw the lines on the parking spots any closer? Ping, another text went off.

My stomach flittered.

Humpty: I'm kind of busy.

Flitter meet Plummet. Could he sound

anymore irritated, and why on earth was he texting me if he's busy? I'm such an idiot. *Don't be reckless with a stroke of luck, Kensington.*

Humpty: Okay, I can be there in thirty minutes.

Wait. I'm confused. He's coming over? Another ping.

Humpty: Sorry, Kensie gotta cut our convo short. Talk to you soon though. ☺

What's below a plummet? That's where my heart just fell. He wasn't texting me, well not knowingly. He had texted me on accident. I should be embarrassed for him, but I was humiliated for myself. I stared at the messages thinking about telling him he texted the wrong person, but I chose to let it go. I didn't want to come off as being too concerned, even though my mind was already running a marathon of possibilities. Who was he meeting in thirty minutes?

Rejection teased my thoughts. If a miscommunicated text message brought it out, I couldn't imagine how I would feel if he didn't want to be with me after learning about my past. This is exactly why I didn't let anyone penetrate my carefully constructed wall. The possibility of being rejected terrified me.

"How did it go? How did it go?" Lennon excitedly greeted me when I walked into the room. Her excitement was contagious and reminded me what a great morning I had.

"I got the job! I start tomorrow teaching the dance class."

"Say what?" she exclaimed, "Kensie, that's perfect for you. Good things happenin' Kens, good things."

"It's just a job Len." But it felt like more than just a job. In a way, it was a piece of that fresh start I'd been after since moving away for college.

"A new job, and new man, maybe a new sexual appetite will follow?" She grinned waggling her eyebrows at me.

"I'm not frigid. I'm picky, and I don't have a new man." I couldn't help but sound a bit disappointed after the way my conversation with August had turned out.

"Oh, you've got him. The guy can't keep his eyes off you...or hands." She waggled her finger at me this time, "Did you hear from him anymore today?"

I felt ridiculous admitting how excited I was about my texts with August, but I did. I told Lennon about the flittering I got in my stomach after each ping from my phone. The room fell silent when I told her about the texts I got that weren't meant for me.

I waited for Lennon to say something, anything. I watched her pace the room kicking at the short rug with her boots. Her silent contemplation was awful. *I saw him with a ho bag slut* would do.

She abruptly stopped her pacing and turned to look at me. "Should I grow my hair out?"

"What?" I yelled at her. She was exasperating, but she laughed. She knew what was going on in my overactive imagination.

"I don't think you have anything to worry about, Kensie. He could have been texting Wes, or Capri, or even his mother. It's really not as big of a deal as it feels to you." She reassured me.

The thing is I agreed with her. Deep down I knew it was a simple mistake. I needed to hold onto that brief moment of doubt though. I had to grab on tight to it because I couldn't deny the truth of my attraction to August. He made me want to fall, and see where I landed.

"Seriously though, should I grow my hair out?" She asked. I laughed and fell backwards onto my bed.

"Okay, I'll stop thinking now. Hand me my iPod will you?" I needed a little help in not thinking. Only my music and a little mental choreography could take care of that.

***

I didn't hear from August the rest of the night. Although, I had gone to bed firm in my decision to keep our relationship on a friend only basis, I ached with regret. I pathetically woke up throughout the night and checked my phone in case I missed a text from him. I hadn't. Somewhere between dusk and dawn, amidst hope and disappointment, I settled into indifference. I'd found it to be a place where truths were easier to bare.

My alarm clock buzzed at me for the third time. I set it thirty minutes before I had to be up, so I could push the snooze button a few times before dragging my ass out of bed. Lennon insists my method of rising only increases exhaustion. I disagree. No matter how you slice it, being forced to wake up sucks balls. Yawning, I pulled myself out of bed, and schlepped my way down to the community bathrooms.

I soaked in the shower longer than usual letting the steam soak up my disappointment. I must have been more upset than I let on because I stayed under the spray until the hot water ran out. Even that was refreshing, though, a reminder that relationships often grow cold.

Tiptoeing back into my dim lit room refreshed and ready to tackle the morning I caught the sight of the message light on my phone blinking. Shit, I hope I remembered to turn the ringer off. Lennon loathed wakeups just as much as I did.

"Answer his damn messages." A muffled noise came from the heap on pillows and blankets on Lennon's bed. "The obnoxious thing won't shut up." Oops, ringer was not off.

"Sorry." I whispered to Lennon and checked my missed messages. Surprisingly there was one missed call and a missed text message from August. *A little too late*, I thought to myself.

Humpty: Sorry for calling so early. I wanted to apologize for yesterday. I hope to hear from you today.

I found myself satisfied by his apology, but not any more convinced that we should try anything other than a friendship. I opted to ignore his text for now. I had a job to get to.

***

"This one will be where you teach the dance classes." John unlocked the doors to one of the rooms I had seen situated off to the side of the gym. "Not much, but nothing here is. Stereo is in the corner, and a storage closet in the back you can store your things in."

"It's perfect." The hair on my arms rose as my eyes took the room in. The small space appeared larger with an entire wall of mirrors. The stereo sitting on a tiny table next to a metal folding chair. I closed my eyes and took in the faintest trace of resin meandering around the room. It was perfect.

John chuckled from behind me. "Alright kid, if you say so. I'll be down the hall if you need anything. The girls should be coming in within the next half hour. Good luck."

It had been a while since I had danced in this kind of environment. Unfortunately with my attempts to create a new life for myself, I had neglected this part of it. Dance wasn't something I needed to change. It was my one saving grace and constant. I should have never let that stray over the last three years. Being back in a space dedicated to dance felt like coming home.

I walked over to the stereo and sat down crosslegged next to the table. Loading the playlist I compiled earlier, I heard a commotion of hoarse voices mixed with the kind of high pitched giggling that only comes out of the teenage girl species. I peeked over my shoulder at the door and grinned at three girls solely focused on one of the boys.

"Oh c'mon, Gabby. You'll like it." The boy

told the tallest of the girls who tittered shamelessly.

"You said the same thing last time." The girl's voice teased him. They had to be talking about video games, or a new slushy flavor.

"And you seemed happy when you left." He teased back.

"I guess you'll just have to prove that to me won't you, Jordan." The teenage girl swiped my grin with her suggestive words. They were not talking about slushies. I pushed up from the floor to go stop them before she offered anything more, but their banter already dissipated.

The trio shuffled in whispering and laughing with each other in tightly wound bunch. Perhaps if one broke away from the herd their survival rate dwindled. When the taller one stopped the other two stumbled to a halt behind her stared at me.

"You the new teacher?" the tall girl said as the others peered around her from each side.

"Yeah, I'm your new dance instructor. You can call me Kensie." I straightened my posture and lifted my chin up to give me the appearance of some sort of authority figure. I'd known being young would be a disadvantage to me, but I'd hoped to earn their respect by showing them how much I respected them in turn.

"I'm Gabby." The tall one responded. "These are my besties, Jasmine and Mia." She pointed to each of the girls next to her. Besties? More like minions. Jasmine was a petite girl with frizzy brown hair pulled back in a tight ponytail. Mia was the curvier one of the three and had beautiful long chestnut hair that highlighted her green eyes.

"Nice to meet you ladies. I'm excited to be working with you." I hoped they'd look forward to coming here and learn to trust me as someone to confide in.

Gabby and her minions strolled passed eyeing me up and down and placing their bags along the back wall. "Well, the last lady who was here made us dance to show tunes." The horror. No show tunes. No flips of the wrist, no grapevines, no sashays, none.

I smiled thanking God I brought my show torture free iPod. "Bruno Mars and Jason Derulo, okay?" I asked. The girls grinned and looked between each other nodding. "Okay then, spread out and let's do our warm up."

The majority of the class went better than I could have expected. The girls laughed and went full out with every eight count. I even caught Gabby making pouty lips at herself in the mirror during a hip isolation move.

Although, heading into the last eight count that all changed. Gabby began grumbling and mumbling to her minions who nodded at her and watched me warily at the same time. Readjusting my dampened ponytail I looked at her through the mirror, "Gabby, do you have something you need to get off your chest?"

"Yeah Ms. Kensie, some of the steps are legit, but this dance ain't really my thang." She complained with her hands on her hips.

"And what would be your thing?" Although in my head I said thang with a swivel of my head. My choice of song and choreography fit their age group. Nothing too risqué, but I still incorporated a lot of moves they'd be familiar with. In fact, I hadn't even had the steps solidified when the bundle of them shuffled in today. I choreographed on the fly, with the feel of the moment and the beat. At the moment what I had given them matched their adolescent attitudes, emphasis on adolescent and attitude.

"I don't know. Somethin'…somethin'…More sexy you know?" Oh dear.

"No, I'm not sure what you mean Gabby." Deep breath, I could handle this.

"Sexy like, you know, more twerkin'." Hell to the no. Tossing ones ass around like a hot water bag did not define sexy to me, nor was it happening in my class. Teenagers can be so misguided. I certainly was at that age.

"I think you and I have a different idea of sexy, Gabby. No offense, but I think your idea of sexy might be borderline slutty." The girls gasped and I mentally chastised myself for my choice of words. "Let me explain myself. See, when I think of sexy, I think of a woman who realizes her potential. I think of someone who is independent and in control of the choices she makes. She doesn't act to gratify others, but behaves in a way that gives her the most dignity and self-respect possible." The girls all stared at me.

"So like, girl power?" Mia piped up from next to her leader.

"Kind of, Mia. What I'm saying is…don't let music, or TV, or the guys you like determine what makes you sexy. You own sexy. It's how much you love and respect yourself." I tried to clarify for them.

"So, to be sexy to Jordan I need to like myself?" Gabby asked.

"Yes Gabby, and if Jordan doesn't find your confidence se...er... attractive then he's not worth your time." I repeated the words I needed to hear at her age, but I couldn't be sure they would have changed much for me. Sometimes I think a person needs more than words to guide them. Sometimes they need some kind of salvation.

All at once, the trio beamed from hooped ear to hooped ear. Pride welled up within me over how fast they caught on to my wise advice. I sat up a bit straighter, but startled when a throat cleared from the door.

I whipped my head to glance over my shoulder, throwing myself into a dizzy spell when I saw him. August stood in the doorway with his arms above his head pushed into the corners. His white shirt was soaked in sweat. Typically I'd be revolted. Today, my eyes clung to the image of his abs outlined under the damp cotton. Today, I rejoiced for sweat. Hallelujah, sweat.

I pried my vision from his stomach and redirected it to his eyes, but not before I stumbled over his parted lips panting in exertion. I caught the tips of those lips pulling up into a smile before I connected with his scintillating stare.

Then I beamed from studded ear to studded ear. Damn.

"Hey, Mr. Hunter! " The girls chimed together.

"Mr. Hunter?" I questioned as I took a

calculated aloof sip of water. My tongue was reduced to sand paper in the last five seconds.

"Hello, ladies. Looks like you had a good class today. Kensie." August's grin faltered a fraction when his eyes zeroed in on the dribble of water that missed my mouth completely. The water traitorously made a road map straight to my chest the pointed at August as if to say, *'you, we pick you.'*

"I'm pleased to find you're the new dance instructor." August pulled his eyes from their happy place and locked back on to mine.

"And I am equally, if not more surprised to see that you are the *what* here?" I set my water down on the floor next to me and crossed my arms over my chest, *down girls*. Gabby and the minions whispered to one another behind me as I moved in closer to August by the door in an effort to keep our exchange private.

"I'm the sports coordinator." He pulled his arms down from the doorframe and crossed them over his chest mimicking my stance. Though his sweaty nipples could pick me all day. I'd not be offended.

"Heads up, Mr. Hunter!" A voice shouted from behind him. August turned and caught a basketball before it nailed him in the back.

"Easy, Jordan. You trying to take me out in front of the ladies?" August joked with the boy Gabby had been talking with earlier.

"No sir, just missed my shot." Jordan huffed in exhaustion and wiped sweat of his forehead. "But while I'm here I'd love to say hello to my woman. Hi, Gabby." He lowered his voice a full octave from around August and waved at her.

Gabby fluttered her fingers at him. I rolled my eyes at the exchange; these two were trouble. August caught my concern and tossed the ball back to Jordan.

"Get back over to the court. I'll be there in a minute." His interaction with Jordan seemed effortless, and something about that was so very sexy to me. "Kensie, I'll let you get back to the girls? Catch up with you later?" He arched an eyebrow at me.

No. "Yes." I replied. Dangit, I have no restraint when it comes to him. He grinned and turned to jog back over to the center of the gym with the group of boys. With my restraint already on hiatus, I peeked around the doorframe to watch him, but was caught when he turned and looked over his shoulder at me one last time. The damn smile he gave me stole my breath.

"You feeling sexy Ms. Kensie?" Jasmine asked from behind me. I couldn't help but laugh.

"Alright you three. Great job today. Clean up and head over to the study room. I'll see you on Wednesday." With only a few minutes left in class I let them out early. I needed to recover and regroup on my own.

I couldn't recall Capri ever mentioning where her brother worked, but there had never been a reason for her too. How was I going to keep this platonic when I had to see him at work now? I wasn't in denial about being attracted to him. I didn't want anything to come of it. I couldn't let anything come of it.

I finished cleaning up the room and headed

to the storage close to pack up my bags when I heard my door squeak open. "You girls forget something?" I shouted.

"Yeah." I jumped when his deep voice spoke from behind me. I turned around and came face to face with August. He stalked towards me in the small closet, determination firm in his eyes. He came to stand in front of me so close that I could taste the scent of his sweat on my tongue. Is there a church of sweat? I need to go.

My eyes remained trained on his, which softened when he started to speak. "I was an ass yesterday." He whispered so close that his breath brushed down my face, "I shouldn't have ended our conversation so abruptly."

"It's okay," I whispered back dropping my gaze to his chest. He placed his finger under my chin and lifted it up forcing my eyes to meet his again. "I realize how my rushed goodbye must have seemed. I was anything but ready to end our conversation. In fact, I thought about it, about *you* all night." He dropped his hand from my chin and reached behind him. I smelled it before I saw it. He smiled and brought up a Mr. Lincoln with leaves and thorns still attached. A giggle bubbled up from inside of me.

"Did you pick this from the bushes out front?" I asked taking the rose from him and placing it in front of my nose to breathe in the soft scent.

"Yes." He replied.

"So you bring me my favorite flower freshly picked and I'm supposed to forget about yesterday?" I ask teasingly.

"No." he said, "I don't expect that at all, but

I would love to spend more time with you. I had a really great time talking with you at the game, and I'm hoping this sad excuse for a rose just gave another chance at getting to know you more." He grinned hopefully at me. Little did he know, he had that chance the second he entered my classroom, and the perfect rose sealed it.

"Well, I was going to head over to grab a cup of coffee if you'd like to join me?" I asked him mentally slapping myself on the wrist.

His smile grew causing his eyes to crinkle at the corners. "Done."

"Okay then," I exhaled all the tension I had coiled up inside. "I'll meet you up front in ten minutes?"

"Ten minutes." He said about to turn around, but then stopped himself. He turned around and closed in on me again. I startled at his change in direction, but instead of moving away I instinctively moved forward. The damp heat from his clothing warmed my skin. With my head tilted up, he brought his nose closer to brush against mine. I sucked in a sharp breath and held the air dancing in my stomach. His eyes glanced down towards my mouth causing his eyelashes to tickle my forehead. My eyes fluttered closed involuntarily when he leaned in the fraction of a space left between us. He placed the sweetest and most torturous of kisses on just the corner of my mouth with his soft lips tickling mine. My insides spiraled with such force my stomach clenched in a spasm.

"Ten minutes, Kensie." He backed away taking all his warmth with him. I was left standing in a storage room closet with my eyes still closed, pulse pounding, and a platoon of butterflies wreaking havoc in my gut. I was not going to survive him, and I was going to relish every moment of my downfall. Rejection be damned.

CHAPTER 5

The car ride to the coffee shop was torture, and I'm not worried about being dramatic. I literally could not get the thought of kissing August again off my mind. His smile when I approached him at his truck made me want to smash my lips to his. The flex in his forearm as he opened my car door had me imagining what they would feel like gripped in my hands while he ravaged me. Cuz he would, in my mind he would be so consumed by wanting me, he would ravage me. His delicious scent blew at me when he turned his heater on and I pictured burying my nose into his neck. Even his awful singing to the words on the radio made me want to devour him. Okay, maybe just to shut him up.

"Kensie, can you open the glove box and pull out that bag of gummy bears for me." He asked casually.

"Sure." I answered as casually and opened the glove box trying to still my shaky hand. I handed him the bag, and our hands touched briefly before I quickly brought mine back to my lap. I watched out of the corner of my eye as August tilted his head back and poured a few into his mouth. His muscles in his neck rippled when his lips formed the perfect pout to chew.

His tongue darted out of his pucker, nipping at the tip of his lips before retreating back into his mouth. I sucked in a sharp breath, and drew my gaze away to stare out the window.

"You okay? You've been quiet over there." He turned and asked me as he parked his truck. The mischievous grin on his face told me he knew exactly where my thoughts were the whole way here. Damn him and his kiss.

"I'm good. Just thinking about how I can suggest voice lessons without sounding too rude." I joked with him as I climbed down from my side. He chuckled as he rounded the front of his truck to get me.

"Singing may not be one of my talents, but I've got plenty of other skills to make up for it." He winked and headed to open the café door for me.

"Oh, do you now?" I asked looking at him up and down as I passed by into the shop. "And what might some of the talents be?" I turned toward him. I don't know what had gotten into me lately, but August was bringing out playfulness in me. It felt good to flirt again, and not just for the attention, but because I was enjoying myself.

"Well, for starters I can turn any song into a Vegas lounge version, which you've been lucky enough to see first-hand. You're welcome." He grinned. "I can turn rainbows into Skittles, puppies love me, and I have been known to write poetry while watching the setting sun."

A loud laugh burst from my lips. "Wow, that's impressive Mr. Hunter. I'd love to hear some of this poetry sometime."

Truth in Wildflowers 97

We moved toward the line at the front of the shop where August positioned himself behind me. The line was fairly long even with the morning rush over. I made sure to not stand too close to the person ahead of me. I didn't want to be that bitch that you could feel breathing down your neck in line.

"Roses are red." He startled me as he spoke closing the gap between us and standing directly behind me. I guess August didn't mind being that bitch. "Violets are blue." His voice dropped to a rough whisper as he pressed his front side against my backside. This, I loved when he this. When he moved in closely invading my space like he too couldn't resist the pull. He wrapped one of his arms possessively around the front of my hip gripping the other hip with his hand. Holy heart tremor.

My breath hitched and quickened its pace as his strong fingers sunk into my sensitive skin. He lowered his lips until he grazed my ear sending chills throughout my body. My eyes closed involuntarily and waited for the next line, but it never came. Instead I felt him tense behind me.

"I lied, I suck at poetry, but the truth is you feel really damn good this close to me." I shuddered. With his admission and I had to agree. I felt really damn good that close to him. He placed a gentle kiss behind my ear and stepped back into his own space. As my eyes fluttered open, I took a deep breath dragging me from the depths of his touch. "Go ahead and grab us a seat, Kensie. I'll order the drinks." He placed his hand on the small of my back and gave me the gentle push I needed to get my legs moving.

The coffee shop I frequented was large, but very cozy. Nooks and crannies made out of bookshelves and potted plants scattered the space. I headed towards one of the tiny tables in the back corner beside one of the bookshelves, and tried to regain my bearings. The touch of his hand and hoarse whisper plucked me from the boisterous shop and landed me into a realm of peace. He had consumed me in that one moment, and I had let him. I felt liberated and wary at the same time. My soul allowed him to possess me without ever asking my permission.

August took his seat across from me at our little table. I cleared my head and smiled at him as if nothing had just happened. "Truth or dare?"

He laughed at my attempt to drum up a new conversation with our familiar game. "So it's my turn now, huh? My ego is still trying to recover from my karaoke dare the other night, so how about truth?"

He was so cute that night. I was embarrassed for him and his sucky singing, but he was so damn cute. I liked that we already had memories between us too. I hesitated a minute thinking about it, but I wanted to create more memories for us. We already had our jobs at the youth center and our connection through Capri in common. The thought of seeing more of him from now on made me happy, really happy.

"How'd you wind up at S.Y.C.?" I was curious. Working with teens wasn't something you did unless you really wanted too. Most people couldn't handle the constant combination of bickering and flirtatious teasing between the kids. Then you have their predatory skills. They sense weakness and will sniff it out before an attack. Only the strong survive.

"I kinda fell into it. My dad went to college with John, you met him?" I nodded, "He asked me to help out with one of the fundraiser basketball tournaments. I filled in as a community member on one of the teams with the kids. By the end of the night, he had offered me a job as a recreation leader."

"You must have impressed him." I said.

"Nah." He smiled up at me. "John tried to play it off like I was helping him out, but he was stepping up for me. He knew I didn't have much going on in my life at the time." His smile wobbled and I thought about his tattoo again. I wanted to know more, but before he redirected the conversation back at me, "What about you? How'd you wind up there?"

"I needed a change. I've worked on campus since I came here. The job was okay at first, but lately I've been restless. I saw this job on the help wanted board on campus, and thought it was worth a shot."

"Was it? Worth the shot?" He asked, but by the intensity of his stare he seemed to be asking about more than my job.

"So far. It feels, I don't know, right." I tried to find the words to describe how the last two days had been for me, but came up short.

"Fate." He said plainly, but hadn't lost the intense stare. "In more ways than one. Don't you think?" I darted my eyes down to my fidgeting fingers. The sudden surge of August in my life wasn't something I could ignore, or wanted too. I had thought of the term fate myself a few times, but could fate be trusted? I hoped so.

"I think." I lifted my eyes to find his again. The intensity faded and softened into the sweetest gaze. His eyes reflected the same hope I felt in my heart. True hope, the kind that only comes from living without it.

Our drinks were ready shortly after we sat down, and August and I talked the two hours we spent there. The entire two hours. I'd learned all about his family, a lot of which I already knew from Capri, but I didn't stop him. I liked hearing him talk. I liked hearing his thoughts and his voice. I liked the way his eyes danced when he told stories about him and Wes standing up for Capri as kids. I liked the adoring smile smeared across his face when he mentioned how his mom and dad have been married for thirty years and still stayed up late at night talking. I laughed at the wide eyes and fake grin he plastered on when he said they even still make out.

As much as August told me, I still sensed him holding back. For one, he never mentioned anything after high school directly related to him. I enjoyed his tales of mayhem and mischief, but I found it odd he never mentioned a story from the last five years. Not that I was in a place to judge.

I opened up more to August in those two hours than I had with most people in years. I talked a lot about my mom, Lennon, and even gave him some good back mail material on Capri. I mentioned briefly that I had a strained relationship with my dad, but not much more. I didn't want him to pity me or worse, stereotype me as someone who'd become too dependent on him.

The thought reminded me of Nolan. I rarely thought of him anymore, if at all. The words he had said to me when he broke my heart had somehow still stayed with me.

"C'mon Kensie, don't get all upset." I smeared the tears from my cheeks and glared at him. Upset? How could I not be anything less than ripped to shreds? I gave him my virginity two weeks ago, and now he's breaking up with me.

"I thought you loved me?" I didn't mean for it to come out as whiny as it did.

"I did," he said more sympathetically now and reached up to touch my face. I jerked away from his deceptive touch.

"I don't get it. What did I do wrong?" I thought we were happy, both of us. When Nolan and I started dating six months ago I never imagined it ending like this, or at all. Maybe it was naive of me, but I really hoped we would last. I needed for us to last. I had fallen in love with him, and I needed more than anything for him to never leave me.

Nolan put his hands on his hips and huffed looking up to the dark sky, not a star to be seen through the cloud cover. "You got so clingy, Kensie. You always want to be with me, and if you're not you want to know where I am or what I'm doing. I'm feeling suffocated."

A fresh set of tears poured from my eyes. I loved him. I had fun with him. Of course I wanted to be with him. I held on too tightly though. I held on so tight; afraid of the day he would leave. Well, now here it is.

"You're a great girl, Kensie," he started to say, but I turned and walked away at that. No pity. I don't like pity or reassurance. I heard him sigh from behind me, but didn't stop. I walked until I got into my house, and then I went straight to my room, to cry. Alone.

I hadn't allowed myself to get close to anyone since Nolan. Emotionally anyway. I set out on a mission shortly after he broke up with me to prove that I wasn't clingy starting with his best friend. What followed was a series of one-night stands that held no value to me, and no risk of abandonment. The disconnection and isolation I got from those moments became addicting. Only then was I able to forget all the shattered pieces inside of me.

There is no doubt that August changed things for me. Rather than walking away, I feel pulled to him. He's woken up a person inside of me I thought had been long gone. All this time I'd thought I wasn't ready to trust again, but now I see that I've always wanted that. I just hadn't found the person to inspire me to. Now I've found August.

"I need to get back to work." August said with a groan and glance at the clock. "You wanna come back with me? Hang out a bit?" He grinned hopefully.

"I'll pass." I scrunched up my nose.

"I see you've had enough of me, huh?" He stretched his arms above his head. My eyes followed the muscles in his arm lengthen and contract. *Not enough in the least.*

"Not at all, but I have had enough teenagers for one day." I thought about calling my dad back too, although, that would only take up ten minutes of my time.

"Ah, yes, they take some getting used to." He stood and held his hand out to me, "C'mon pretty girl. Let's get you back to your car."

CHAPTER 6

Lennon was in class for another hour, so I had some alone time after getting home. I sat cross-legged in a mish mash of black sheets strewn all over the bed. The phone in the palm of my hand taunted me with a shining a blue glow across my face. My finger hovered over the call button when the screen went black. Being this nervous over calling my own father saddened me. I touched the keypad reigniting the light. I had to do this, if for anything to know I did what I could to repair our relationship.

I hit send.

Ring. Maybe he won't answer *Ring.* I should hang up and make my bed first. *Ring.* Why is he not answering? A heartbeat before I hung up, he answered mid-ring.

"Hey, kiddo," his voice was hidden below the shouts and cheering in the background. The deep rumble of my childhood both soothed me, and nauseated me. It was hard for me to believe the man who could heal a bad day at school with a bedtime pow wow, had become the source of years of hurt.

"Hey Dad, sounds like your busy. I can call you back later?" It was also hard for me to believe the man who comforted me, was now one that made me nervous.

"Just a minute, Kensington." I cinched my eyes closed ignoring the urge to correct him, and listened to the noise drift further away.

"Hey, kiddo. We're at Parker's play-off game."

"S'okay dad, I won't take up too much time. I wanted to let you know I'll be at Thanksgiving dinner this year." I don't know why I'd decided to go. Spending time with August had me looking through different lenses. I'd spent the last three years avoiding my dad, so perhaps I was part of the blame for our disconnected relationship. One dinner couldn't make things worse. I heard more cheering in the background, but no response from my dad. He probably wasn't even paying attention.

"Dad?"

"What? Oh yeah, sorry Kensington, I don't know what to say. I'm pleased you're going to be with all of us this year. I'll let Jodie know so she can plan dinner.

"Cheers erupted through the line again. "Atta boy, Parker! Nice corner shot!" My dad shouted into the phone. I guess my fabulous athlete of a stepbrother is saving the game again. "I need to get back to the stands, kiddo."

"Bye, da.." and he hung up.

I stared at my screen trying to decide how the call went. On a scale of Tom Cruise jumping on a couch, to a Brittany Spears fan ugly cry, I sat comfortably at a Kristen Stewart halfsy smile.

"Roomie, I'm home." Lennon bounded in the

room, but paused in the doorway with grocery bags in hand, "Wait, what happened? You're abusing you're cheek."

Lennon had been my roommate since freshman year. I will never forget walking in and seeing her hanging her band posters all over my side of the room. She had already decorated her bed in purple and black linens and hung black roses from the ceiling.

"What are you doing?" I asked her as I watched the pint size black haired beauty standing on my mattress.

"Decorating our room," she answered without stopping what she was doing.

"Who's to say I want to wake up to Austin Carlisle every morning."

She dropped her poster clay on my bead and stared at me in disbelief. "Do you have a vagina?"

I choked on my spearmint gum. "Uh, yes...." I waved my hand across my nether regions.

"Then you want to wake up to this man every morning. I'm doing you a favor. You can even play with your snatch a little while he smiles down on you." She continued to hang up the other corner of the poster. I immediately liked her. She was sassy and unguarded, and everything I had hoped for in a roommate. I wanted real, and it seemed that Lennon kept it real.

"Well, I guess I should be thanking you. I'm trying this whole born again virgin thing, so Austin will do a nice job of keeping me occupied."

Lennon's eyes widened at me in disbelief and jumped off the bed to plumage through her boxes. "Oh honey, here I have an M. Shadows one for you too sweetie. Sounds like Austin might need some backup."

From then on, we were best friends. She's the rocky to my road, and the vodka to my tonic. She's quick to call me out, and even quicker to have my back. Put simply, Lennon is the best friend I've ever had.

"I called my dad." I peered up at Lennon hoping she'd put some calm to my unease. She also had the ability to add a little extra tenacity too it, so much so that I often wished I could bottle it up to use for myself. I may need it when I visit my dad.

"And," she dropped the bags in the doorway, and sat on the bed beside me. "How'd it go?"

"Okay I think. I mean, He was at Parker's game so obviously he was busy, but he stepped away to take my call." I shrugged my shoulders. Gratification never came with the call, but neither did regret.

"Oh sweetie, that isn't bad at all. That's actually pretty decent of your dad. Did you talk much?" Lennon placed her hand on my knee offering me comfort. For someone who was so fierce, she never shied away from affection.

"No, not really. I told him I'd be there on Thanksgiving." I flinched when I bit my cheek too hard leaving a metallic seeping in my mouth.

"So, you're going? Why'd you decide to go this year?" A wave of panic washed over me that Lennon recognized immediately. "No...don't over think Kens. This could be a good visit for you two, and if he breaks your heart again, I'll shower his beloved Beemer in tampons and maxi pads."

"What?"

"Don't question my retaliation techniques. Go with it." She kicked her boots off letting them fall to the side of the bed in a clunk. "I am curious though, why the change of heart?"

"I wouldn't go as far as to say a change of heart, more like a last chance."

Lennon regarded me closely, "I think I like this plan. It's like you're reaching out, looking for something to grasp. It's good." She smiled wickedly, "You should start with grasping August," she nudged me with her shoulder, "Eh? Eh?"

"Well..." I trailed of and looked coyly over my shoulder.

Lennon's eyes widened, "Did you grasp that? You grasped that didn't you? You little floozy!"

"No!" I shoved her away from me laughing, "But I did see him today. If you can believe it, he works at the youth center I got hired at. He's some kind of leader. Fate's a slick bitch." I was starting to like her, and the welcome predicaments she placed me in lately, like the storage closet.

"There's more. Spill it woman." I groaned. What was she a savant? "And before you call me a witch or some crazy ass thing, your face is the shade of Capri's lipstick." Of course, my blush never lied.

"He kind of kissed me." I didn't even try to conceal my smile, "On the corner of my mouth."

"Like, on purpose, or did he miss?" She

asked confused.

I laughed and threw my pillow at her. "On purpose. At first I thought he was being a gentleman, but now I think he was trying to tease me."

"Well, hot damn. Your dad wasn't King Douche and August is lighting a fire in your pants." She pulled a bottle out of one of her grocery bags. "Margaritas and chick flicks. Let's do this."

One *Mean Girls* viewing and way too many tequila shots later, Lennon and I were roasty toasty. We came up with a game where we would take a shot every time the other person could quote a scene word for word. We had watched the movie over a dozen times together, so that equaled a lot of shots. I wasn't much of a drinker anymore, but I decided it was okay since I was in the safety of my dorm room with only Lennon. There weren't any guys around to lose myself to tonight. Unless the RA came knocking on our door, but I'm pretty sure my body wouldn't be compelled to launch itself at the five foot two calculus major.

"So," Lennon began while wiping her entire hand across her face, "lemme get this straight." She slurred a little at me. "He has kissed you on the corner of your mouth, and your cheek. Not butt cheek, as you clarified for me."

I giggled. "Yes, all in one day. Thas a lot of body parts for one day. Don't you thin?" I looked up at her from where my head dangled upside down off the edge of my bed. Thank God I wasn't slurring like she was.

"I thin he should be able to do better, sweet

cheeks. How could he not want to smother you with kisses even after only an hour? We should call him. Tell him you need more kisses. Smothering."

I rolled over onto my stomach and reached out to grab my phone off the side table. I missed my grab and sent it tumbling to the floor. "Shit, my hands aren't working." Lennon and I both giggled uncontrollably. I was going to regret this in the morning. "Maybe I'll sext him."

Lennon sat up as quickly as her sluggish body could move and her wide eyes sparkled at me. "Yes! Let's sext." She clapped her hands together like a schoolgirl, although she missed her palms a few times smacking her wrists. "Oh, I'm so excited Augie came along to help you get your groove back."

"I've always had my groove, Lennon." I stood up from my bed and swayed my hips in a half hazard assumingly sexy way. "I've had it under lock and key. I'll give August the code." I raised my eyebrows and Lennon crinkled her nose at me.

"No more cheesy jokes for you. That was lame." Lennon's comedic bone must lose its blood supply when she drinks, cause I'm freaking hilarious right now.

"Okay, so how should I do this? How does one sext?" I must approach this task and professionally as possible.

"I think you have to say some dirty things and send him a picture of your nipple."

I looked at Lennon in disgust. "My nipple? Who wants to see a nipple?"

"Okay, the whole boob?"

"I'm not sending August a picture of my boob. He needs to earn boobage."

Lennon and I ran some ideas back and forth and even Googled. "How to sext?" After wiping the tears form our endless laughing, I had it.

"I know Len! I'm going to send him pictures of all the new places I want him to kiss."

She did some version of the MC hammer dance across the carpet, "You're a genius, Kens. That boy's not gonna know what got into you."

"Okay, what first?"

"You should start small, build his anticipation."

"Anticipation. Yes, he needs anticipation. Okay." I thought for a moment. "How about my shoulder. That could be sexy?"

"Perfect! Hand me your phone and push your strap over."

Lennon grabbed my phone from me and took to picture.

"Okay, now what do I say?" I thought and came up with something suggestive but not too revealing.

Me: You've missed a couple of spots.

"Oh that's good," Lennon squealed over my shoulder.

"Quick send another one before he can respond."

Next she captured my neck. Snap. My collarbone snap, and got in one more of my jawline, snap, before I got my first message tone from August.

Humpty: Oh?
Humpty: Shit Kensie...
Humpty: Okay, what the hell are you doing?

Lennon and I laughed as his texts flew in one after the other. I thought to make a snarky remark about accidentally sending him those texts, but I decided honesty would be the best. Even in my intoxicated state, I was clear about not wanting any blurred lines between us.

Me: I'm sexting you.

I waited a few minutes with no response. "I shouldn't have told him that." I clicked on the message I sent him frantically trying to delete it. How is it that my phone can talk to me, but can't delete a message I just sent? Someone needs to get on that.

Lennon patted my shoulder. "I think he's taking care of some business with his bottle of lotion, if you know what I mean. Lotion for the motion."

The blood in my veins chilled numbing a few fingers and toes. I had said too much. I misread him today. He could be laughing his ass off right now too. No, that's not it. This is hot. My sexting is so hot. Another text came in.

Humpty: I'm so on board with this.
Humpty: Seriously though, can you send me more?

Lennon and I shrieked together. We'd better keep it down or the R.A. really would make an appearance. "Okay, more provocative now, Kens. Can you do this?"

She placed both hands on my shoulders and looked into my eyes, "I can do this" I replied completely amped up. If August was in, I was in. Does he want to jump off a bridge? Done. Swim with some sharks? I'll bring the wetsuits. Wrestle an alligator? I'll prepare myself with extra lunges to better clamp its head between my thighs of steel.

Next came a love handle shot. Yes, I have them, and tonight I'm showing August how hot they are. Next up, my hipbone. Snap. Lower back. Snap. Upper thigh. Snap.

This time August's texts didn't wait.

Humpty: Kensie….

Humpty: Fuck.

Humpty: Wait…are you drunk…

Me: Define drunk

Humpty: Well, now I can't say anymore. I don't want to take advantage of the situation.

Me: Take advantage. Humpty: I would never take advantage of you.

A stab nicked my self-esteem. Here I was putting myself out there, in a sext session no less, and he was denying me.

Me: So…you don't like my sexting?

Humpty: Oh no, I like this. I'd prefer to see you in person though.

Me: Yeah?

Humpty: Yeah, so I can kiss every one of those places on you, and then some.

"Oh Jesus, I need some fresh air. You two are making me all hot and bothered." Lennon fanned herself as she headed toward the door. "I'm gonna run and grab a bottle of water and give you some privacy. Want one?"

"No, thanks." I was left alone with August on my phone.

Me: Define some.

What can I say, I was feeling brave.

Humpty: Well for starters I'd kiss that perfect little ass I held in my hands the other night at Tommy's.

Me: Yeah?

Humpty: Yeah, then I'd kiss the soft spot behind your knee.

My knee? I wanted to clarify, but I wasn't going to ask questions now.

Humpty: Then I trail my lips up your thigh. Maybe I'd nibble a little on my way up. Would you like that Kensie?

Me: Yeah.

I think I'd really like that. I like the sound of it a lot.

Humpty: I'd stop at that spot right at the top of your thigh. You know the one I'm talking about? Right where my lips would graze the outer edge of you.

Holy shit.

Me: Yeah?

Humpty: Would you like that Kensie?

Me: A lot.

I was getting worked up now, and anxious for his next message. His end of the line remained silent longer than I expected though.

Humpty: Sorry Kensie, I had a call come in.

What?

Me: Ok.

Humpty: Shit, I'm really sorry, but I've got to go.

What? No, no!

Me: Ok

Humpty: Trust me Kensie, best night of my life. Thank you for these pictures. I'm never deleting them. Ever.

Apparently not good enough to ditch whatever the phone call requires and finish this off with me.

Me: You'd better not show Wes my goodies.

Humpty: Not at a chance. Now go drink a bottle of water and take two aspirin. You're going to feel like shit in the morning.

Me: Bossy.

Humpty:Goodnight, pretty girl. Goodnight frustrating boy.

I fell asleep before Lennon made if back to the room that night in a swirl of August and a wary smile on my face.

CHAPTER 7

I will never eat cotton balls again. I rolled over in bed and buried my face into my pillow groaning. Oh right, I didn't eat cotton balls; I drank 'te kill ia'. I attempted to sit up, but my head weighed my body down.

"Rise and shine, sleeping beauty." Lennon chirped from somewhere above me. "Two aspirin and a bottle of water. Dr. Hunter's orders."

Cold plastic assaulted my face. "What is he? My dad?"

"On the contrary, princess. He is a man smitten by you and who wants you to feel well. Your father would lecture you on the statistics of binge drinking." Lennon forced open the palm of my hand and placed the two pills in it. "You've got work in an hour. I'd hate to see you explain to a room of teenagers that you were late because you were hung over after sexting your boyfriend all night."

"He's not my boyfriend." I mumbled before mashing the pills into my mouth.

"Sexting is overrated," if you're wasted and a novice, maybe next time I'll be more seductive. What am I saying? I won't allow a next time, unless he liked it. Then, perhaps I'll arrange a next time. I'm not sure what has gotten into me, but I think I like it. August was someone special for sure, if he's causing me to bloom when I thought I had already withered.

***

Turns out, the water and aspirin worked wonders. Points scored for August. I strolled in to youth center at eight am and ready for the day. I signed myself in at the front desk and waved hello to the receptionist. Her hair was a faded pink today. Only her eyes looked up at me from where she was working on supply orders. I almost missed the judgment in her eyes. Awareness. Recognition? She knew I'd sexted. My pulse accelerated and I darted my eyes around the room. Clock. Chair. Skittles wrapper on the floor. Her throat cleared and I made contact with the judging eyes again. They narrowed at me and read all my secrets. Then I took off.

I scurried down the hall so fast, I nearly missed John's hello from inside his office. I slowed down and poked my head in on my way to my classroom.

"Morning, John."

"Kensie," He waved me over with one hand while patting his chewing mouth with the other. "Slow down. I brought you in a breakfast sandwich and some coffee. Figured since I'd tortured you with opening on a Saturday, I'd treat you." Huh, how thoughtful. My stomach growled in appreciation as it caught scent of the breakfast sandwiches.

"Thank you. I'm starving."

I tossed my dance bag in the corner of his office and plopped down in the chair across from him. He slid the sandwich and coffee towards me inhaling another bite. My dad wasn't a dainty eater either. "No worries, kid. I like to take care of my staff. You guys work hard."

I'd never had a boss like John. He ruled with a supportive hand, and took care of his employees like family. I'd even received a voicemail last night to let me know the girls had nothing but great things to say about the class. His words were, "You've successfully got them excited about something other than watching those boys play basketball." I grinned all night after the unexpected call. It's amazing what a few kind words can do to a tired soul.

"Any special plans for the holidays?" John asked before taking a bite of his half eaten sandwich. The youth center closed for a month in winter. The goal was to keep the gym open so the kids had a place to come hang out, but for now funding was low.

"Spending time with family." I said putting the sandwich aside when my stomach became uneasy.

"They around here, or ya have to travel?" John kicked back in his chair.

"My mom is about an hour north of here. My dad and his family aren't too much further." John nodded his head a considered a minute before responding.

"So divorced, huh? Gotta be rough during the holidays." He didn't sound pitying, thank

God. He spoke like divorces happen every day, and I guess they do. People are walked out on all the time.

"Not really, I mean, it's mostly just been me and my mom. I visit my dad every now and then." I mumbled the last bit and took a sip of coffee.

"Hm." was the only response I got. I couldn't tell if John didn't say more because he felt sorry for me, or if he picked up on my distaste for this topic of conversation. Whatever the reason, I was glad he let the discussion end.

We sat in silence for a few minutes sipping coffee and John chewing his food. He finished his in record time crumpling up the wrapper into a tight little ball and made the basket into the trashcan on the opposite side of the room.

"So, August seems to be pretty taken by you." John said patting his rounded belly. I nearly choked on my attempt at another bite of sandwich.

"He's bossy." I mumbled behind my food, but didn't make eye contact with him, "And he's an awful singer with even worse dance moves." I added for good measure.

John laughed with a snort and slapped his thigh. "Thought so. I saw the way you looked at the boy, and don't think I didn't catch you two driving away in his car yesterday." Crap. I hadn't considered that employees might be prohibited from spending time together outside of work.

"I'm sorry, John." I rushed to explain, "The outing was harmless really, just a friendly cup of coffee." I shook my head to reassure him and myself. I tried to keep the thoughts of what I did last night away. August threatened my sensibilities. Keeping this job was important to me, and I couldn't lose it over guy.

"Well, that's too bad. I'd hoped you were finally the one to make him come around." He said unexpectedly and squinted at me. I assumed to hear a lecture on risks of dating a coworker, not the promotion of it.

"What do you mean?"

"He hasn't had a girlfriend since he started working for me three years ago. He's a nice looking kid, well mannered, responsible. It can't be that girls don't want to date him. So he's been holding out for some reason. Then, you came along."

I let John's words sink in. I guessed he didn't have a girlfriend because Capri would have told me. The three years part stumped me though. August seemed confidant, and I had first-hand experience in how charming he could be. Oh God, what if he's a man whore? Wes is a man whore, I think. They probably run in packs, and hunt. I'm being hunted by August. I'm his prey. Huh, that doesn't sound half bad.

"Watcha ya contemplatin'?" John asked, when he noticed I was lost in my thoughts.

"Maybe I'm not special. What if I'm one of many?" I remained collected. I didn't want John privy to my thoughts on August.

"Don't doubt your worth. I'd be honored to have any of my boys date ya." John's words touched me. He'd known me less than a week and he'd already had such kind things to say to me. He sat back up in his chair and leaned towards me. "Hear me when I tell ya this. August isn't a playboy. You're special."

Special. I allowed the word to roll around in my mind and knock against the hardened ridges. Perhaps if I let it stay long enough, it could chip away and soften them some. *Special.*

***

After breakfast with John, I retreated to the classroom to prepare for the morning. I sought solitude to reflect on our conversation. One step into the room and the scent of fresh wax and Windex loosened my wound muscles.

I walked to the stereo kicking my flip-flops off along the way. One tug of the hair tie securing my hair and the wavy tendrils fell wildly around my face. Settling on a song, I plugged my phone into the stereo. The lyrical tune filled the classroom breathing life to all four walls. I rolled my head and kicked one leg out stiffly with a flexed foot. My arm and hand followed the same stiff motion.

I set out in a series of slow rigid turns across the spans of the floor. I relished the sting left across my cheeks after each whip of my hair. On the final turn, I spun to a knee towards the floor, but made a change last minute and wound back up to my feet. I lifted another leg in front of me in an attitude position and held firm. Every muscle in my body contracted to hold the stiff pose until the disjointed beat broke into a fluent rhythm.

My leg slackened and my bones followed. Every extremity gave into the swaying and reached back and forth loosely. My head tilted upwards and rocked side to side with the beat.

"Ms. Kensie!" A tempered voice snapped me from asylum I'd created. I tilted my head down towards Gabby with her minions standing in the doorway. I help up a finger and rushed over to turn the music down.

"That what we're doin' today?" Gabby nodded up at me.

"No, no. I was messin' around." I wrapped a protective cloak over my movements.

"Hm." Gabby crossed her arms over her chest and her minions mimicked her. "That's cool, but that stuff's too Emo for us. We too street for it."

"I'm street." I said having a hard time maintaining my straight face. The girls exploded in fits of laughter. We started class shortly after, where I proved to them how street I could be. According to the all-powerful and wise Gabby, I had some work to do.

As class ended, I said goodbye to the girls I was becoming very proud of. I blew my hair out of my face and sprawled out on the ground. I'd worn myself out. After a few minutes on my back soaking up the chill of the ground, I reached over to my bag feeling for my phone. I hadn't heard from August since last night. I feared my attempts at intoxicated seduction might have scared him off.

Oh what the hell, I sexted the boy I might as well call him. I powered up my phone and immediately got a voicemail alert. To my surprise, I had a message from August. I smiled to myself getting a dose of the giddies.

The bubbled excitement in my stomach turned to nervous pangs when I began to listen to the message. It was August, but he hadn't called me on purpose. The muffled voices and static told me he had dialed my number on accident.

That wasn't the worst though. The worst part was the unmistakable mumble of a female. I should have hung up, but I'm a glutton for punishment. I kept listening for the entire five-minute message. First there was the giggle, not mine, not Capri's, not anyone I know. It was followed closely by August's mumbled chuckle. My stomach dropped. She'd made him laugh.

I bit my thumbnail unable to stop the message. Next, I heard a mumbled thank you from this mystery woman. There was a moment of nothing, a few clicking noises, and the rumble of an engine. He was in a car with her. I could barely hear above the beating of my heart swallowing my ears. My temples pulsated so strongly I squinted my eyes closed. Then, silence, a click, maybe a seat belt? I strained to hear anything steadying my breathing so the whooshing didn't drown out the faint sounds on the message. Then, an abrupt and audible, "Want to come in?" In her voice, and the line went dead.

CHAPTER 8

"That son of a bitch!" Lennon cursed throwing her tiny Bug into park while I crawled into the back making room for Capri in the front. "What the hell is wrong with your brother?" Lennon barked at Capri making her jump and hit her head on the door jam.

"He's a man." Capri shrugged as she flipped the make-up mirror on the visor down and smeared on a layer of shiny lip-gloss. "What did he do anyway?" She flipped the visor back up and turned towards me smacking her lips together.

I opened my mouth to answer but Lennon cut in, "He butt dialed Kensie while he was with some ho-bag this afternoon."

Capri held her lips together tightly. She squinted out of the passenger window and watched the coastline pass by. "Spill it, Capri," I said watching her through the mirror. "Who is she?" I watched her squeeze her eyes closed and silently cursed myself for never asking her if August was involved with someone else. Capri took a deep breath and turned back around locking her August brown eyes on mine.

"Kensie, he's not seeing anyone else. I don't know who was in the car with him, or why, but

I do know you are the only one he is interested in." The tightly packed air I held in my lungs whooshed out.

"Bullshit." My fiery friend piped up as she flipped off the car that had just passed her. "You don't see Kensie driving around with any other men do you? No, you don't." She answered before Capri, "'cause Kensie is a class act. When she likes someone she's committed from day one."

"I am?"

"You are. You don't know this because you haven't given yourself the chance to be in a relationship, but you are very faithful."

"Thank you." I crossed my arms and nodded to myself very pleased with her assessment.

"But tonight that changes. Tonight you are going to sample the platter a little bit before you order from the menu." Lennon's car screeched into the beach parking lot sending Capri and me into the doors. Capri straightened up and turned back toward me.

"Kensie, I'm serious. This is all new to August, so I can't promise he will make all the right choices, but I can promise you he really likes you. Don't do anything that will hurt him." Lennon's head whipped around to stare at Capri at the same time I sucked that air back into its cage in my chest. I'd never intentionally hurt August, and having Capri warn me not to, offended me. I wanted to tell her I was the one who should be worried about getting hurt, but something about the wary tone in Capri's voice told me to just leave it be.

Against Lennon's encouragement, the only

tasting I'd be doing tonight would be in the form of S'mores. Even in my current limbo of emotions, there was not a male soul I'd want to spend time with other than August. So while Capri spent time with her latest boyfriend at his frat's bonfire, and Lennon buzzed around the crowd, I'd be gorging myself with graham crackers, chocolate, and marshmallows.

Chocolate.

August.

Chocolate August.

Oh well, I tried.

Walking towards the party, a group of shirtless guys shuffled by us with a table and ice chest. One of them barked at us as they passed. Lennon barked back. In the distance, coeds cheered when a set of girls mastered the keg stand. A few couples scattered the sand with legs and arms tangled around each other.

As we neared the fire, Capri's new guy swooped in giving her a side hug and holding his red plastic cup in the other hand. I tried not to judge his hugging technique. Though in the category of girlfriend greeting, he gets a two.

"Tanner, these are my friends Lennon and Kensie. Girls, this is Tanner." His hug may have been lame, but he was exactly what I'd learned Capri's type to be. Clean cut, polo shirt, khaki cargo shorts. His hair was blond and just long enough he had to flip his head to the side to clear the strands from his eyes; again, and again, and again.

Lennon stuck out her hand and gave Tanner a firm handshake. "What are your intentions with my friend?" Capri and I rolled our eyes at each other before Tanner yanked his hand away wrapping it around Capri's shoulders with another flip of his hair.

"Nothing but good times," *hair flip*, "and good love." *Hair flip accompanied by a wink.* Yuck.

"So, how'd you two meet?" I asked Tanner trying to steer him from his sleaziness. He flipped his hair again. Who am I kidding? He can't even save himself.

"Funny story," he laughed. "I was in the Student Union talking to this girl." "You were hitting on her." Capri interrupted.

"Don't cut me off babe," Lennon and I tensed. I could feel the pulse of her fists clenching and unclenching through the space between us.

"Don't talk to me like that, Tanner." Capri grunted to him, although not as forcefully as I would have liked. Still, I'm glad she spoke up.

"Okay babe, sorry, so anyway." He continued on, "This other girl kept ignoring me. So disrespectful. That's when Capri walked by with her long legs and tiny shorts. I left that other girl where she sat and followed after Capri." He placed a kiss on Capri's cheek and winked at us again.

"That was a funny story? I'm not laughing," I whispered to Lennon.

"No, I wanna high kick his balls off, but I'm not laughing." She whispered back.

"So, you only like her for how hot she is?" Lennon spoke up to Tanner. *Hair flip* "You didn't even mention how sweet, kind, or easy going she is." *Hair flip, hair flip, hair flip.*

"Nothing about who she is, only what made your dick jump?" *Spastic, rapid hair flip.*

Tanner remained silent, but his hair spoke volumes.

Lennon made him nervous, which she had intended to do. As much as I'd love to watch her make him squirm a bit more, Capri had enough. She tapped her jeweled sandal in the sand sending up a puff of fine dust around her legs.

"Alright Capri," I said, "why don't you two head over to the party and we will catch up with you in a bit. I want to find a friend of mine from psych real quick and say hi." She mouthed a silent *Thank You* to me and pulled a still seizing Tanner toward the party. Without missing a beat, he reached down and gave her butt a hearty squeeze.

"He's a tool bag." Lennon said to me while glaring them walk away.

"Yeah, he's not my favorite that's for sure, but we've only just met him."

"How is it you have so much faith in others and none in yourself?" Lennon asked grabbing my hand in hers and yanking me towards the party. I stumbled along, my feet tripping over her words.

***

I'll never pee in a frat house again. Lennon and I found ourselves ambushed by two of Tanner's fraternity brothers. Hunter and Jake currently enlightened us about the peepholes they had drilled into the walls of the bathrooms in their frat house. I doubt they would have divulged such information had they not spent the last hour at the beer pong table. Lennon seemed to enjoy dragging the dirty little secrets out of the inebriated twosome. I, on the other hand, mentally vowed to seek a bush rather than the bathroom at Casa de Sigma Chi.

Midway through their blueprint of how to be a peeping tom, Jake jumped up and tripped sideways on his bare feet. "That's where I know you from!" Oh shit, I'd already used the bathroom there.

"I had biology with you freshman year." Crisis averted. I couldn't remember the guy at all though. Nothing about him was familiar to me. He swore we even talked on a few occasions. "I even asked you out once." He told me as we sat together on a log in front of the fire. Lennon busied herself by placing requests with the aspiring musician who had shown up with his guitar.

"You did?" I doubt I'm the one he's remembering.

"Yeah, I asked you if you wanted to go out for pizza with some of my buddies. You straight up told me you didn't date." Well, that sounded like me.

"I did?" I did. I probably shared a likeness to Keanu Reeves dodging dating requests in slow motion.

Here comes a date! Quick, backwards table top!

He laughed at my confusion and scooted a little closer to me on the log. "Yeah, you did. I told you it wasn't a date, just pizza with some friends, and you told me pizza leads to sex."

I barked out a laugh at that. Yep, that was me. "I remember now. Sorry about that. I was a little callous for a while." I wouldn't admit the truth, that I had been callous a long, long while. Up until very recently, up until a tall dark haired, chocolate eyed, dangerous mix of sexy and sweet August showed up into my life. He had me reconsidering my stance on dating. Had being the operative word, because after my voicemail today I wasn't so sure August and I had the same idea when it came to dating.

"No hard feelings." He scooted again until his thigh touched mine. I scooted away. "I'm just glad I ran into you again. You seem good now. Happy." He scooted back towards me, and he was right. I was happy. The fuzzy view of my life had started to come into focus.

My interest in August was clear. My visceral reaction to him had peaked my curiosity to begin with, but the time we had spent getting to know each other is what really let my carefully placed veil slip a bit. The voice message I heard today blurred my thoughts on what to do about those blossoming feelings. I wanted to trust him, and I wanted to see where things could lead with us. Those desires alone were monumental for me, but want and assurance were two very different things.

I was so preoccupied by my thought of August, I thought I saw him walking out of the parking lot towards the party. I had it bad. Whether I trusted him or not, my mind could have cared less. It watched the stranger navigate through the crowd and imagined August searching for me. *Frantically he bobbed and weaved, until his eyes locked on me across the sand. With determined strides he made his way to me and pulled me passionately into his arms before his tall bearded friend could catch up.* Wait, tall bearded friend?

I realized my mind wasn't dreaming him up, but he was actually here. I wanted to ditch poor Jake and dash from this log to August's forearms. My soul leapt towards him attempting to pull my body along. As if he felt the same tug, August looked up from where he was scanning the crowd for me. We were too far away to make any eye contact, but I knew the moment he saw me. I felt it like a zap of electricity on my skin, and I saw Wes stumble into him when he halted his steps. I forced myself to turn back toward Jake, who had been talking to me this whole time.

"Maybe," Jake started. "Maybe, I could take you out for that pizza? No friends this time. Just us two?" Oh hell, I hadn't seen that coming. Before I could politely decline, a deep voice I knew so well spoke behind us.

"No can do, Romeo. She's spoken for." August reached between us grabbing my hand and pulling me off the log to his side. Jake stood and threw his arms in front of him in surrender. "Sorry man, I didn't know she had a boyfriend."

"She doesn't." I yanked my hand away from August's and started stomping off in the sand away from the fire. How dare he be with another girl today, and then claim me? I didn't get the chance to claim him, instead I had to listen to someone else make him laugh.

"Kensie!" August called behind me. "Kensie,

wait up. What's this all about?" He caught up to me and gently grabbed my hand. My mind told me to keep stomping off into the night, but the warmth of his hand shot straight to my heart.

"This," I gestured to the fire and the group of people that were now either stumbling, singing along to the musician's songs, or flat out in the sand, "is a party, August."

"I know this is a party." He looked disappointed in me for my avoidance. "What I mean is, why did I get a call from my sister telling me to come straighten out the mess I made? Why did you not answer any of the gazillion calls I made to you in a panic? Why did I show up here to see you snuggled up with some other dude?" He still held my hand in his and the confusion swimming in his eyes nearly drowned me.

"I wasn't snuggling up with anyone, August. I'm just hanging out at a party."

"Okay, so why haven't you answered any of my calls? I was worried." Guilt gnawed at my firm stance.

"I was busy. No big deal." I'm such a bitch. August's eyebrows pulled together and he takes his hand from mine. The chill left in my palm a stark contrast to his effect on me.

"No big deal? Well, it's a big deal to me, Kensie. It's a big deal that I can't get you off my mind. It's a very big deal that I want to spend all my time with you. It's a very big fucking deal that I drove all over town like a madman thinking you were... that something bad had happened to you." His chest heaved just inches from me. I wanted to give into his distress, but I couldn't ignore what I'd heard earlier.

"If this..." I gestured between the two of us. "is a big deal, August, then why were you with another girl this afternoon?" I asked quietly breathing in enough of his anger for the both of us.

A look of recognition sparked in his eyes. "I was with another girl today," he began, but didn't finish as I cut him off.

"No shit, you butt dialed me and I got to listen to five agonizing minutes of it. Five minutes of trying to rationalize who it could be, why she was with you, and why you hadn't mentioned it to me." Screw this. I turned around and plodded kicking up sand on my way towards one of the small coves on the beach.

"I butt dialed you?" He yelled from behind. I could hear his footsteps pressing into the soft sand from behind me, but I didn't stop walking. Just as I reached the solace of the cove, his hand made gentle contact with my forearm. Damn him and his long legs.

"I butt dialed you." His voice cracked over a hidden laugh. I whipped around and glared at him.

"Yes! It's not funny." I propped my hands stiffly on my hips.

"No, no. Not funny at all." He said shielding his face from me in the darkness, but I caught the smirk on his face shining in the moonlight.

"You were with someone else, and she made you laugh." The jealousy and hurt I'd been holding in all day wanted escape, but I held those betraying feelings hostage.

His eyes flicked back up to me and they

widened in understanding. "I hurt you." He said taking a step toward me.

I took a step back. "I'm not hurt. I'm angry."

"I'm sorry I hurt you." He said taking another step toward me.

I took another step back. "I'm not hurt..." I started to say again, but he cut me off.

"I know, you're angry. They're kind of the same thing though, Kensie." He said taking another step toward me and I remained still. "You're angry because me being with another girl today hurt you." He said taking advantage of my immobile stance and moved another step closer until he was in front of me. "I'm sorry." He said lifting his hand to me, but then pulled it away before he made contact. My cheek cooled in rejection.

"It's no big deal." I shrugged, but I knew I didn't fool him. He was right. I was livid because I was hurt. It hurt to know that he was spending the same kind of time with someone else that he had spent with me. What was a huge step for me became devalued in that voicemail.

He cocked his head to the side and watched me. Closely. Under the white glow from the moonlight his brown eyes had a molten quality to them. I fidgeted under the intensity of his stare and looked away from the heat searing between us.

"Fuck it." He said before his hands were on me gripping my waist and his lips smashed into mine. My breath hitched in my chest, but my body was paralyzed by his touch. His hands yanked me into him breaking me from my shock and punching me with desire.

I opened my mouth to him in a moan and he didn't waist a second invading my mouth with his tongue. I met his immediately, and lifted my once limp hands around his shoulders pulling myself further into him. Our tongues tangled wildly, our mouths moving roughly against each other.

This kiss was all lust, passion, and pent up desire relishing its release. I couldn't get enough of him, of his mouth against me, of his taste in me. He devoured me.

The urgency wrapped between us was almost too much to take. I rose up on my toes to align the center of my body with his, but he was too tall. I lifted one leg and wrapped it around his waist digging my heel into him. August growled and wrapped his hands around my thighs turning us towards the ground until I was under him in the sand never breaking away from the frenzied kiss.

I welcomed the cool sand against my heated skin and released his mouth to suck in a breath of fresh air. August's lips never left mine, simply hovering over my lips. The atmosphere surrounding us stilled silencing the waves and muting the stars. The only thing I smelled was the hint of mint on August's breath. The only sound was the mingling of our panting and heavy breaths. The only thing I felt was the soft, teasing passes he made against my swollen lips with his own. Brushing, nipping, pulling.

The distant sounds of the party seeped in and out with each breath I took against him. Slowly, the sound began to build until a loud cheer came from far off sucking me out of that kiss and tossing me back into reality. I huffed in a deep breath and wiggled under August until he pulled away and sat up onto his knees above me. He squinted at me under the moonlight and his hair was disheveled. Adorable.

I sighed at sat up brushing the sand from my hair. August fell back onto to sand. "Wow." He said running his hand through his hair.

"Wow." I nodded agreeing with him. We sat together, quietly, and oddly enough comfortably.

He nodded down towards the space in the sand next to me. "Can I? I want to explain something to you." I laughed at that. I'd just let him practically eat my face and he was asking to sit next to me.

I nodded and pat the sand. I could continue to pretend I didn't care, but the truth was, after that kiss, nothing was the same. That kiss changed everything, and I needed some answers. If he was the kind of guy that dated multiple girls at once, I wanted to know, because if that was the case I'd need to step away for good. "So tell me. Who were you with today?"

"I was with a friend. I've known her forever, and we are *just* friends. What you probably heard on the voicemail today was me giving her a ride home from her job. She doesn't have a car right now, so she occasionally calls me to give her a ride home. What you also probably heard was the conversation on the way to her apartment where I told her all about a beautiful, smart, sweet, funny, strong woman that I had just met and was crazy about." He paused waiting for me to reply. "Is that crazy?" He asked.

"Which part? This new girl in your life, or that you are telling me about her?" I couldn't help it. I was not amused by this confession.

August tilted his head back in a laugh. When he looked back at me his the moonlight caught his eyes in an angle the reflected his humor back into the night. "I'm talking about you. You're the one I've been crazy over. Ever since your pretty little self walked into Wes's tattoo shop. I thought I would have had to stalk the shop day and night waiting for you to come back in again so I could ask you out. I haven't been able to get you off of my mind. When I'm not with you, I think about being with you, and when I am with you, I think about how great it is to be with you."

"Me?" I squeaked holding my hand up to my chest.

He nodded and shifted in the sand so that he was facing me with his knees bent up.

"So, okay, wait. Me?" I asked again trying to see through my fog of confusion. It was pretty dense though.

Or maybe I was the dense one.

"Yes you, jeezus. It takes everything in me just to keep my hands to myself when I'm around you." I could relate. It took everything in me just to avoid his hands when I was around him.

"Do you wonder if it's just physical though?" I asked truly curious. I'd wondered the same thing myself, but the more time I spent with

August the more I saw that the physical was just a doorway to a deeper connection I felt with him. I worried he wasn't feeling the same.

"That wasn't just physical." He said gesturing to the disturbed blanket of sand around us. I raised an eyebrow at him. "Okay, it was very physical, but there was more to it. I didn't just kiss you because I wanted too. I kissed you because I needed too. Because, something in me is so enraptured by you that I have to have you."

Okay, that was good. So good I couldn't figure out how to respond, but thankfully he kept talking.

He took both of my hands in his. "Kensie, I'm going to be honest here. I haven't done this in a really, really long time. I'm not a fuck around kind of guy, but I am definitely rusty in what to do here. I'd like to spend more time with you, see where this goes."

"You would?" I was shocked. Hearing those words fall from his lips filled me so completely with happiness, there was no room for hesitation. I wanted this too. I was scared, I was nervous, but I was one hundred percent positive that I wanted to explore our connection.

"Yeah. I would." He smiled hopefully, and almost vulnerably squeezing my hands in his.

A small smile crept across my face. August saw this as a good sign and let out a breath I didn't know he had been holding. "Whattaya think? Should we date, see where things go?" He asked as he brought one hand up to stroke my cheek with his thumb.

"It's only going to be me, right?" I had to

makes sure August's definition of dating matched my own.

"It's only ever been you. I just didn't know until I met you." The words were sweet and a bit slick, but I believed every syllable of the statement. I had to because I felt the exact way.

CHAPTER 9

I hate economics. I don't even know why I'm still in this class. I had the brilliant idea of signing up for it at the last minute in the beginning of the semester. I remember watching a show on TV one night where people pitched these ridiculous and yet so very necessary inventions to investors. Right then and there, I decided that I needed to be an entrepreneur and make millions on one idea alone. Never mind that I had no experience in anything business related, or that I was lacking the drive to start my own business. Now, I am kicking myself and lost in a haze of production, consumptions, and all things that make me want to bang my head into my tiny lecture hall desk.

The constant drone of the professor's voice was wearing on me. I was losing my mind. I could feel it. The walls began to creep in on me slowly. Every time I looked up toward the professor, I saw them slink towards me out of the corner of my eyes. The fluorescent lights began stabbing at my eyes causing me to squint, and the solid plastic chair was driving its metal bolts into sensitive parts on my back. The whispers and giggles of the sorority sisters behind me slowly morphed into a nagging clucking. I reached back and felt my hair. Did it just move? I swear their feathers were ruffling it. I was under attack. I began to strategize an escape plan. The tiered desks made it difficult to make a crawling getaway. Sweet Sara, who always shared her notes with me, was to my left and giant lineman, Mike, was in front of me. To my right was some kid who slept through the whole class, although now I presumed perhaps he had already suffered at the hands of boredom. There was only one option. I was going to have to launch myself over the class and crowd surf my way to the door...

"Class dismissed."

Oh thank you, Jesus. I threw my notebook into my bag haphazardly and made haste to the door pushing it open as the fresh air embraced me. I took a deep cleansing breath in and savored my freedom. As I soaked in the natural sunlight, I heard a low chuckle next to me. Without even looking, I knew it was August because of the chill bumps coating my arms.

"It's not funny. I almost perished in there."

He pushed off the brick building he was leaning against and came toward me wrapping me into the crook of his arm.

"I'm so glad you made it out alive. I would have really missed you." He kissed me on the top of my head leading me away from my almost certain death.

"So, what are we doing today?" Before leaving me at my dorm room with a goodnight kiss, August asked me out on our first official date. We agreed on doing something after my class today since we both had the night off. I lied in bed all night anticipating what August would plan.

It may appear silly to an average college girl who had gone on dozens of dates, but for me this one date was a first of sorts. It would be my first date since I'd banned myself from guys my last night of high school. Although, those encounters were never dates.

I looked up into August's smiling eyes and my stomach dropped. He was so handsome, and this was so easy. This thing where he picked me up from class and we bantered together strolling through campus, it was easy and natural. I'd toiled over the quick progression of our relationship a bit last night, but I'd come to one conclusion. It may be fast, but I was too fond of the wind in my hair to worry. Rather than holding tight and bracing for a crash, I was going to ride with my arms in the air and August by my side.

"What are you grinning about, pretty girl?" He asked me. I wasn't aware I was smiling, but not surprised. The smile had become a recent addition to my fall wardrobe.

"I'm just happy. Happy to be with you, and to get to spend the rest of the day with you." There was a time when I would have skirted around that question, but it had come and gone. I was no longer afraid of what would become of us. I was too busy enjoying what *was* us.

"Me too. Very happy." Before I could register what was happening August had me spun around with my back pressed against his truck. I was completely stunned and immediately turned on. All I could focus on what the feel of his determined hands gripping my hips and his feet stepping in between mine. My breath hitched when his legs brushed against my inner thighs. I wanted to tell him to hang on a minute, that people were staring, that I would happily let him manhandle me in private, but all I could muster was a breathless, "Hi".

"Hi," he whispered back before he recaptured my mouth in his. His sweet assault nearly brought me to me knees. With every swipe of his tongue, my heart pulsated and I lost all sense of time and place. Completely absorbed in the feel of him pressed against me, I wrapped my arms around his head lacing my fingers through his hair and drawing him in closer. He let out a groan when I rose onto my toes brushing myself against just the right spot. Placing a couple gentle pecks on my lips, August pulled away and placed his forehead against mine whispering again, "I don't think I'll ever get enough of you."

I was still catching my breath and couldn't utter a single response. I just stared wide-eyed and thoroughly kissed, as he reached behind me to open my door and help me in.

***

August's idea of our first official date was one of the carnivals that came into town a couple times of year. Even though I had passed them driving here or there, I hadn't actually been to one since I was a kid. Most of my fun now was that of the college brand; parties,

Tommy's, and maybe a concert on occasion.

I was relieved at his choice. A carnival surrounded by families and kids didn't invite any opportunity for me to get caught up in him. Though I was comfortable with being exclusive so quickly, the physical momentum of our relationship needed to move slowly.

I'd been impetuous so many times before, intentionally losing all my thoughts in those moments. This time I wanted it to be different. I wanted everything with August to be meaningful. I needed to come out on the other side overflowing rather than drained, and I wanted to grasp every thought and feeling he conjured up in me. Deep down I knew that any level of intimacy with August would be momentous. I knew that it would have the likelihood to either unravel me or put me together. I hoped he would be patient with me.

My reflective thoughts weren't the only things that August's kiss had spurred. The entire ride to the carnival, he and I both were taking any chance we could to touch or kiss each other. We held hands over his center consul and took turns leaning in for momentary kisses at stoplights. They were a welcome distraction from my introspection, and I reminded myself that no one really lives life fully if they are continuously thinking about it.

I gazed out the window and admired the sky in an attempt to calm my restless mind. It had rained the night before and there was always something beautiful about the day after rain to me. Everything was more alive after the rain. Puddles pooled on sidewalks replaying the sky above through their ripples. Birds sung more, or louder, I've never been sure which. The scent in the air was more aromatic and fresh like a single downpour had the ability to wipe clean all of nature's transgressions. I breathed in deeper the day after the rain. It was a perfect day to wonder the carnival outside with August. The translucent sky had only a hint of storm clouds in the distance.

August brought up my hand interlaced with his and placed a kiss on it. I smiled at him and wondered how I got so lucky to be sitting here with this wonderful guy. I don't think I ever did anything extraordinary that would have persuaded Karma to bring him to me, but I wondered what he was like before me. I imagined an adorable boy in grade school with messy brown hair and a smile that lit up his toothless face. I found myself wanting to know everything about him, not just the him *now*, but what made him the magnetic and enticing man holding my hand.

"What are you so deep in thought about over there?" He asked as he tucked a stray hair behind my ear.

"You. The you before me to be specific. I want to know everything about you."

He tensed a moment and swore under his breath. My eyes widened in surprise just before he slammed on his breaks.

"Shit, sorry Kensie, are you okay? People around here don't know how to drive with a little rain left on the street." I nodded my head and wondered if his discomfort was from my curiosity or almost rear ending the car in front of us. Before I thought too much about it, he answered my question.

"Well, I was a little punk in high school." He laughed at the stunned look on my face.

"You?"

"Me." He grinned at me. "Imagine Wes at fourteen years old, but with a little more sense."

"Is that even possible?"

"It is. I was a living breathing oxymoron." He laughed and told me about he and Wes in high school. They really did get themselves into some trouble. I never would have imagined a young August covering his science teacher's car in silly string. Wes all the way, but August I'd expect to be the kid who stayed a little late to help the teacher carry his supplies.

The further he got into his reminiscing, the more his stories turned from the practical joke variety to experimental. He told me about the first time he and Wes smoked weed and wound up in his gutter eating a box of croutons. He even so kindly told me about ditching class to practice his 'skills' with his girlfriend behind the gym bleachers. He obviously noticed that my mind was visually bitch slapping the ho, when he rubbed my knee and said, "It was a long time ago."

As we neared the carnival, I wondered what had cause him to turn his life around. I suppose just growing up and getting older would make a person who was once careless, find some direction. I had been in a similar place in high school though, and for me, I had to want the direction. It wasn't a natural shift just because I grew up. I had to come to a place where I realized the way I was sloppily coasting through life was not going to land me in a good place. Even still, life didn't turn the way I'd wanted.

CHAPTER 10

I hadn't been to a carnival since I was a kid. It all looked exactly how I remembered it to look. Rows and rows of games with prizes to be won, rides that tilted and twirled, and food trucks lined up and emitting the smell of all things sweet and fried into the air. Every ride and game tent was adorned with lights that would eventually cast a glow into the sky for a couple miles once the sun went down.

"So what first?" August came up from behind me wrapping his arms around my body and placing his chin on my shoulder.

"I'm starving. I say we sample some carnival cuisine first." I swear I could smell the chocolate sauce smothered funnel cake from here.

August cringed at my suggestion. "We can't eat first Kensie, we'll lose it all on the Tilltorama."

"Who said anything about the Tiltorama? I don't do tilting. No tilting, twirling, spinning, plunging, none of it. They make me sick. I will, however, ride anything that moves at a steady pace in one direction, eat as many fried Oreos as I can get my hands on, and kick your ass in all the games."

August laughed at me, and grabbed my hand leading me toward the food trucks. "Does this ass kicking come with and sort of incentive?" He rubbed his hands together and raised an eyebrow at me. "I'd be willing to forfeit, in the event that you kiss it and make it all better."

I rolled my eyes at him. "Oreos. Now."

Three corndogs, two bowls of chili cheese fries, one funnel cake draped in chocolate, five deep fried Oreos, and one fried Twinkie joined us at a picnic table under some Oak trees. We may have gone a little overboard, but it had been so long since I had any of this. August was happy to make all of my artery clogging carnival food dreams come true.

Halfway into my chili cheese fries, I noticed a young dad with his daughter at the ring toss game. She had to have been around five years old all dressed up in a purple dress with a tutu skirt and her hair in a tiny braid. She waited on bouncy toes as her dad tossed ring after ring into the sea of bottles.

He tossed the last ring and it clanked around one of the bottlenecks. The little girl squealed in delight and wrapped her little arms around her daddy's legs smashing her cheek against his thigh. He laughed and reached down to pick her up so she could point out the stuffed animal she wanted to take home. It was the sweetest sight and reminded me so much of how my dad and I were when I was young. I was a daddy's girl through and through. There wasn't anything I believed my daddy couldn't do. I silently hoped that this dad and daughter kept their bond much longer than I was able to hold on to mine.

The ringing of another game snapped me out of my memories. I looked over to August who was watching the same scene take place. Where I watched reverently and even with a shadow of a smile, August watched with a different expression. His eyes were far from the crinkled smiles I usually saw and seemed to be forlorn. I wondered what he saw when he watched the pair to cause such a lost look.

As far as I knew, he and Capri had a great family and their upbringing was as close to perfect as it could get. Whatever caused it, I was sure he would reveal to me in time.

Even though we had an instant connection, we were still just getting to know each other. For now, I was determined to take the sad out of my handsome guy's eyes.

I nudged August with my shoulder breaking him from his daze. I could see him silently shake himself, and then my playful August came back and kissed me on the tip of my nose. "Let's go, pretty girl, I'm gonna win you a teddy bear."

***

I remember seeing a news report once about these carnival games. Apparently they rig them so that it is nearly impossible to win. At least, that's what I'm going with right now as August attempts the fifth game of the night. He missed every shot in the basketball toss, he couldn't get a ring to wrap around a bottle, he fell off the ladder climb time and time again, I watched ping pong balls bounce off the edges of fish bowls to the wood chipped ground, and right now we are waiting our turn for the water gun game. As the last round of players clear the seats, August and I sit down side by side. I quickly notice we are the only two playing this round, so odds are in our favor. Question is, do I let him win, or do I kick his ass?

"Okay, Kensie," August squat down beside me, "It's really pretty easy." I held back a snort at that. As easy as the last four games I wondered? "The trick is to keep both eyes open. People always want to close one eye when they aim at the target, but you get a more accurate shot with both eyes focused on the clown's mouth. Once you get the shot right, just hold the gun steady until the balloon goes up to the top and dings the bell. Got it?" Did he really just explain to me how to play one of the world's simplest carnival games? Decision made. I'm kicking his ass.

"Okay, so do I hold it with one hand or both?" I asked innocently as he climbed back into position at his seat. He laughed at me, "Both, Kensie. Both." Duh, but I wasn't going to tell him my dad taught me to shoot when I was eight and that I had a better shot than most of his friends that went shooting with us every weekend. No, I was just going to enjoy this ass kicking.

The carny announced one last time that we are about to begin in case any passersby wanted to join in. It was still August and I when he began his countdown, and on three, two, one, the buzzer sounded. I took quick aim shot steady stream of water straight into my clown's mouth all while August fumbled with his gun. He shot a couple way ward streams, even hitting my target once before he hit his target in the clown's mouth.

I was inches away from winning, so I took a second to glance over at August who wasn't following his advice very well. He was hunched over with one eyes closed and his tongue sticking out of the corner of his mouth. He looked so focused and so damn cute. Not even a second later my bell went off signaling that I won.

August jolted from his concentration and looked around dumbstruck. Then he zeroed in on the dinging light above my bell and looked over at me slowly.

"I guess I won." I shrug my shoulders and smiled sheepishly at him.

He shook his head and grinned in disbelief. "You played me, Kensie. Not only did you play me, but you kicked my ass."

I laughed as we got up from our seats. "Sorry, you were so determined to help me understand the game, I didn't have the heart to tell you I had this in the bag."

Judging my his smirk I could tell he wasn't buying that, and that he knew my true intentions were to show him I was just fine winning on my own.

"Alright, but I still get to pick out your prize for you. I need to feel like a man at some point and give my woman a damn stuffed animal."

"Fair enough, cave man. Drag back something pretty." A couple minutes later August returned to me with the most adorably hideous stuffed dog I had ever seen. It was an awful shade of lime green with one eye sewn a little low and to the left. There was a puff of stuffing coming out of the stitching at its rear end that I pulled out when he handed it to me with a cheesy grin on his face.

"For you, woman," he huffed and pounded his chest.

"It's perfect," I laughed and took his hand into mine while snuggling my new pup under the other arm.

"Where to next?"

"I think I'm done with the games." He looked at me sheepishly. "Maybe some rides?" I opened my mouth ready to remind him about my standards for carnival rides but he spoke before I had a chance too.

"I know, slow and steady, no twists, no turns, no upside downs and inside outs. I got it." Then he leaned over and placed a soft kiss on my lips causing a momentary jolt on me. I'd have to become immune to those lips at some point. They were constantly throwing me for twists and turns.

August was true to his word and we only went on rides that would have received a senior citizen approval rating. We currently waited in line for the huge Ferris wheel and I was admiring how beautiful it looked all lit up now that it was dark. Earlier this evening, it was nothing but a big hunk of metal creaking and groaning as its cars went up and around. Now it was a spectacular canvas of lights that seemed to streak across the sky, leaving tails of color as the carts went around.

It was almost enough to take my mind off how terrified of heights I was. Almost. But my nagging fear was making itself known as we inched up in the line. August must have noticed the change in my demeanor and my sudden bout of silence.

"Hey, everything okay?" He asked as he turned me around to face where he stood behind me in line. He wrapped his arms around my waist and looked down at me in worry. For a brief moment the safety of his arms vanished my fears, but then I looked up.

"Yeah, fine. Good, I mean. Well, maybe I'm not good. I mean, I'm good; I'm having a great time with you tonight. I'm just at this moment..."

"Okay," he cut me off mid ramble, "You're obviously nervous about something because you're doing that adorable speed talking thing you do. So what is it?"

"I'm scared of heights. Petrified." I just stared up at him wringing my now sweaty palms together.

His face softened and he pulled me into him placing his forehead against mine. His gentle eyes searched for mine to connect and when they did he started to talk, "We don't have to go on this, Kensie. It's not a big deal, but if you do want to give it a shot, I promise I won't let anything happen to you. You will be just fine."

Not only does he remind me that I have the option here to not ride this ride, that it's my choice, but he also encourages me to try it out without making me feel forced. Rationally I know nothing is going to happen to me, and I've grown to trust August enough to know that he wouldn't willingly let anything happen to me. That's the thing with true fear though, rational doesn't matter; the fear completely takes over. Somehow wrapped in August's arms, I found the courage to face my fear.

I took a deep shuddering breath as the line moved forward again. "Okay, I'm owning this ride."

August let out a low chuckle and kissed my forehead before pulling away, "That's my brave girl. We got this." He held up his fist in front of him and I obliged by pounding it with my own.

A few minutes later it was our turn to climb into the tiny cart. At that point, I was already so withdrawn inside myself from fear that my movements were on autopilot. I didn't pay close attention to anyone or anything, just to my inner chant; *I'm fine, I'm fine, I'm fine.* Sensing I wasn't mentally present, August helped buckle me in and pulled me closer tucking me under his arm. "I've got you," he whispered in my ear while I focused on a spot of old tarnished gum on the metal floorboard.

The ride jolted us as it began its ascent and my eyes jumped to his in pure fear. "I can't do this," I whispered, pleaded to him.

"You already are doing this." He spoke calmly to me. As we rose higher into the air my pulse began to pick up and my fear started to engulf me completely. The world closed in on me sitting in the tiny cart next to August. My instinct was to run, jump, and get out *now*. The need to flee became overpowering, but I was trapped. We rose higher still and my vision turned spotty. That's when August peppered my temple and cheek with soft delicate kisses. His lips made their way to my neck and nuzzled into the crook nipping and pulling at the sensitive skin. Caught up momentarily with the feel of the cool air fanning across the freshly kissed spots, I leaned my head into him. August must have taken this as his sign and pulled away to kiss my hair. I sighed in protest and he chuckled at me.

"Want to hear a story?"

"A story?" I whipped my head around. "Now?" I looked up and realized we were now at the top of the Ferris wheel. I became paralyzed when my breath caught in my lungs and squeezed onto the metal bar across my lap.

"Once upon a time," he began. This was absurd. I was miles in the sky about to fall to my death and he wanted to tell me a story?

"There was a beautiful dandelion swaying in the breeze on a lonely hill. One day, the wind came to the dandelion and told her he was going to carry her away from her lonely hill. The dandelion was scared at first, but the wind told her that he would take care of her and that she could trust him, that he would show her things she never thought possible." What the hell kind of story was this. Where was the princess or the little elves that come to your house and bake you cookies? I took my hands off the bar and folded them across my chest as he continued.

"Not wanting to be alone any longer and curious as to what she would see, the dandelion gave her trust to the wind. When the dandelion let go the wind blew she fell apart piece by and was carried away with him."

"Wait, why did she let go? She didn't even know the wind." I asked him.

He laughed and pulled me in closer. "She trusted him. Even though she hadn't known him long, she knew she could, and she was brave enough to let herself."

I scrunched up my face and looked at him disbelievingly. "Oh okay, that's realistic." He shook his head smiling and continued.

"First, the wind carried her past a little girl playing hide and go seek with her mom in the field. Then, the wind carried her by two young boys fishing together in the pond. Next, the wind brought her over a young couple kissing wildly in the back of a pick-up truck, followed by the front of a house with a middle aged couple rocking in their chairs on the front porch. Finally, he floated her slowly over an elderly man placing a bouquet of daisies in front of a headstone."

I placed my hand over my heart, "Oh my gosh. That's so sweet."

"Isn't it?" August grinned down at me.

"The wind brought the dandelion to rest on the top of a new hill that overlooked a new valley. When the wind began to leave the dandelion begged him not to go for she had seen more with him than she ever knew existed. The wind told the dandelion that he was only a breeze away and to remember all the love he showed her on their journey. If she would hold onto that then she would never be lonely again and would be able to experience the new view from this new hilltop."

I stared at August with my jaw slack and now both my hands held each other gripped over my heart. "That's a beautiful story. The wind showed her what it was to live a life full of love." I paused a moment. "I want wind."

August smiled down at me and I saw the stars reflect in his beautiful wise eyes. "I'll be your wind."

With that, I threw my arms around his neck and pulled him down crashing his lips to mine. But once I felt him against me, the kiss that began quickly turned slow and intentional. I wanted to feel every part of August in the kiss, but more importantly I wanted him to feel me through this kiss.

My stomach rolled with each leisure and deliberate motion between us. August held my cheek in his hand while his velvet lips tenderly brushed mine. I placed my hands on either side of his face and held him to me while I drank in this heartwarming moment.

I gave every bit of me in that kiss. I wanted him to feel my gratitude for getting me through my fear, for not forcing me, but for encouraging me. He stayed in the moment with me and guided me through it with nothing but compassion and care. I was completely overwhelmed by this feeling. I had searched for it, I had craved it for so long an in this solitary moment August managed to give me a pillar to lean against.

He held me in his arms and told me a tale of love while bestowing on me an act of love I thought I'd never come across again. As we broke apart, a tiny tear tickled its way out of my

eye. August dabbed it away with his knuckle.
"What is the tear for?" He asked softly.
"You."

CHAPTER 11

August and I called it a night after our adventure on the Ferris wheel. We headed for the gates with our little lime green pup that I had named Sir William in tow. When he questioned my choice, I explained to him that he needed a regal name to make up for his lack of confidence in his looks. He poked fun at me for that, but August's teasing and laughter came to a halt as well as his steps when we walked by the picnic tables on our way out. I looked up at him in confusion and saw him fixated on something to the right of us with his jaw clenched.

My gaze followed his and was met by two teenagers making out on one of the benches. Actually, making out might have been an understatement. They were hot and heavy, the girl straddling the boy and a mess of tangles limbs right there in the middle of a carnival. I thought I understood August's irritation based on that alone, but it took me a second to recognize the couple. Gabby and Jordan were the compromised couple. I was one second too late in my recognition because August had already descended on the couple. A cloud of dust kicked up behind him.

It took me a second to recover from the gag reflex that happened when Jordan's scraggly arms reached up and tugged at Gabby's wiry hair, but when I did I scurried after August. I had never seen that look on his face before. The look of anger, disgust, and disappointment all swirled together to create a beast of a man that made me nervous for the two teens.

August reached the couple before I did and I watched in anxious suspense as he grabbed Jordan's shirt collar and pulled him out from under Gabby. Gabby shrieked and fell away from Jordan who was in a fit of curses before he realized who had separated the two.

As I approached them I caught the anger August spat at Jordan. "Don't you *ever* let me catch you mauling a girl like that in public again?" His authoritative and fierce demeanor sent Gabby back a few steps. "Not only is it disrespectful to her," he pointed back at Gabby without removing his treacherous stare from Jordan, "it's disrespectful to all the families that are here and don't want their children watching soft core porn next to the slushy booth."

"Dude, relax," Jordan cut in. Not wise Jordan, not wise.

"Relax?" August's stern voice lowered an octave. "I can't *relax* Jordan when I see you two kids, because that's what you are kids; when I see you over hear engaging in something that will easily go further than you expect it to, Jordan. *So easily*, and I don't want to see you, a smart kid with a bright future, ending up a dad before you've even had a chance to grow up. You can't take something like that back, Jordan." August took a deep distressed breath and ran his fingers through his hair.

I somehow managed to will my stunned feet to move and went toward a very pissed, and yet ashamed Gabby. "Gabby, I don't even know what to say," I told her, and I didn't. I was shocked, stunned that we had just caught two of our kids in such a compromising position. I was equally stunned at the way August was reacting. He had always been so calm and collected, establishing an air of confidence and responsibility around him. This August was a frazzled mess of fury, irritation, and something else I couldn't figure out.

I noticed August had visibly calmed and pulled Gabby aside so he and Jordan could have a minute alone. I could tell there was more he wanted to say to him, but not in front of Gabby.

"Gabby, you really have to be careful." This was new for me. I'd never given advice in this situation before. Although, I'd never received it either when I should have.

"I'm not some slut, Ms. Kensie. I know that's what you think." Tears began to well up in her eyes.

"That's not what I think at all, Gabby. At all. Look at me." I wanted her to see the genuine concern on my face and know that it was coming from a place of love, not disgust. When she looked up from where she was running the toe of her shoe in the dirt I continued, "What I think is that you are a person who got caught up in the moment with someone you care about. I think you are a beautiful, smart, and funny girl. Obviously Jordan has caught on to that too, because he likes spending time with you. I think you guys do, however, need to start setting some boundaries in your relationship. You two are clearly attracted to each other and Mr. Hunter is right, that can turn a harmless make out session into something much more very quickly."

"I'm not stupid. I wouldn't let it get that far." She looked irritated at me now.

"I don't think you're stupid at all, but I do know I was your age a very short time ago." I wasn't sure how much of my personal life I wanted to divulge in that moment, but I felt like this was an opportunity for me to really connect with Gabby. I took a hesitant breath and pressed on, "I know first-hand how quickly a situation like what I just saw can become more." Silently, I hoped I wouldn't regret divulging that little piece of me.

"You do?" Gabby looked at me in disbelief now that made me laugh a little bit.

"Yes, I do. I can tell you from experience that going that far should not be done hastily or in the heat of the moment. It should be saved for someone truly special and you guys should be well prepared for it. You should want that to be meaningful for yourself and to not regret it when it's over because you can never take it back," I stopped myself a minute, "and I would prefer you wait until you are much older because it is really difficult when you are young to trust the people who you think care about you."

I chanced a glance over at August and Jordan who were now sitting together and in deep conversation on the bench. He looked up briefly to me, and our eyes met. I still saw that same look before that I couldn't name, although now it resembled something like anguish. I wondered what had gotten my sweet steady guy so worked up. He smiled a small forced smile and nodded his head at me, letting me know he was wrapping up his talk with Jordan. I looked back at Gabby whose eyes were anywhere but on me.

"Look, Gabby, I know that must have been embarrassing. I'm sorry things happened like that. Mr. Hunter and I both care about you guys and want to see you have the promising futures you deserve, with as few detours as possible."

"Yeah, okay." Was the only response I got from her. I could only hope she took some time to herself to think about the event that just played out and gain some understanding from it.

***

The walk back to August's truck was uncomfortably quiet. Neither of us said a word once we left Gabby and Jordan at the scene of the manhandling. August was especially somber, and I wanted to do something to help break him from his mood. I suggested the only thing I could think of that had worked for me countless nights when I contemplated how to overcome the abandonment I felt from my father. I suggested we head to the cliffs for some fresh sea air and a stroll to help work out whatever was going on in his mind. I knew I wouldn't be able to erase it, but I wanted to try anything to help him work his way out of it.

When we arrived at Sunset Cliffs only the cars that belonged to the impressive waterfront homes were left parked on the street. Not many people lingered around too long after the actual sunset. August turned off the car and looked over at me. "So, your secret place is one of the most popular tourist attractions, huh?"

I swatted at his arm. "Just because it's popular, doesn't mean it can't be a secret. Only I know what is in my head when I'm here, no one else. And I usually come on cloudy days when not many people show up. No one likes to watch a sunset when you can't see the sun."

"I suppose not. And they obviously don't hang around for the after party with the moon either." He waved his hand and gestured to empty parking lot.

"They don't know what they're missing." For me, an empty beach that was lit by nothing but the hazy moon was the most breathtaking moment to be on the sand.

There was no better place to release the culprits of our personal downfalls. I always felt that what pollutes a person from the inside out was easily washed clean by the encompassing sound of the crashing waves.

They roared louder at night for some reason. As if the waves knew they had to put in an extra effort while people slept to wipe away their doubts and fears. I was hopeful that August would find the same sort of purification here that I did.

August went ahead of me and held my hand

down the steps that led to the sand. We both kicked off our shoes and left them near the last step. Heading down to the water's edge, I inhaled the heavy scent of the ocean. I felt August's intake at the same time. I looked up and smiled at his closed eyes as he breathed in the same air. He opened his eyes and peered down at me. "See something you like?"

I laughed and shoved into him as we walked. "Yeah, actually." I smiled up at him and thought that I more than liked him. I'm not sure what people call the middle ground between like and love. Hope maybe? I'm in hope with August. He wrapped his arm around me pulling me close.

"You cold? I think I have an extra sweater in the truck. I can run back real quick and get it?" He asked me.

"Nope, I'm perfect." I answered snuggling myself in closer to his side.

After a few minutes of comfortable silence I spoke up. "So what happened tonight with Jordan?"

He winced at my question and bent down to pick up a seashell before tossing it into it low crashing waves.

"I'm sorry, Kensie."

"You don't have to apologize. I'm bound to see you upset at some point. Everyone gets angry for one reason or another. I'm just surprised at how quickly you snapped."

"I overreacted," he huffed out a distressed grunt, "with Jordan. God, I'm an asshole."

I thought for a minute about reassuring him, "You aren't an asshole, far from one actually. You did have a moment of assholery though." I looked at him warily when a huge grin broke out across his face.

"Assholery?" he chuckled, "Well my moment of assholery was uncalled for. I apologized to him when I calmed down, I just hope I wasn't too hard on him."

"Sometimes kids need someone they respect to be hard on them. I think it's okay as long as it comes from a place of love and you do it with intentions of strengthening them and not breaking them." I tried my best to reassure him.

August smirked me. "You're really wise. Owl status." "Owl status?" I scrunched my nose up at him.

"You're my wise little owl." He said and leaned over to kiss me softly on the lips.

"Hoot?" I shrugged up at him kicking up cool sand with the tips of my toes.

A loud chuckle burst from his chest mixing with the sound of the waves. "And she makes me laugh."

I beamed at him as I watched him look at me with awe in his twinkling brown eyes. He looked at me with such admiration and warmth. I basked in it, and soaked up all I could. I hoped he saw the same in me when I looked at him, because I wanted to make him feel as cherished and valued as he made me feel.

"What did you two end up talking about anyway?" I asked him as we stopped to admire the moon hover over the ocean.

"Girls." He grinned at me. "Wanna sit down for a while?"

"Sure." I answered and sat down in the

cool sand with August sitting behind me. He pulled me between his legs and wrapped his arms around me, nuzzling his nose into my neck. He placed a kiss there before resting his chin on my shoulder and looking back towards the water with me.

"He told me he wasn't sorry for being all over his girl, but that he regrets doing it that 'hardcore' in front of all the kids. He said that he loves her. I told him that there is nothing wrong with loving on your girl in public, but that I want him to make sure he's responsible for the physical part of their relationship. In short, I told him not to knock her up."

"Do you believe him?" I asked.

"Believe what? That he will be careful? Yeah, I think I put more fear into him than an episode of Teen Mom." I could hear the grin in his voice.

"That's something." I laughed. "No, I mean about being in love with Gabby. He's only fourteen."

"Completely."

"Really? You think a fourteen year old understands love?" I asked disbelievingly. I guess I didn't necessarily agree.

"As much as a fourteen year old can love, I believe they do. I don't think love is a static word. I think it's more of a dynamic feeling that morphs and changes throughout life." He kissed me above my ear sending chills down my neck before continuing. "I think love at fourteen is different than love at twenty three, and love at twenty three is different than love at seventy three. It has to be with all the lessons the movement of life brings on, but just because they are different levels of love doesn't mean it isn't love."

I let his response soak in. If I had allowed myself a chance at love when I was Jordan's age would it have been different than if I fell in love with August? I couldn't even imagine being in love with anyone. At one time in my life, I thought I'd loved Nolan. For some reason it didn't matter now.

"Hoot?" August broke me from my thoughts and I let out a giggle.

"Yes, hoot. Who's the owl now, oh wise one?" My thinking had brought on a question I wanted to ask August, but wasn't sure I wanted to hear the answer to. I wanted to know everything about him though, so I banished away my worry and asked anyway. "Have you ever been in love?"

"Yeah." He didn't even hesitate. Well hell, I take that back. I didn't need to know everything about him. My heart twisted at the thought of him in love with someone else.

"Don't worry." He whispered in my ear, taking turning my jealous tension into lust filled anticipation. "It was a fourteen year old kind of love."

"Was she a high school girlfriend?" Inconsequential love or not, I still didn't like it.

"Yeah she was, but we don't have to talk about it. I want you to know, though, that what I felt for her at the highest point of our relationship doesn't even compare to how I feel about you now."

My breath caught in my chest with that

admission. How he felt about me now? Was he feeling just as strongly as I was for him? I hoped so. God I really hoped so. I didn't know how to use words to express how glad I was to hear that to him, so instead I turned my head and brushed my lips against his. As I pulled away a little, he leaned in and pressed into my lips more firmly. I kissed him soft and slowly trying to show him the sincerity of my feelings for him. When we pulled away I leaned my forehead back against his cheek.

"Tell me about it."

He took a steady breath before beginning. "Bree and I started dating freshman year. We were a pretty reckless couple in the beginning. I guess that's why I was so hard on Jordan, because I had made the wrong choices at his age. We partied a lot together, skipped school most days to go back to her place while her parents were at work. We decided we were in love fairly early on. Looking back on it, my love for her was based more on a physical connection than anything else. I don't think that means I didn't love her though. We experienced a lot of firsts together, and a lot of heartbreaks together, and through it all I know I loved her in a way only my teenager heart could love."

Maybe I shouldn't have encouraged him. Jealousy gnawed at my heart causing me to rethink this discussion. His description of how he was in his relationship reminded me a lot of my careless self, except for one notable difference. He was in a monogamous relationship, and I was not.

"Look, Kensie, I think I should..."

"No, August." I cut him off, I didn't want to hear anymore. Maybe I was being immature, but I didn't want to hear any more about his life before me with another girl. I wanted to drop the topic altogether and revert to the moment where it was just the two of us.

"Kensie, let me explain this part. It's important." He huffed out a frustrated breath behind me.

"No really, I just want right now to be about me and you, nothing else." I felt him tense. "Please. Enjoy this moment with me, before I make you go for a moonlight swim in the ocean." I smiled at the last part and was relieved when I felt him relax and started to laugh.

"You would too."

"I so would." I laughed along with him glad that we could so easily shift back to this effortless banter.

"Are clothes involved? 'Cause if you tell me we leave our clothes here on the beach, I'd probably…no I'd definitely be up for it."

I turned and shoved his arm. I'd be up for it, too.

CHAPTER 12

"You have a special visitor." August's voice reverberated through my classroom and into the storage closet I was putting the broom back in. Even after all the time we had spent together, the low tone of his voice got to me. We'd been inseparable since our first official date at the carnival, spending nearly all of our free time together. Three years ago, I'd have intentionally put some space between us so he wouldn't get tired of me. Now, I was taking any and all of August I could get.

"Does this visitor want some special attention in the storage closet again?" I hollered and laughed to myself thinking about that first time he kissed me. I wiped the hair from my eyes and stepped out in a huff. I looked up and saw my mother standing in the classroom with August smiling behind her.

"Mom?" I questioned enthusiastically. "What are you doing here?" Seriously. It was a school day, and I just propositioned a guy in front of her.

"Today was a teacher work day so we could put grades in. I got out early, so I thought I'd surprise you and take you to lunch. If you have plans with this handsome young man in that closet you just came out of, I can wait up front." She smiled a cheesy mom grin at me. One of those ones mom's do when they are trying to have some sort of awkward adult friendship with their kids, no thanks.

"No, Mom," I rolled my eyes and walked up to her for a hug. "Thanks for coming. It's a nice surprise." I stuck my tongue out at August over her shoulder eliciting a suggestive eyebrow waggle from him. "I see you met August." I stepped away and gestured towards him as he leaned against the doorway in his tight white undershirt, pulling at his lean muscles in just the right places. Playing basketball everyday with the kids was working out nicely for him, and me. The way he had his arms folded across his chest made the veins in his forearms pulse with his heartbeat and I was suddenly wishing it wouldn't be terribly awkward to have my mom wait up front.

"I did meet him. He greeted me when I came in, and when I told him who I was he was kind enough to invite me to sit with him until your class was over. We had a nice chat didn't we, August?" She looked over at him conspiratorially.

"Yes we did, June."

"Oh, you're on a first name basis already?" I cocked my eyebrow in question at him. I pretended to be irritated by it, but I was really relieved to hear that they have already hit it off so well. One awkward parent meeting done and one more to go; the latter one I would postpone as long as humanly possible.

"We are." He pushed off the doorjamb and

strolled toward us in the middle of the room. "I was even invited to lunch with you guys, but John has to leave early today so I said I'd close for him."

"Did he say why?" I asked a little worried. John never left early. I'm sure he was here more than he was home.

"He said something about Bear being sick all night and taking him into the vet today."

"Oh no, I hope the old guy is okay." Bear was John's golden retriever. He had spent many days with John here at the center snoozing away in his office. Bear was all John had since his wife had passed away from breast cancer three years earlier. They had never had kids, so Bear was their dog child.

"I'm sure he will be. The old guy is pretty stubborn. The last time John rushed him into the vet because he got stuck in the dog door and John thought he was having a stroke. Turns out, he just had a thorn in his back paw and didn't want to put any pressure on it."

I laughed at that. For some reason, I could picture John coddling his dog to the point that the old guy yipped like a puppy just for attention. August kissed me before saying goodbye to my mom and I. "Call me tonight, pretty girl?" He turned and asked before he headed out the door.

"Of course." I smiled and turned towards my mom whose grin was of shit eating proportions.

"Come on Mom, I'll introduce you to John on our way out and then you can tell me exactly what you and August talked about."

I tapped quietly on John's door. It was rarely closed. I worried he was having a rough day worrying about Bear. "Yeah," his voice vibrated from behind the door. I poked my head in first, but didn't see him in his usual spot at the desk.

"John?" I called hesitantly.

"Right here, Kensie." I screamed and jumped back colliding with my mom sending us both back against the hallway wall. I scrambled trying to stay upright, but lost my footing further smashing into mom and sending her sliding down the wall to the ground.

"Crap." John bounded from behind the door to catch my arms just before I fell on top of my poor mom. "Sorry, didn't mean to spook ya. You two okay?" He reached down toward my mom and helped her up. "I was looking for one of the kids' files back here. Shoulda' warned ya."

I helped my mom brush herself off and straighten out her clothes. "You okay, Mom?" I couldn't keep down a little laugh while I took a dust ball out of her perfectly hair sprayed bob. I didn't even know how the thing managed to attach itself to that sprayed coat of armor on her head.

I stopped laughing when my mom failed to answer. "Mom?" I asked her afraid maybe she really did get hurt in the tumble. She absentmindedly brushed her hands down her grey sweater staring at John. Her mouth opened and closed, but no sound came out. She looked like a stunned goldfish. "Mom." I elbowed her.

"Oh!" She jumped. "Yeah, I'm fine, sweetie."

I looked back and forth between the two of them. John was grinning at my mom like a fool. They were seriously attracted to each other. I guess after years of encouraging my mom to date again I never considered what her type would be. With his warm cornflower blue eyes, tall thick build, and that smile that lit up his face, my mom clearly liked what she saw in John.

"Mom, this is my boss John." John reached out for my mom's hand and brought it to his lips kissing her knuckles with a slight bow. When did he get a regal on me?

"A pleasure to meet you. I had no idea Kensie's beautiful mother was paying us a visit today."

I rolled my eyes. My mom was June Brennan, age fifty, schoolteacher, and master scrabble player, not the Queen. Men do one of three things when they are attracted to a woman. They turn up their testosterone dial and become cave man alpha males, they charm the pants of her with kind words and undivided attention, or they bring out their inner Rico Suave. John was going for number three. Thankfully for me, August went with number two, but my pants were still intact.

"Well, she sure didn't tell me her boss was such a fox..." My eyes widened as my mom proceeded to ramble, "...Oh, I mean so good looking, and so strong.... or such a gentleman rather, but you're strong too. I'm sure you're strong, I mean I felt it in your hands. You must work out your hands."

"Mom!" I had to stop her embarrassing rant.

God, I wondered if that was what I sounded like when August made me nervous. I hoped I'd never tell him he had strong hands. Or call him a fox. How is that even a compliment? A fox is small and hairy, and scurries through the forest. I don't want a small hairy scurrying man.

"Oh sorry, sorry. It's nice to meet you, John." My mom finally responded with an appropriate introduction. John chuckled in amusement at my mom and it was hard to miss the way his face lit up as he watched her gain her composure. I had never seen that look on John's face before. I had some match making to do, although, it seemed the hard work was already done.

***

Mom and I settled into our booth at the little deli down the street from work. I talked John up the whole way over, not that he needed it. John was one of the good ones, like August. August mentioned John was training him to take over the director position as soon as he completed his degree this spring. I couldn't imagine a better man to take over the position that a great man was leaving behind.

"So, August seems nice," my mom said as she stirred sugar into her iced tea. I knew it wouldn't take long for him to come up. I was close to bringing him up myself because I was dying to know what they had talked about before my class had ended.

"He is." I smiled at her knowing my short and detail free answer was torture for her. My mom wasn't the kind of mom who dug for information. She typically checked in on me with vague questions leaving me room to fill in the blanks. I could see now that I worked with the kids at the youth center, that it was her way of giving me the responsibility to express as much or as little as I wanted. It was her way of gaining my trust without pushing me. In the end it didn't matter how much or how little I divulged. Like some type of clairvoyant, she always knew everything anyway.

I remember the day in high school when she took me to my doctor to get on birth control. She just sat me down and said, "I know you are having sex now or at least thinking about it. I want to make sure you are safe and smart about it." I had been a little embarrassed by the whole conversation, but more than that, I was ashamed. She assumed I had found one boy that I developed a relationship with. She had no idea that I had slept with that one boy and four of his friends within a month. So maybe she didn't know everything after all.

"From what I gathered during my brief chat with August, he's smitten." I grinned while she paused to take a bite of her BLT, "and I can't believe you didn't tell me you were dating someone." She mumbled around her food.

"We literally just started dating Mom." I picked the onions off my sandwich before taking a bite.

"Well, you must have spent some time with him, enough for him to start falling for you." She said before taking a sip of her tea. I froze mid bite and lowered by sandwich back down to my plate.

"He's not falling for me, Mom. It hasn't been long enough for that."

My mom shook her head and tsked me, "Love is an emotion, not a thought. Whether he knows it yet or not, that boy loves you."

"What did he say to you anyway, that has you thinking he's in love with me?" Now I was really curious.

"He told me how much he's enjoying spending time together, and how grateful he is to have met you. It's not what he said though, sweetie, but the look in his eyes when he said it. When he talks about you his eyes glow as if his soul has just woken up." I'd seen that look in August's eyes, and I'd taken notice because it resembled the light I'd felt in my heart. If I could find the courage within me to trust it, then our hearts would be a reflection of one another.

My mom said I woke up his soul. There was no question a part of me had awoken the day I met him. Suddenly, all the pieces of myself I was trying to orchestrate into a meaningful composition all these years were starting to find their place. They had been there all along, but August affected a place deep within me that made me feel like grabbing hold and finally making sense of it all. It was like he gave me a reason to move again. To go forward in what I had always wanted for myself, including what I had only dreamed of for myself, with him.

CHAPTER 13

Thursdays had become our own version of a Saturday night. Wes worked late on the weekends at the shop, and August and I were usually at the youth center all weekend too.

Tonight, Tommy's was hosting an open mic night for local talent. Lennon mentioned something about her friend Milo playing tonight, and that she wanted us all to go with her to check it out. She was always scoping out up and coming musicians, and while the whole band scene was more her style than mine, these open mic nights were always a lot of fun.

August invited the group over to BBQ at his house before going to Tommy's. We'd spent nearly all of our free time together over the last few weeks. If we weren't together at work, he'd come hang out with me on campus or at my dorm. We spent casual nights together at the movies or grabbing a bite at the pizzeria down the street. Though it seemed mundane, those were the moments when our relationship really took shape. I could spend hours doing everything, or simply nothing at all with him and genuinely enjoyed every minute. I missed him when we were apart, and felt whole when we were together.

It was one night earlier this week when we were walking through the mall hand in hand that we ran into a friend of his from high school and he introduced me as his girlfriend for the first time. He squeezed my hand at the introduction silently asking if it was okay, and I squeezed back letting him know it was perfect.

August picked me up from my dorm early and we went to the store together to pick up all the food before setting up at his place. He parked his truck in the driveway of his tiny bungalow. I was shocked when he told me he owned his own home. What twenty six year old college student has a house? He explained to me that after high school he didn't go straight to college, but got a job at the local grocery store full time. He had worked a lot and saved all his money to put a down payment on the tiny two bedroom, one bathroom house. When he and Capri's grandfather passed away three years ago, August used the inheritance his grandfather left him to pay off the mortgage.

"This is adorable." I told him, walking through the red door straight into the living room. The kitchen was open to the small space making it appear to be larger than it really was. It was modestly furnished with a simple leather couch and chair. Of course, there was flat screen TV hanging on the wall above the small tile fireplace. There were a few family photos spotting the walls and some empty spaces where it looked like he was going to be putting up some new ones.

"I don't think any man wants his house referred to as adorable." He said as he took the grocery bags from me and went to put them in the kitchen. It was a very small space just like the living room. It had beautiful red Spanish tiled floors that looked like they had been there long before August moved in. The appliances were all updated, but nothing over the top. He had a small dark wood table in the corner by the door that led to the backyard. The whole space was surprisingly clean, but I didn't expect August to keep his house like a typical bachelor pad. It felt warm and cozy, like a home.

"Sorry, this is a very manly place you have." I said while rubbing my chin and furrowing my brows. "Lots of solid looking wood and strong ..." I looked around, "and strong doorways."

He laughed at me while putting the groceries away taking extra care in placing his economy size bag of gummy bears on counter. "All the better to pin you against." He said while head first in the fridge.

Oh? I looked over at the doorway and imagined myself pinned against it with August leaning in close and his hands propped on the wall on either side of my head. I fanned myself with my hand.

"You okay over there?" August asked with a knowing smile on his face while he bunched up the grocery bags and tossed them into a drawer.

"Uh? Yeah, yeah. It's hot in here."

"What are you thinking about?" His face went from playful to serious when stalked towards me.

"Just um, I was just um, looking at your strong walls." My voice trailed off as he moved in closer to me.

"Know what else is strong?" He waggled his eyebrows at me with a cocky grin. I rolled my eyes, knowing exactly where he was going with that.

"Not a clue." I said smirking at him.

"The counter." He grabbed me and lifted me up turning towards the kitchen counter. I squealed and wrapped my legs around his waist grabbing his shoulders. He set me down on the countertop and stepped between my parted legs placing his hands firmly on the counter on either side of me halting my giggling.

"The way that shirt hangs of your shoulders has been driving me nuts all afternoon." He nuzzled into the crook of my neck and nipped and the sensitive skin. "I want to touch you, Kensie."

"Yes..." I whispered breathlessly. He swiped his tongue along the sensitive spot below my ear sending shivers racking through my body. We'd spent a lot of time kissing and caressing, but hadn't gone much further. I knew it wasn't because he wasn't attracted to me. I felt his attraction every time we were pressed together heatedly. I sensed he was waiting for me to give him the go ahead, and I was ready for something more. I brushed my hands up through his short cut hair and brought his head down further into my neck inducing a groan in him.

"You're so sexy, Kensie." He breathed into my ear. I tilted my head to the side giving him access as he trailed kisses up the side of my jaw to my lips. He took my mouth in his and I greedily pushed my tongue in. I couldn't control the way my stomach fluttered at the feel of our mouths devouring each other. I pressed myself against him trying to appease the need he had created deep within me.

The sweet friction was becoming more than I could take, I had to have more. As if sensing my desire, August reached for the bottom of my shirt and pulled it over my head. He placed wet open kisses along my collarbone and unclasped my strapless bra sending it to the floor.

He stared at me. I wiggled. I've had a lot of guys see me naked, but none of them looked at me. August was the first man to see me. "Don't." He moved my arm from where I draped it across my chest. "Don't hide yourself from me. You're beautiful. So beautiful." He looked up into my eyes. "My beautiful girl." My heart skipped a beat at the sincerity in his eyes.

He trailed down to my sensitive nipple that was perked up begging for attention. He flicked his tongue over it teasing me and making me whimper with need. He closed his mouth over it sucking and tickling with his velvet tongue creating a puddle between my legs.

The moans escaping my lips could not be controlled. I'd been possessed by lust. With a pop he let go and moved over to the other nipple giving it the same delicious attention. I yanked on his short hair gripped between my fingers and ground myself against his hardness.

"Kensie," August panted out my name the desire dripping from his voice. I was ready to beg him to take me to his bed, but a loud knock shook the door just a few feet away.

"No fucking way." August let out a frustrated, very frustrated groan and let his head fall onto my shoulder. I laughed softly and trickled my fingers up and down his back. "Hold that thought." He whispered and gave me a sweet kiss on the lips. He adjusted himself in his pants and headed towards the door with another frustrated grunt mumbling under his breath.

Now that I had some physical space from him, I was able to think. I couldn't believe I almost let it go too far without telling him about my past. I was terrified of what his reaction would be, but I wanted him to know about that part of me before we went further. I had better come up with a way to tell him fast.

I prayed he'd still want me after he knew the truth. My biggest fear was he wouldn't want me after hearing the shameful details I've been trying overcome. Then he'd leave me.

I shook the nagging thought from my mind and hopped off the counter. My shirt and bra went back on messily when Lennon came bounding in. She looked up at me about to say something and stopped. A lazy smirk pulled up on one side of her face. She grabbed my hand and pulled me through the living room.

"August?" she yelled at him, "Where's your bathroom? I've to help Kensie wipe the freshly fucked look off her face before your sister gets here. That'll really freak her out." August laughed at Lennon and pointed down the hall.

"First door on the right." His smiled softened when he looked at me and I smiled back.

Lennon flipped on the lights and pulled me into the decent sized bathroom. I took a quick look around. August had a simple white shower curtain and grey towels on the racks. They were definitely used, not the towels girls hang up to look pretty and don't touch. My glance continued around the room and then landed on myself in the mirror.

Damn, I did look freshly fucked. My lips were swollen and already chapped. My face was flush and tiny red marks, evidence of August's nipping, were trailing down my neck towards the edge of my t-shirt that hung off my shoulders. I ran my fingers through my hair ignoring Lennon's grin through the mirror. "Hmph."

"See, I told you." She said putting the toilet lid down and taking a seat. "This is getting pretty serious with you two." She said looking at me with sincerity.

I just nodded my head while still straightening out my hair.

"How serious? Like serious, serious?" I knew what she was asking. Lennon knew why I had sworn off all sex and that I was waiting until I was in a serious and legitimate relationship. She was asking me if this was *that* relationship. She was asking me if I was going to sleep with August. It was the decision that meant I had healed enough to move forward with my life.

"Serious. As serious as I can be." I said with conviction. She grinned one of her rare sincere smiles at me.

"I'm so happy for you." She got up to give

me a hug. When she pulled away she looked at me in the eyes and said, " I have a good feeling about him, Kensie. I think you may have found your one....but I want you to know, that if for some reason things don't work out, it's okay. You will be okay, and everything was worth it.

Because the way I see you now, you are stronger and more confident in yourself than I have ever seen. That's worth something. That's worth everything." She took a deep breath prompting me to do the same, "but you two are going to get married and make a lot of really cute babies, so we don't need to worry about that last part."

I breathed out a laugh. She was right. I had grown to forgive myself and love myself enough on my own that I would be okay if things didn't work out. Did I want to live without August, *hell no*, but I knew I could. I couldn't help but think about my dad too. I had spent so much of my life up until this point consumed with what his abandonment had turned me into. I wasn't going to let that fear of being left take over anymore, or even give it the power to exist.

Lennon turned around and opened August's mirrored medicine cabinet above the toilet. "What are you doing?" I asked her completely confused. Was she looking for aspirin? Did she have a headache?

"Snooping." She stated nonchalantly while pulling out his medicine bottles one at a time and reading the labels.

"Len." I growled out in a whisper and looked around over my shoulder. What is it with doing something you know you shouldn't that causes a person to be so paranoid? As if there are a bunch of tiny little munchkins hiding in the walls watching our every move and reporting back to August.

"Now I know why he has such stellar teeth. " She mumbled more to herself than me. She pulled out a bottle of mouthwash, a pack of dental floss, and whitening strips. "He even has a water pick...I've always wanted one of these." She pushed the button shooting a stream of water onto the wall.

"Lennon, stop. We shouldn't be looking through his things." At this point she was next to me on her knees and pushing me out of the way so she could better access the cabinet under this sink. She opened the doors and stuck her head inside letting out a low whistle.

"Somebody plans to get lucky." I dropped down to my knees next to her and shoved my head in under the cabinet. "Who?"

"An economy size box of condoms." She slid the box towards me and pats the top of it. "And ribbed for your pleasure. How sweet."

I poked around the box making sure it really was unopened.I guess I was hopeful he bought them strictly for me. If this was the case, as it appeared to be, than he either had planned on sleeping with me often, or for a long time to come. Maybe even both? Both sounded good to me. When had I become such an optimist?

Oh, his cologne! I love the way August smells. I wanted to take this home and douse my sheets in it so I could smell him all night. Not creepy at all. I popped the lid off and closed my eyes with a deep inhale. It smelled so good, but nothing compared to the way it smelled on his skin. This clean scent mixed with his natural musk was delicious.

"Knock that off." Lennon grabbed the bottle out of my hand. "You're gonna get high."

I rolled my eyes at the ridiculousness. "I am not going to get high from sniffing my boyfriend's cologne." Then I glanced around the tiny dark space we had shoved ourselves into and thought about the lack of ventilation. I put the lid back on the bottle and set it aside.

The bathroom door burst open from behind us sending us both jumping and slamming our heads into the bottom of the sink that sat above us. "Fuck!" Lennon cursed.

"Well, well, well." Great, Wes had caught us snooping. "What do we have here? This is a view I wouldn't mind seeing more often."

I grunted and pushed myself out from under the cabinets, but Lennon was faster and I heard a smack followed by Wes's, "Ow!" I stood up from the ground while Wes rubbed the back of his head. "Stop looking at my ass." I glared at him.

"Close the door you pervert before anybody sees us." Lennon shoved him aside and closed the door, but not before peeking back and forth down the hallway.

"Look, Kensie," Wes began and held his hands up in surrender, "I'm flattered, really, I mean I'm not one to disappoint, but August would kick my ass." I looked at him confused. What was he talking about? "But, Lennon," he looked at her and clicked his tongue on the roof of his mouth, "I'm down. Let me just say now I don't want this changing anything between us. It's completely casual, no strings attached, and Kensie...I don't mind if you watch. I mean, if you like that kinda thing." Oh gross. He though we were in here propositioning him... together. Now it was my turn to smack him. I shoved him in his gut causing a grunt.

"Sick, Wes. My vajajay is not that desperate." Lennon reached up and pinched his arm.

"Ouch. Damn, you two are abusive." He whined rubbing the spot Lennon attacked.

"We're snooping through August's shit." She told him. I thumped my hand against my own head at her bluntness.

"Awesome." Wes replied doing a fist pump. "I'll take the medicine cabinet! You girls get back on your knees."

I thought about smacking him again, but it was no use. Wes opened the cabinet and pulled out a larger bottle. "Gummy bears!" He popped the lid off and dumped a handful into his hand. I grabbed the bottle from him to read the label wondering what heck August was doing putting gummy bears in his bathroom.

"Wes wait! They're gummy vitamins." Too late, he was already chewing his handful and just shrugged at me. "Princess gummy vitamins?" August had princess vitamins?

"Yesssss, I get all the Jasmines!" Wes grabbed the bottle back from me.

"You only like Jasmine because she's half naked. What about Belle who reads, or Mulan who kicks ass?" Lennon's voice was muffled from under the cabinet.

Wes stopped chewing and looked like he was thinking.

I guess he can't do both at the same time. "Okay...Ariel. I get all the Ariel's. Ariel is my girl." He held the bottle up and peered inside.

"That's even worse." I told him. "She only wears a seashell bra and," and what else did she wear. Did she have a skirt or pants, or...no...she didn't wear anything else. "She doesn't even have any pants!" I yelled in disbelief.

"Who doesn't have any pants?" August's voice spoke from behind me.

"Shit!" I jumped.

"Fuck!" Lennon cursed from under the sink as her head clanked into it again.

Wes was busy rustling himself into the shower and closing the curtain.

"Wes, I saw you go in there." August said to him leaning against the door way with his arms crossed over his chest.

"Dammit!" Wes cursed shoving the curtain aside and climbed back out. "They made me do it!" He shouted and pointed at us.

"She made me do it." I pointed at Lennon.

"You guys suck." Lennon said.

"Didn't you guys think I would notice that I was the only one left out in the kitchen...and that you were all in here together?" He reached out and pulled me into him wrapping his arms around my shoulders and kissing my temple. I loved how often he touched me, especially when he didn't seem to notice he was doing it. It was just second nature for him to hold me. "Did you guys find anything good?" He asked us.

"Princess Gummies?" I looked up at him in question.

"What? They were on sale." He replied back, "I don't like to swallow those big ones."

"Kensie does." Lennon patted my shoulder and Wes chuckled to himself. "Looks like you were planning on figuring that one out soon enough judging my the economy sized box of condoms under your sink." She waltzed passed as while my face grew warm. "Get her, tiger." She winked at August and disappeared down the hall.

I felt August's chest shake in silent laughter and I turned in towards him wrapping my arms loosely around his neck. "That is an awful lot of condoms." I pressed a series of kisses to his lips.

"And we are going to use every one of them." He mumbled in between kisses. I needed to tell him soon.

Wes cleared his throat from where he stood behind us. "At the risk of sounding like a pansy, you two are really cute." He smiled genuinely at August who smiled back. They seemed to be having some weird silent bro exchange when Lennon shouted from out in the living room.

"Capri and Tanner are here!"

Wes's faced morphed into a grimace. "Why'd she bring him?"

"Um, cause he's her boyfriend?" August questioned puzzled by Wes's hostile reaction. I wasn't confused at all. I caught on a while ago that Wes, whether he knew it or not, had a thing for Capri.

"He shouldn't be. Drives me nuts watching her with that fuckwad." He huffed passed us. I could feel the tension pulse off him as he rounded the doorway headed towards the living room.

August's body froze and he looked down at me in question. I nodded my head and rubbed my hands up and down his biceps letting it sink in. "Huh? How about that?" He still looked like he was trying to figure it out. Maybe trying to piece together how long Wes had been interested in Capri.

"Let's get back out there before Lennon decides to start snooping through your kitchen too." I gave August a peck on the lips and headed towards the living room.

***

When it was time for us all to head out to Tommy's, Wes suggested he ride with Capri and Tanner in order to help with California's gas emissions. I'm not totally convinced he knew what he was talking about, but he weaseled his way into riding with the two of them. Capri tugged Lennon along in their car leaving August and I to drive alone in his truck. Quietly. Silently.

He parked his truck next to Tanner's car at Tommy's, but the foursome had already made their way into the bar. He turned off the car, but didn't move to get out. "You okay, Kensie?" He turned towards me and worried his lower lip between his teeth.

"Yeah, I'm fine." I lied. I had been deliberating how I wanted to tell him what I was like a few years ago. My conversation with Lennon helped me to see it was time he knew. I couldn't keep it from him any longer if I wanted to have an honest shot at a relationship with him, and I did. I wanted everything with him. If he wasn't all in with me, then I needed to allow him this chance at an out.

"Then why are you chewing on the inside of your cheek? You do that when you are thinking." I smiled at the fact that he had picked up on that about me, "Is this about what happened in the kitchen?" He reached over and grabbed my hand.

I shook my head. "No, no that's not it. Well, not entirely it." It was the counter incident that brought me to this point where I've realized our relationship is moving towards the next level. "It's just, that was a big step for me... a really big step. I mean, we almost... you know? When it goes further." Crap I was rambling again. I chanced a glance up at him and saw his eyes widened in shock.

"What? Wait, Kensie, are you a... are you? Have you never?"

I started to laugh when I realized what he was trying to ask me. "No, I'm not a virgin." *Far from one.*

A look of relief washed over his face as his body relaxed. "Oh okay, good. I mean if you were that wouldn't have been a big deal. Well, it would have been, but you know I wouldn't have minded. Actually, I kinda like the thought of me being the only one to touch you." He grinned proudly to himself as he thought about that, and my stomach did a somersault making me ill. How was I going to tell him that not only was he not my first, but many, many guys had touched me before him? I cringed at the reality of it all. I summoned one deep breath and any amount of courage I had within me.

"I'm so sorry, August." A stray tear fell from my eye.

"Hey, it's okay, Kensie. Whatever it is, it's okay."

He squeezed my hand and smiled, but it didn't reach his eyes.

A steady sprinkle of rain had begun to dot the windows as we sat there in his truck. I stared at it quietly watching it splatter. "I lost my virginity when I was fifteen." There was no going back at that point. "I lost it to a boy I dated for six months. Then a week after he broke up with me, I slept with his best friend in the back of a car. A few weeks after that there was another one at a party. That was only the beginning. I slept with *a lot* of guys throughout my four years in high school. Except for the first time, none of them were relationships. None of them were planned or thought through. None of them were special. I don't know how many I slept with in all. I stopped counting after twelve because it was easier to not keep track."

I thought about looking up at him to gauge his reaction, but I couldn't will myself to do it. I didn't want to see the look of disgust that I knew was on his face. "I've thought about it a lot since then." His hand gave me an encouraging squeeze. "High School was a really rough time for me. My relationship with my dad crumbled. We completely disconnected. I felt lost and, I felt abandoned I guess. I was plagued with thoughts about what I did to make him leave, and what I could do to bring him back. I constantly compared myself to his kids, and always found myself not measuring up."

The rain outside had begun to pick up and the drops were audible pitter pats on the truck. They perfectly reflected to erratic pace of my heartbeat. "The only time I ever stopped thinking, or stopped worrying, and stopped....feeling, was when I was with someone. It became my escape, an addiction." I scoffed at my realization. "I was addicted to sex at fifteen." I grimaced inside. I was disgusting.

My tears flowed freely now along with the rain on the truck. I went to pull my hand away from August's to wipe my tears and he let me. My heart broke. I looked over at him and shattered at what I saw in the glow of the streetlight. He worried his lower lip between his teeth and his eyebrows were furrowed together. "What are you thinking?" I asked.

"What made you change? You said that was how you were in high school, so when did you stop?" Now I understood the look of concern on his face and hoped my answer would be enough.

It was graduation night. I went to a party with my friend Chelsea.

"You look hot!" Chelsea yelled above the music at me. She was my sidekick these last four years.

"Thanks!" I yelled back at her. I had to

agree. I looked pretty good in my red mini dress I bought with the money dad sent me to use on a graduation dress. It's a good thing he didn't make it to my ceremony today to see that I was wearing the same one I wore to his wedding. I tried to act like I didn't care that he wasn't there, but I did. What kind of father doesn't go to his kid's graduation? I didn't even know he wasn't there until I found my mom in the crowd after. The sympathetic look on her face said it all.

Apparently he had been running late at work and got stuck in traffic. He went home to shower and get ready for my stepsister, Bethany's, graduation that was being held later that night instead of coming to see mine.

"Let's go find the garage. Someone said that's where the kegs are." Chelsea hollered and grabbed my hand pulling me through the crowd.

"She was my partner in crime." I told August. Looking back we were really unhealthy for each other. She never told be to stop when I should have and I never told her either. That night I wish she had stopped me, I wish I had stopped myself. I was so set on forgetting the day. I usually drank, that was part of the reason why it was so easy for me to get lost in the sex, but that night I went overboard.

Chelsea had gone in to talk with my ex and his friends. I stayed behind and sat on the couch sandwiched between Matt and Jase in a satisfyingly numb state. Jase took a swig of his beer and leaned over snapping his fingers in front of my face. I lazily looked up towards him. "You should take Kensie back to one of the rooms." He told Matt. "Yeah? She down for that?" Matt asked. They were talking around me like I wasn't even there. I didn't care though. I wasn't there.

"She's always down," Jase said. "Hooked up a few weeks ago with her at Jen's house and Danny said he did last month after the game. She won't even nag you after about calling her and shit. She's cool like that." Cool like that, is that what I was to them? Cool? I doubted it, but again, I didn't care. Matt shrugged his shoulders and grabbed my hand pulling me up from the couch. I followed him unsteadily towards the back of the house.

The rain was heavy outside now, covering August's truck in a blanket of water. I wondered if that's why he hadn't left me yet, because he was waiting for the rain to die down. "So you slept with him I take it?" August asked flatly. Not a hint of emotion in his voice. I sucked in a breath trying to ease my aching heart.

"Yeah, I did. I didn't remember any of it though. That was scary. I always remembered whom I slept with, using protection, getting dressed, and leaving. I always remembered. I didn't remember that night though. I just woke up the next morning without knowing what I had done.

I cringed my closed eyes and rubbed my palms over them. I usually felt like shit, but that morning I was feeling extra shitty. I opened one eye and looked around freezing when I didn't recognize where I was. I sat up quickly and my head spun causing me to feel like I was going to be sick. I took a few breaths and looked around again. Matt from my calculus class was lying next to me sprawled out on his back and snoring. Shit. I shoved him. "Matt." he snuffed a grunt and rolled over. "Matt." I shoved him harder that time.

"What?" He asked irritated.

"Did you we use a condom?"

"Fuck, I don't know."

I panicked. This was not happening. I always used protection. "I don't know…" I whispered to myself.

"Oh great. Now I have to go get checked for gonorrhea and chlamydia and all that shit don't I?" He grumbled as he sat up and put his shirt back on.

"I don't have any STD's, you asshole."

"How do you know? You get around enough." That hurt. He was right though.

"I always use protection." I bit back at him. He finished getting dressed and stood up stretching his arms above his head.

"So, you wanna go get coffee or something. How does this normally work with you?" Was he for real? How did this normally work for me? He managed to make me feel like a third class hooker in a matter of minutes.

"Just go." I muttered at him still wrapped up in the sheet. No way was I letting he see me naked.

"Yeah, okay. Later, Kensie." And with that he walked out the door. I sat huddled on someone's bed in a stranger's house naked in more ways than one. I had resorted to this behavior to forget how I felt, and at that moment I didn't think I could have possibly felt more alone.

"So after I left the house, which turned out

to be Jase's, I went to the drugstore and got the morning after pill to make sure I didn't get pregnant. That afternoon I made an appointment with my doctor to get tested for STD's too. I spent the whole day trying to fix what I had done, and as I sat there waiting for my prescription I realized I wasn't really fixing anything. That I was so completely messed up inside. I didn't want to be that girl I had turned myself into anymore. I wanted to be worth something. That day I vowed to not sleep with anyone again until I was in a serious, committed relationship. I stopped drinking because the alcohol aided me in letting go. For the first time in years, I didn't want to let go. I wanted full control." I looked out the window at the rain that was lightening up.

"You really scared yourself that night." August said. I just nodded my head while looking down at my hands that were tangled nervously together. I felt lighter though; relieved that I finally told him. Now I had to prepare for what he had to say to me.

"Come here." He said to softly to me.

"What?" I wiped my damp face with the back of my hand and looked at him confused.

"Come here, Kensie." He said with more force, grabbing my arms and pulling me across the center console onto his lap. I went willingly and listlessly straddled him.

"I understand if you don't want to be with me anymore. I wouldn't blame you for being disgusted by me." Though I sat so intimately close to him, I still couldn't look him in the eye.

"Why would you think that?" August asked.

I shrugged my shoulders and shook with silent tears that were picking up speed again.

"Kensie, look at me." He tilted my chin up with his hand. He brought up his other hand and cupped my face in them forcing me to look into his eyes. "I'm shocked. I'm shocked that the woman I see now who is confidant, and funny, and smart, was at that place once in her life." I hiccupped on a sob. "And I'm angry." He continued, "I'm angry that you had to go through that, that the feelings your dad's absence put in you drove you to need that kind of distraction. I feel helpless that I wasn't there for you then, and that you have those memories now. I feel sad, sad for my beautiful girl that had to experience that."

I fell into his chest and continued to cry. "What I definitely do not feel is disgust, Kensie. I am so in awe of you. You've turned your life around in such a short amount of time and are the most amazing woman I have ever met." I sobbed in relief. He didn't find me disgusting. He still cared about me. "Thank you." He said while stroking my hair as my tears slowed down. "Thank you for telling me that. I want you to know that you can share everything about you with me. I want to know it all because I want to know the girl I am falling for. You can trust me, Kensie. Always. I'm not going anywhere." He kissed the top of my head. "And I'm really pissed at the fuckers that took advantage of you. So mad, I'd like to beat the ever living shit out of them." He said the last part in a heated growl.

I pulled up and looked into brown blazing eyes. "But what about, what about..." Oh God, I didn't know how to ask him." What about how many?"

He placed his finger over my lips. "All I care about is that I am the only one now." He removed his finger and gave me a sweet gentle kiss sliding his tongue in briefly. "And that I am the only one from now on." I smiled and nodded my head up and down.

"That's why I wanted to tell you, why you needed to know. You're the only person I want to be with."

He smiled at me and leaned his forehead against mine. "You're it for me, Kensie." I laughed because I didn't know what else to do. He was it for me too.

CHAPTER 14

August gave me a few minutes in the truck to clean myself up before we went into Tommy's to catch up with the rest of the group. We had been out there a while, but Lennon knew August and I had some talking to do, so I'm sure she was the one to make sure we had our privacy.

I hadn't opened myself up like that to anyone since that night. Capri and Lennon knew minor details, but I had never told anyone the whole story. I think not talking about it was my way of leaving it in the past and moving on. I'd realized keeping it in, did just the opposite. My shame had become a poison, eating my value away from the inside, and feeding me lies that I wasn't worthy. August was my anecdote. I was healed the moment I set the shame free, and he cared anyway.

"There they are?" Lennon shouted to the group as we took our seats at the table. "I hope you two just made me an aunt!" August froze next to me. Yeah, I wasn't ready for that either buddy. I rolled my eyes at Lennon as she gave me a playful smirk that morphed into an unspoken question. I nodded my head letting out a relived breath. She grabbed my hand and gave it an encouraging squeeze under the table.

"It's about time." Wes grumbled from where he sat on the opposite side of Lennon.

"What's the matter with him?" I asked her. "He's pissed he didn't get made into a Wes sandwich. He wanted to sit between Capri and Tanner, but she wouldn't let him." That explained the pouting. He was going to have to work harder than that of he wanted a shot with Capri.

"C'mon, let's go get some drinks dude." August patted Wes on the shoulder noticing the pity party too. That was August, always looking out for everyone and taking care of what was his. "Want anything, pretty girl?" His whisper tickled my neck sending shivers down my spine.

"Just a coke, please." I smiled up at him before he kissed me on the lips softly and turning towards the bar with a grumbling Wes behind him.

"So, when's Milo up?" I turned towards Lennon who was scanning the crowd. The low-key space was considerably more packed than usual. On a normal night, the small hazy bar was speckled with small groups of friends, but tonight it was wall-to-wall leading me to believe Lennon's friend was a legit musician.

"Should be any minute," she answered. "I went back to see him a little while ago and wish him luck." I didn't miss the blush that she tried to hide from me by turning away. I don't think I'd ever seen Lennon blush. Not even the night she tore a hole in her black skinny jeans from droppin' like it was hot. Where my blush came on like a wild fire across my whole face, hers just tinted her soft ivory cheeks.

A trickle of clapping began and grew into a healthy applause as Milo took the stage. I looked around for August and caught sight of him already looking at me from the bar. He smiled at me while Wes ranted on. It looked like they would still be a while.

Milo cleared his throat bringing my attention back up to the small stage. He welcomed the crowd and joked with them while his eyes scanned the mass of people. They stopped abruptly when he spotted Lennon and he smiled with a lick of his lips. "Whoa." I whispered to Lennon, "I think he just eye fucked you a little."

When she didn't respond I looked over at her and saw that the dainty blush from her cheeks could now rival my wild fire one. "Ummm," I laughed.

"Drop it, Kensie," Lennon clipped back. I guess Milo was off limits for now. I could respect that, but I wouldn't keep quiet for long. Even though he wasn't' my type, I'd be blind to not see how attractive he was. He had dirty blonde dreads that were tied back at the nape of his neck. I couldn't see the color of his eyes from where we sat, but I could see a slight slant to the shape of them. His black t-shirt clung to his body in places where he was already beginning to sweat, and it was clear he worked out.

He was tall, but not quite as tall as August...August? August stood to the side of the stage saying something to Milo who bent down from his stool towards him. Milo nodded his head and laughed at something August said before sitting back up to readjust his guitar. I hadn't realized August knew Milo, but I hadn't met anyone he knew outside of our group either.

My eyes traced August as he weaved his way through the crowd back towards our table. I caught sight of several girls glance back at him as he strode passed, completely oblivious to the attention he drew. He looked especially gorgeous tonight in a plaid shirt paired with dark wash jeans. He was steadily carrying a beer in one hand and my Coke in another.

"I'm going to start off with a request. I don't usually do this, but seeing as this is a friend of a... friend." Milo's rasped voice stumbled over the word friend. He cleared his throat again, and began to strum a tune. I knew instantly what song he had begun to play, and my heart swelled.

Milo's sultry voice sang out the first few lines of Dave Matthews, Crush when August's hand appeared in front of me. "Dance with me?" He asked even though he didn't have to. I'd take his hand anywhere.

He led me to the tiny dance floor that didn't actually have anyone dancing on it, but instead people watched Milo put his own blue grass twist to my favorite song. August pulled me close wrapping me in his arms. I nuzzled my head into his chest and let him lead me in a soft sway to the music. He didn't say a word to me, and I didn't utter one to him. We didn't need words in this moment. Being close to one another was all I needed from him. Just to be held.

August brushed his hands up and down my back letting his head lean against mine silently giving me the comfort he knew I needed. His arms told tales of our happily ever after. I imagined us just like this, wrapped up in each other and dancing on our wedding day.

Milo was midway through the song when I noticed we were no longer the only couple dancing. "Look what we started," I said up to August, but he had stopped swaying and was staring at the bar.

"Hmm, sorry, what did you say?" He asked, but didn't take his eyes off whatever had caught his attention. I turned around to follow his line of sight, but it was too crowded to see exactly what had him so concerned.

"What is it, August?"

"Go sit with my sister, Kensie. I'll be there in a minute." He nudged me towards the table.

"August?" I asked again, but he was already moving purposefully toward the bar and still hadn't looked at me. I willed me legs to walk, but my eyes stayed trained on August weaving in and out of the boisterous crowd until I lost sight of him.

I was still looking for him when I got back to our table. "Hey, lover girl, "Lennon greeted me, "Where'd your boy toy stalk off to?" About to ask her if she saw where he went, I spotted him up at the bar with Wes.

"Oh, there he is." I pointed. "Up there with Wes and some girl. Maybe Wes needed some reigning in. He's pretty out of it tonight." I made a point to look over at Capri on the last part. She didn't reply, but her suddenly stiff posture suggested she wasn't unaffected. I suppose she wouldn't have said much regardless with Tanner tapping his foot along to the music right next to her.

"Dang, look at that trashy temptress." Lennon nodded towards them. "She's all sorts of fucked up." Capri's head whipped around at that and she glared down the aisle that seemed to magically part between us. She stared up at August and his company when her eyes widened. Her mouth dropped open and she gasped, "That bitch!" She shoved out of her chair, "be right back, Tanner," and turned to walk away. He flipped his hair out of his eyes to follow where she was going, and redirected his attention back to Milo.

"What's going on over there?" Lennon nodded towards the bar. Capri was already in front August digging her finger into his chest and spouting what appeared to be heated words. August nodded his head unaffected by Capri's outburst, as if she was expected to be that upset.

"Why is she mad at him?" I asked confused. I thought she went up there because she was mad at Wes for letting that girl hang all over him, but now she was waving her arms wildly clearly pissed off at August.

The trashy temptress hung hers arms sloppily over Wes. The girl in no way could compete with our beautiful friend. Where Capri was tall and slightly curvy, this girl was tall and rail thin. Her blonde hair looked brassy and brittle lying tangled down her back. Even from this far away, I could see the black make-up smudges rimming her eyes.

Wes shook his head at her and folded his arms across his wide chest. The temptress shrugged her shoulders one at a time causing her arms to flop along with the movement. Then she promptly turned and clunked her head down on the bar top spreading her arms out on either side.

"Is she alive?" I asked Lennon. I probably should have made a move to go see if August needed any help, but the scene Lennon watched with me, and never once glanced back towards Milo who was still swooning the crowd, was riveting to me. "I'll be back. I'm going to go see what's up." I told her. She nodded, but then quickly grabbed my arm and a look of what I can only describe as, *oh shit,* painted her face.

"What?" I turned in time to see the trashy temptress draped across a broad chest, *my* chest, August's chest. Her arms were wrapped lazily around his neck while she looked up at him.

"What...the...fuck?" Lennon drawled out next to me. As we watched the temptress run her fingers through dark brown hair, August's hair. What the fuck exactly. August froze and turned his head locking eyes with me. The nervous look in them was all the motivation I needed to get that sloppy bitch off of him.

"I'll be right back." I told Lennon and stood up so forcefully the chair squeaked on the wood floor before falling over.

"Wait," she grabbed my hand, "Are you jealous?" She asked incredulously with a hint of a smile. Was I? Watching that girl touch what was mine sent sparks flying in me. I was ready to go all Fourth of July on her scrawny ass.

"You know what, I think I am." I said, a grin spread across my face. Lennon and I shrieked together and jumped up and down laughing. "Oh my god. I'm jealous!" I rejoiced.

"You're jealous!" Lennon held my hands while we bounced together in tiny circles. I'm sure we looked ridiculous, but I didn't care. I had never been jealous. I had never felt protective enough over a relationship to feel threatened. It sounded ludicrous even to me, but I was so proud of myself.

"Now excuse me while I go claim what's mine." I turned on my heels and my best *bitch back off glare*.

"Atta girl!" Lennon encouraged me on.

August peeled the trashy temptress from him maintaining eye contact with me as I approached. She tried to fall against him again, but he put his hands up and shook his head at her. "Kensie," he said when I took my place next to him, uncertainty lacing his voice. I broke my stare from him and redirected it to the temptress.

"Excuse me, " I said in the sweetest of pissed off voices. She looked up at me with heavy eyelids and waved her finger at me. I think she meant to hold it steady, but her intoxication had it waving in front of my face.

"This her, August?" She asked finger still waving. Two more seconds and I was going to snap it off.

"Yep, this is me," I said relieved she finally put her hand down. I didn't think an assault charge would go over well with John. "I'm Kensie." I told her stepping my body in front of August effectively cutting her off from touching him anymore. I'm pretty sure I heard him chuckle, but I had more important things to deal with than his finding humor in this.

"August's new girlfriend." She said flipping her straw like hair behind her shoulder.

"August's girlfriend," I told her flipping my silky soft hair behind my shoulder intentionally leaving the word 'new' out of it. I wasn't new. I was *it*. She clicked her tongue on her teeth and cocked her eyebrow at me. I'm sure she was trying to look intimidating, but with her intoxicated state she just looked like she had something in her eye.

"You gonna give me a ride home, August, or what? You know I can't drive like this." She looked directly at me when she spoke to him behind me. I felt August's body tense when he cleared his throat to speak, but I beat him to it.

"The only one who is getting a ride from August is me." I glared at her, "and lucky for him I can drive. Really well." I smirked back at her. August choked out a cough behind me and tapped my arm gently pushing me aside. At the same time, I heard Wes mumble behind me, *"Lucky Bastard."* I had almost forgotten he was there.

The temptress opened her mouth to retaliate, but August cut her off. "Enough of this. I've wasted enough time away from my girl tonight. Wes will you call her a cab?" He looked over to Wes who nodded and August grabbed my hand in his, pulling me away from her. I maintained my glare on her from over my shoulder tripping over myself and falling into him.

He marched us right past Lennon and Capri, who had made it back to the table at some point. They both stood and clapped. I released August's hand and stopped to bow before he took my hand back and continued to stalk away shaking his head at me.

When we got outside, he led us directly to his truck, and still hadn't said a word to me. He unlocked and opened my door for me when I turned to face him. "What's wrong?" I was confused, shouldn't he be proud of the way I handled the temptress? I was so proud of myself I felt euphoric, but August was tense.

"Get in the truck, Kensie."

"But,"

"Get in the truck, Kensie." He repeated again, but didn't wait for me to move. He swept me off my feet and sat me down in the passenger seat. Then he climbed up on the running board and hovered above me in the doorway.

"Move over."

I did as he said, not sure what the hell was going on. I opened my mouth to ask what was wrong again, but was completely caught of guard when he climbed in on top of me pushing me down across the seats.

His mouth came crashing down on mine and my lips immediately parted to absorb the growl that erupted from his chest. He kissed me hungrily and I returned the need. He pulled away to nip and suck on the spot just below my ear. "That was so hot, Kensie." He said breathing on me, sending heat flooding through me. "So damn hot." He pulled down my shirt and nipped and sucked across my chest. I wriggled under him. "All jealous and territorial. So hot." I giggled a laugh that turned into a moan when he adjusted himself and pressed against me in just the right spot.

We went on like that long enough to fog up the windows of his truck, and long enough for me to be certain that I needed more, that I needed him. I pulled away and looked up at August whose eyes were heavy with desire. I wanted him to take me home, back to his home and his bed. My heart stopped. No, I needed more time, more time to make sure.... My heart started beating again.

He stared down at me his breath panting against my skin, when a hint of a smile touched his lips. He ran his finger down the side of my face and I closed my eyes instinctively laying my cheek into his palm. Everything with him was instinctual. I should stop holding back, and just let things happen. If I shut my mind off long enough I could hear the crackling pull between us. Or maybe it was just lust? If lust had a sound I can imagine it crackling and burning. This wasn't just lust though. My heart crackled and burned for him, but it also beat for him. My heart stopped. I didn't just have a need for him physically. I needed him completely. I looked up at August and felt my heart beat again.

"What on earth is going on in that head of yours?" He touched my lips with the tip of his fingers and I let out the breath I hadn't noticed I was holding in. I reached up and grabbed his face in my hands and pulled him down to my lips. I had to feel him, to feel it was real. Sure enough with our lips moving together my heart beat at a new pace, one I had never experienced before.

August's heartbeat pulsed through me. Our alternating beats thumped back and forth, one after the other.

Pound, pound.

Pound, pound.

Pound, pound.

In one swift moment, when we both parted to inhale a breath of each other's air, they synched together forming a singular steady beat. I can't imagine anything ever being more real.

August cleared his throat and pulled himself off of me. "Let's go somewhere."

"Right now?" I asked running my fingers through my hair.

"Yeah, why not? Unless you're too tired; it's been a long day." He stretched his arms behind his head and his stomach peaked out above the waistband of his pants. I honed in on the outer edge of whatever he wore under his pants. That sliver of bare skin was one of the most attractive parts of a man, and right now my eyes were riveted. I wonder if he wore boxers or briefs.

"Boxer briefs." He groaned as he finished his stretch.

"I said that out loud? "I asked.

"Well, you whispered it...out loud." He smiled crookedly. "What about you? Lace? Cotton?" He shook his head. "Wait, no, Thong or the butt cover kind?"

"The butt cover kind?" I laughed at him. "You mean bikini?"

"Whatever, it either covers or it doesn't." He watched me anticipating my answer.

"Wouldn't you like to know?" I teased back.

He grunted and opened the door to hop out of the truck. He closed it behind him and I watched as he ran around the front of the truck toward the drivers' side. Boxer briefs. Good answer.

CHAPTER 15

"This is your favorite place to go?" I asked staring out the front windshield into the dark.

"Yep." He said from his already opened door. He came around and helped me down from my side of his truck. We walked together through darkness to a chain link fence at the end of the parking lot.

"So." I started, but stopped when he jumped at the fence grabbing on half way up. "What are you Spiderman now?" I heard him chuckle as he scaled up and over the fence before he jumped down on the other side. He linked his hands on the fence and leaned in toward me, so I walked up and did the same.

"Your turn."

"No, uh uh." I said and let go of the fence where we stood backing away. "I don't like heights, August. I'm not climbing over the fence." What kind of surprise was this anyway? When he said he was taking me to one of his favorite places to go, I assumed it would be somewhere by the beach.

"It's not that high up, Kensie. I can come back and help you over if you need me to." He cocked an eyebrow at me.

"No, I can do it by myself." I said walking slowly up to the fence and placing my hands back on it just above my head. I never did like being offered help. I'd much rather do things myself and prove that I can. I looked up just a couple feet above me knowing from the top the view would be miles from the ground.

"Hey." He said from directly in front of me making me jump. "You can do this Kensie, and *if* you need help, I will help you."

"This is ridiculous." I muttered as I started my climb. Thank God I wore my cheetah print flats and not the ridiculous hooker heeled boots Lennon suggested. "We aren't even supposed to be here after hours." My foot slipped through one of the holes and my heart fell. I readjusted it and kept climbing. "I just saw my life flash before my eyes by the way." I could hear him snickering below me, but I was too nervous to look down. "If I get arrested and go to jail you'd better bring me candy bars every day." I threw one leg over the top and straddled the pointed chain links. Falling now would be very uncomfortable. I took a chance then and looked down at August who was lying on the dirt with his hand propped behind his head and watching me with a wide grin. "Oh come on, really?"

"Lace huh, and a thong? I'm a lucky man."

"What?" I held on tight with one leg on either side of the top of the fence and tried to look back at my pant line, where sure enough my red lace thong was half way up my back. Trader panties. I swung my other leg over and began my steady descend back down the other side of the fence one foot at a time.

"You know, you're only a few inches from the ground now. You can just hop off the fence." His voice spoke up from right behind me and was laced in amusement.

"Don't rush me." I yelled behind me still taking one step at a time. When my foot made the last step onto solid ground I took a breath of relief and turned towards August. "There. Happy now."

"With you? Always." He said grabbing my hand in his. "You did good, pretty girl." He leaned down and kissed my forehead. "Maybe a little faster on the way back? Especially when the police get here. I don't think I can afford all that chocolate."

I knocked my hip into him and rolled my eyes. We both turned and looked out at the acres of rolling...dirt. "So the flower field is your favorite getaway spot? I imagine it's really beautiful, when there are actually flowers." I teased.

"It is." He said still staring out at the dirt. "It's beautiful. Rows and rows of solid color, like a rainbow you can run your hands through and actually catch." I watched his face in the moonlight, and the peace this place brought him was almost tangible. I reached up and ran my hand down his cheek to see if I could feel it. He leaned into my touch and smiled as he turned to face me. "Want to walk through the flowers?"

"Sure," I waved my hand out at the empty space in front of us, "give me the grand tour."

We walked together hand in hand through the empty flower fields and talked casually. He told me about his parents and how they volunteer as a family every year to serve Thanksgiving dinner at the local woman's shelter. That nurturing trait I always see in August ran in the family. I wondered briefly if he would introduce me to them as his girlfriend anytime soon, but we had only been dating a short while so I wouldn't mind if he waited on the parent meeting. I felt anxious enough lately worrying about Thanksgiving with my dad. Meeting August's parents now would likely lead me to all sorts of nervous and embarrassing ramblings.

We stopped and sat down at wooden bench along one of the paths. August sat down first and then pulled me down to sit on his lap. He folded his arms around my waist and set his chin on my shoulder. "Why do I always want you closer?" He asked me. My stomach heated at his admission. "When I'm near you I have to be touching you, but even that's not enough."

"It aches." I whispered knowing exactly what he was talking about because I felt it too. The need to be with him was so consuming, his touch alone was never enough. I felt the urge to physically crawl inside him just to try and satisfy the desire.

"Exactly." He said and pulled me in closer to him. We sat like that, as close to each other as we could get for now, and watched the breeze blow up swirls of dust across the field. They twirled and spun occasionally catching just the right angle of moonlight creating sparkles in the air. "That reminds me of you." He whispered.

"What?"

"The way the dust dances." I sighed and leaned back into him further. It reminded me of myself too, but only recently had I felt the way the dust moved. Only since meeting August had I felt free again, and beautiful. I'd always assumed I needed to feel whole before I would find the one person I was meant to be with, but maybe I was wrong. Maybe you aren't filled completely until you meet them.

"Truth or Dare." He asked me softly.

"Hmmm, I think risking my life climbing the tallest fence ever was risky enough tonight. Truth."

"You know I would have caught you if you fell, right?" He assured me.

"I know." I told him, and I did. I knew he would always catch me. I'm not sure how he planned on doing that while lounging in the dirt mocking me, but I he'd figure it out. He was Spiderman, after all.

"So, truth? Let's see." He drawled thinking up a question. "Why dance?"

"Why dance?" I asked him not sure what he meant.

"Yeah, when most people dance it's because it's fun, or in my case because I've had one too many beers. For you it's different though. The way your body moves, the way the blink of your eyes slows down, and it's like you're…"

"Somewhere else?" I finished his thought.

"Yeah." He nodded behind me. Moving the hair that had blown across my neck aside so he could kiss me there. I shivered and he wrapped me up tighter in his arms, not knowing it wasn't from cold. He seemed to have a way of making the simplest of kisses feel so intimate. Or maybe it was just because they were from him.

"I remember when I was really little, two I think, I liked to dance around the kitchen. The floors were so much better for spinning." I smiled thinking about my mom stopping to twirl with me in between chores. "My mom called me her tiny dancer." When my parents argued, which was often, my mom would tell me, 'Go on tiny dancer, and go twirl in your room.' I didn't see it then, obviously, but she wanted to shield me from the arguing as best she could. She did that a lot when it came to my dad. She spent a lot of years making excuses for him until I was old enough to tell her I didn't need them anymore. She still made them.

"So, I'd go twirl around in my room and listen to the arguments escalate. Usually to yelling and my dad leaving the house." He was always a runner, quick to walk away before putting up a fight. "I learned to zone out while I danced in my room. When they argued, I liked to imagine I was a fairy dancing on a petal or a princess dancing at a ball." August shifted under me, and I moved to sit beside him. He pulled me right back down on his lap.

"Just an itch. Go ahead." He urged me to continue, so I did.

"I think it was safe place for me to go. Especially as I got older it became a place to go reconnect with myself when I felt overwhelmed with life." I laughed mirthlessly, "Kind of sad really. Something I love to do began as a way to occupy me while my parents fought." I had never realized that before. Not even my love of dance was untouched by the pain my dad had caused me. The reminder of his abandon had even seeped its way into my safe place.

"It's not sad at all. You love to dance because of the way it makes *you* feel, not because it's what someone told you to do. Regardless of how your love of dancing started, it's yours." He was right. Dancing was mine. I loved it because it gave me strength when I couldn't find it on my own. It centered me when I felt like I was teetering off an edge. It was mine, and it always caught me before I fell. It was a lot like August.

"What about you?" I asked him, "Why is this your favorite place?"

"It's pretty." He said in a falsetto voice making me laugh. "No really though," he continued, "my granddad lived on a small piece of land in the central valley that Capri and I visited every spring break. We spent hours playing in the wildflowers. My granddad sent us out in the morning with bottles of Kool-Aid and sandwiches because he knew we'd be out there till dark." He chuckled to himself over his memory. "As we got older and visited less, I could never lose the memory of how I felt out there." He quieted and we stared at the empty field together.

"We shouldn't let life take that feeling away." I said quietly. He hummed agreeing with me. We let the field of wildflowers we ran through as kids, slowly dwindle into nothing more than a couple of stems in a mason jar. I wanted that feeling of possibility and freedom back. "I want wildflowers." I whispered to myself. No more jars, just fields and fields of wildflowers.

"I think we might have found them." He whispered back. I think he was right. Suddenly August picked me up off his lap and set me on the bench next to him. He stood up abruptly and did a slow spin with his arms out wide. "But this," he stopped and pointed out towards the field, "is not even close to those fields. Why do I even come here?" He asked thoroughly confusing me.

"Huh?" I squinted. "You just said to remind yourself of them."

"But its nothing like them. I think I always wanted this place to feel like that, but it never has. It's manufactured. People put seeds in the ground. When it doesn't rain, they water it. When they bloom, people pick them; they sell them, and then it's empty again. Nothing about this place is natural and free. There's an undeniable truth in wildflowers, a promise that when it appears nothing can survive, something beautiful spontaneously blooms. There is nothing spontaneous here."

"So, we don't like the flower fields anymore?" I asked him cautiously.

"We don't," he laughed. "They suck." Well, this sure did take a drastic turn.

"Maybe we should have just raced through the dirt or something. All this deep talk just crushed your happy place." I smiled at him as he walked back towards me and sat down on the bench again.

"Happy place crusher." He teased me and poked me in the side making me jump.

"You crushed your own happy place buddy, I'm just a bystander." I raised my hands in front of me in defense.

"Oh Kensie, you're anything but a bystander." He reached his arm around my shoulders and squeezed me to him. "You *are* the wildflowers."

The only movement I could summon was the blinking of my lashes. By my definition, he just told me I was freedom, possibility, and hope. I was his new beginning. The thought bewildered me. There was no doubt August was my new dawn. I had no idea I was his, or that he even needed one. I opened my mouth to ask more, but I was stopped when he continued talking.

"You were completely unexpected," He said still looking out ahead of him. "I always knew you were out there, but I didn't know I was ready yet to find you." I held my breath then. "When I met you, I knew I had to have you. Whether I was ready or not didn't matter. I wasn't going to let you go."

He turned toward me and reached up to hold my face in his palms. He softly ran his thumbs over my cheeks looking into my eyes in a way that arrested my heart. The longer I looked into his eyes, the more my own vision became blurred. He closed his eyes and leaned towards me gently placing his nose beside mine. With the brushing of his breath on my face, my eyes closed and tears gently rolled down my cheeks. He slowly and tenderly nodded his head up and down brushing his nose against mine. *I love you,* my heart spoke.

"I love you, Kensie," he whispered and everything in me melted. I fell into him with the softening of my soul and sniffled. "You don't have to say it back, but I had to tell you. I know without a doubt I do and I don't want a day to go by that you don't know it. I love you." He said again and hiccupped and giggled all at once.

Then he kissed me. It was the sweetest, most honest kiss I had ever had. We kissed slowly and almost lazily. There wasn't the fire of lust behind this one, but the afterglow of love. Even though I couldn't tell him yet, I hoped he could feel my heart returning the same love he was giving me.

CHAPTER 16

This has to be a joke. I poked the button one, last, hopeful time and nothing happened. So then I punched it, a few times. After no sign of life, I brushed my hair out of my face huffing. How could the coffee machine be out of service? I didn't sleep at all last night. I was too high on August and replayed the moment he told me he loved me over in my head a gazillion times. I kept thinking I should have said it back. I knew I loved him, without a doubt, but for some reason I was terrified to tell him. Even after hearing him tell me, I couldn't let the words fall.

"Excuse me." I called into the kitchen.

"Yeah?" One of the cooks popped his head out.

"Is there any coffee?"

"Out of service." He answered in a bored tone. I guess I wasn't the only one searching for coffee this morning.

"I saw that, but is there a pot or an old coffee maker that you could brew some in?" I asked innocently. He looked up at me and cocked his eyebrow.

"No."

"But, I really need it."

"Me too, kid." Ugh. "The café on the other side of the campus is open." He couldn't really expect me to move my body that far without a jolt of caffeine. The smart thing to do would have been to go crawl back into bed, but I had to go to the library to study for my child development final.

August sent me a text at an ungodly hour and said he had family stuff to take care of today. I worried at first, but Lennon and Capri were out working on a project so it couldn't have been an emergency. I remembered him mentioning something about his parents remodeling, so I assumed he was helping out his dad. He told me he'd be out all day and to head to his place when I was done studying to wait for him. I should have gone to his house this morning and studied there all day. He's a smart man. I bet he had coffee.

***

I powered up my laptop in the quiet corner of the library to check my Facebook account. Procrastinating? Maybe, but my child development class was one of the few I actually enjoyed and I wasn't too concerned about my content knowledge. I probably didn't really need to study at all, but with August, Lennon, and Capri busy all day, I didn't have much else to do.

I scrolled through the posts on my profile. I passed up a post from a friend I knew in high school about her dinner last night. Really? Why do people need to post pictures of all of their meals? I didn't join social networking site to see how your meat and potatoes get along.

I kept going and read a quick post from Kate who lived on my floor, "Worst night ever." That was it. She was notorious for posting cryptic messages, and Lennon was as notorious for commenting on them. Under the post Lennon wrote, "Let us know what episode of *Sex Sent Me to the ER* you'll be on." I love that girl.

I saw a post with a picture attachment from my stepsister just under Kate's. The photo of a smiling Bethany, Parker, Jodie, and my dad in in front of a mountain covered in snow had the comment "Great family weekend in Big Bear." Burn. I pursed my lips and bit back the singe. As much as I tried to feign nonchalance, and as much as I tried to move past it, it hurt to see my dad in a family I wasn't a part of.

Call me a glutton for punishment, but I continued to scroll through her pictures from the weekend. The next few were more of the four of them, but then there was one of dad with my grandpa by a large fireplace. *My grandpa.*

The next photo had Parker playing chess with my grandpa. It looked like they were in a living room and I could see a kitchen in the distance full of people. I clicked on the picture to enlarge it and zoomed in on the kitchen. Bethany sat at a kitchen counter with a girl donning a head of brown curls piled on top of her head. It couldn't be. They wouldn't do this without me there.

I zoomed to the right of Bethany, and there behind the counter stood a painfully familiar woman. I tried to swallow, but my throat caved in. The fuzzy enlargement of my aunt standing at the counter talking to Bethany and my cousin Shaylee emphasized my exclusion from the family reunion.

I clicked up to the top of Bethany's page and quickly unfriended her. I couldn't control what they did without me, but I could control whether I had to see it or not. I chose to not witness my own father's abandonment through someone else's happy memories with him. Memories that should have been mine to share.

Trying to ignore the pain in my chest I continued to scroll through my newsfeed when a new friend request popped up. I wouldn't be surprised if it was Bethany already realizing we weren't friends anymore.

I clicked on the icon and a name popped up that I hadn't expected to see. Chelsea Baker, my best friend from high school. I hovered over her name contemplating whether I wanted to accept her request or not. Our friendship wasn't strengthening to me back in high school, so why would I need it now? People change though, and Facebook doesn't even make us friends anyway. We'd be two people who were once close, now getting to spy on each other's lives now. *What the hell.* I clicked accept.

I immediately went to her page to initiate my stalking. The first thing I noticed was that she had a beautiful baby boy. I smiled, proud of my former friend for becoming a mother. We may have had a toxic friendship, but I didn't doubt she was a wonderful mother.

I scrolled through a few of the photos that proved me right. She was a great mom with a happy child. I proceeded to click quickly through the photos, one of his first birthday, one of a camping trip, and one of Christmas with his dad I assume. *Wait.* I went back to the Christmas photo and stared blankly at the page with my heart pounding up into my neck.

There, sitting with Chelsea's baby on his knee was Nolan. I had no idea they kept in touch all these years. Though, why would I since I all but disappeared from that life. Still, he must be really close with her family to have spent Christmas with them. Something told me to stalk further.

I went to Chelsea's posts and scrolled through looking for anything Nolan related, then I slammed my computer screen shut. What was I doing this for? It didn't matter how close Nolan was to Chelsea's family. I shouldn't bother me in the least that they even still know each other. I tapped my fingers on the top of my computer and chewed on my cheek.

Then, I popped it back open and continued scrolling. That's when I found it, the one post that rocked me where I sat. Chelsea was engaged to Nolan. Not only were they engaged, she posted a loving comment about how happy she was to be engaged to her high school sweetheart. The one she shared a beautiful boy with. The one she first "hooked up with" at Tawnie's party.

The last sentence had my stomach rolling. Tawnie's party had taken place the week Nolan pulled away from me. I distinctly remember mulling over what had gone wrong that night to cause such an abrupt change in our relationship. Well, now I knew. My boyfriend had cheated on me with my best friend.

I slammed my computer shut again and shoved it into my bag. I had to get some air. I rose from my chair and mindlessly headed for the stairs. My legs stumbled and collided against themselves and all that was in their path. Movement had become a foreign concept to my body. With the exit doors in sight I skipped and tripped over the last few stairs on leading to the bottom floor zeroed in on the porthole of freedom ahead.

I exploded through the doors leaving my purgatory to replay on the third floor. A cleansing burst of fresh air stopped me in my tracks on the step. Still numb, my arms flopped to my sides sending my backpack falling off my shoulder onto the concrete next to me. The faint smell of sea air loosened the tightly wound fibers within me, and flopped down onto the step. I rested my head between my knees and practiced the slow steady breathing my high school counselor had taught me years ago.

How could I not have noticed my best friend was sleeping with my boyfriend behind my back? Too enchanted back then, and too hopeful for a fairytale, I'd left myself blind to truth. I'd foolishly embraced my personal love story, until he started to pull away. He wanted to go out more often, and I wanted to stay in. He wanted to drink more, and I was afraid too. Chelsea was everything he wanted me to become. Now I clearly saw Nolan's retreat from us coinciding with the time they spent working on their biology project together.

I sat against the stucco wall of the library and stared up to the tops of the palm trees.

They were so tall, so out of sight. If you didn't stop to look up you'd miss the quiet ruffle of the tips of the leaves in the ocean breeze. I squinted my eyes and watched the pointy tips wave stiffly thinking about how far I'd come since high school. As much as it hurt to find out now, I'm glad I didn't know then. It would have torn me apart to lose my boyfriend, and what I thought was my best friend at the same time. With the shock receding, I thought clearly.

My heart broke for the girl I was then. She had so much abandonment in her life. Nolan and Chelsea had gone on to live their lives together, and from what it looked like, happily. My dad moved on and took an entire half of my family with him to a new one. While all the people who had left me moved forward, I had been stuck in place, trying to move on from the hollowness left in their wake. Now what? *I suppose you keep moving.* The words echoed in my tired mind, and suddenly there was only one place I needed to be. Moving forward with August, and leaving it all in the past.

***

I could have sworn he said it would be under the rock by the front door. Yet, here I stood with the rock in my hand staring down at the empty spot in the planter without a key. Once I had calmed myself down in front of the library, I came immediately to August's. I'd hoped he'd be home, but when I arrived his truck was gone. After the afternoon I had I just really needed to see him. He grounded me. I needed to be pulled back down to what mattered more than anything at that moment, but August wasn't home and the damn house key was missing.

When I first showed up I saw Wes' classic Chevy in the driveway. I knocked on the door for a few minutes without an answer before I decided to hunt the spare key down. It wasn't until I'd checked under a dozen rocks and scratched myself searching through the bushes that I realized Wes probably had used it to let himself in.

I sat on the front stoop with my head in my hands and cursed this awful day. I reached over to the flowerbed and picked up one of the rocks. I gripped it in my hand and sent my frustrations through my arm and into my white knuckles clutching the stone. Then, I chucked it, hard and fast into the grass with a grunt and watched it bounce springing about dirt. It felt good.

I stood up and reached down picking up another rock repeating the same action sending it pummeling into the sod. I continued to throw rock after rock grunting and cursing. When I'd thrown the final rock and stood satisfied and heaving with my hands on my hips. I blew a piece of hair from my face and crossed my arms over my chest looking at August's grass littered with angry rocks. I may need to consider kickboxing. It's probably a more appropriate form of anger management than rock chucking.

I leaned over to search out my bottle of water in my bag. Anger is exhausting. I took a few gulps and pulled out my pack of mints. I opened the case to find they were all gone. Ugh.

What the hell. I chucked the metal container into the grass.

The clicking of the door sounded behind me. I turned around to Wes finally opening the door. I was beginning to wonder if I needed to call emergency services to make sure he was alive in there.

"This is just pathetic." Wes said leaning against August's open front door with nothing but a towel wrapped around his waist.

"How long have you been standing there?" I asked both relieved, and irritated that he was in the house I was locked out of. "And where are your clothes?" This matter seems more pressing.

"Here? In this doorway, about five minutes, but I watched you through that front window," he pointed to the window that was just behind the planter, "for about ten minutes or so." He watched me and my temper tantrum the entire time? How embarrassing. "And my clothes are in the wash. Some newbie upchucked all over me at the shop."

"You watched me?" I asked nervous about seeming a bit unstable at the moment, although, he completely enabled my outburst. He could have let me in and stopped my tirade and any minute, but didn't. "Did you even think to let me in?"

"I did." He nodded like it was no big deal. "But you are really entertaining when you're raging." He turned and walked into the house.

"Gee, thanks." I said to myself agitated with him. I leaned down to pick up my bag and followed in behind him.

Truth in Wildflowers 235

"I couldn't wait to see what you would do next. " He said loudly padding into the kitchen. "You just kept going, rock after rock." I heard the refrigerator door open. "That shit was impressive. And your cussing," he walked back into the living room with taking a bite from an apple. "Your creativity is top notch. I mean, you called a rock a Ho-waffle. I admire that." He mumbled behind his full mouth.

"At least I've got that going for me." I rolled my eyes and tossed my bag next to the front door. I staggered over to August's couch and fell face first onto it.

"I have mints in my car if you still wanna make out?" Seriously? I willed my head to the side and glared at him.

"I don't *wanna* make out with you, Wes." He shrugged and sat down at the desk turning towards the computer.

"Your loss. I taught August everything he knows." I giggled to myself a little and watched him as he looked over his shoulder at me and grinned.

"What are you doing over there anyway?" I asked him not anymore motivated to move.

"Just looking up some stuff to sketch for some sessions next week." He said taking another bite of his apple. "This Pinterest thing is like crack."

"You're on Pinterest?" I laughed and pushed myself up. Tired or not, this I had to see.

"Yeah, this chick said she pinned the tat she wanted, so I jumped on to check it out real quick. Next thing you know I'm looking at beards, then fedoras, then mint green high top

Chucks, and now I'm looking at weddings." I leaned over his shoulder to take a look. "Why am I looking at weddings?" He looked at me mystified. I couldn't answer him. Pinterest did the same thing to me every time.

"Wow, did they have an In N Out food truck at their reception?" I pointed to the picture on the screen.

"Badass, right? And look, the dudes wore superhero shirts under their tuxes." He clicked on another picture. "Such a cool wedding. I call dibs on Silver Surfer at your wedding." He turned quickly to look at me. "Tell August I have dibs." I nodded my head to reassure him, grinning at his reference to a wedding for August and I. It was the ultimate stamp of approval from his best friend. That, or he just wanted to wear a superhero shirt under a tux.

After Pinning his heart out, Wes brought out some of his sketches for tattoos he was working on. He and I sat Indian style around August's coffee table that was already strewn with colored pencils and sketch paper. He asked me if I wanted to help him color them in so he could give his customers some options. I think he caught onto how mopey I was, and how often I was checking my phone for missed alerts from August. Jumping from the couch toward the door when I heard a car door outside didn't help either. Peering through the peephole I saw it was a neighbor, and that's when Wes waved me over to the table.

"So you wanna talk about what's got you down?" Wes asked not taking his eyes off the sketch he was working on. I, on the other hand, stopped coloring the koi fish he had given me and tilted my head at him.

"What do you mean?"

"You've colored almost every picture I've given you in shades of black and grey." I twisted my face and looked down at the pile of sketches I had been coloring. He was right, even when I had used color is was dark and depressing like oxblood and navy. "Huh."

"So, we talkin'?" He asked again still not looking up at me.

"It's nothing. I had a lousy day."

"And now August is late getting home, and you haven't heard from him." He said putting his pencil down and looking across the table at me. I averted my eyes from him.

"There's that too. I wanted him here so I could maybe talk to him about it." I shrugged and went back to my coloring. I didn't typically talk about things that bothered me and instead tried to work through them on my own, so him no being here struck a nerve with me. I tried to not be mad at him because he had no idea that I needed him, but I was growing more and more frustrated over not hearing a word from him yet.

"Lay it on me." He said and went back to his sketching. I thought about not bothering him with it all, but quickly decided that I couldn't let it fester. There wasn't anywhere for me to dance out my frustration so if Wes was kind enough to listen, then I was going to take him up on it. "Tell me about this awful day so you can start giving my customers some color in their tats." He waved his hand towards him inviting me to speak up.

I didn't hesitate to fill him in on my horrible

day start to finish. I blubbered on and on, and Wes simply listened nodding at all appropriate places. He never spoke to offer advice or solutions. I wouldn't have ever pegged him for being such a great listener. "Damn, sounds like your day was a healthy dose of bullshit with a side of what the fuck." I did, however, count on the fact that he would lighten the weight the day had placed on me.

I laughed, "I really could have done without the what the fuck."

He shook his head and laughed with me. "No joke. That shit's gonna piss August off though. He's all sorts of protective over you."

"He is?" I put my pencil down and leaned back against the chair behind me folding my arms over my knees. I knew how August felt about me, but I had never witnessed him being protective over me. He seemed to let me take care of myself, and I liked that. The thought of him all caveman, though, peaked my interest.

"Yeah, that first night we saw you at Tommy's some dude tried to dance with you," I nodded remembering that guy. He was attractive, but I hadn't been interested. "And the second he left the dance floor, he came back up to the bar and said something to one of his buddies about you being a tease." I gasped but Wes put his hand up motioning for me to hear the rest. "Next thing you know August's fists were gripping this dude's shirt. I don't know what he said, but dude looked scared shitless. Just nodded his head and when August let him go, he took off."

I probably should have been a little upset at

being called a tease, and maybe shocked that August nearly physically assaulted someone for me, but I wasn't. He stood up for me before he even really knew me, I couldn't be anything but grateful to have him in my corner now.

I smiled proudly. "That's my man." I told Wes and he threw his head back and barked out a laugh.

"He is." He said and smiled to himself. "You make him really happy, Kensie." He said more serious then. "You've come along and brought him back to life." I sat up straight at Wes's choice of words. I was confused by what he meant. The August I knew was happy, independent, and determined. Nothing I knew of him suggested that I had come along and caused any profound changes in his life.

I leaned forward and was about to ask Wes what he meant when he spoke up looking back down at his sketches again. "Don't overthink it, Kensie. You guys are lucky to have each other. Some people spend their whole lives looking for what you two have."

I settled back down against the chair behind me. He was right; we were happy, really happy. We were in love.

"Uh, Kensie." Wes said almost painfully with one of the sketches I had colored in his hand. He ran the other hand through his hair and winced. "You made this rose look like a vagina."

"What?" I sputtered in shock and half laughed. I reached out and yanked the drawing from him. "It's a rose. I don't know what you're talking about. It's not my fault you can't get the female anatomy off your brain."

"No, look you colored the inside of the rose a different color than the rest." He pointed down to where I had used a dark violet color on the otherwise red rose.

"I was shading." I said a bit defensive over my artistic expression.

"Well, you gave the rose a labia. Shade with a more similar color next time. No one wants a vagina on their shoulder."

I laughed at him and tossed the drawing before it fluttered back onto the table. So maybe I wasn't an artist, but I was good with kids. I'd been thinking a lot lately about a possible career working with kids. I was looking forward to discussing my plans with August.

I stood up and went toward my bag to take out my phone. I wasn't going to sit here all night waiting for him. I pulled the phone out of my bag and sent him a text, encouraging myself to be more proactive in my life.

Me: Will you be home soon?

I didn't say anything else. I thought about telling him that I needed to talk to him, but I didn't really. I didn't *need* him, but I wanted him here to talk to. I had no doubt that if I told him I needed him here with me now, he'd drop whatever he was doing and come home. But, I was okay right now. Wes was doing a good job of distracting me.

He'd surprised me tonight. The time we were spending together allowed me to see that he wasn't only a big goofball, but a genuinely good guy. I could see why he and August were such good friends for so long. They really did take care of each other, and that reminded me of the girl we ran into last night at Tommy's.

"Hey, can I ask you something?"

"Shoot." Wes said scribbling away with one pencil and another one placed behind his ear.

"That girl last night," I started and Wes paused but didn't take his eyes of his paper, "Who was she?" I had been thinking about her off and on since last night. They obviously knew who she was, she even seemed like she somehow knew about me. I meant to ask August last night, but got swept up in the moment with him.

Wes looked up at me and twirled his pencil between his fingers, "Who was she?" He repeated what I asked.

"Yeah, you guys knew her, and she said she knew who I was. She seemed interested in August too. Too interested. Should I be worried?" I cringed at my question. I hated that I even felt like I needed to ask him that. Of course I didn't need to worry. Even if she was all over August, he didn't reciprocate. And I'm pretty sure I made myself clear. If I were her, I wouldn't mess with me again. "Never mind." I said shaking my head. "I'm being silly."

Wes put down his pencil and pouted his mouth in a look of sympathy. Great, he thought I was being silly too. "She's just an old friend. You don't have anything to worry about. Everything August does is for you. Remember that, kay?" Weird.

"Okay." I thought back to last night and how he removed her every time she touched him, and how he took me out of the bar when I got too upset with her. Wes was right. August always looked out for me. I had nothing to worry about, and I was being silly for even thinking about it.

***

Wes left sometime around ten thirty. He stayed so I wouldn't be alone waiting up for August, but I could tell he was tired. Well, it was obvious when he passed out on his last sketch of a mermaid and drooled all over her tail. I woke him up and assured him I would be fine. He nodded his head at me and mumbled something unintelligible before sweeping up all his sketches in a messy pile and stumbled out of the house.

Locking the door behind him, I peered out the window to make sure the chilly air woke Wes enough to drive home. When music loud enough to rattle the window frame blared, and Wes bobbed his head with furious intent, I knew he was fine.

A ping on my phone alerted me to a message. I glared down at my bag that lied inches from where I stood. If it was August, I'd be both happy to finally hear from him and angry it took this long to finally hear from him. I reached down and pulled the phone out of my bag and sighed when I saw the message.

Humpty: I'm sorry. I didn't plan on being this late. I'll be home soon. Can't wait to see you.

I tossed the phone back into my bag without replying. I'm not sure if I had a right to be mad being that I also hadn't messaged him all day, but I was. If I hadn't been so tired I would have just gone back to my dorm. Instead, I turned on his TV and laid on the couch.

I turned on some show about people who had costume fetishes. Odd. Creepy. Sometime after one couple went to a bed and breakfast dressed up as giant Teddy bears, I zoned out. The weight of the day began to take a toll and catch up to me. I laid my head back on the pillow and stared up at the ceiling.

I don't think I would ever be able to put into words the kind of pain someone feels when they are abandoned by a parent. The hurt he instilled in me long ago created a chasm within me. I can't pinpoint a time when the pain was ever greater than a time before, but instead it has just always been a constant in me. Slowly over time it eroded, leaving me a hollow and empty shell.

Staring at the family photos today I knew I should have been broken, but I was just the same as I've always been. Not one single moment in time has hurt me, but the hours mixed into days, mixed into years...hurt. Somewhere along the way I learned to accept it as a part of my life. I even made excuses for the way things were. I was too independent, I was always closer to my mom anyway, but in the end I just hurt.

I got up to grab a box of tissues when my breathing became stuffy and my eyesight blurry. I picked up my bag on the way, figuring I might as well put my stuff in the bedroom. I halted in the doorway of August's room rethinking my sleeping arrangements. I wasn't sleeping in here with him tonight, and frankly I didn't want my stuff in there either. I needed to distance myself, even if it was only with material objects.

I turned around and went across the hall to the only other bedroom in the house. I opened the door and gawked in semi horror. August's guest room was yellow; don't forget your sunglasses yellow. I'm sure I'd wake up with a tan after a night in here. A tiny twin bed sat against the far wall, but I couldn't imagine anyone actually getting any sleep in here. Maybe that was the purpose, to make sure Wes didn't overstay.

Taking the box of tissues I found on the bathroom counter, I went back to curl up on the couch. I pulled my knees into my chest to resume my trip down pity lane.

It made me nauseous. I lived a lie believing I was the only one for Nolan, just as he had been for me. The days I kissed him, he wasn't only kissing me. When he pulled away he made me believe it was because I was too clingy. I believed him. I trusted him. I trusted both of them. This was why I couldn't trust myself to lean on people. I always chose wrong. I somehow always ended up alone in the end.

I lie there on the couch and cried, for a long time. It felt good to let it all out, but at the same time it felt completely isolating. I really wish August had been there with me. I really did need him. To hold me, to listen, but he wasn't.

A while later I was awakened by soft kisses down the side of my cheek. I sighed, inhaling his clean scent and rolled toward him, but felt myself slip just before he caught me.

"Come to bed." He whispered and continued to pepper me with kisses. I must have fallen asleep on the couch waiting up for him. I groaned in irritation thinking about how late I had stayed up.

"No." I mumbled and rolled back over to face the couch cushions. Then I felt his arms reach under me as he prepared to pick me up. I swatted his arms away from me. "No. Mad." I mumbled again.

He sighed and I felt the seat dip in next to me. "I'm sorry. I should have called."

"Hmmhmm."

"I didn't expect to be so busy today. I would have much rather have been here with you." I felt his hand trail lightly across my arm and I batted him away again. He chuckled a little at me that time. "Still mad?"

"Hmmm."

He sighed again. "I'm sorry. Outside of letting time get away from me and being an asshole, I don't have a good excuse. You were on my mind *all* day though, and I couldn't wait to get home to you."

"Sleeping," was all I mumbled to him. Truthfully, I was letting him sweet talk his way into my good graces, but I didn't want to talk to him about it when I was half asleep.

"Come to bed with me." He asked softly. "Please." He almost begged. I couldn't though. I wanted him to know how much he had hurt me, and I wasn't going to give in.

"No." I mumbled again and snuggled down into the throw pillow I was laying on.

He sighed again. "Okay." and I felt him leave the couch. I listened to him walk down the hallway towards his room and immediately felt empty. I wanted him with me even when I was upset with him. Maybe I should have just gone in there with him. I still wouldn't talk to him until the morning, but at least I'd get a good night sleep. As silly as it sounded though, I didn't want my first night in August's bed to be like this. I didn't want to start off sleeping back to back and not talking. So until we had talked about the day, I'd stay put on his couch.

I snuggled myself back into the pillow when I heard the sound of his bare feet padding down the hallway. I followed his steps all the way up until they stopped beside me. A heavy quilt gently fell across my body, and the couch sank in next to me. He laid down next me. I opened one eye and saw his long eyelashes flutter closed inches from my face. "What are you doing?"

"I'm sleeping with you." He said and climbed over me to the other side closest to the back of the couch.

"That's better."

"No, you're not." I said looking over my shoulder at him now.

"Yes, I am. If you're sleeping on the couch, I'm sleeping on the couch." He pulled me down and settled me into the front of him.

"We are not both sleeping on this couch. Go back to your bed." I whispered to him behind me.

"Only if you come with me."

"Not a chance." I said more determined than

when he had first woken me up.

"Then neither am I. Now stop talking to me so I can sleep." The smile in his voice should have irked me, but it didn't. I smiled a little to myself. "You're so stubborn." He said wrapping his arms around me and pulling me tighter against him.

I was very stubborn, and he let me be. I sighed and settled into him on the tiny couch. If I was going to wake up and put on my mad face again I needed to get some sleep. Just as I started to doze off wrapped up in his arms, I felt August place a kiss on the side of my head just next to my ear. "I love you." He whispered, and I was wide-awake again.

CHAPTER 17

The smoky scent of bacon and my stomach's grumbling reminder that I hadn't eaten much the day before. I stretched with the added space on the couch now that August was no longer on it. We slept curled up together all night, and I slept soundly until now.

I lumbered off the couch and shuffled into the kitchen. August stood at the stove shirtless wearing nothing but a pair of basketball shorts. I watched his back flex and ripple with the simple movements he made cooking up breakfast. I smiled at the grease spot he left smeared on his hip when he reached over to scratch himself mid pancake flip.

I pulled out a chair to sit down, and August turned when it screeched against the tile floors. "Good morning." He smiled and my heart fluttered. God I missed him yesterday. One day apart and I missed him.

I smiled back. "Good morning."

"You hungry?" He asked me scooping the last bit of eggs onto a plate.

"I'm starving actually. This all smells really good."

"You still upset from yesterday?" He asked

me and I saw a bit of brokenness in his eyes.

I nodded. "Yeah, but let's talk after we eat." I patted the chair next to me inviting him to come sit. Relief loosened his face before he turned around to pick up our plates and place them on the table.

We sat at the table in silence except for the noises our utensils made against the plates. I know he'd woken up and did this for me. Our first morning here together wasn't as he had imagined, but he was trying.

Placing my hand on his thigh I rubbed circles with my thumb. It was a simple gesture, but I wanted him to know he was already forgiven. Without even explaining what happened I already forgave him, even if he didn't want my forgiveness. I trusted him that much.

He put down his fork and looked down at my hand with a sad smile. He picked it up in his own and brought it to his lips before kissing my knuckles. "You're too good for me." He whispered painfully before putting our hands down and picking his fork back up. I couldn't take my eyes of the disappointment he shrouded himself in. I zoned in on the wall behind him questioning the source. The one that nagged at me, was the fear that he may think I became too dependent on him. I feared he would see my reaction to his absence yesterday as something to run from.

I helped August clear the table and wash up the dishes when we'd finished breakfast. I couldn't handle the silence between us anymore, so I made small talk telling him about my night with Wes. He smiled and laughed with me, especially when I told him about my skills and turning harmless tattoos into porn.

Once the kitchen was cleaned up, we sat down on the couch in the living room. August sat at one end, and I saw the hurt on his face when I sat down at the opposite end. All I wanted was to curl up next to him, but I needed my physical distance from him to say what I needed and to protect myself if I didn't like what he had to say.

"Okay," I said more to myself than him and turned to face him down at his end. "I don't know why I didn't hear from you yesterday. I thought a lot last night about how maybe it wasn't my place to know. Maybe demanding you tell me where you are, or that you check in when you are gone so long is too clingy." I cringed at the term Nolan once used to describe me, "But then I decided no. No, I have a right to know. I'm your girlfriend. I don't deserve the brush off. If for some reason you have decided that you don't want to be with me with me anymore, then you need to tell me."

"Kensie, no," he cut me off, "Don't jump to that conclusion just from one day of not hearing from me. Of course I want to be with you."

"No," I said firmly, "I get to jump to that conclusion. What else am I supposed to think? You didn't even call me, and you only texted me after I wrote you because I was worried about you. I was sitting here in *your* house, where you asked me to come wait for you, and you never showed up." He leaned forward onto his knees and dropped his head into his hands.

"You're right." I heard him mumble.

"I have been walked out on one too many times August. Too many times, I have trusted people to only have them leave me. I don't want that from you. It would hurt the most from you." I was crying now. "I want you to be the one to stay." My voice cracked when I realized it wasn't August being gone all day that had me so upset. It was the realization that he had the ability to leave me, and that it would hurt more than any other abandonment I had faced.

I had begun to cry so hard that I didn't see through my blurred vision when he had crawled across the couch and pulled me onto his lap. He wrapped his arms around me and I wrapped mine around his neck holding him to me. "I'm not going anywhere," he said, but that was all. He held me while I cried.

When I calmed down, I lifted my face from August's shirt. "I made your shirt all wet." I said and wiped at his shoulder. He took my hand and kissed it before putting it down to my side. He stared at the coffee table biting on his lip. It took a few minutes before he finally spoke.

"I'm an asshole," He said shaking his head. "I can't believe I did that. I can't believe I made you feel that way. I thought I was...I was trying to...I thought..." He stopped and looked at me suddenly with such desperation in his eyes it broke me. "I fucked up, but its not going to happen again." He grabbed my hands again and held them tightly. "I promise you this won't happen again." He nodded his head and looked back towards the table. "Not again." He said resolutely, but I had a feeling it was more for his reassurance than my own. Something inside me told me there was much more he needed to say, and more questions I needed to ask. But of course, I ignored it.

"Hey," I whispered to him and ran my fingers through his hair while he sat fixated on the table in front of him. I didn't want him to worry about where we stood. I believed him when he said it wouldn't happen again. He leaned his head into my hand while I continued to run my fingers through his hair and lightly scratch at his scalp. His body sagged and he sighed contentedly.

"Damn woman. You have magic hands." He said and his smile was back. I loved that smile. I loved a lot about him. "Can you massage my shoulders?" He asked sitting up straighter and I obliged. "A little lower," he said and I moved my hands down his back. "Lower." I massaged down to his lower back, "'Kay a little lower now and towards the front," he said and I stopped.

"Excuse me?" I asked and he snickered to himself. I swatted at his arm but he caught my hand before I made contact. He pinned it down on the couch next to us, laying me back as he crouched over me. "This is exactly why women steer clear of massages. You men are always turning them into something dirty."

He smirked and shrugged his shoulders above me.

"Can't blame a guy for tryin'." Then he leaned down to kiss me. As our lips met, I laid all the way back onto the couch and brought him down on me. He adjusted himself so that he was between my legs and continued to kiss me senseless. We laid like that until we became a tangled web of 'can't get enough' when August abruptly sat up.

I brushed my hair out of my face. "What?" I asked trying to catch my breath. That's when I heard the doorknob jiggle and the sound of keys. "Who is that?" I hissed and shoved him all the way off of me trying to regulate on my frizzed out hair. Capri floated in carrying a tray of coffee cups. She kicked the door shut with her foot at looked up at us.

"Oh!" She said eyes wide and teeth in a clenched grin, "Um..." She shrugged her shoulders sheepishly, "I brought coffee." I jumped off the couch and ran towards her snatching a cup out of her hands as she waltzed into the kitchen.

"Cock blocker." August coughed as he got up from the couch too and halted Capri's steps. She turned slowly and squinted her eyes at him. "What did you just say to me?" She asked slowly dragging out her words. He lifted one shoulder. "I called you a cock blocker." He said casually and walked up to her grabbing his coffee off the tray.

"I hate that word." Capri said gritting out each word slowly and I swear time slowed down. There should have been old western music playing in the background. Capri turned toward the table and set down her coffee while August sipped and looked around the room deliberately casual. "I hate that word," she said again, "and you know it."

She walked up to him and before I could register what was happening Capri dove towards his legs. August caught her before she grabbed him and locked her under his arm. Capri screamed while he rubbed his fist on the top of her head sending her blonde hair flying. She made a good effort at swatting at his legs, but she wasn't getting much accomplished.

"Ummm," I said holding my coffee to my lips, but afraid to take a sip like life was normal. Was this normal? As an only child, I wasn't too sure. They let go of each other panting and laughing when I asked, "What just happened?"

"She hates that word." August walked by me and placed a kiss on my lips.

"I guess so." I said following him into the kitchen.

He stopped and leaned up against the kitchen cabinets smirking at Capri when she walked in and took a seat at the table. "Especially when Wes says it. She really hates it then." He said and Capri's face glowed crimson. I couldn't help the giggle that escaped me, but quickly shut up when she snapped her head my way and glared at me.

"I hate that word 'cause it's crude, and you," she pointed at August, "have a bedroom. If you don't want to be interrupted then go in there." She sat back into the chair, all traces of her embarrassment leaving her face when August replied back.

"What fun is that?" He grinned crookedly at me, "I own the house. Why use the bedroom when Kensie and I can use the couch," Capri scrunched up her face, "and the doorway," he continued and Capri covered her ears, "and the shower," she plopped her head down on the table and groaned, "and that table." He said and

Capri sat straight up looking at the table in horror.

"You're disgusting." She said standing up and heading the sink and wash her hands, and her forehead.

I, on the other hand, was left with visions of August and I in all the places he had just listed. I didn't even realize I was fanning myself when he pushed up of the counter and sauntered towards me. He grabbed my hand in his and leaned down to whisper in my ear, "And the counter too." I shivered before he kissed me on my neck and went to throw his coffee cup away. I like the counter. The counter and I got along real well last time.

The rest of the afternoon was spent hanging around the house with August and Capri. She said Tanner was out working all day, and didn't seem to care too much about it either. They were an odd couple. The girls and I had plans that night to head to Tommy's for a girls only happy hour. It had been a while since the three of us got together, and I was in need of a little fun with them.

Capri and I rode together to Tommy's to meet up with Lennon. I almost didn't make it out of the house when August found me in the hallway all dolled up and pinned me against his bedroom wall begging me to stay. I'm sure his reaction wouldn't have been the same had he known I was wearing one of Capri's dresses. She'd brought one over for me since I didn't make it back to my dorm that day.

As tempting as August was, and he was *very* tempting, I couldn't ditch out on girls night. I had a lot to get out of my head that I wanted their take on. I chastely kissed him on the mouth and blew him a kiss when I walked out the door.

***

"Wow, what a shit-tastic day," Lennon said taking a sip of her beer.

"I know, thank God it's over." I agreed and sipped from my iced tea. "Is it weird that I was bothered by Chelsea and Nolan being together?" I asked the girls. It's something I worried about. I tried not to care about finding out my ex and former best friend not only got together behind my back, but were also still happily together. For some reason, I couldn't get it off my mind. "I mean if I'm this happy with August, it shouldn't bother me right?"

"Not necessarily." Capri said taking a drink from her Cosmopolitan.

"Yeah, I'd be pissed." Lennon interjected, "No matter how long ago it was, they still screwed you over." Maybe that's what was bothering me so much about it. Not that they were happy. I wasn't jealous of them, not at all. I was irritated that they hid it from me. I felt a little naive and foolish, and that's what I didn't like.

"When you give your heart to someone," Capri cut into my thoughts, "friendship or more, they always have the ability to hurt you."

"Huh." Lennon and I said at the same time.

"It doesn't mean you have feelings for him now," Capri continued, "it just means that you made yourself vulnerable to him back then. There isn't anything weird about that. It means you're human." Capri finished and went back to sipping on her drink like she didn't just say something profound.

The three of us sat there drinking in silence digesting her words. I didn't like being vulnerable to guys like Nolan still, but I think she was right. Loving him had made me vulnerable to him. Even now, though not in love with him, I still feel a tinge of pain when I think about what he did to me back then. "What did August say when he finally came home?" Capri asked me.

"He promised it wouldn't ever happen again." I told her squeezing more of my lemon into my tea.

"Ever? Like never ever again?" She said leaning forward suddenly very interested.

"Yes, I assumed that's what he meant. Why, you don't think he means it?" She was a little too eager in fact. It made me nervous.

"Oh no," she set back into her seat, "no, I believe him. I'm just really happy to hear that. He needs to make sure you know how serious he is about you. So that's good. I'm glad he said it, and meant it." She was rambling a bit too much. Lennon must have caught on to the unease it put me in because she quickly found a way to steer the conversation in a new direction.

"So, how's Tanner?" Lennon asked Capri causing her head to whip over in Lennon's direction.

"Good." Capri said and shrugged a

shoulder. I wasn't interested in how Tanner was. After seeing her get uber embarrassed over the mention of Wes earlier, I couldn't keep my curiosity to myself anymore.

"How's Wes?" I asked Capri casually and she froze with her martini glass in the air half way to her mouth. Lennon let out a whooping laugh next to me and shoved my shoulder. Capri took a deep breath and set her glass back down on the table without ever taking a sip. "Why would I know how Wes is?" She said as calmly as possible, but the blush that covered her face gave her away.

"Oh don't play coy with us," Lennon said. "We know you have a thing for him." Capri shook her head and looked down at the glass she was twirling in her fingers.

"It's okay Capri. He's actually kinda sweet." I said remembering how he sat with me all night.

"And hot." Lennon said making Capri flinch.

"You can admit it." I said trying to give her nudge since she was still fixated on her glass. She nodded her head slightly.

"Okay, yeah." She said without looking at us. "I've had a crush on Wes since I was a kid, but that's it. Just a harmless crush." She looked up at us then. "He's not my type at all, but yeah, he's hot." She agreed and smiled leading me to smile too. She and August had the same infectious grin. I wondered what he was up too at that moment. I suggested that he and Wes have a guys' night, but he informed me guys don't do that. They don't make plans for a guys' night out. They either hang out or they don't, and its always spur of the moment. Noted.

"What about you?" I asked Lennon, "How's Milo doing?" I was still curious to know what was going on between those two. Lennon avoided talking about it like the plague, but I figured since we dove into topics of Nolan and Wes, it was only fair that I grill her a bit.

Lennon took a long drink of her beer that turned into a few gulps. "He left on tour last week." She said and set her empty bottle down on the table.

"What?" Capri and I asked together. I had no idea he was that serious of a musician, or that he was leaving.

"Yeah, he's touring right now, getting his name out there. We talk, but we are living two different lives now." She propped her elbow up on the table and rested her head on her hand. She actually looked a little sad. I patted her knee under the table. The supportive gesture must have snapped her out of her self-pity because she sat upright and added. "And he's just a good friend. We had a lot of fun with music."

She didn't fool me though. She liked him, I could tell. I could see how it would be hard to have a relationship with someone who is living his kind of life now though. Lennon was larger than life herself, but deep down she was a big homebody. All that travel never would have suited her.

"What about you though Kensie," Lennon deterred the conversation back to me, "Capri said she walked in on you two boning." I scrunched my nose at her word choice.

"We weren't...we were just kissing. She's over exaggerating." I played with my straw in my drink thinking. If Capri hadn't have come in when she did, we may have been... doing *that*. I don't know.

"You're blushing." Lennon pointed at me and looking towards Capri who agreed, "So, have you?"

"Not yet." I told her. She sat back and folded her arms over her chest watching me with her head tilted.

"Why?" she asked. I stopped playing with my straw and looked up at her. Why? I wracked my brain, but couldn't come up with a good reason anymore. "He loves you, Kensie," she said this time more sympathetically, "he's not going anywhere. It's okay to enjoy what you have with him."

"I know you love him," she said now and Capri awed next to me. I nodded my head and bit my lip. I did. I loved him, tremendously so.

"I do." I said quietly.

"You do what?" Lennon asked me smiling.

"I love August." I said with more conviction.

Capri squealed next to me and leaned over wrapping her arms around my shoulders. "You guys deserve this." She said before pulling away.

"But you haven't told him yet." Lennon stated as a fact and not a question. I nodded my head again, but couldn't find words to explain why.

"Trust yourself, Kensie. You trust August

enough to love him, so trust yourself enough to know that it's okay." I sucked in a quick breath and held it. Was that it? Was it myself I was having a hard time trusting and not August? How was I supposed to make sure that I was making the right choice in loving him? That's just it though. Loving him wasn't a choice. I didn't wake up and decide to fall in love with August, but I did choose to constantly fight it. I didn't trust myself.

"But what if he leaves me." I said to them gripping my glass as if it held the ability to keep me together when I felt like I might fall apart.

"He's not going to leave you, Kensie," Capri said rubbing my shoulder, "You're it for August." She said then squealed making Lennon and I jump into one another. "You're gonna be my sister in law." She clapped her hands today excitedly. I rolled my eyes, but couldn't hide the smile the crept across my face. They were right. I needed to trust myself and let myself love August. I didn't even really have a choice.

CHAPTER 18

Baking has never been a strength of mine. I once made my mom a birthday cake from scratch. After a couple of bites, she asked if there were sprinkles in it. Nope, egg shells. Sorry mom. I warned John that I wasn't the best choice of employee to bake the cupcakes for the holiday party, but he insisted I would do fine.

I picked up August on my way over so he could help out and make sure I didn't burn down the kitchen. I may or may not have bribed him with a bag of gummy bears.

We were just finishing up the frosting on the last batch of cupcakes when August walked over to my purse to pull out his bag of gummy bears. "See, you did fine. The kitchen is still standing and all the cupcakes appear to be edible." He walked over and jumped up to sit on the counter next to me.

I put down the last cupcake and looked over my little masterpieces. I had gone with plain white frosting not wanting to get too adventurous. In my head I imagined a table covered in little edible snowballs with a fluff of frosting on each one. Looking across the counter I had cupcakes of all shapes and sizes.

Some overflowing their paper cups, some not even reaching high enough for me to frost. The frosting was crusted all over the edges of the silver paper. Note to self, frost after they have cooled to avoid melting. My imagined fluff was smeared across the tops and dripping onto the counter tops. So maybe masterpiece was a little of an exaggeration.

"Maybe I should have gone with the brown frosting." I contemplated and pointed my icing covered spatula at the cupcake.

"Kensie," August said in between chews, "they're perfect. Kids won't care." He was right I suppose. They wouldn't care what they looked like. They were just happy to even be getting this party. With the center shutting down over the holidays, we decided at an employee meeting that we should give them a celebration to honor all their hard work over the semester. John had most of the food donated through a local catering company, as well as a DJ. My girls were really excited about that. We were using the tables and chairs at the center and spent a small amount of money on some decorations and tablecloths.

I put down my spatula and sighed wiping my hands on my apron. I hoped there weren't any hidden sprinkles in them. "What are you eating?" I asked August and looked up at the exact moment he tilted his head back to pour the gummy bears into his mouth. "No!" I yelled at him causing him to jump and choke. He tilted leaned over his knees and coughed while I patted his back.

"What the heck, Kensie. You don't yell at a man mid gummy chew." He cleared his throat and poured a few more into his hands before popping them into his mouth. I watched as his mouth formed the perfect pout and began its slow circular motion. Little Red Gummy was teasing me in there I knew it. I felt my jaw loosen and breathing accelerate when he licked his lips mid chew leaving at a shiny gleam on them. "What are you ..." August started to say, but stopped when he realized what I was gawking at. His puckered lips turned up at the corners and his chewing became slow and exaggerated. He threw his head back and moaned, "Mmmm."

I narrowed my eyes at him and untied my apron from around my waist to throw at him. It pelted him in the face before landing on a few of my sad cupcakes. Oh well, no real loss there. "Knock it off." I scolded him and picked up the apron to smooth out the damaged frosting.

"How long has this been going on?" He leaned back placing his elbows on the counter.

"I don't know what you're talking about." I turned around and busied myself with cleaning up my supplies.

"Oh, you know what I'm talking about." He said, "How long have you been lusting over my gummy bear habit?"

"I'm not lusting," I said and heard him jump off of the counter. "Your chewing is annoying." I listened as he walked up behind me.

"It is, huh?" He asked much too close. He touched my arm and guided me to turn around toward him. I rolled my eyes when I looked at him still smirking at me.

"Yes. It is." I said and poked my finger into

his chest.

"Is not." He said and swiped his finger across my nose. The moment he touched it I smelled the scent of vanilla and felt the coolness of the frosting smear.

"No you didn't." I said and wiped the frosting off of my nose.

"I did." He said and grinned at me. If I wasn't so irritated by his chewing and my frosting nose, I would have felt my heart pitter pat and the sweetness in that grin. I reached back toward the bowl I had just placed by the sink and swooped up a glob of frosting. Still too proud of himself, August didn't see it coming when my hand reached up and swiped the glob across his cheek.

His grin fell instantly and I couldn't hold in my giggle. Before I could stop him August reached behind me simultaneously pinning me to the counter. He smeared a streak of frosting down the side of my face while I shrieked and laughed trying to wiggle free. What ensued was a frosting fight of epic proportions. We ran around the kitchen laughing and throwing globs of icing at each other. He hid behind the island when and I used a cookie sheet to repel his shots.

I thought I was sneaky when I faked left and dodged right, but really I was stupid. I slipped on a smear of icing on the floor and flailed for a few seconds trying to gain my balance before falling flat onto my back. I was still laughing lying on the frosting covered kitchen floor when August crawled over to me.

"Shit, Kensie," he said, not laughing

anymore. "Are you okay?" I slowed down my laughing and smiled at his handsome face with eyebrows pulled together in worry.

"Yeah, I'm fine. A bruised ego maybe, but fine." He sighed and dropped his head onto my shoulder letting the rest of his body relax from where it hovered above me. I sucked in a sudden breath with the feel of his weight suddenly covering me. That made him lift his head and look at me again.

"Hi." He said lying on top of me with frosting speckled across his face and clumped up in his perfectly messy hair.

"Hi." I smiled back up him feeling my heart swell at the same rate as my increased pulse.

"You have a little something here." He said and leaned down kissing under my jaw. I reached up and wrapped my arms around him, "and here" he kissed a little lower onto my neck. I leaned my head back welcoming his lips, "and here" he kissed my chin and I sighed at the nearness of his lips to mine.

"You missed a spot." I whispered when he pulled away too look at me again.

"I did?" He looked around investigating my face and I laughed at his playfulness.

"I think I have some on my mouth." I said and ran my tongue slowly across my bottom lip. "Yeah, there. I can taste it." I whispered and watched his eyes grow wide when he inhaled a deep breath.

"I got it." He said before crashing his lips down onto mine. I welcomed his kiss and let his tongue swipe across mine immediately. He tasted like cherry and vanilla. I let my legs fall apart so he could fit in between. We groaned together when he settled against me and I couldn't control my hips when they rolled up toward his. I slid my hand up the back of his shirt and gripped his back when his hips began to mimic the motion of his tongue within my mouth.

"Hmhmmph." A voice cleared from directly above us and we froze mid hip thrust and lip locked. "If you get her pregnant on my kitchen floor, you're dead." John's voice was stern. August nearly leapt off of me back onto his feet. He reached down for my hand to help me stand up, but didn't take his startled eyes off John who was standing in the doorway with his arms folded across his chest.

"You hurt her, I kill you. We clear?" John said to August who nodded his head. I covered my mouth to hold in the laugh that wanted to escape and watched John turn to walk out the door, but not before winking at me.

"I think I heard you gulp," I said to August. He breathed out a sigh of relief and hung his head letting out a low, frustrated chuckle.

***

I look like a nineties grunge rock hooker. At practice earlier in the week I didn't expect the harmless bet I made to end with me in baggy boyfriend jeans, a plaid lumber jack looking button down wrapped around my wait, and a crop top that might as well have just been my bra.

This was not good.

"I can't believe I let you guys talk me into this," I said coughing into a cloud of hairspray Mia was spraying on my teased hair.

"You made the bet Ms. Kensie." Gabby pointed out while smearing on her mocha colored lipstick. God, she was right. I made the bet. When they spent nearly half the class completely distracted by the boys in the gym, I came up with the not so brilliant idea of making them a bet. I was desperate to regain control over the practice that had been sabotaged by the basketball game August set up. When the girls weren't stumbling over each other mid dance to peek of the classroom door they were making ridiculous excuses to leave the classroom. My favorite was when Mia told me she heard her car alarm going off. "Mia, you're fourteen. You don't have a car. You don't even drive." I had clarified for her before she pouted at me and stomped away.

I told the girls that if they couldn't keep away from the boys all practice, I got to hand pick all of their outfits for the holiday party. The look of sheer horror on their faces should have been enough, but then to make it extra painful I described in detail what I had in mind. Tapered legged jeans and "sensible" t-shirts made them groan, but when I mentioned cardigans and a stylish pair of Keds, I swear I saw Gabby gag.

As a fair betting woman I allowed them to come up with what I would do if they did in fact keep clear of the boys. I was so sure that there would be no way they could resist the young men, that I agreed to perform with them at the party, and wear what they chose.

So now, here I was dressed like a Nirvana

groupie and waiting with the girls to perform the dance they had been practicing for the last few days. I was making myself sick with worry just thinking about it. "I didn't realize part of the bet included," I waved my hand around myself, "all this."

"Well, yeah." Gabby looked back at me over her shoulder waving her mascara wand at me, "All that is called performance attire." Wow, she named it and everything. She had one thing wrong though. I don't perform. I never did. Performing insinuated pretending. I danced the truth. Whatever I felt, I put it into what I danced. So tonight, I had to find some piece of myself that was a little nineties grunge rock skank and let my truth be told.

"You know there was money in the budget for whole t-shirts right?" I asked her and tugged my shirt down. It was no use.

"Ms. Kensie," Gabby put her mascara back in her make-up bag and walked towards me. "I'm disappointed in you." She stopped in front of me and crossed her arms over her chest. Mia and Jasmine came up and flanked her on either side mimicking her stance.

"Why, what did I do?" I asked looking around them at myself in the mirror. What on earth did they do to my hair?

"You aren't looking very sexy right now." She said and popped her hip to the side.

"No, no you're right Gabby. I'm not looking sexy at all. I'm looking trashy." My voice rose, but the girls remained unaffected.

"You taught us that who we are is what makes us sexy." Jasmine piped up.

"Yes, that's right, and you are three brilliant and beautiful girls who don't need to dress half naked to prove it."

"We aren't trying to prove anything Ms. Kensie. We don't have too. These are just costumes." Mia said opening her arms up passionately. "We don't let what other people think of what we wear, or how we act influence how we feel about ourselves. You taught us that. You taught us that we are brilliant and beautiful no matter what."

I was so touched that they had taken all of the pep talks I had given them to heart. I didn't just teach them how to dance; I also helped guide them into being self-respecting women. I was so proud of them, and a little proud of myself too.

"Come here, "I opened my arms and motioned for all three to come in for a group hug. When we all circled up and held each other in love and support and all our womanly bad assed-ness I whispered between tears, "I'm so, so proud of you."

I felt the pitter patter of their hands patting my back. "Good luck, Ms. Kensie," Mia said to me. "Who needs luck, when I've got you girls." I told them and pulled away. All their uptight, prima donna, hormone-parading moments were forgotten to this one sweet moment right here.

CHAPTER 19

August

Sitting next Jordan I scanned the gym bouncing my legs. I hadn't seen John since that afternoon, but I wasn't sure how he was going to react to me. To say he caught me ready to rip Kensie's clothes off would be an understatement. I didn't even care that we were in the middle of a frosting covered kitchen at work. I would have taken her right then and there. I was trying really hard to be patient, really hard. I knew she wasn't ready, and a part of me knew it wasn't right to be with her when she didn't know everything. The other part of me, specifically the one in my pants, couldn't behave around her and was growing really impatient with me.

"The girls are gonna look so hot, "Jordan said next to me and stuck out his fist at me. I shoved it away.

"Dude." I said, and raised an eyebrow at him. He shrugged his shoulders at me and moved his baseball hat so the bill was behind his head.

"Don't act like you ain't excited to see Ms.

Kensie in the outfit Gabs picked out."

"What outfit?" I asked him and he nodded up to the make shift stage in the middle of the court the guys had helped me set up the day before.

I hissed in a breath and felt Jordan nudge my arm, but I was too paralyzed by what I saw. She looked so damn hot. Her flat stomach was completely bare, and perfect. Her brown hair was messy. Messy like she just got out of bed, or just rolled around in bed, oh hell... Kensie had freshly fucked hair. I felt my pants getting tighter. Kensie had freshly fucked hair and she focused on me with her big brown eyes. She smiled slightly and her lips puckered to the side while she nibbled the inside of her cheek. Yep, pants were tight. Kensie with freshly fucked hair, nibbling, puckering, *fuck me.*

I cleared my throat and wiggled in my seat trying to adjust myself nondescriptly. Thankfully all the kids were watching the stage waiting for the dance to start. I scanned back up to the stage when I caught him glaring at me. Fuck, John was glaring death lasers at me. He pointed two of his fingers at his eyes and back towards me letting me know he was 'watching me'. *Great.* He probably saw my tight pants.

I looked back up to Kensie and caught her smile just before she turned around. My heart stuttered. God, she was beautiful. I remember the first time I saw her walk into Wes's shop. I flinched when I saw her come through the front doors with the sun shining behind her highlighting her petite frame and long hair. She was the light in my otherwise dark day. Wes thought I was in pain from the tat and stopped to tease me, but he followed my stare and smirked at what had captivated me before pounding me on the back where he was working.

Dipshit.

She was so cute and determined looking at the pieces hanging up on the wall. She had a scowl on her beautiful face that said she had no clue what she was doing there, but she was going to figure it out. I think I fell on love with that part of her right then.

I was used to the way her eyes scanned me when she first noticed I was there. I had seen it plenty of times before with other girls, but they usually looked at me, inviting me to make a move. Kensie looked hesitant, and caught off guard. The vulnerability that slipped through peaked my interest. It should have scared me off, but it didn't.

When she quickly shoved it back down, and put on her brave face again, I had to know her, but it didn't feel right, wanting to hit on a chick that day. I wasn't there to pick up on a girl, so I let her run out of the shop, but smiled watching her the whole way.

The beat of the music started and my eyes attached themselves to Kensie's hips moving slightly with it. She whipped around suddenly and the look on her face was fierce. The nervous unsure girl, who was just smiling sweetly at me a few minutes ago, was now a confidant force to be reckoned with. I couldn't take my eyes off of her as she popped her shoulders to the beat. Beyoncé' was singing something about girls being in charge, and I believed it. I believed it because Kensie did, and it was written all over her body. I had never in my life seen anything sexier than when Kensie danced.

I'm so happy I let Wes talk me into going to Tommy's that night to get my mind off of things. When we found Capri at the bar with none other than the little firecracker Kensie had been with earlier that day at the shop, I was convinced this girl was worth my time. The look on Lennon's face when she saw Wes told me I wasn't the only one who couldn't get over our meeting.

I remember Lennon didn't even say anything to me, just laughed loudly and walked over grabbing my arms to point me into the direction of the dance floor.

Then I saw her, hair flipping around and her arms above her head. Time slowed down as if to allow me this moment to focus on the girl who would steal my heart before I was ready to give it away. I was blown away how beautiful she was, completely lost in the moment. She danced with a frustration and a longing that I knew all too well. It was like she was dancing for me. Then, some meathead walked up behind her and pulled her into him.

Without thinking I made a move to march out there and yank him off of her, but Lennon stopped me by grabbing my arm. I looked at her both confused, but when she nodded towards the dance floor I saw what she meant.

Kensie had kindly danced away from the jackass, and began to head back toward the bar. She looked up and smiled when she recognized Lennon and Capri. Then she saw me, and that smile fell from her face. I saw her glow pink and my heart picked up its pace. I smirked while taking a sip of my beer. That was the moment I knew I had her, and she had me.

With the music blaring, Kensie dropped on her knees and moved in way I hoped she'd show me in private later on. I felt Jordan's hand close my jaw that apparently had fallen open. Oh god, now she's lying down. Shit, did she just thrust? Fuck yeah, she thrusted.

I jumped from my seat and ran out of the gym without looking back, and I heard the boys whooping at me from behind. I felt bad leaving in the middle of her performance, but no way could I sit there and harmlessly watch that. Next time I watch one of these, I need to make sure she is wearing a potato sack and only spinning in slow circles. Who was I kidding, Kensie would look gorgeous in a potato sack and my horny ass would be trying to catch a peek of what was underneath.

***

Kensie found me a few minutes later sitting against the wall in the hallway. I had calmed down for the most part.

"Hey," she smiled and kicked my feet standing in front of me.

"Hey, pretty girl." I said and smiled back. At the risk of sounds like a pussy, I think I'd smiled more in the last few weeks than I had in the last few years. She did that. She brought my smile back.

"So..." She trailed off and tied her hair behind her head, "What did you think?" She asked looking nervous.

She was adorable.

"I thought it was great," I said grabbing her hand and pulling her to sit down next to me.

"I saw you rush out of there pretty quickly. I wasn't sure you liked it." She bit the inside of her cheek and I chuckled to myself.

"Liked it? Oh, I liked it. A little too much," I said and pointed to my lap making her form a little o with her lips. "Too much. I needed a little breathing room, but it was great. I can't believe those girls actually complied enough to make a whole dance. I didn't think they did anything other than giggle at the guys and complain."

She laughed at that. "Well, that's still what they do," she said, "but I am pretty proud." Her smile beamed at me and I forgot to breathe. I reached my hand up and ran my thumb across her lips. "You should be. I am." I whispered and leaned in to kiss her.

She tasted like salvation. That was the only way I could describe what I felt every time our lips met. When I kissed her I tasted hope, forgiveness, promise, even love.

She hadn't told me she loved me yet, but I knew she did. I felt it in her kiss, and in her gaze. When I told her I loved her, I meant it. I think I'd loved her long before that, but right then in that empty field I saw things so clearly. I saw how I had fallen completely in love with Kensie, and if there is anything I had learned in life it's that you always make sure the people you love know it. So I told her, and I became free. Saved.

I didn't expect her to say it back, and I am kind of happy she didn't. Kensie has had so many people she loved abuse it, and not appreciate it. It's a good thing I hadn't met her dad yet because I'd have a few words with him. I couldn't imagine doing that... I couldn't imagine.

That bullshit with that asshole Nolan and all of his friends had me beyond pissed. When she told me about how they took advantage of her when she was trying to just hang on. I almost lost it. I have never been a violent person, but hearing that someone abused my girl made me want to beat the shit out of 'em. In fact, if I ever come across any of 'em, I probably will. There is no doubt she had some real pricks in her life. I know she's scared, but I hope she sees that falling in love me would be a gift to me, and not a risk for her.

When Kensie pulled away from my kiss she was flushed as usual. That made me grin. I'm not gonna lie. Knowing I could make her like that from just a kiss was a pretty good boost to my confidence. "So, I was actually thinking." She started and I felt nerves buzz with excitement. *Please say you want me to take your clothes off, please, please, please.* "I think I really like working with the kids." *Oh.* "I went to talk with my academic counselor the other day and we discussed changing my major to Adolescent Psychology." She waited and looked at me expectantly. I could tell she was excited about this, it was written all over her face, but she wanted my approval.

I didn't know if I was glad my opinion mattered so much to her, or disappointed that she might have thought I wouldn't be supportive. "That's perfect for you," I said and couldn't contain the grin that filled my face. "Perfect." I said and she breathed a sigh of relief. "Yeah?" She asked still hesitant.

"Yeah Kensie, completely. You are a natural at working with these kids, and I can tell you love it. I think it's a perfect choice for you."

"Yeah," she said more confidently this time, "yeah, I think it is too." She started to giggle and her laugh was so contagious I found myself chuckling along. "I'm excited," she said. "I get to do this forever." Suddenly I had visions of watching Kensie on the stage like I had just witnessed forever. I squeezed my eyes shut and leaned my head back against the wall and groaned. I couldn't take it. "What?" She asked still smiling.

"I'm going to have to learn to work with blue balls, aren't I?" I opened one eye and peaked over at her. To say she was glowing would be an understatement. She was radiating and I was happy to bask in it. In fact, I couldn't get enough. I'm not sure I ever would. She shoved me in the arm and her giggling picked up again. "Dancing with the girls was a one-time thing."

Well damn.

CHAPTER 20

Kensie

Well, the kids even ate all of the cupcakes I made, and didn't complain about any extras in the batter. August and I stood off to the side of the gym most of the night monitoring the dance floor. We wanted the kids to have fun, but not too much fun. Any dancing that looked like it could produce off spring was quickly broken up.

I glanced around all the happy faces the filled the room and smiled softly to myself. This was where I was supposed to be. With the kids, making them smile, with August who always made me smile, with my amazing best friends, my mom, and I couldn't forget my newest surprise friend Wes. Even John had wiggled his way into my heart and had become a great role model and source of support for me. Things were really falling into place. The one missing piece, I'd be spending Thanksgiving with tomorrow.

I was a nervous wreck about seeing my dad. I had tried not to think about it, but it was inevitable that my worry seeped into the quiet moments like right now. August noticed the change in my demeanor instantly. I felt him touch my elbow, "You okay?" He asked and I nodded my head biting the inside of my cheek. He smiled sympathetically at me, "Come with me." He turned and headed for the gym doors. I followed him into my dance room where he waited for me to go in before closing the door behind us.

"I thought you said you couldn't handle any more of my dancing?" I teased him, but sounded unsteady.

"Ha, ha, funny girl." He motioned me to follow him to sit against the mirrors. I slid down and sat so closely too him our sides touched. "You nervous about tomorrow?" He asked and brushed a loose strand of hair out of my face.

I inhaled deeply, "Yeah, so nervous." I'm not sure why I was so worried. Not much could go wrong that I hadn't already dealt with. "I just feel like I'm in such a good place right now, and really happy. I don't want seeing my dad to affect it." August nodded, understanding. I was feeling protective over my new life and I didn't want my dad's nonchalance towards me to infiltrate my bliss.

"I hope it goes well Kensie, I really do, but if it doesn't, know that I am here for you, that we all are here for you." He said and reached under him to pull something from his pocket. He handed me a folded piece of paper but stopped me when I tried to open it. "Not yet," he said, "I don't want you to open until you feel like you need me. Since you won't let me go with you." I rolled my eyes at that. He asked, no begged to come with me to my dad's house, but I insisted I go alone. I appreciated his support, and loved his desire to be there for me, but I had to do it on my own. He seemed to understand that, but didn't like it.

"I want you to have a piece of my with you, so I wrote you this. It's not nearly as tall, sexy, or charming, but I think it will do." I laughed at that and leaned over to hug him. I melted into him and sighed when he nuzzled into my neck. While his kisses set me on fire his hugs put me at peace. "I love you." He whispered into my hair and my heart trembled. *I love you, too.*

***

I pulled up to my dad's large colonial home in a quaint little neighborhood. It was a beautiful place, huge with an open floor plan, but it never felt as inviting as the tiny bungalow my mom and I had shared growing up.

I called my mom that morning to wish her a Happy Thanksgiving and catch up before I left. She reassured me that everything would be fine today, and that I was always welcome to go with her to my grandmother's house if I changed my mind. I had to go though. A small part of me hoped that the upswing my life had been on would filter into my relationship with my dad, and that maybe we could begin to repair it.

I sat in the car and looked at the red painted door trying to steady my shaky breathing. I reached over to the passenger's seat to grab a side dish when I remembered Jodie had told me not to bring anything. I looked behind the seat to pick up my purse, but realized I only brought my wallet. So, I turned forward and tapped my fingers on the steering wheel. I needed something to carry in. My empty hands were suddenly making me feel very alone.

I opened my center console looking for a mint when I saw the folded up note August had given me. I plucked it out and held it in front of me. He told me to open it if I needed him, but I hadn't even walked in yet. I had more courage than this. I took a deep breath and tucked the note into my pocket. I wished he was here, but I didn't need him. I could do it on my own. I climbed out of my car and nervously approached the house.

I took another deep breath, though shaky this time, and lifted my arm to knock on the door. Sad, but I was knocking on my own father's door. I didn't even feel comfortable enough walking in. I shook my head and knocked once before the door flew open.

"Happy Thanksgiving!" Jodie cheered wiping her hands on her apron. "Come in sweetie, come in. Dave, Kensington's here!" She hollered in the direction of the living room. I didn't even get two feet into the house before she pulled me into a tight squeeze. "We're so glad you could come." I pulled away feeling a little awkward with her display of affection.

"Thanks. Thank you for inviting me." I said, and my heart tinged briefly remembering the family reunion I hadn't been invited too.

"Sweetie, of course," she said smiling at me, "and don't you look beautiful." I forced a smile and brushed my hands down my sweater dress.

"Kensington." My dad's voice boomed as he

strode in from the living room, but he stopped in the entryway. "You look beautiful, kiddo."

"Thanks, Dad." Was all I managed to say and the tiny tiled entry way fell silent. God, it was uncomfortable.

"Well," he continued, "Parker and I are watching football, but I'm sure Jodie and Bethy could use some help in the kitchen." He said looking towards his wife and she nodded brightly.

"We'd love some help. C'mon in." Jodie motioned for me to follow her. My dad smiled and walked back into the living room where I heard Parker yelling something at the television.

I followed Jodie and tried to shake of the disappointment of being dismissed to the kitchen to help with dinner. On the way here, I had daydreamed about my dad swooping me up in a hug and leading me into the living room to sit together on the couch and catch up on what we've missed with each other. Wes was right though; I had a really great imagination.

Bethany was perched up on one of the stools at the center island rolling out the piecrust when I walked in behind Jodie. "Happy Thanksgiving, Kensie." She smiled at me. It was so hard to hate my dad's new family when they were all so genuinely nice.

"Happy Thanksgiving," I said and smiled back. "I like your sweater." I said and pointed to her gray wrap around that looked great with her smoky blue eyes. "Thank you." She said brightly.

"Come on over here Kensington and we will get you to work on the green bean casserole,"

Jodie said, and I walked over to the opposite side of the island from Bethany. Jodie put all the ingredients on the counter in front of me and I got to work throwing it all together. It wasn't hard to make, so I got the feeling Jodie was just trying to find something for me to do. I was thankful for having something in my hands though. It made me feel like I had a purpose there after all.

"So, are you dating anyone new?" Bethany asked me filling the piecrust with cinnamon scented apples. I laughed at how straightforward she was, but she had always been that way. Anytime I saw her, the first and last thing, well, the only thing she ever wanted to talk about was a guy.

She was two years younger than me, and far more boy crazy than I had ever been. Though, I'm sure I had more experience than she had. Her passion for guys was very innocent, mine had been very…sad. Things had shifted for me lately though. I thought about August and his family working together at the women's shelter. Maybe next year I could go with them.

"Oh you're smiling, there is a guy." Bethany said excitedly and put the bowl of apples down. "Tell me," she said leaning placing her elbows on the island and resting her head in her hands. The hearts in her eyes glowed at me from across the counter. She had seen too many Disney movies as a kid. Hell, she probably still watched them.

"Yes, sweetie," Jodie said standing next to Bethany now, "any guy that makes your face light up like that is worth gushing over." I couldn't disagree with them there. August was gush worthy.

I began to fill them in on how he and I had met and all of the coincidences that led to us getting together. I told them all about how amazing he was and how perfect we are for each other, but I spared the details about my struggle to trust him, or myself. I felt more at home in that house than I ever had when I was talking about August.

"He's a lucky guy." Jodie said smiling at me and patting my hand before getting back to her cooking. She had that all wrong. I was the lucky one.

***

After spending the majority of the afternoon in the kitchen with Jodie and Bethany, we all finally sat down for and early dinner. My dad took the seat at the head of the table with Parker and Bethany flanking him on either side. I sat down at the opposite end across from Jodie. We bowed our heads while Parker said a quick and to the point Grace before we each grabbed at the dishes.

We helped ourselves and passed the bowls around the table between ourselves. I was scooping the mashed potatoes onto my plate when my dad spoke up from down at his end of the table, "So kiddo, what have you been busy with lately?" I stopped and looked at him with the heaping scoop of potatoes half way between the bowl and my plate. It was the first thing he had said directly to me since walking through the door and it caught me off guard.

"Ummm," I said before I felt the potatoes slip from the spoon and land in a messy lump on the table, "Oh crap, I'm sorry Jodie." I said and scooped them onto my plate with my spoon like a kid in a sand box. She smiled and shook her head at me letting me know it wasn't a big deal. While I was scooping I was trying to come up with something substantial to say to my dad. I wanted to say something that he would be interested in, or proud of. "Ummm, well, I just changed my major to Adolescent Psychology." I said shuffling the potatoes around on my plate now too nervous to eat.

"Hmm," he mumbled while chewing, "but you're a junior right? Shouldn't that have been decided a while ago?" His questioned scraped a little piece of my heart off.

"Yeah," I said loudly and awkwardly trying to sound confidant, but I only made Bethany startle next to me, "but I've had some trouble figuring out what exactly I want to do, so I've just now figured it out." How did I go from telling August about this enthusiastically yesterday to telling my dad about it now like it was embarrassing?

"So, what is it you just decided you want to do?" He asked cutting away at his turkey with his brows furrowed. He didn't look very confident in me at the moment, but I'd hoped he would be when I finished telling him about it.

I told him all about S.Y.C., and about the girls in the class I was teaching. I felt so much pride in filling him in on all the details of the great things the center was doing for these kids, and how I was helping with it. "I have always been most interested in my psychology classes," I told my dad finally taking a bite of my dinner. "It just took finding this job to help me put the pieces together." I said around my food, watching him eat away at his plate, but not really making any eye contact with me.

"You know," he said looking up and pointing his fork towards Bethany next to me, "Bethany is going to be a teacher. Maybe she could fill you in on the program and give you some pointers." He said before taking another bite. I stared at him dumbfounded. Had he just missed the whole part where I told him about the youth center and how passionate I was about working in a place like it? Or maybe it was the part about me that he missed, that this was about me and not Bethany.

"I'd love to help you out." Bethany said enthusiastically next to me. I tried to smile at her, but it came out as more of a grimace.

"That's okay," I said within my tight smile, "I'm actually pretty certain that I'm gonna to stick with this."

"What are the benefits like working at a place like this youth center?" My dad asked me, "And job stability? You know teachers have great benefits and job stability, right Bethy?" He smiled affectionately at her when he used his special nickname he had given her. I realized then that my choice was not going to be enough for him, and made the decision to keep quiet rather than defend myself. If he couldn't or didn't want to understand it, then I didn't want to explain it anymore. Another piece of my heart chipped away.

I picked at my dinner the rest of the meal while everyone chatted with each other. They talked about school and work. Both topics I had no knowledge of when it came to them. At one point, they even brought up what a great time they had at the family reunion with no mention of my absence.

I watched as they laughed together and finished each other's sentences reminiscing over that weekend they spent with my family. They smiled adoringly at one another and teased each other. I suddenly felt like I was watching from the outside looking in. They had become the happy family in a holiday commercial, and I was simply watching it on the television set alone.

This was how things had always been, so I shouldn't have felt so left out but I did. I was hopeful to find a new place for myself in this family, but sitting there watching them all fit seamlessly together I realized I was the piece that belonged to another puzzle. Still, he was my dad, I was his daughter, and I didn't fit. Another shard of my heart crumbled. I stood up slowly and walked toward the bathroom.

They hadn't even noticed when I left the table. I shut the bathroom door behind me and leaned against it letting go, and let the tears fall.

What I had hoped would the turning of a new leaf in my relationship with my dad had turned out to be nothing but heartbreak. I was still unwanted. I reached into my back pocket and pulled out the letter August had written me. I needed it. I needed him. I sat down on the toilet and sniffled. I opened up the letter and instantly felt comforted by his handwriting alone.

Truth, I love you.

Truth, I will always favor you over the red gummy bears. Don't be jealous.

Truth, meeting you has made me a better person. You inspire me with your determination and heart.

Truth, there isn't anything I wouldn't do for you.

Truth, you are braver and stronger than you give yourself credit for.

Truth, you are the greatest dancer EVER! Truth, you are brilliant.

Truth, I had forgotten how to live, but then I met you. I didn't know what true love was, but then I met you. I couldn't see past today into my future. Then I met you. You are my future.

Truth, you are my wildflower.

I sobbed, I hiccupped, I laughed, and I inhaled. I took a deep breath and felt August with me. I felt his support, I felt his strength, and I felt his love for me. I don't know why I deserved him, but I do know I will never take a day with him for granted.

I stood up and looked at myself in the mirror. I traced one of the remaining tears down my face and smiled. August had given me tears of joy where there once had been tears of sorrow. I folded up my letter and kissed it before putting it back into my pocket.

I walked out of the bathroom and peaked into the dining room on my way toward the front door. I thought briefly about going back to my place at the table, but then I stopped and watched my dad interact with his family. I saw him get up momentarily from the table and walk into the kitchen.

Still, no one had commented on where I had gone. When my dad came back, he had the wishbone from the turkey in his hand. I grinned remembering our tradition from when I was a kid.

Every Thanksgiving my dad would save the wishbone until after we finished dinner, then he would walk over to wherever I sat at the table and kneel down next to me. He'd hold out the wishbone hanging onto one side as I grabbed the other. Then he'd say, 'Who needs luck, when I've got you.' just before I pulled on the bone.

I stepped into the dining room, but halted when I saw my dad kneel down by Bethany. My blood ran cold, *don't say it, don't say it, don't say it.* Then, he said it. He held the wishbone out to Bethany and said, "Who needs luck, when I've got my beautiful family."

I turned on my heel and bolted out of the living. I ran out of the house so quickly I didn't even know if I shut the red door. The chill of the air brushing swiftly across my face as I ran to my car, was a welcome reminder that this was real, and that reality could be cold.

I stopped at my car and fumbled with the keys dropping them once before I finally got in. I left without taking a second glance at the house. I saw the blur of red retreat out of the corner of my eye and realized I had in fact closed the door.

***

I drove quickly and mindlessly towards home. I probably wasn't in any condition to drive, but I was on autopilot, and my one direction was to get away from my dad's house. My vision was clouded the entire drive back, but not from tears. In fact, I didn't cry a single tear on the way home. I breathed unevenly with sporadic deep breaths woven between tiny pants, but I didn't cry.

My mind was blurred from hurt wanting to rationalize the pain, and wanting to forget it all at the same time. I didn't even notice how I ended up parked in front of the youth center, but it was the perfect place for me to end up.

After punching in the code on the alarm keypad I let myself in, but didn't bother turning any of the lights off. I walked through the dark musty scented hallways and felt more at home than I had the whole day. I slipped my key into the lock of my classroom door and hurried in shutting the door behind me. I propped my hand against the frame and breathed a sigh of relief. I didn't have any of my dance shoes or clothes, but that didn't matter.

I sat down against the door and unzipped my boots setting them aside. An eerie sense of calm washed over me with the only sign of my anguish coming in gentle breezes. I'd be silly to think I was feeling better though. The moment of peace was just the eye of the storm. What was to come next would rival the storm surge I had felt on my way here.

I cued up the music on my iPod and walked to the middle of the room shaking out my legs and arms. The song began slowly with only piano notes and I rolled my head reaching my arm out in one direction while stretching my leg out in the other. I spun in a slow soft circle letting the peace whirl out of me. I kept my eyes closed as the beat began to pick up.

My spinning picked up speed as a single hearty sound of a guitar came in repetitively. I reached my arms up above my head losing my clam altogether when the clash of the drums erupted. I stopped spinning and threw my arms to my sides jumping to the heavy beat. I lashed one arm out to the side abruptly and tossed my head in the same direction. I repeated the same move on the opposite with my eyes cinched shut and gritting my teeth.

I continued with a series of kicks and leaps making use of the entire dance floor. After a turning leap I went to the ground. I rolled a few times arching my back and extending my leg. My movements slowed, but I continued to pant as I stepped up from the floor dragging my back leg into a slow spin on the way up. I tucked my arms into my chest and continued drifted around the floor brushing my feet with my head hanging down. I did another slow spin to the ground and stayed crouched there as the music died down.

I watched the drops land onto the floor below me and burst apart with contact. One, after the other, after the other, after the other, until they were falling so fast that I couldn't catch the moment they landed through my blurred vision.

I let myself cry then, for the little girl who never knew her daddy could leave, and for the woman now, who has lived through it and is surviving.

CHAPTER 21

August

There was one car in the parking lot, and I swear it looked just like Kensie's but she was at her dad's house. If I didn't know how important this dinner was for her I would have insisted she come with me to help my parents at the Women's shelter. Who am I kidding? I can't introduce Kensie to them. I want to, God, I really want too. I know they'd love her. I can't until I tell Kensie the truth, though. My parents have no clue that the girl I've fallen for doesn't know. But I'll tell her. I will.

The lights were all still off, so I concluded it was a stray car from the billiard next door. The last thing I wanted to do after a long shift at the women's shelter was drive all the way back to work, but I had forgotten my wallet in John's office. I usually locked it up in one of his desk drawers when I was working, and out of habit I had put it in yesterday before the party.

I unlocked the front door and immediately I heard the muffle of music coming from the back of the building. With all of the lights still off I crept down the hallway. The closer I got to the music the better I could make out the melancholy tone of the song. That turned on a light switch in my head and my cautious steps broke out into a sprint. I pushed open the door and halted.

Kensie was on the ground in the middle of the floor dancing. She took my breath away with her slow, languid, and sad movements. Rolling to her knees she tucked them into her chest.

It took a few seconds for me to realize she wasn't dancing anymore. Her body silently shook and I knew then she was crying. I was gonna kill him. Whatever happened with her dad to put my beautiful, strong, Kensie on the floor like that was something I couldn't stand by and allow.

I leaned over to set my wallet down next to the door. I didn't want to startle her, and honestly, I think she needed this moment alone. Those moments crying by yourself are the most honest moments of sadness. You have to allow yourself to be consumed by it completely before you can move forward. That's how it was for me at least.

My keys slid out of my pocket just as I let go of my wallet, and landed noisily on the ground before I could catch them. Kensie sucked in her sob and whipped her head around. If I thought seeing her dance a few minutes ago was torture I was wrong. This was heart shattering. Her wide eyes were puffy and swollen. The warm brown color that always seemed to smile was lost to a red tinge. I wanted to kill him for taking the joy from her eyes. "I didn't mean to scare you," I said so softly I wondered if I had even spoken the words.

She rushed up from the floor and ran to launch herself into my arms. I caught her as her body slammed against mine and then collapsed in silent sobs. I held her to me as tightly as I could. Where she no longer had the strength to stand, I had plenty to hold her up. I'd hold her there for as long as she needed me to, and I'd kill him for making her crumble.

I rubbed her back softly and peppered her tear soaked cheeks with kisses. I tried to find the right words to say, but I couldn't come up with any to soothe her. I didn't think words could anyway, but I was frustrated with myself for not knowing how to make her feel any better.

I could feel when she started to regain control of her body again. Her spine straightened up, and she put weight back on her legs. She pulled away then and looked up at me with big sad doe eyes wiping her tears with the palms of her hands. I reached up and pushed her hands away to replace them with mine. She smiled a soft smile and closed her eyes leaning her cheek into my palm. I rubbed it with my thumb and asked quietly, "What happened?"

She shook her head in my palm, but didn't open her eyes. When she spoke her voice was scratchy and forced. I'd kill him for taking away her sweet voice. "It was awful." She said and her bottom lip started to tremble again. I panicked not wanting her to cry again and swooped in with a quick kiss. When I pulled back, I was about apologize when a soft giggle bubbled from her. She opened her eyes and they twinkled back at me.

"I should go clean myself up." She said, but leaned in to hug me again, this time with all her strength returned. "Thank you." She whispered and turned walking out of the classroom.

Thank you? For what? I didn't do anything, but I was thankful I found her when I did. Thinking that she could have still been sitting here alone in her sadness made the anger churn inside of me.

While Kensie was in the bathroom cleaning up I heard her phone vibrating in her bag. I ignored it the first two times, but on the third one I peaked inside. I wasn't sure what the boyfriend protocol was for helping yourself into your girlfriend's purse, but I was wary. I knew first hand some crazy shit lurked in them.

I pulled the bag open with one finger, as if that was any better than just diving right in. I glanced in over my shoulder and saw the screen of her phone light up. *Dad*, showed up in black letters across the floral background. Just the man I wanted to talk to. I took her phone out of her bag no longer concerned with the protocol. She could get mad at me all she wanted. I wasn't going to let her near him again without setting him straight first.

Kensie

I cringed at myself in the mirror. I looked awful. My hair was strewn about except for the parts that were matted to my wet cheeks. My eyes, yikes, I looked like Lennon when we found out she had a shellfish allergy, but I did feel better.

I knew dancing would take away some of the sting from dinner at my dad's, but what I didn't expect was for August to be the most soothing. My body ran towards him before my brain even realized he was standing there. The real kicker was that I completely let go of myself the moment he caught me. I'm always consciously making the effort to control how I feel so others don't have to feel bothered by it, but with August I was able to let it all go.

Just the feel of him allowed me to fall apart. I was safe with him. I wasn't judged but supported, I was strengthened, and I was loved in his arms. He unraveled me and stitched me back together. He didn't even have to utter a word to comfort me. In fact, I preferred that he just held me.

I straightened my shoulders and raised my chin up with one last sniffle before walking back to my classroom. I wasn't looking forward to relaying what had happened at my dad's, but I knew he wanted to know. I was just glad I would be able to tell him about it without breaking down now.

When I stepped into the room August was holding my bag for me. "Let's go, pretty girl. I'm taking you back to my place." He met up with me and wrapped his arm tightly around my shoulders. I looked up to meet his lips in a kiss and let him guide me out of the building to his truck. I was thankful he was taking me with him, because I really didn't want to be alone tonight of all nights. I don't know that I would have even called him had he not shown up. I probably would have just waited until the next morning not wanting to disturb his holiday with his parents.

"What brought you here anyway?" I asked him as we pulled away from work.

"I forgot my wallet last night. Seems I was a bit distracted then." He smirked over at me and I giggled at the memory of his panicked face when he ran out in the middle of my dance. " I'm glad I was here, though," He said taking my hand into his, "I know you would have tried to shoulder that on your own if I didn't show up, but I want to be here for you. Even if I'm not, I want you to find me. Always come find me." He said, and I knew he wasn't just asking me to lean on him, but to let him know when I needed to.

I appreciated that, especially after the other night when he came home late. I'm sure things would have turned out differently if I had just told him I needed to see him. The thing is, I didn't trust myself to need him then, but things shifted the moment I fell into him tonight. I didn't just leave my sorrow over the abandonment of my dad on the dance floor; I also left my mistrust of myself. Everything I went through created this stronger woman, and put me on this new path. How I could I not trust myself? I was a warrior when I needed to fight, and I was champion when I didn't accept defeat. I not only survived the hollowness I burrowed myself into, but I pulled myself out.

***

I told August every horrible detail about my horrible Thanksgiving dinner right down to the red door. His demeanor was colder than I had ever witnessed from him before. In particular, he got most agitated when I told him my dad spent the afternoon watching the football games with Parker and sent me off to the kitchen. "Are you kidding me?" his nostrils flared and his knuckles whitened on the wheel.

"I wish I was," I responded much more calm than I was earlier.

"He never sees you. How could he spend that time when you were right there, right under his own roof not paying any attention to you?" August asked me seeming genuinely distressed for me. "He should never take advantage of his time with you like that. *Never.*" He gritted out the last part and I found myself comforting him with a rub on the knee.

"As much as that hurt," I said, watching the streetlights pass by, "I think the worst part was when he gave Bethany our tradition, even down to the same words. I foolishly thought those words were reserved just for me. I thought they were special." Now he was the one rubbing my knee in comfort, "Even with an emotional separation that could rival the Grand Canyon, I've still held onto those memories. I've kept them in a place where they are untouched by the pain and bitterness I battle with. Now, he's sabotaged those too. He won't even let me have those."

"He's the one who will lose out, Kensie." August took his eyes off the road and looked at me earnestly, "One day he will realize all he's missed out on, and there won't be anyone to blame but himself." I smiled a weak smile at him. He was probably right. There might be a day when my dad sees the error of his ways, but I wasn't going to put myself through the pain anymore. I was making a choice for myself and for my future to not put myself in the position to be hurt by him. It seemed as though I had already been phased out of the family, but now I was making the choice to bow out.

August stopped by my dorm on the way to his place so I could run up and throw together an overnight bag. Once we got to his house, he directed me to take a shower and relax while he ran out to go pick something up for us to eat. Bossy.

On my way down the hall, I paused outside the yellow room where I was going to put my things. Just as I touched the doorknob to go in, I changed directions and went to August's room instead. I tossed my bag on the floor next to his bed and looked around. I thought briefly about snooping through his room, like we did in his bathroom, but without Lennon there to egg me on, I didn't have to gumption to follow through. Instead I wondered around and took in what was on display.

His room was actually quite simple with pale grey walls and dark blue bedding. He only had two pillows on the bed, which told me he must have decorated it himself. If Capri had a hand in this room, there would certainly be an obscene amount of pillows stretching out to the middle of the bed.

He had a wooden dresser with some loose change scattered across the top. His converse lied tossed by the side of the bed and a basketball was in a corner.

A picture hanging on the wall next to his window caught my eye. I walked up to it to get a better look. It was a simple sketch of a man sitting at a table holding a bouquet of flowers. What really caught my attention were the words scribbled on the picture. There was a haunting quote about someone always having place here when they are gone, and Keaton Henson signed it.

It seemed a little morbid, but I guess when someone you admire creates art, you aren't picky about what it's of. Dave Matthews could color a picture of a blade of grass and I'd proudly display it in my house.

I tossed my bag onto his bed and pulled out my comfy clothes. I usually slept in my boy short underwear, but tonight when I threw my stuff together, I thought twice. I pulled out a lacey pink thong along with my grey sweats and a fitted white t-shirt before heading back down the hall to the bathroom.

I was stripped down and in that steaming shower faster than it took my dorm one to even heat up. I leaned over tipping my head under the showerhead and moaned in satisfaction. Through the noise of the steady spray plodding on my head, I heard a deep voice in the house. I thought briefly about telling him I was in here, but I'm sure he would figure it out. I had, after all, began sighing and groaning obscenely as my muscles relaxed.

I heard the door to the bathroom click open and a stifled cough. "This shower feels amazing. It's just what I needed after tonight." I told him moaning in approval when his shadowed stopped outside the pixelated shower door.

"Ya know, Kensie, we really need to stop meeting in these situations." He spoke and I screamed covering all the important parts even though he couldn't see in.

"Wes! Get out." I demanded, but he continued on like he didn't hear me.

"First you proposition me with mints, and now you're pleasuring yourself in the shower. I'm not complaining, but I'm telling you August would kill me."

I turned around and squished myself into the corner of the stall. His voice alone was obtrusive enough. "Get. Out." I said again getting a chuckle out of him.

"Relax Kensie, I'm not here to see your goodies, I thought August was in here too. He asked me to stop by."

"Wait," I turned and looked at his figure still standing outside the door. "You thought August was in here with me, and you still thought it was a good idea to come in?" I knew they were close, but this was ridiculous. It was silent long enough that if I didn't still see him standing there I would have thought he left.

"That is kinda weird, huh?" He asked contemplatively and I silently nodded my head.

"Sorry Kensie," he said as his figure retreated away from my door, "next time I'll make sure August's alone." I heard the door click shut.

I finished up my shower quickly and shook my hair dry with my fingers before slipping on my pajama boxers and tank top. A chill night with August on the couch watching a movie was exactly what I needed tonight, but it was obvious that was not happening when I walked into the kitchen and saw Wes leaning against the cabinet texting on his phone.

He nodded at the table, "Brought the goods." About ten liters of Coke and a giant pile of king sized candy bars sat on the kitchen table. Before I could ask why it looked like he robbed a gas station a loud pounding reverberated through the house from the front door.

I peeked through the peephole and saw a mop of bright red. The second I unlocked the door Lennon pushed herself into the house with her little arms overflowing in bags of chips and peanuts. "Is there a sale at AM PM?" I asked trying to help her catch the bags that were falling from her arms when Wes swooped in and took the junk food from the both of us carrying it all into the kitchen.

"Ha, you try to find a place to get food on Thanksgiving night."

"What?" I asked her completely confused about what was going on here.

"Ask your lover," she said patting me on the shoulder before making her way into the kitchen with Wes. "He's a very convincing man." She yelled at me from behind her before I heard her scolding Wes for already opening a Snickers.

I shook my head trying to make sense of our two friends sitting in the kitchen with a pile of gas station junk food when I heard the doorknob jiggle again. I turned in time to see

Capri breeze in with a tray of coffee and a bright smile on her face. "Happy Thanksgiving." She said coming towards me, but was quickly interceded by Wes taking the coffee out of her hands.

She stammered a thank you to him and then came up to give me a hug. "What's going on?" I asked her still squished in her embrace. That's when I heard the front door click shut. Capri pulled away and smiled at August who had just walked in with a bag of gummy bears. I had to raise my eyebrow at that making him laugh.

"Just hanging out." August said looking a little unsure.

"Oh please," I heard Lennon yell from within the kitchen. "He called me and told me that if I didn't show up here in thirty minutes with something to eat that he would replace my Austin Carlisle poster with giant pictures of Wes while I slept." I looked at August in confusion.

"Damn," Wes said in the kitchen, "now, that's a good morning." I heard a smack followed by a grunt.

"He called up all of us and asked to meet you here for Thanksgiving Dinner." Capri grinned at me and then touched my arm as she walked passed me into the kitchen. I looked up at August who raised his eyebrows in a grin at me.

"You called them?" I asked

"Yeah." He looked down and shuffled his feet.

"And asked them to bring some of my favorite junk food?" Was he real?

"Yeah." He shrugged his shoulders and peered up at me bashfully.

"Why?" I knew he and Capri already celebrated their Thanksgiving with his parents, and Lennon said she was going to her uncle's house. I couldn't wrap my mind around them coming here.

August shrugged his shoulders again. "I wanted you to have a nice Thanksgiving, with people who love you and want to be with you." I lowered my eyes and felt my heart swell to proportions that I couldn't contain. It overflowed with gratitude and love for these people, for August. It poured out of the corners of my eyes and streamed down my face. I couldn't look up at him yet though, I was too consumed in the feeling. He took the chance to keep talking,

"If it's too much Kensie, I can ask them to go home. I know you've had an overwhelming day," he sounded apologetic, but I couldn't find the words to tell him this was okay. This was amazing, and he was amazing, "I just wanted to try and show you how special you are to me, and to all of us."

I looked up at August when he took the few steps bringing us face to face. I smiled through my tears, and he let out small chuckle with his own breathtaking grin. He placed his hands on either side of my face and stroked my tear-streaked cheeks with his thumbs. "You good?" he asked quietly. "For a minute I thought you were mad at me."

I shook my head. "I love you." I told him and there wasn't a shred of doubt within me. I loved him something fierce. In this moment seeing the lengths he went to just to make me happy, and the fortress of support he built around me when I had crumbled; there wasn't anything I was afraid of anymore. I shouldn't have waited so long to tell him in the first place, but spending the afternoon with my dad made me realize that I was a different person now than I was back then. I was stronger and wiser, and because of that I knew the love I had for August was one that I could count on, and one I could trust.

August pulled my face to him and kissed me senseless. Somewhere between my pounding heart, August's lips, and my hands gripping the front of his shirt in my fists, I heard cheering in the kitchen.

I giggled into his kiss and he pulled away looking down on me with such those chocolaty brown eyes and puffy lips. He smiled so wide his eyes crinkled in the corners in the way that I loved. "'Bout time." He teased me and I shoved him pushing on his chest laughing. "I love you, Kensie." He said grabbing my hand back and pulling me in for one more kiss.

"Can we eat yet?" Wes yelled form the kitchen, "I'm starving." he whined.

August looked at me and rolled his eyes, "Wes, didn't you eat at your mom's today?"

"Yeah, like three hours ago, dude. I'm a growing boy." That made be burst out in a laugh and August led me into the kitchen by the hand. What followed next was the best Thanksgiving dinner I have ever had. I was surrounded my best friends, old and new, and eating all of my favorite junk food. We laughed and joked around and even fit in a game of truth or dare that ended with Wes getting covered in a whipped cream bikini, or whipkini as he called it. He really needed to work on specifying who had to do what.

At one point, Capri had gotten up to take a call from Tanner. She said he was spending the weekend at his parent's house. Wes kept squirming around and leaning back in his seat trying to eavesdrop on her conversation in the living room. Lennon winked at me seconds before she kicked Wes's chair mid-lean sending him falling backwards onto the floor.

August and I couldn't contain the fits of laughter, when Wes got up and brushed himself off like nothing had happened. "She won't be with him forever." Lennon reassured him and he scoffed at her taking his place back at the table.

"Just looking out for her, right Augustus? We keep an eye on Capri." He nodded towards August who looked at him perplexed. "Sure buddy," and he rubbed my knee under the table.

Not long after Capri rejoined the group, we decided to call it a night. Wes was the first to leave, surprisingly, telling the girls that August and I needed some alone time and not to overstay their welcome. That elicited a groan of disgust from Capri who followed his exit.

Lennon hung around a bit longer helping me clean up the trash left over from our feast while August showered, but left soon after before he was even out. She gave me a quick hug telling me how happy she was for me sincerely followed by "now go get your groove back," and a swat on the butt.

CHAPTER 22

I was picking up the last of the trash when August came in from behind me and wrapped me in his arms. I sighed into him and tilted my neck so he could kiss me. "Did you have a good Thanksgiving?" He asked me.

"I did, the best." I told him and turned around in his arms to look up at him. "Thank you." I said earnestly and leaned in to kiss him, but he stopped me holding his finger up in between our lips.

"One more thing." He said and walked over to one of the bags he brought in when he got home with Capri, "Here it is." He turned and came towards me.

"A donut?" I asked.

"There's not much left at a gas station at seven o'clock at night on Thanksgiving." he shrugged. "Here take one end," he instructed me and I did as he said while he held the other end feeling my bottom lip wobble when I realized what he was doing. "Luck is for pussies," he said and my wobbling lip burst out in a laugh, "we make our own happiness." With that we pulled apart the donut and each took a bite.

I smiled up at August's powder covered

mouth and knew this was happiness that we were making. No amount of luck could create this. Fate? Sure, I think we were meant to find each other, but it was up to us to make it happen. I was going to continue making happiness with him, forever.

"I say this should be our new tradition." I mumbled around my donut.

He nodded his head and swallowed his, "The first of many."

August sat back down in one of the kitchen chairs. He was so tall, the way his legs sprawled out across the floor almost took up the entire kitchen space. He stretched his arms above his head and held them there watching me wash the powder from off of my hands. I peeked over and eyed him, heat flooding my cheeks.

"Come here." He said holding out an arm to me.

I dried my hands off and put one in his letting him pull me toward him. "I need you closer." His voice sounded raspy and he grabbed my other hand pulling me down to straddle him on the chair. When my body connected with his, I gasped at the immediate tremble it caused within me.

He lifted a hand and ran it softly down the side of my face. My eyes fluttered closed and my body pulled toward his hand magnetically. He continued brushing his hand down my jaw line and to my neck. When his hand kept going I opened my eyes to see his watching the journey of his hand. "You're so beautiful," he whispered to me, but was fixated on his hand as it descended to the outline of my chest. His fingers trickled over it sending a shiver through me that ended where our bodies were touching.

His fingernails grazed the rest of the way until he held my hip firmly in his hand. I was so transfixed on the feel of him, that I hadn't spoken a word. Though physically, I was saying so much more than I could ever voice. He looked up into my eyes then. The ache in his caused a throb in me so powerful I thought we may not even make it much further.

"Say something." He told me bringing his lips so close to mine I could feel him breathe in me.

"Yes." I whispered back.

In one motion, August stood up with me still attached to his waist. He held me tight to him with his hands gripping under me. Fluttered kisses along my neck had me dropping my head reflexively to the side to give him better access.

He placed me on the edge of his bed when we got to his room and I looked up at this amazing man, my everything. He was my hero, my partner, my joy, and my love. He was more than I could ever define. August was my one.

"God Kensie, you're gorgeous." He ran his hand through his hair as if he was nervous. "I've thought about this moment since I met you." He knelt down on the floor in front of me taking one of my bare feet into his hands.

"So, you've only ever wanted in my pants?" I asked, far more nervous than he could possibly be.

"Your pants are just an obstacle in the way of where I want to be." He grinned up at me, but without the usual sparkle in his eyes. This time his grin was lazy and his eyes held an intensity that sent a welcome shiver through my body. It coincidently began at the place on my inner foot he'd just brushed his lips against.

"But to answer your question, no." He placed a wet kiss on my ankle before trailing his dampened kisses up my calf. "I've wanted into your mind, *kiss* I've wanted into your heart, *kiss* I've wanted into your soul, *kiss* and I've wanted to be buried between your legs.*" kiss*

With his head tilted, he lingered the last kiss behind my knee and slipped his warm tongue across my sensitive skin behind it. A direct current ran from that spot to the place between my legs that ached in anticipation.

"Oh." Fell from my lips a bit breathless and unrestrained. I heard him chuckle lowly, completely aware of what he was doing to me. The vibrations of the laugh that first got my attention only added to my need. I reached down to the hem of my dress to pull it off when his hand came over mine to stop me.

"Uh, uh." He said removing my hand from my dress. "I'm taking my time. I'm going to kiss every inch of this body I've been dying to take. Don't rob me of that." His hands grabbed onto my dress in the same place mine had just been evicted from and pushed it up around my thighs.

He brushed his rough hand down my thighs away from where I wanted them causing a small, uncontrolled whimper to escape my lips. When his hands reached my knees he gently pushed my legs apart and ran those teasing hands along my inner thighs adding a shudder to my second whimper.

He brushed them slowly up under my dress and gripped each of his hands around the uppermost part of my thighs. So close I could feel the heat of his hands through my lace underwear. So close, that when I shifted slightly to the right his knuckles graced torturously close to where I needed him.

He swiftly ran his hands back down toward my knees. I groaned in frustration and slapped my hands onto his leveling him with me stare. "You're in, August. You're in my mind, you're in my heart, you're in my soul, and now for the love of God, get in me."

He chuckled and smirked at me. He reached for the hem of my dress again and this time pulled it effortlessly over my head. I leaned forward and repeated the same motion his shirt. My mouth panted open at the sight knelt down in front of me. I breathed out and he smiled bashfully running his hand through his hair again. I reached out to run my hands across his stomach, and he obliged but only momentarily.

He grabbed my hands from where they traced over each ripple and gripped them in his own. He rose off his knees and pushed me back onto the bed. He climbed onto the bed to cover me, still holding my hands in his and pinned my arms above my head. "Don't move," he whispered into my lips, "I'm still taking my time." Son of a bitch.

He let go of my hands and reached under me to unclasp my lace bra. I arched my back so he could slide it off of me, but the move had my already sensitive nipple brushing against his chest through the lace. I sucked in a sharp needy breath when he whispered, "Don't worry, I'll take care of those," as he pulled my bra off and tossed it to the side.

Just as my back relaxed back into the mattress, August's velvet tongue licked across one puckered nipple. My back regained its arched pose. He flicked his tongue across the perked mound and my legs shuffled at the sheets with need. The combination of warm and wet, rough and delicate, sucking and kneading had my body begging for him to crawl into me.

When I thought I couldn't possibly take a second more, he slipped one rough finger into my folds and so gently traced circles around my entrance. My head fell back in a moan at the same time my legs fell apart. I pushed myself up towards him to force the motion I was desperate for.

He nuzzled into my neck and kissed along my jawline when he slipped a second finger in. I turned my head toward his, nudging against his jaw with my nose. He brought his face up to mine. "Kiss me," I demanded breathlessly unable to breathe with the swirling of his fingers.

His mouth covered mine and mimicked the motion of his fingers. His tongue circled mine as they did. His tongue stilled teasingly when his hand did. His lips sucked and pulled at my own when his thumb massaged me on the outside. Then he hooked his fingers and hit a spot that halted my breath. My hips arched upward and my mouth fell open, but I remained motionless waiting for more, praying for more, and silently begging for more.

Suddenly I was empty. My body fell back onto the mattress. I inhaled a breath I desperately needed and looked around the room for August. He stood just at the end of the bed quickly stripping off his jeans and gazing at me under hooded eyes. Finally. Thank fucking God.

When we were exposed and bare together the beat of my heart began to thrum in my ears. My breath mixed into the beat as reeds while my body created its own soundtrack.

I pushed myself back onto the pillows at the top of his bed in slow graceful slides, August following my lead. His eyes remained fixed on me in a hungry yet patient stare that only fluttered away when he brushed his body onto mine. He dipped his head then, gliding his breath from my stomach up to my neck until our lips connected.

I placed my palms against his chest and rocked into him when I felt his arousal against my skin. My heart skipped then, and the truth washed over me. I was more connected to August now than I had ever been to one single person. After this moment there was no going back. He would own me inside out, and I would be helpless to control the way my heart moved for him.

Sensing my shift August brushed his nose against mine and reached down to clasp our hands together. "I got you, pretty girl." His breath whispered across my skin so softly it buried deep within my being.

He reached over to his nightstand and cued up a familiar song. "Augustana?" I asked, and then I heard the tearing of the foil packet. "Yeah, but this song's all for you. Lose your fears to it, Kensie. Lose your fears to me. Let me become your safe zone. I promise I'll take care of you." My soul collapsed to him sending my body softening against his as he pushed into me. My heart's cadence grew as did the volume and rhythm of my breath, and we moved together effortlessly with to tune of the music and our bodies.

He slid slowly rocking with me in time without heavy breaths. We were completely in tune with one another. Each pump, each glide, felt better than the next. When I moved, he moved. When I raised my leg, he caught it and slid his hand down to where our bodies met. Needing more of him, I pushed my legs out further gliding my toes along the sheets. He buried himself into me in a deliciously slow circular motion. My body obliged moving uninhibitedly in the same motion.

"You feel amazing," August uttered in my ear sending a shiver through my spine. If I could think I may have said something back. My mind was silent though, and my heart was shrouded in what I can only describe as peace. I had completely given myself over to this moment with him and found safety to let go. He had become my safe zone.

Everything began to build simultaneously within me. My heart beating, my breathing turned into panting. The heightened sensation of hard against soft within me became more arousing with each thrust. Everything around me disappeared, and the noise of the world silenced. My mind focused solely on the place where our bodies joined.

I moaned his name with each dip as he gave me more. My body pulled and grabbed at him more urgently trying to find relief. "*More.*" I whispered to him, not even sure of what I needed more of.

He groaned and he pumped into me deep and hard, but deliciously slow. *One*, and I cried out, my legs spread wide begging. *Two*, and my hips arched up to meet his thrust pressing him into me firmly. *Three*, he buried as deep within me as he ever could be.

My body and soul squeezed and pulled around him in the most addicting and delectable relief. The force in which I had just given myself to him swirled around me, and I was released with each satisfied thrum of my body.

August continued to rock more gently into me as my heart rate slowed to a softer beat. His arms were wrapped tenderly under me and mine were gripped around his shoulders. I leaned my forehead against his chest and placed a soft kiss on him. He leaned down to catch my lips into his and we kissed slowly and sweetly still joined together, as we would be forever.

***

The following morning I was sore in the most liberating way possible, that only forty-five minutes in the most amazing shower ever could handle. August woke me early with feather light kisses telling me that he had to go into the youth center to finish up some administrative paperwork, but to make myself at home until he got off at noon. I planned on staying in the exact same sprawled out position I was in on his bed until eleven fifty nine am, but then I heard the shower turn on. I supposed that was my cue to get my ass out of bed.

August's heavy footsteps stopped beside the bed when he leaned down to kiss me one last time before leaving. "I heated up the shower for you," he whispered into the crook on my neck before pulling away and walking towards the door, "and you're a cover hog." He added scurrying out of the door like a coward.

"Am not!" I grumbled and threw a pillow, though he was long gone and it simply slid down the side of the wall. "You snore like a freight train." I added to myself. Thank goodness he wore me out or I certainly would have been up all night envisioning myself as a damsel in distress strapped to a railroad. Although instead of a cowboy coming to save me on a strapping mare, it would be August in a giant truck. I think he'd still wear leather chaps though, and a cowboy hat; definitely a cowboy hat.

We'd have to work out some sort of deal where he needs to wear me out properly every night. I smiled to myself remembering just how properly he had last night, and hopped up to go to my shower.

There was something completely comfortable about being alone at August's place. I occupied myself with washing his sheets and tidying up the kitchen a bit more from the previous night. Other than that, I hung out on the couch watching old episodes of Dawson's Creek. I never felt awkward, or out of place. I felt at home, like it was natural for me to be there doing nothing at all.

After getting something to eat and making August's bed I sat on the couch with my laptop. I was set on finding some new music to put some dances to for the girls when they came back after the holidays. Choosing songs they liked was a sure way to keep them motivated in the routines.

I sampled some of the latest songs on the hip hop top one hundred charts, and realized I had already known most of the songs; I mentally high fived myself for being so cool. A couple of songs into my search my phone lit with an incoming call. I smiled when I saw Lennon's name knowing exactly why she was calling.

"Hello." I answered.

"How does it feel to be a woman?" She asked enthusiastically above the sound of her little car's engine revving in the background.

"Don't you become a woman when you get your period?" I asked purposely avoiding what she was trying to get at.

"No, you become a hormonal bitch when you get your period." She replied and I heard her honk and swear under her breath. "You become a woman when you finally hand over your vagina maintenance to a man." I cringed at her crude response, but was in no way shocked.

"My vagina has been maintenance before, thank you very much. In recent years by myself much better than any man, but if you're asking how my night went then yes, I am feeling very womanly this morning." I grinned to myself powering off the television.

"Hallelujah!" She cheered, "I should get August a box of cigars or something." She mumbled loudly into the phone.

"Slow down, lady. Cigars are for babies, and I'd appreciate it if you didn't congratulate my boyfriend on finally nailing me." I rolled my eyes when I heard her tsk at me. I was about to ask her where she was going, but sat up when the lock on the front door began to jiggle. "Hang on a sec a Lennon, I think he just got home." I pulled the phone down from my ear and began to stand up when *she* walked in the door.

"Oh." She said bitterly. "You're here."

I could barely hear her above the pounding of my heart and I sat back down on the couch suddenly unable to feel my legs. *She has a key.* "What are you doing here?" I asked though it came out patchy since my mouth had become completely dry.

"Is it August?" I heard Lennon's far away voice and brought my phone back up to my ear watching my visitor walk into the kitchen. *She knows where the kitchen is.*

"She knows where the kitchen is," I repeated out loud to Lennon.

"Who?" She yelled through the phone. "Who's over there, Kensie?" She asked but *she* cut off my answer.

"I thought August would be home." She grumbled loudly from the kitchen and I heard her open one of the cabinets. For some reason that snapped me out of my shock. I didn't know why she had a key or what she was doing here, but something about her helping herself in August's house pissed me off.

I stood up from the couch and barged into the tiny kitchen, "I'll ask again." I said sternly, "What are you doing here?" I could still hear Lennon's shrieking from the phone that was now held in my hand to my side. I picked it up and told her I'd call her back later.

"Who is it?" She asked.

"Trashy Temptress." I said staring at my visitor whose mouth dropped open at the name and I hung up on Lennon while she screamed a steady stream of explicative.

The temptress recovered quickly replacing her look of offense with a smug smirk, "Clever." She told me and I couldn't help but notice she was more lucid than the last time I had seen her. At least she had that going for her because she looked like she had just rolled out of bed with her long hair tangled down her back and her large dark sunglasses still on. I cleared my throat letting her know I was still waiting for my answer.

"I left something here," she said obstinately, "I just came by to pick it up." She tossed her snarled hair like it had anywhere to go. I tried to ignore her obvious attempt at riling me up.

"Who are you?" I asked bringing a genuinely shocked look to her face followed by a sinister turn of her lips.

"Oh, so he hasn't told you?" she asked.

"Obviously not." I told her growing irritated by her games.

She leaned one boney hip against August's

counter, "I'm Bree." She said and my heart began its hammering in my head again. I remembered that name.

"August's old girlfriend?" I asked trying my best to appear unruffled when I was anything but. Inside my heart and head were finally on a united front of chaos and disorder.

She cocked her head to the side studying me. "He really didn't tell you, did he?" She asked sounding a bit put out. What hadn't August told me? I tried to tell myself that this girl was clearly unstable. The first time I saw her she was a wreck, and even now, though she could form a coherent thought, she was looking rough. I tried so hard to dismiss any crazy notions that were trying to get at me inside my head.

I trust August. I trust him. I trust him, but why does she have a key? Why does she know her way around his house? I looked at the tall thin girl in front of my with sharp cheek bones that held up her heavy sunglasses, and skinny arms the produced jagged angles where they now sat folded over her chest. She's Bree. "Didn't tell me what?" I asked her warily disregarding any attempt at ignoring her. Her mere presence had my certainty over my relationship with August decomposing, and my insecurities sprouting again.

"About our daughter." The words flowed out of her mouth freely, but each one entered my head independently punctuated by a splintering in my chest. The moments after the words were uttered, slowed into a blur. Bree had already lumbered past me by the time I had processed what she said. Her mouth moved as she went by, but the only thing I heard was the echo of the word *daughter.*

August had a daughter. Bree was her mom. August and Bree had a daughter, together. It's weird how when you are thrown into a situation that rocks you to your core, your brain latches onto the simplest thoughts in order to function. It was like some transcendent survival technique, where my brain knew that if it searched further beyond the most basic of facts, that my heart wouldn't withstand it.

I turned to follow Bree down the hall towards the bedrooms. "Your daughter?" I spoke up not knowing where she had gone, but then heard her voice come from the yellow room.

"Yeah," was all she said? I walked slowly toward the room afraid of what I would find, even though my mind was beginning to put together the pieces. I stood in the doorway and watched as Bree rifled through the white closet that stood out against the colored walls. She pulled out a pink tutu and turned hastily on her heels exiting the room quickly and swiftly, bumping against me in her scurry.

I stared unblinking at the open closet with a handful of little dresses hanging so obviously on the rack. The sound of keys startled me and I turned walking mindlessly back toward the living room.

"Yeah, daughter." Bree spat out at me more wounded now. "I don't know what's worse for you. The fact that your relationship is obviously not as solid as you assumed, or that you are with a man who doesn't acknowledge his own daughter." With that she left the house slamming the door behind her and I collapsed to my knees in the living room.

CHAPTER 23

August

There wasn't much to do at work with the kids all being gone for the holiday, so the staff had the time off as well, except for me. John had me scheduled this morning to go through some of the work orders we had made throughout the past year to make sure the inventory lined up. It wasn't a typical task for a general center leader, but he had been training me more often in tasks that I would take on when he retired and I took over as director.

As I finished up the last supply form review my phone vibrated from in my back pocket. I checked the caller and answered. "Hey, Capri."

"What the hell did you do, August?" She sounded flustered.

"What are you talking about?" I asked folding the papers back into the manila folder. I was used to Capri blaming me for things. Very used to it. She once blamed me for the high and tight haircut she gave her Barbie dolls, claiming I wouldn't let her play with me if they didn't look like my army men.

"She won't answer any of our calls, August."

She sounded increasingly more panicked.

"Who won't? Calm down, and tell me what's going on." I held the phone between my head and me shoulder locking up the file cabinet.

"Kensie, August!" She shouted at me and an unsettling feeling began to churned stomach. "Lennon was on the phone with her and someone showed up at your house. She said it sounded like a girl."

My heart rate jumped a beat, but I ignored the discomfort. "It was probably one of the girls from the youth center, Capri. We keep in touch with them while they are on break. She probably had one of them come over to check in." Yeah that had to be it. Gabby must have stopped by for a visit. Kensie was always so attentive to them and making sure they stayed on a solid path.

"Oh, ya know what?" I quickly added, "It could be her mom too. She stopped by once unannounced to take Kensie to lunch. Yeah, it might have been her mom."

Capri sighed from the other end of the line, "Don't be an idiot, August. You know exactly who it was. I thought you took Bree's key away?" Her panic had subsided some.

"I did," I told her. "Just after I met Kensie, but she still knows where the spare key is hidden." I ran my free hand through my hair while I locked up John's office. "It couldn't have been Bree though, Capri." I reassured both her and myself.

"How can you be so sure?" She asked me, and I wasn't. I wasn't completely sure if wasn't Bree, but for Kensie's sake I hoped it wasn't.

"Look, I'll give Kensie a call and clear all this up. I'm headed home now anyway." My chest warmed at the thought of Kensie being home waiting for me. I couldn't wait to ask her to move in with me now that we were honest about how we felt toward each other. Things were moving in such a positive direction for us I was anxious to take them even further. I knew she needed me to move at a slower pace, but if I could have her wearing my ring my tomorrow I would. There was no doubt in my mind that I wanted her to be my wife, but she wasn't ready for that yet. I'd just enjoy the ride of getting her there for now.

My truck rumbled to life and I picked up my sunglasses from where they bounced around on the dashboard. I set my phone down in their place and hit speakerphone-calling Kensie. It rang a few times and went to voicemail. *Come on, pick up.* I hit redial and listened to the unanswered ring tone again. *Shit.*

Kensie

August's carpet was Berber, and it had five different colors of thread in it ranging from eggshell to a chocolate color similar to his eyes. At some point, I pulled myself up from the floor and went in to start clean some dishes I had used throughout the day.

I had convinced myself that Bree was spouting lies. It was obvious to me at Tommy's when we ran into her that she had feelings for August. This had to be an attempt at getting me away from him. I turned on the faucet, and I squeezed soap onto the blue sponge. I swiped it across a plate watching a rainbow of bubbled splattered in its wake. They all popped burst on their own accord at completely random moments. *She had a key.*

If Bree was in the past as August had let on, why would she have a key? I dropped the plate into the sink and stared at the wall. She not only had a key, but she knew her way around his house. He told me he bought the place three years ago when his grandfather passed away. So Bree had been here, often, within the last three years.

His relationship with her had gone beyond high school, which wasn't something he told me. He led me to believe it ended then. Or maybe I just assumed that? Assuming was my tragic flaw. Maybe I had just concluded that their relationship ended then, but really they remained friends after.

I tried hard to convince myself that I was overreacting, but I couldn't deny the obvious. I tossed the sponge into the sink and wiped my hands on a dishtowel making my way to the yellow bedroom. I stopped at the doorway and looked in. The twin sized bed I assumed to be Wes's late night crash spot, now looked the perfect size for a little girl.

I walked into the room and paid more attention to it than before. There wasn't anything on the walls. In fact, they looked oddly bare. There were, however, nails dotting the surface leading me to believe there were things hung up around the room at some point.

I ventured to the closet looking at the tiny tutus hanging up. I touched the purple tulle on one and smiled when the image of a tiny little girl twirling in circles in it crossed my mind. I pushed the tutus aside and saw a pile of frames leaning against the wall in the back of the closet.

I knelt down and began pulling back the frames one at a time. Each one held the artwork of a small child. One was what looked like to be a fairy, or something with wings. Another was just scribbles, and the third was a picture of a rainbow.

My heart was pounding at this point, but my mind had yet to catch up. For some reason I felt like I still needed more proof? I didn't want to believe what I was seeing yet. I stood up and bumped my head on the clothing rod and felt some boxes fall from above onto the floor behind me. I stepped out of the closet and turned around to see what I had knocked over.

Fate was cruel a cruel bitch. There on the floor in front of me, mocking my disbelief was a scattering of photos that had spilled out of one of the boxes. They were pictures of August, Bree, and a little girl. I knelt down and took a pile of photos in my hands. I looked through one at a time feeling my pulse in my thumbs.

Most were of the little girl who looked to be around two or three. She had blonde hair and a sweet scrunched up smile that made me grin. That fell when I locked on her eyes, her beautiful chocolate colored eyes. They were exactly like the ones I had come to know so well. The next few photos were of him with her, and the last one in my hand was of August,

Bree, and the little girl together at the zoo. This changes everything.

I fell back and stared at the picture of the happy family in my hands. The pounding of my heart silenced in my ears when my brain kicked in, telling me I had all the proof I needed right here. I dropped the picture into the pile on the ground and stood up. I was suddenly overcome with the urge to run. I needed to get away from that room, that house, from everything.

CHAPTER 24
August

The door was unlocked. That was the first thing I noticed. My house was immaculate, that was the second thing. The kitchen was clean, sparkling really with not a dish in sight. The living room was organized with all the furniture polished leaving a lemon scent in the air. "Kensie?" I yelled, but didn't get an answer.

I took one step into my hallway when I saw the golden hue from Ella's bedroom lighting up the hallway. "Kensie?" I called again more urgently as the silence in the house didn't sit well with me. I stopped at Ella's door. My eye's zeroed in on her little tutus hanging in the open closet. *Please no, please no, please no.* I approached the closet and saw photos scattered across the floor.

The one on top both broke my heart and mocked me in one successful blow. It was a picture of Bree, Ella and I on one of our monthly trips to the zoo. My heart froze sending chilled blood through my veins. I picked up my phone and dialed. Capri picked up immediately. "She knows." I said without waiting for Capri to answer. I was already half way out the front door when she spoke.

"Bree was there, August." She snarled and I cringed. "I know."

Kensie

I cued up a rock station on my Pandora ignoring the ringing of my cell phone on the seat next to me. The rapid heavy beats and hoarse screaming from the speakers was exactly what I needed to hear. I left August's in such a hurry, I couldn't even remember if I had shut the door behind me. A few miles from his house my shock started to fade and fury was left in its wake.

I cursed myself for knowing better. If I had listened to my head all along I would never be in this situation. I had learned not to trust men, and subsequently built a small fortress around myself, but I ignored those defenses. I surrendered myself to trust, and because of that I was made blind.

I tapped my thumbs to the frenzied beat of the music and stopped at a red light. My phone began its incessant ringing again. I reached over and shut it off without looking at the caller before shucking it into the backseat. I was suddenly slapped with the memory of August's mystery phone calls and texts over the last few weeks. I excused them away so easily, and now I see how stupid I was. The signs were there, and I played to part of the oblivious girl perfectly.

I watched a group of friends cross the street in front of me just before the light turned green.

They were laughing with each other and talking wildly with their hands. It made me angry. Angry that they were smiling and I wasn't. Angry they were out having a good time with their friends. Where were my friends? Did all of them know about this? There's no doubt Capri and Wes did.

I was so embarrassed. I grit my teeth together and the thought of Capri betraying me, and betraying our friendship. She never once told me about August having a daughter, hell, she never even mentioned having a niece. The second August and I showed an interest in each other, she should have warned me. Friends take care of each other, they don't throw you into a fire and watch you burn. I never once thought I'd have to guard myself against my girlfriends, but I guess I should have taken notice to the fact that they can shred you too, after I found out about Chelsea and Nolan.

Chelsea was never a stellar friend though. She was someone who entered relationships for her own personal gain. Capri wasn't like that. She was kind and sweet, and never once gave me a reason to be weary of her loyalties. Until now.

Loyalty. I scoffed aloud at the word August had once used to describe himself. If loyalty meant completely misleading someone you claim to love than color him loyal. I physically ached at the thought of love. I believed he loved me, and I let myself love him. How could he not tell me he had a daughter? That's not something that just doesn't come up. Its part of who he is, it's a part of the person I fell in love with. So if I didn't know he was a father, did I really even fall in love with him? If he kept this from me, what else could I have not known?

I glanced in my rearview mirror and saw flashing lights in the distance behind me. I began changing lanes to pull off the side and let the emergency vehicle through. I changed the station on my radio to one with a little less anger on it. The passing sirens reminded me that I was driving and needed to calm down.

August

"You should have told her, August." Capri calmly scolded me, "You said you were going to tell her." I still had Capri on the phone when I drove to S.Y.C. to look for Kensie.

"I was." I sounded frustrated. "I am." I said. I had planned on telling Kensie so many times. Just when I worked up the nerve or found the perfect opportunity, I would choke. I should have told her from day one about Ella, but I was so taken by Kensie. Nothing else mattered when I was with her, and for once I let myself get completely wrapped up in someone else.

"A little too late for that." Capri chided me.

"She doesn't know everything. I need to tell her everything." I heard her sigh on the other end of the phone.

"I know. I hope she will let you tell her."

I hoped so too. If she never wanted to see me or speak to me again I would understand. I was a lousy piece of shit for never being honest with her, but I couldn't live with myself if I let her think I was like her dad. She had come so far in moving past the damage his abandonment had done that I didn't want her to think it was all in vain. Above all that though, I needed to tell her I loved her. I had to make sure she knew that wasn't a lie, but was the truest thing that I had said in years.

I pulled into the parking lot at work and let out a stream of curse words when I didn't see her car anywhere. "What?" Capri asked still on the phone.

"She's not here." I said letting my head fall onto my steering wheel. "I thought maybe she would have come here to dance. She likes to do that, to dance out her frustrations. She's beautiful when she dances, but she's not here." If she wasn't here I didn't know where she could be.

"Oh, August." Capri sounded sympathetic on the line. "Let me call Lennon and see if I can figure out where she would have gone, and I'll call you back." She hung up before I could say goodbye, but I wasn't going to sit there and wait for her to call back. I needed to find my girl.

I got back onto the main highway and drove. I had no idea where to go, or where I was going, I just needed to do something. I called Kensie's phone again and it went straight to voicemail telling me she had turned it off.

I heard sirens in the distance and could see the blue and red from behind me. I pulled to the side of the road to let them pass trying not to look, but it was no use. I was slammed with the unwelcome memories that made my stomach turn.

Sirens, so many.

My neck began to sweat as my vision became spotty so I pulled completely off the road. *The smell of gas, Bree unconscious. Ella. My Ella.*

I opened my truck door on the side of the road and vomited into the street.

Kensie

I drove slowly passed the accident that had noticeably just happened. Two cars were smashed together head on, and a stream of gas slithered across the road in front of me. I heard the sounds of more sirens coming, and I said a silent prayer for the safety of all the people involved in the accident.

Once I cleared the scene there was nothing but open road ahead of me until I made it to my mom's house. I sent her a quick text to let her know I would be showing up, but didn't explain anything else. I was done running away from houses that wrecked me, and more than ready to run to a house that somehow always put me back together.

My rage music was no longer pounding through my speakers. The open, empty road had inspired a more melancholy song choice in me, or maybe it was my mood. The more I drove, the lonelier I became. The reality of what had happened really started to sink in and take root.

For the last three years I tried to rearrange my life and create a template for myself to start over. When I met August I had thought I'd finally found a reason to begin again, and the person I was meant to be with. Now, I was doubting everything.

Three years ago, I was attempting to rebuild my broken spirit after constant abandonment. Now I was back in a place of brokenness, but this time it was so much worse. I wasn't being abandoned. No, I was the one aiding in the abandonment. I was a Jodie. August had never once mentioned his daughter to me, and I in turn became the woman he started a life with away from his little girl. I could never forgive myself for that.

August

I shuddered at the roadside trying to regain my composure before I started driving again. I hadn't had a flash back like that in a while. In fact, since I met Kensie I hadn't had one at all. Being with her didn't cover up the past; it just enabled me to see a future. Maybe that's why I could never bring myself to tell her about Ella. I was so desperate for that feeling of hope and promise that being with her gave me, I was afraid to lose it. That had to make me some sort of sick bastard.

I turned my eyes to the road when I heard another set of sirens coming up. My phone rang and I was thankful for the distraction as the ambulance passed me. "Did you find her?" I asked Capri hoping Lennon had helped.

"Len said she probably went to her mom's." Capri told me that she didn't go there often, except for when she needed a break.

"What's her mom's address?" I asked fully prepared to drive there immediately regardless of where it was or how long it took me.

Capri sighed before she spoke, "I don't think you should go, August." Was she crazy? Of course I should go.

"I'm going." I said sternly.

"I think you should give her some space. She has a lot to take in." Capri suggested, but I wasn't interest in giving Kensie any kind of space. I needed to see her.

"I'm going, Capri. I have to explain. " I surprised myself at how desperate I sounded, but that's exactly what I was. I had first-hand experience in how quickly Kensie jumped to conclusions and how easily she overacted. Right now, I just needed to make sure she was okay and not caught up in her head.

"I know you do, but why don't you let me talk to her first, just to calm her down and see where her head's at. The last thing you want to do is show up and make her even more upset." Capri had a point. I needed to explain to Kensie what happened, but more than that I needed her to be able to listen. I wasn't so sure tonight was the best time to tell her everything.

"Ugh, I think you might be right," I said regretfully, "but as soon as you see her text me and let me know she's okay." If there was anyone I would let go in my place it was Capri.

"I will." she assured me.

"I'm going to her mom's first thing tomorrow." I told her firmly.

"I know you are." She replied and I sensed

a smile in her voice. She would take care of Kensie tonight, and I would be there in the morning to see if I could repair the damage I had done to the love of my life.

CHAPTER 25

"What do I do, Mom?" I sat at my mom's kitchen table twirling my coffee cup in my hands. When I arrived I was a tear stained emotional disaster. Now, after a cup of coffee and pouring every last detail out to my mom I was feeling better. Exhausted, but much better.

"Honey, I can't tell you what to do. Only you know what is right for you in this situation." She sat down across from me stirring sugar into her mug. "What I can tell you though, is to make sure you know all the details before you make any decisions."

Oh, I knew details. Though there were few, they were incredibly influential. Since I hadn't spoken to August I was left to my own devices to come up with the rest. Knowing myself, that wasn't the best scenario. I had a pattern of jumping to conclusions. Even August had once asked me to come to him first if I ever had any doubts. I was definitely having doubts, but I hadn't gone to him, and now I was left with the worst possibilities swirling around in my head.

"I hate it when you do that you know." I said smugly to my mom and took a sip of my coffee.

"Do what?" She asked smirking.

"Tell me what to do, but make me think I came up with the solution on my own." She laughed at that.

"I don't tell you what to do, I merely make suggestions and your own brilliant mind figures out the right thing to do." She reached across the table and patted my arm. So maybe she was right, and I did need to hear the whole story, but not tonight. I was still unsure of where I stood.

"So, what if his reasons for not telling me are justifiable ones? I can't be okay with dating someone who doesn't have an active role in their child's life, Mom. That hits too close to home." I couldn't respect a man who didn't take care of his daughter, and I couldn't respect myself as the woman in his life who allowed that. "I won't stand by and live my happy life with him while his daughter misses out on it." I folded leaned back and folded my arms across my chest.

"Oh, honey," my mom's eyes grew soft with sympathy, "I hate what your father has done to you." She took a sip of coffee and set it down on the table leaning forward to unwrap my arms from their position across my chest and held my hands in hers. "You listen to me." She said firmly. "Your dad is a confused man who has his priorities mixed up and always has. Jodie tries to guide him in the right direction, but he is responsible for his choices, not her or the kids," I nodded my head to that. I never really blamed them for any of the attention they took away from me. It was never their fault that my dad didn't know how to include me.

My mom continued, "I don't know what the

story behind August and his own daughter is, but I do know that I don't want my own daughter to fear falling in love and trusting a man because of where her own father placed her in his life. Over the last few weeks I have watched you go from a guarded young woman who was afraid of what she deserved, to one who has finally allowed herself to truly be happy. Love and trust aren't things we come by naturally; they are gifts we give ourselves. For some reason you needed August to make you feel worthy of those gifts, but make no mistake of the fact that you gave them to yourself. Only you can take them away. Don't be afraid of them because of your father's mistakes, and don't hold August responsible for his mistakes either. He is his own man, and one who has proven to love you very much regardless of what you discovered today."

I let go of one of my mom's hands and wiped the few tears that had fallen from her words. "I love him so much mom, I don't know what to do." I whispered somehow unable to speak above the ache in my heart.

"You keep loving him sweetie," she squeezed my hand, "and after you talk to him you decide if that is enough to get you through this and move forward with him." I nodded.

Of course I would keep loving him. I didn't know how not to. Even if I couldn't stay with him, I knew I'd continue to love him. That's the thing with love that I had learned. In my carefully orchestrated plan to get my life on track, love taught me that there are some things you can't plan or coordinate. They show up in your life like a torrential downpour and have the power to either wipe out all you had, or bring new life to it. Up until this afternoon, loving August had been the latter.

My mom's cell phone rang from the kitchen counter. She looked at me, and I nodded letting her know I was okay. She got up and patted my shoulder on her way to pick it up. "Hi, John." She answered and my head whipped around. My mom smiled sheepishly at me. "Yeah, she's here." I threw my hands up in the air in question at her and she just shrugged her shoulder at me. John? My mom was talking to my boss? This day couldn't get any more complicated. She talked a few more minutes before hanging up and just looked at me.

"John, Mom? Really?"

"We've only been talking on the phone honey, hardly anything to claim yet." Yet? So my mom wanted to claim John. I shuddered at the thought and shook my head to get the damaging visions out of my mind. "He is wonderful though, Kensie," she started and I waved my hands in front of me to stop her. I knew where this was going and I wasn't prepared for it, but she kept on rambling, "He is so attentive and charming. And sometimes he calls in the middle of the night just cause he can't get me off his mind," she blushed, but couldn't stop herself, "I mean, we don't you know, not in the middle of the night, or not on the phone, not completely anyway, but in person..." My mind, my poor defenseless mind.

"Mom! Stop!" I yelled above her rambling, "Oh my god, seriously?" I asked her and she shook her head covering her face with her hands. "I'm happy for you, Mom, and John is a great guy, but the last thing I need to hear is anything about your late night phone calls."

"Sorry." My mom said sheepishly before we both burst out in a laugh. She had successfully taken my mind off the dramatic shift my life had just had, but where she lead it wasn't a welcome direction. At least she had made me laugh. There was that.

***

I had managed to calm my nerves enough to eat some pizza with my mom. Okay, that's a lie. My nerves were still a chaotic mess, but I never can turn down a pizza. My mom snuck off to wash my sheets for me. I told her it wasn't necessary, but she insisted a fresh pair of sheets would help me sleep better that night. I think as much as she encouraged me to take care of myself, she was still finding anyway she could to take care of me, clean sheets being one of them.

A knock at the door came not long after she went back to my bedroom. "Pizza's here Mom, I got it!" I yelled down the hall. It was the least I could do for the woman who was always there for me.

I opened the door counting the cash out of my wallet, "Thirty-five?" I asked pulling out the money.

"If I charged, you can bet it would be more than that." Her sweet voice surprised me.

"Capri?" I didn't expect to see her here. In fact, I don't think I'd ever brought her home before. Which means only one thing, Lennon told her where to find me.

"Hey," she said flashing me her sweet smile. "Can I come in?" She asked and I stepped aside to let her through the door. I was still upset with her, but I couldn't help the smirk that crept across my face when I took in her appearance.

"You're in the same outfit you had on last night." I said recognizing the tiny coral colored sweater dress she wore to August's last night, except, it was a bit more stretched out than I remembered. A blush crept across Capri's face and she lowered her head to the take in her outfit.

"Yeah, yeah it is." She was definitely nervous and I couldn't hold in the laugh that escaped.

"Have a good night with Tanner?" I asked her still laughing.

"No, I broke up with him last night." She said defensively. That was surprising. Not that she broke up with Tanner, he was tool, but that she broke up with him and still came over looking like she had a good time with someone.

"So, he's not the one who had such a hard time getting that dress off that he stretched it eight ways from Sunday and even managed to put a tear in the back," I pointed behind her to the rip along the seam and she whipped her head around too look at the tear she clearly didn't know was there. Her face was completely blushed over now, but she maintained her stern face.

"I'm not here to talk about my dress, Kensie." She pointed her manicured finger at me, "I came to check on you."

Of course she did, I knew that. I also knew August most likely sent her, but what I didn't know was why he didn't just come himself. It was very unlike him to stay away and let someone else do the talking for him. As if reading my thoughts, Capri spoke up helping herself to a seat on my mom's sofa. "August wanted to come, in fact he was half way here this afternoon without even knowing where he was going, but I told him to let me see you first." I felt a pang of guilt picturing how worried he must have been, but then I thought of the box of photos I found and my guilt conveniently went away.

I sat down next to Capri tucking my legs underneath me. "I don't really care to see anyone at the moment," I told her feeling a bit mean for how I was talking to her, but she had betrayed our friendship. "I get it, Kensie," she began, but I quickly cut her off.

"You get it? You get that my boyfriend lied to me about having a daughter and an ex that is well acquainted with the house I was staying at. You get that I was made to look like an idiot by my friend who knew all along and never said a word to me? You get that just after twenty-four hours of telling him I love him, he ripped my heart out? You get it?" My voice had become so loud that my mom peeked her head in to make sure I was okay. I waved at her to let her know I was fine and she nodded to Capri.

Capri looked so defeated sitting there in her tore up dress and ratty bed head. How did I not notice her hair? It was always flawless and now it looked like hell in a hurricane all piled up on top of her head. Dang, she really had a good night. I bit back my smile to maintain my anger.

"Kensie, I'm so sorry. I don't know what to say other than I feel awful for keeping it from you. August promised me he was going to tell you and I never intervened because I assumed he would. When it became clear you still didn't know, I wasn't sure what to do. I was stuck between my best friend and my brother. It's August's story to tell, and still is, but yesterday I told him if he didn't tell you soon, I would tell you this weekend." I hadn't thought about the position Capri was in. She was August's sister, and one of my best friends. I would never ask her to choose, but in my anger that is exactly what I expected from her.

"I'm sorry, I should have thought about the position we put you in when we got together." She shook her head to stop me but I continued, "It wasn't your responsibility to tell me it was his."

"I don't know what I could have done differently, but I'm sure I could have figured something out to save you from getting hurt. I'm still sorry, Kensie." I appreciated her apology even though it was unwarranted, and now that we had talked I was glad she came. She made it clear she wasn't going to tell me about August's daughter, but maybe she could clue me in a little on Bree.

"It still hurts that I found out from that girl Bree, but thank you for apologizing," I told her and watched her relax back into the sofa.

"I hate her." She said quietly surprising me. I didn't think it was possible for Capri to hate anybody.

"What's up with her?" I asked, not sure if she'd tell me or not.

She sat back up and shrugged her shoulders. "I can't say too much because I think you need to hear the whole story from August, but I can tell you they haven't been in a relationship since high school. August lost his respect for her a long time ago, but she just won't go away." I imagined not, since she was his daughter's mother. She would always be there, but I was relieved to hear that what he told me about their relationship ending years ago was true.

Capri and I talked a little bit more before she got up to leave. I tried to get the name of the guy she spent the night with, but she was tight lipped and insisted it wasn't what I was thinking. She encouraged me to talk to August and hear him out, which I had fully intended on doing anyway, just not tonight.

CHAPTER 26

August

I'm such a creeper. If I got out the second I saw her emerge onto the patio I wouldn't be as big of a creeper, but I was still one considering how long I had been sitting in my truck outside her mom's house. I promised Capri I would wait until morning to see her, and that was what I planned on doing. As soon as the sun peaked up over the roof I was going to be knocking on the front door.

I watched her sitting on the bench with her head tilted back resting on the side of the house. She was even more beautiful than I remembered from just that morning. I think the fear of losing her got to me, and suddenly everything about Kensie was more.

She was certainly more than I deserved, but I always knew that. I had planned on sitting in the truck and watching her until she went back into the house, *see... creeper*, but I couldn't physically watch her just yards away and not be near her. She startled when I shut the door to my truck and jumped up to her feet. I walked around it and leaned against my headlight watching her look around to find the source of the loud noise.

I knew the moment she recognized my truck because her whole body went stiff. That wasn't a reaction I particularly liked, but it was a well-deserved one. It was the reaction she had when she saw me in front of it, that gave me hope.

There was no hesitation from her when she walked out toward me. Her arms reached me, but she quickly reigned them back in as she got closer. "August?" She spoke the words so softly, but I could hear the heartbreak in her voice. I ran my hand through my hair and gritted my teeth. I was such an asshole. I tried so hard to protect her from the worst of my past that I threw her right into the line of it without ever realizing. I had to make this right.

"Kensie," her name came out rough and gritty so I cleared my throat. "We need to talk." She jerked back at that, and I cursed myself for already screwing this up.

"Of course we need to talk," she said, "about something that we should have talked about weeks ago."

The words came out stiff and clipped, which I was thankful for. Angry Kensie I could handle, sad Kensie would break me in two.

"Can we go somewhere?" I pleaded with her.

She shrugged her shoulders, "There's not much around here," she waved her hand through the air gesturing to the rest of the neighborhood, "and I'm not getting into your truck with you."

I sighed, so maybe this wasn't going to go as well as I thought. "Then we'll talk right here, cause I'm not leaving your side until you've heard the whole story, and after that I'm hoping you'll let me stay by your side forever." Her rigid stance softened and she nodded her head towards the street. "There's an old playground over there we can walk to," Then she turned in that direction without saying another word.

The silence on our short walk to the park was much too loud. The only sound was the crunching our shoes made on the old gravel. There were no dogs barking, no crickets chirping, I imagined everything around has had come to a standstill to watch this all play out. *Is that western music I hear?* Great, Kensie was wearing off on me. I smiled and chanced a glance at her a few feet in front of me where she insisted on walking. She was a stubborn one all right.

I watched her hair bounce on top of her head where she had it wrapped up in some knot thing. A few loose strands trailed down her neck. In a natural progression, my eyes darted straight down to her ass that was bouncing left and right with each step she took. I watched it move back and forth like a spectator at a Ping-Pong match before I realized the word *Pink* was written in gigantic letters across it. In pink no less. The images of everything pink on Kensie that I'd seen last night flashed through my mind like a strobe light, and suddenly I was coughing, no choking, I was choking on my own saliva.

Kensie didn't stop walking, but looked over her shoulder and scrunched her face up at me. I just waved her off letting her know I was okay. There was no way I was admitting to choking on my spit while gawking at her ass on our way to determine the fate of our relationship. That would not go over well.

I followed her into a small clearing at the end of the block, and by clearing I mean overgrown horror movie playground. "Does your mom live in Chernobyl?" I asked taking in the old rusted playground surrounded by tall grass and weeds. Kensie laughed and my pussy heart grew wings.

"Most the people in this neighborhood are over fifty-five, so the playground doesn't get much action." She still hadn't looked at me, but walked over and sat down on one of the swings. I couldn't decide if I should sit down on the one next to her or stand by in case I had to save her from being crushed by the swing set. I chose to sit next to her; I think I'd always choose to sit next to her.

We swayed back and forth on the swings together, but where I was going side to side she was going in a tiny circular motion. After the brief distraction on our stroll to the park, I was struck with the reality of why we were sitting there. My inability to let go of the past had left Kensie in a position of confusion and doubt. If I wanted to have any chance at removing it, I needed to start talking. That was easier said than done, because I'd never told anyone what had happened since that day.

"So," Kensie started us off and I put my feet on the ground to stop my swaying and look directly at her. I needed her to hear this first.

"Before I tell you, Kensie, I need you to know that nothing about how I fell in love with you, and nothing about being head over damn heels in love with you *now* is untrue because I kept something from you. In fact, the way I feel about you is the truest thing I've felt in years. Everything about us is still real." I watched her lift her hand to her cheek and fake an itch, but I had already seen the tear fall.

"Kensie." In a risky move, I grabbed her hand and was relieved when she let me, "You didn't think I was honest about my feelings for you, did you?" I had put so much doubt in her. All I ever wanted was to be someone she could always count on, and I had shown her the exact opposite.

She nodded her head, then shook it, "I don't know, I don't," she was stumbling on her words, "I don't know. I feel like I don't know anything." I shook my head at her and climbed off the swing to kneel in front of her. I reached up and held her face in my hands. "Know that I love you."

She laughed and sniffed, "You make it sound so simple." I wiped away another tear that had fallen with my thumb.

"It is simple, pretty girl." I stood up and sat back down on the swing next to her. It was time to start talking.

"The winter before I graduated high school, Bree and

I found out she was pregnant. I was shocked, but I shouldn't have been. We were never careful, but I didn't think something like that would ever happen to me. Ella was born seven months later and changed my world. I had never thought about being a dad at that age, but I think I fell into the role pretty quickly.

That little girl had me wrapped around her finger."

I smiled thinking about how tiny she was all bundled up in her pink blanket and blinking her eyes up at me. In that moment, my priorities had flipped upside down. Goofing off with Wes and sneaking around with Bree, took a back seat to spending every available second I had making that little girl smile.

"I did the best I could to take care of Bree and Ella, choosing to take a job at the grocery store for the benefits and steady income, instead of going to college here like I had planned. Between becoming new parents, and having a baby so young, my relationship with Bree suffered. We ended it when Ella was just a few months old, but vowed to keep things between us friendly for her sake.

With Bree and Ella moving out, I found myself working longer hours more often to make sure I had enough money to take care of Ella at both houses. That's where I was the night of the accident. I was at work on a night when I was supposed to have Ella with me. I took an extra shift and asked Bree to keep her that night instead."

"Accident?" Kensie's voice spoke up from in front of me where she was sitting in the grass. I hadn't even realized she had gotten up and sat down there, but I was glad to have her sitting closer. I slid off my swing down to the grass too and sprawled my legs so that she fit perfectly in between them.

"Yeah." I cleared my throat trying to hide the way it cracked. "This is hard," I admitted, "I haven't talked about it since it happened."

Her eyes widened in surprise. "If you don't," she began, but I cut her off.

"No, I need to tell you. I want you to know, just as much as I need to say it aloud." Part of me felt a sort of an anxious relief in finally having someone that I could unload the weight of this with. I had my family, but their pain was just as tangible as mine. Capri still couldn't walk into Ella's room after all these years. Having Kensie was like having a second skin. I was stronger now that she had burrowed herself into my soul.

She nodded her head and grabbed my big hands into her small delicate ones holding them between us. I swallowed around the lump in my throat and looked down at our clasped hands. "I was breaking down boxes in the receiving room when I got the call. It was Bree on the phone. I knew by the caller ID, but not by the sound of her voice. It was weak and shaky. The only words I could make out were accident and Ella's name."

I felt my heart tick reminding me that it was still beating when I saw the blinking of the red and blue lights ahead of me. I didn't remember leaving work or how I got here, but I found the accident and that's all that mattered. I ran towards the emergency vehicles at dream speed. I willed myself to move as fast as possible, but it felt as though I wasn't moving at all.

Ella.

My heart ticked again when I watched my feet splash into a stream of gasoline that reflected a murky rainbow back at me. I followed the stream with my eyes to see where it began, but fire trucks and ambulances were in the way. Ella.

Another tick of my still beating heart and the clicking of a gurney being rolled to the back of an ambulance had my legs moving again. The person lying down wasn't whom I was searching for, but I knew her.

Bree. I threw myself into the gurney tripping across a fire hose. I felt the whooshing of air in and out of my mouth and the vibration within my throat, but I couldn't hear a sound. Ella...

The ticking picked up its pace making me anxious. Bree stared up at me wide-eyed and vacant. Her eyes blinked, but she wasn't behind them. Her chest rose and fell with each steady breath she took, but without purpose. She was both alive and she was dead. Her body was there, but her soul was gone. Ella. Ella. Ella.

My search became frantic mimicking the rapid ticking of my heart. I was sucked out of my body and became merely an observer. My mind placed a guard over my heart, so that it could better withstand what I knew was coming.

People were everywhere, running, yelling, focused on each task. Lights were flashing reflections off the trees, yet everything was silent in me. The rigid hands of fear had grabbed a hold of my lungs and gripped tight.

The ambulance Bree had been loaded into pulled away and opened a curtain onto the vehicles smashed into one another. The ticking in my heart paused abruptly, and when my vision tunneled in on the paramedic pounding on the chest on the tiniest lifeless body, my world exploded.

    I couldn't put into words how it felt to have my child taken away from me. Words were meaningless. There weren't any that existed for that kind of pain, because no parent should have to endure it. In an instant, my whole world imploded. I had no more meaning, no more purpose, and I was felt helpless to the little girl I swore to always protect. I was her daddy, and I couldn't save her.

CHAPTER 27

Kensie

I was nervous about what to expect when he began speaking, but I never would have guessed this was what August was keeping from me. I couldn't even say with certainty anymore that he was keeping it from me. I think he was keeping it from himself even more. He was protecting himself from reliving that night. My heart broke for him, in such a tangible way that I felt it bleed through our tears.

I climbed into August's lap and wrapped my arms around his neck. He buried his head into my chest and wept. Sad, slow, hushed tears that were so calm they must have been familiar tears to him. Though he said he had never repeated what happened the night of the accident before, I don't doubt it has played through his mind endlessly. As if sensing the sadness, the sky began to weep along with him in a gentle sprinkling.

"Thank you for telling me." I whispered into his dampening hair. I couldn't think of anything else to say except to thank him for opening his wounds to heal my own. I caught a glimpse of the tip of his tattoo under the collar of his shirt.

"The scars?" I asked rubbing my thumb in across the back of his neck.

He looked up at me and I think I gasped at the depth reflected in his eyes. They spoke of the kind of wisdom that only comes from enduring such great pain. "I got the first one on the first anniversary of Ella's death. It was a reminder that even though I appeared to be functioning on the outside, on the inside I was scarred forever." He was getting a third scar added to his back when I met him for the first time. "Three years?" I asked making the connection. He nodded his head and adjusted me lifting one of my legs over his so that I straddled his lap on the grass.

"And the lyrics?" I asked. I remembered they were from an Augustana song. He surprised me when his lip quirked up on one side and let a chuckle slip out.

"Yeah, they were one of my favorite bands," he said rubbing circles with his thumbs on my hips. "The song always made me think of her and how she gave my life meaning. I used to sing it to her as her bedtime song." I smiled and ran my hand down his back over the place his scars were. He leaned into me and placed a kiss on my shoulder. "After she passed, the song took on even more meaning for me because I knew then what it meant to really be afraid of love."

"And you love me anyway?" I asked, in awe of the capacity of his heart.

He smiled at me then and it was his face consuming, eye crinkling one. "No Kensie, I don't love you anyway. I love you, all the way. I love you to my core, and with every cell in my body. I have so much love for you, there is no room for fear."

My heart broke then, in the sweetest possible way. I leaned my head to meet his and watched his eyes flutter closed before I brushed my nose along his. I pressed a soft kiss to his lips and whispered, "I love you." He grabbed my face in his hands and pressed my soft kiss into a heavy one. It was desperate and restorative with slow, deep strokes of his tongue against mine. When we broke our kiss, I kept my eyes closed and brushed my open mouth against his. We inhaled each other's exhales combining our independent breaths into one, and I felt fearless.

The drizzle from the clouds was light but steady and our clothes quickly became uncomfortably damp. We walked back to my mom's house down the dark street. Unlike our walk to the park, our walk back from it buzzed with a little more life. Lights were on in houses and engines of cars coming to life could be heard in the distance. That was the thing about retired people. For some reason they were up before dawn, even when they had nowhere to be. When I got to that age, I was sleeping in. Well, if August's snoring allows it.

I glanced up to where he walked next to me holding my hand and smiled at him, but I felt it stop short of my eyes. I was more connected to August now than ever before, but there was still a nagging in the back of my mind. Sensing my mood August squeezed my hand, "I should have told you from the beginning, about Ella and Bree. I should have told you." I nodded my head unable to disagree with him. He should have told me, but I understood why he didn't. Talking about Ella wasn't easy for him, but there was more to his relationship with Bree than he had initially told me.

"Tell me about Bree." I said feeling ashamed of myself for asking him to tell me more, but I had to know.

He rubbed his free hand down his face and looked up to the night sky that was hiding the stars under a blanket of clouds, but no longer weeping. "Bree has had a difficult time grieving. Almost immediately she started self-medicating with the painkillers she was prescribed after the accident. I've tried to help her throughout the last few years, but she's only gotten worse. She drinks a lot now too, like what you saw at Tommy's." I nodded remembering the mess of a woman I saw being too friendly with August. If I had known then what I know now, I wonder if I would have looked at her differently.

"So, all those phone calls and texts?" I asked linking those moments that caused a dose of hesitation in me with Bree. "Last Sunday?" I whispered as if not giving it volume would make it untrue. It was true though. He nodded his head, but didn't say anything. I felt a hammering of agitation in me. "So, it was another girl." I confirmed aloud for myself.

"It wasn't another girl, Kensie," He replied hastily. "It was Bree."

That wasn't working for me. "Bree or not, another women took your time and attention from me." I told him not caring if I sounded irrational or jealous. I hated the thought of any other woman taking time with August away from me.

"She's usually not that bad," he said starting to make excuses for her. "Ever since I told her about you, she's gotten worse." I snapped my head from where I was looking at the ground and glared at him.

"Of course she's gotten worse." I tried to control my voice, but it grew with my irritation, "She doesn't have your full attention anymore."

He shook his head as we walked up to his truck in front of my mom's house. "It's not like that, Kensie." He told me beginning to sound frustrated himself.

"Oh, it's not?" I asked him taking a step away and throwing my arms up to my side. "Then tell me how it is, cause from where I'm standing it looks like she takes advantage of your loyalty to her, and you let her." I remembered then, his self-described biggest flaw. Loyalty. It made complete sense, but if he knew he was loyal to Bree to a fault, why was he being defensive now?

August leaned back against his truck and pinched his eyebrows together with his fingers. "Look," he sighed, "I know I've enabled her over the years. I know I haven't helped by being available to her, but I don't know how else to make it up to her or Ella."

I dropped my arms from where I had crossed them defensively over myself. "Make up what to them?" I asked him sounding much calmer than before. He looked off into the distance unable to make eye contact with me.

"If I hadn't had taken that extra shift, I

would have had Ella with me that night." He said clenching and unclenching his fists at his side.

"And then she would still be here?" I asked finishing his thought for him.

August nodded and then pinned his pleading eyes back on me. Pleading me to what? Agree with him? I stepped into him closing the gap between us and tilted my head up to maintain the connection of our eyes. "That is not your fault." I said and held his hands in mine when he tried to shake it. "No, listen to me, August. It was an accident. You didn't do anything wrong, and helping Bree hurt herself isn't going to solve anything."

I lowered my hand from his face and held both of his hands in mine. The next part I was going to say was going to be the hardest, but I had to do it. I had to for me, for August, and for the future that we both deserved together. I chewed on the inside of my cheek trying to find the words. "Say what you're thinkin." His voice came out in a rough whisper.

"I love you." I told him first because that was the most important thing I had to say, or would ever have to say to him. "I love you, but you need to work out things with Bree, and set yourself free of her and your guilt. I can't come second to her, and I can't support you in taking care of her." August's throat rippled when he swallowed.

"What are you saying?"

The wavering of his voice had me pinching my eyes shut to hold in the tears that threatened to fall. "I'm saying," I said locking my eyes back onto his and let the pools of tears that refused to subside flood out. "I can't be with you like this."

CHAPTER 28

August

Thud. Thud. Thud. I groaned and smashed my pillow onto my head. Thud. Thud. Thud. I chucked the pillow across my room and forced myself out of bed. When I got to the door, I swung it open and squinted into the sun at the ridiculous man in a fedora. "Dude, your spare key is broken." Wes said shoving his way passed me into my house.

"It's not broken," I grumbled, "Bree still has the key."

I hadn't even bothered to ask her for it back. I hadn't bothered with much of anything over the last few days since I saw Kensie. To say I was crushed, would be the understatement of the century. Crushed insinuated that although in pieces, I still existed. I would hardly call lying on my couch with my outrageously large case of beer existing.

"That's why I'm here." Wes said from halfway inside my fridge. "Dude, do you have anything besides beer in this place?" He peeked up at me from over the fridge door. I shrugged my shoulders. I had no idea. He shook his head and closed the door. "I guess we will buy you some groceries first. You can't bring Kensie back here without any soda and chocolate around."

"She left me, Wes. She's not coming back." I raised my arms up, gripping the back of my head and staggered back a step at the pungent odor that seeped out from under them.

Wes pointed at me and nodded, "You stink." He turned to pull out a notepad and pen from one of the drawers and began taking inventory of my cabinets. "And she didn't leave you." He said opening up bare cabinet after bare cabinet. "She's waiting for you to figure your shit out."

"You think so?" I asked feeling a tinge of hope. I walked over to my secret drawer and pulled out a bag of gummy bears tossing them to Wes.

"Oh, thank God. Sustenance." He said before tearing into it. "For sure, dude. She loves you." He pointed at me chewing a mouthful of gummy bears. "She wouldn't even make out with me when I offered."

"You hit on my girl?" I took my bag of gummy bears out of his hands before he ate them all.

"It wasn't even like that, dude." He defended himself putting his hands up in front of him.

"Then what was it like?" I asked not really worried. Wes would never move in on someone I was serious about, but I was curious.

"I was just teasing her, but still, she didn't take me up on the suggestion. Most girls would jump at it, joke or not." I shook my head and laughed at him. He flashed his dimpled smile at me and waggled his eyebrows.

Maybe Wes was right. Kensie had been so incredibly supportive of my grief over Ella. In a way, she seemed to grieve for my daughter that she'd never get to meet. Keeping my loss of Ella from her wasn't what led her to end our relationship. It was Bree. She said herself that she could never come second to Bree, which flabbergasted me. Kensie would never come second to Bree, or to anyone. She was in a place that was all her own deep within me. My actions over the last few weeks showed otherwise, and I knew now that if I had any chance at saving my relationship with her I'd have to make some changes.

"Okay, what do we need to do first?" I asked Wes.

"Atta boy." He grinned and rubbed his hands together. "First, you're taking a shower. You smell like an overused hooker." I scrunched up my face. I wasn't touching that.

***

She still lived in the apartment we had rented together. I actually still paid the rent. I was anxious about how this would all go, but I had to do it. Wes and I spent all afternoon devising my steps to get Kensie back. After stocking up the fridge with all of her favorites we changed the locks on my doors so Bree couldn't use her key to get in again. I changed my phone number after that and sent out a group text with my new number, only to the people I really needed in my life, Kensie being one of them. I'd followed that with a call to my therapist and set up an appointment.

Yes I had one, or I'd seen him once at my mom's urging right after I lost Ella. I was too proud then to accept that I needed help. Screwing things up royally with Kensie knocked some sense into me. I needed to get myself straight if I had any chance and keeping her, if I got her back.

The final step was to cut Bree off, financially and emotionally. Kensie was right when she said I needed to stop enabling Bree. I had been doing it for so long that it sadly had become a part of my daily life. My guilt about the accident was the sole driving force in my enabling. I had felt indebted to Bree for taking our daughter the night that lead to her being stripped form our lives. Kensie was also right when she said it wasn't my fault.

It wasn't something I hadn't heard before. Capri, my parents, and Wes have continuously encouraged me to let go of my guilt and responsibility towards Bree. It wasn't until Kensie that I believed it though. Maybe because I finally saw a reason to set myself free and move forward, or maybe I was inspired by her own strength in getting the life she wanted. Either way, I was ready.

She opened the door before I even got up to it. "Well, look who it is." She drawled out looking up at me with her big round sunglasses on her face.

"You expecting someone?" I asked her. Answering the door on the first knock, let alone before anyone got to the door wasn't typical. She usually took more than fifteen minutes to hear the knocking and drag her up from wherever she was to answer the door.

"You, of course." She said stepping aside to let me in. *Of course*, I thought. It was definitely time to end this.

I glanced around the apartment making my way to the couch. It looked cleaner than usual, which wasn't necessarily a good thing. She usually cleaned when she was on some sort of bender. "The rent's overdue." She told me sitting down in the old rocking chair we used to put Ella to sleep in. She looked so much different now than back then. She wasn't even a shadow of the girl I used to know. That girl simply didn't exist.

I smiled at the memory of that young unsure mom who sat for hours in that chair afraid to put Ella down because she always woke up when we did. Her hair was always pulled back in a low ponytail, and she didn't have time for make-up then, but her face was always glowing.

Now, her hair and make-up were never done for other reasons, and the glow was long gone. In its place was a dense fog, I'm not sure she could even see out of anymore. I took a deep breath and laid the pamphlets Wes and I had picked up earlier on the table. "I'm not paying the rent anymore, Bree." I told her. She didn't say anything, and I couldn't see her eyes under her glasses, but I kept talking. "I can't do this anymore."

I corrected myself, "I'm not doing this

anymore. It's time we both move on, and I have a chance at that now and I'm not losing it."

I pushed the pamphlets I had set on the table towards her, and still she didn't move, "This facility will give you your chance too, Bree. We will always love Ella, and though we will never recover from her death, we have to live. We haven't been living, and she would want that for the both of us." She leaned forward and picked up the papers. My heart skipped a hopeful beat.

"I can't afford something like this." She said still looking through them.

"They offer a program specifically for low incomes, and they even help you move into a sober living house and find employment after. All you have to do it go, Bree." I knew her journey would be much more difficult than that, but I only focused on encouraging this first one. After this, she was on her own. "I want you to go, Bree. I want you to find life again, but the decision is yours to make. After today, I will no longer be in contact with you." My heart was beating erratically, but I remained calm on the outside. I was setting myself free.

She tossed the papers back down on the coffee table and folded her arms over her chest.

"So, that's it? You meet some new girl and everything changes?" I could hear the curiosity in her voice laced through bitterness. I hoped she took this chance at getting well, so that she too, could find change.

"That's exactly it. I met *the* girl, and everything has changed."

Bree remained silent when I stood up to let

myself out. I stopped at the door and turned to look into the apartment where our little family began for the last time. I would always hold the memories of those first few months close, and hopefully Bree would get to a point where she could remember them too. "Goodbye, Bree." I said, and shut the door.

CHAPTER 29

Kensie

I had only been at my mom's for two nights, but I was already feeling like it was time to go home. She told me I could stay as long I needed to and decompress, but to be honest I was feeling more and more claustrophobic sleeping in my childhood bedroom. Overhearing her late night phone calls with John wasn't helping either. Hearing my mom giggling in the middle of the night made be both smile, and vomit in my mouth a little.

I enjoyed my time with my mom, but I was really starting to miss the girls, being at work, and with August. I really missed August. I knew I made the right decision. I couldn't stand by while Bree suffocated him, and I didn't want to force him to end his relationship with her. I wanted him to do that all on his own. The part that broke my heart was that I wasn't sure he would. I questioned if I was even worth putting him in that position. Bree was the mother of his child. They had a relationship that twisted and turned and dove deeper than the relationship August and I had just begun. I wasn't even sure I could compete with that, but that's why I stepped aside. I shouldn't have to compete, but I still hoped I'd win.

My mom had a curriculum meeting at school today, so I took the opportunity to be alone for a while and took a walk. I found myself at the same playground I had taken August to, and it looked strikingly similar to the way it did at night. It was even just as silent. I sat down at the old picnic table making sure to test the bench first. I didn't need to fall through the splintered wood and onto a rusty nail today. I'll pass on the tetanus shot, thank you. Although it did sound better than going back to see August again.

I wasn't sure how I would handle that. The whole group had gotten so close over the last few weeks, and I'd never put Lennon or Capri in a position where they'd have to choose. It was only a matter of time before August and I were in the same room together again.

I leaned down and plucked a dandelion from the grass and twirled it in my fingers. The only solution was to be the bigger person. I'd have to hold it together on the outside when my insides would undoubtedly be cracking and splintering. I wouldn't be hollow though, which surprised me. The wind picked and the tiny seeds on the flower began to flutter.

Hollow was a feeling I had become acquainted with. My relationship with my dad left me hollow, Nolan hollowed me when he left, and I was even guilty of contributing to my emptiness through my interactions with the guys in high school. After August, I wasn't hollow. I was wrecked, but I was complete. Maybe because August didn't abandon me. I'm the one who left him. A wave of regret rolled through me when the wind swept by in a gust.

I watched as the little seeds that held onto the flower so tight were plucked off one by one and were carried into the wind. *Wind. I want wind.*

My heart coiled up into my throat and pulsed there. My wind. August was my wind. I wasn't empty because being with him hadn't drained me into a shell of myself. He did the exact opposite. He showed me how strong I am, and he showed me how determined I can be. He showed me how to love myself again.

In just the few weeks we had together, he had showed me a world of possibilities. There was the possibility to overcome, to succeed, to come apart and mend, to fall and rise, and most importantly the possibility to love and be loved. He guided me through my fight and carried me when I couldn't move. Not once did he leave me, not once did he walk away or give up on me, but I walked away from him.

I dropped the naked stem of the flower in the grass and ran home. I don't run, ever, but I ran. I had to get back to August. He may have made some mistakes when it came to handling Bree, but he was struggling too. I thought walking away was the best decision, but I was so wrong. August needed me to stand with him and guide him through this like he did with me. He needed me to carry *him*, when he couldn't make a move.

I burst through my mom's front door and was horrified to find my mom under John on the sofa. Legs intertwined, or maybe they were hands, or hand and legs. Oh God, I hope it was only hands and legs. I screamed, they screamed. John jumped off of her and I shielded my eyes. "Oh my God, you guys!" I yelled from behind my hands. "I sit there!" This would be seared into my brain forever. *I'm so sorry brain.*

"Relax, Kensie," my mom's voice spoke up, "We were just making out." *Vomit* "You can open your eyes, everyone is clothed."

I peeked through my fingers just to make sure and breathed a sigh of relief when I saw she was right. I let my hands fall to my side and looked at John, "I can never look at you the same way again, you know." He chuckled and tucked his shirt back into his Levi's.

Vomit.

"Good thing I'm retiring soon." He said and winked at me before kissing my mom on her cheek and whispering something into her ear that made her giggle. He walked by me, and when he went to pat me on the shoulder I jumped back. He raised his eyebrow in a smirk at me.

"I don't know where your hands have been." I said completely serious. He shook his head laughing, "Welp, I'd better go feed Bear. See ya later, Kensie."

"Thought you were at a meeting?" I asked my mom.

"I was," she said, "and then it ended and John took me to lunch." She smiled and sat down on the couch. I stayed standing. I would forever stand in the living room now.

"What has you in such a hurry?" She asked me. I was relieved for the change of subject.

"It's time for me to go home." I said, and she smiled in a nod.

"You ready to see him again?" She asked.

I bit the inside of my cheek and nodded. "Yeah, I need to make some things right." I hoped I hadn't ruined it all. "I never even gave him a chance to set things right. I ran. I was so scared of him leaving me that I left him first." My mom nodded in understanding.

"Loving someone is scary, but it is also incredibly rewarding when you are willing to work through your fears and stand up for it." If there was any love worth standing up for it was August's.

"Thanks, Mom," I said before running into my room to pack up my clothes. Thankfully I hadn't showed up with much, but I did buy a few things because I wasn't sure how long I was going to stay. I unplugged my phone from the charger when I saw I had a missed text. I didn't recognize the number but my heart stilled when I read the first line.

It's August. This is my new number. I changed it so Bree can't contact me anymore... I love you.

I was crying. I was laughing. I was laughing and crying. August was already making changes to his life so that we could move forward together. Of course he was, though. He was amazing, and he was mine. I couldn't wait to get back to him. I just had one stop to make on my way.

***

The Red door wasn't as intimidating this time, maybe because I felt in control. I got out of my car and straightened up my shoulders leaving my purse in the car. This wasn't going to take long.

It took my dad a few minutes to answer after I had knocked. I imagine he was upstairs in his office running numbers, whatever that meant. The look on his face when he opened to door only gave me more ammunition. He was shocked, but not eyes aglow wide smile happy to see me, shocked. He was exasperated with me. "Kensington," he sighed out a grumble and took his glasses off rubbing the bridge of his nose.

My rapid heartbeat did nothing for my already constricting lungs. This wasn't the same nervous energy I felt when my anxiety came on, though. This was vamped by pure adrenaline. My endorphins were working over time with the knowledge that I was about to own this part of my life. "Dad." I said when he opened the door wider and nodded at me to come in. He just nodded. I grunted low in frustration and spoke up, "No, Dad, I'm not coming in."

He stopped mid step and turned around tucking his glasses into his shirt pocket. "Okay, what's up, kiddo?" He sounded a bit more chipper now, but the damage was already done. Long done.

"I needed to come say a few things to you." I started and he cut me off.

"Oh good, I've been meaning to talk to you too, when I saw you next." When he saw me next? He could see me all the time if he really wanted too. Hell, he could call me if he wanted to talk to me.

I put my hand up to stop him. "Dad, please I need to say this."

I closed my eyes then and took a deep breath. "You've been a really crappy dad since you and mom split up. Like, really crappy." I opened my eyes to see his wide eyed and genuinely shocked face, but he didn't say anything. Crappy wasn't really what I had anticipated to come out of my mouth, but I was going with it.

"I have spent years wondering what I did wrong to make you choose to be a dad to someone else's kids instead of me. Your craptastic fathering left me struggling to find any amount of worth in myself."

My dad cleared his throat and loosed the knot in his tie around his neck. I guess I had gotten his attention. Finally. "Kensington, come in and sit down so we can talk about this." He asked me again. I shook my head and took a step back from the door.

"No, Dad. I'm not here to talk this out. I'm not here to ask you to make more of an effort, or to plead for your attention. I'm here to tell you that I'm done doing that. I'm not the little girl who needs her dad's approval anymore. I'm a woman who has realized that what makes a family is not who you are bound to by DNA. It's choosing to surround yourself with the people who love you and support you. I have the most amazing family now, and I don't feel the need to find a way into yours."

I unclenched my fists releasing the pressure

in my palms. That had been the most liberating realization for me, that I was not bound to people who poisoned my life. My dad was most certainly poison, and I wasn't allowing him to contaminate me any longer. He could only hurt me as much as I allowed him to, and I was so done being hurt by him.

He cleared his throat again. "Well," he said scratching his thinning hairline with one hand. "That was what I wanted to talk with you about, although that young man didn't go into that kind of detail when I talked with him." Wait, what?

"What young man?" I asked him, completely confused.

"The young man that answered your phone on Thanksgiving. When you disappeared, we called you a couple of times, but you never picked up. Eventually a young man picked up and told me what an awful father I was, and that I should be thankful to even have such an amazing daughter to spend my time with. He hung up before I even had a chance to ask who he was."

I couldn't help it. I smiled. August really loved me. I couldn't believe he had stood up for me to my dad, but then again I could. "That's my boyfriend." I told my dad proudly and didn't miss the small smile that crossed his face.

"Well, I really didn't appreciate the way your boyfriend spoke to me. I would have preferred a more civil conversation, man to man." I rolled my eyes at that. August would forever be a greater man than my dad. As far as I was concerned, that gave him free reign to address my dad however he chose. "It does, however, make me really happy to know my daughter has a man who isn't afraid to fight for her." I stared at him blankly waiting for him to continue; because quite frankly it pissed me off that after everything I had just poured out to him he had the nerve to offer his approval of my boyfriend.

"That was also what I wanted to talk to you about." He said shifting on his feet. He probably needed to sit down, but I didn't plan on staying much longer. "I didn't realize any of this," he told me genuinely and I knew as much. I just would never be able to use that as an excuse for him because he should have realized. He should have realized when I wasn't at the family reunion. He should have realized when he didn't know anything about my life outside the fact that I was living. "I'm just sorry you feel that way," he said and then he stopped talking and looked at me sympathetically with his mouth turned down.

I waited a minute to see if he was going to say anything else. Maybe say, an apology for how he had treated me. It never came, though. All my dad was capable of was apologizing for the way I felt, as if he had no responsibility in it. I snorted and shook my head.

"That's it? You're sorry for how I feel?" I probably should have been hurt by his disregard, but I wasn't. I had already come to a place where he couldn't hurt me anymore.

"I'd really like for us to try to work this out, kiddo." He said still completely clueless. I was done. I had said what I needed to say to him. I came and set myself free, and now I was just ready to get back to the people who were worth my time.

"Look Dad, I'm done. If you want to call me, call me. If you want to come visit me, come see me. Other than that, I don't know what else to say." I turned and walked down the front steps to my car. Other than a very loud sigh, my dad didn't say anything. That was exactly why I had to come here. I could never change the way he was, but I could change the way in which I dealt with it.

***

The bells jingled against each other. The last time I walked through this door it changed my life, and now I had a reason for a memorable tattoo. The shop was full tonight. I remember Wes telling me they worked the most at night. I guess nobody wanted a tattoo at nine in the morning.

"Can I help you miss?" A guy asked from behind the counter.

"I'm looking for Wes if he's here tonight." I said hoping he was. There wasn't anyone else I wanted to do this tattoo for me. The guy squinted his eyes at me and fiddled with his lip ring, "Depends. If you're here for some work he's in the back, but if you're here to be worked over, he said to send you away."

My mouth fell open at his remark. I guess crude honest was a requirement for working here. I was about to answer when I heard a boisterous chuckle from the back of the shop, "That's just the girl I wanted to see around here tonight." Wes yelled pointing to me as he made his way to the front around the scattering of customers and artists. I looked down at the lip ring guy who was smirking at me. "Shut it," I pointed at him,

"I'm here for a tattoo."

I pushed my way through the saloon door where Wes greeted me with a hug. "Don't tell August I've got my hands on you. He'll kick my ass." I laughed at that, relieved August still had a reason to. "Is it time for that tat?" He asked pulling away from me and rubbing his hands together.

"It's time." I said with my stomach in knots more nervous about the pain than anything.

When I told Wes what I wanted, he stared at me in utter disbelief. I knew my tattoo wasn't entirely unique, but it had a special meaning to me. It wasn't even a rose or a butterfly so I don't know what the problem was. "Seriously?" He asked making me uncomfortable.

"Yes, seriously. Why, what's wrong with it?" He threw his head back in a laugh, "Nothing. Nothing's wrong with. It's perfect. Let's do this."

I straddled the chair and pulled the straps of my tank down. Wes didn't waste any time getting to work on the tattoo on my shoulder. It wasn't as painful as I had thought, although he told me this was one of the least painful spots. The build-up in my mind was even worse than the actual needle on my skin. A couple of spots on the bone had me cringing, but Wes was quick to give me a break when he took notice. We were already half way done with just another hour or so left.

"So glad you decided to give him another chance," Wes mumbled around a green gummy bear. I told him all about my reasons for sending August home without me that night, and about what I had realized since then. I found getting a tattoo was a lot like getting my hair done in that they worked while you spilled your guts. "I just wish I would have given him the chance then. I've missed him the last few days." I admitted, "a lot."

I reached into the bag of gummy bears and passed over a red one. "Open." I told Wes who opened his mouth so I could toss the yellow one in. "You did the right thing." Wes surprised me with that. "We've been telling him for years that helping Bree out so much wasn't good for him." I tossed another bear his way, but missed and hit his eye.

"Oops. Sorry." I giggled, "That's what I'm afraid of, though. This is something he's been doing for years. What makes me think he can let her go now?" I winced on the last part when Wes hit the edge of my shoulder blade.

He stopped the gun and sat back in the chair stretching his neck from side to side. "That's just it." He put the gun down on the table and cracked his knuckles. "We are all permanent fixtures in his life. None of us would leave if he didn't set Bree on her own. Not me, not Capri, not his parents. You can though, and that scares him. He could lose you over Bree, and he wants you more than I've seen that guy want anything."

I may have physically needed to space myself from him, but my heart would never have left him. I hoped we really could get through this, or I'd have to invest in some cats to keep me company for the rest of my days.

"Do you think he'll be awake when I get there?" I hadn't realized how late it was getting. I thought about waiting until tomorrow to go to his house, but that was impossible. I wanted to go home, and August had become my home. Wherever he was, is where I wanted to be.

"Oh, he'll be up." Wes said opening his mouth again like a baby bird. I took a handful of gummy bears and dropped them into his mouth.

"There ya go, little guy." I patted him on the head and tucked the bag back into my purse. He chewed that mouth full like a trooper and then pointed back to the table for me to lie back down.

I heard the buzz of the gun while I situated myself back on the table, but then it abruptly stopped. I looked at Wes over my shoulder. "In all seriousness." The usual glint in his eye was gone now.

"Can you do serious?" I asked making him laugh.

"I'm working on it." He flashed me his dimples. Oh, how the ladies must swoon.

He started the gun again and continued talking, "Losing Ella wasn't just hard on August. It was earth shattering. I can't imagine someone ever gets over losing a child, and I never expect him to. I always hoped he'd find a way to live again though. He did when he met you." I listened intently to Wes's soft words and felt them seep into my heart making it swell and ache simultaneously. "Before you, he was an imposter. He carried on with life, but never meant it. Now, when he laughs, he's really laughing. When he smiles, it's genuine. The best part of all is when he talks about being in love with you, the dude beams. Like, turn that shiny shit down so the rest of us can see." He smirked down at me. "You bedazzled my boy."

I laughed so hard Wes had to pull away from my skin. "You guys had better get some good sunglasses then," I told him because August made me feel just as shiny.

CHAPTER 30

August

I set up the last few cups around the living room and glanced around the survey my genius. Red plastic cups weren't the best choice aesthetically for the flowers, but they'd have to do. I didn't have many options considering how late at night it was.

When Wes called to tell me Kensie was stopping by tonight, I got to work. I couldn't be sure why she was coming over, but I hoped it was to work things out between us. Although, there was also a chance that she was stopping by just to get the sweater she left here the other day. I chose to ignore that reason. Regardless of her visit, I needed to tell her that Bree was officially out of the picture. If that didn't convince her to take me back, then I was optimistic my gesture would aid in my efforts.

I brushed the crumbs of the couch when I thought I heard a thump at the door. I stopped to listen, but didn't hear anything. I swiped my hand over the cushions again making sure all evidence of my *woe is me* couch days was gone.

Another noise alerted my attention back to

the door. I walked to the window next to it scratching my bare chest. I'd showered when I got home from getting the flowers, and was in such a hurry to get them scattered around the room, I only slipped on my workout pants.

I pulled the blinds apart and peered through them to my front yard. I noticed my empty pot was lying sideways in my grass. Odd. There were pavement rocks scattered out of place along my walkway, and what looked like evidence of a struggle with one of my bushes. Then I saw her, sitting on my stoop with her back to me. Her chestnut hair fell softly down her back reminding me how amazing my pillows smelled after she left the other morning. I lied there for far too long with my nose buried in them, only getting up when things became a bit awkward for my mattress.

Yet again, I was a creeper and watched her for a few minutes. I couldn't help it. I memorized the curve of her back, and the gentle way her body moved just in case I never got to see it again. I watched her eat a handful of mints and immediately put my hand in front of my mouth and breathed. If she was eating that many mints, I wanted to make sure I was ready for whatever she had planned. I was more hopeful than I had been since the day she found out about Ella and Bree.

She turned around at stealth speed and glared at the window. I jumped back startled by her quickness making the blinds rattle. I opened the door and looked down at her, and her presence stole my breath.

Her wide brown eyes blinked up at me reminding all the things I'd learned to do to make them fall and flutter. She chewed on the inside of her cheek puckering her lips at the same time. I remembered how sweet they always tasted, but I was willing to bet they were all minty fresh now. I watched her chest fall in an inhale and she pointed her little finger at me. "You guys suck." She scolded me, but didn't sound nearly as determined as I think she intended too.

The sight of me was affecting her too. I was sure of it. I'd learned the way her body responded to me over the last few weeks, studied it. I bit my bottom lip scanning over her in her grey sweater and jeans. Right on cue, I watched as her exposed collarbone prickled up. "I didn't leave you out here as a joke," I said and ran my fingers through my hair waiting for her parted lip response. There it was. "I just was just being creepy and ogling you." Why deny it?

She closed her lips and sucked in a quick breath through her nose, that was a new one. "Oh." She breathed out.

"Well, can I come in?" She asked me like she needed to. That irritated me.

"Of course you can come in, Kensie," my voice clipped and she shrunk back. "Don't say stuff like that. I want you to feel at home here. You can come and go anytime you want." I softened my tone thinking about having her here with me all the time. She nodded and I stepped aside to she could come in.

The gasp she sucked in was my first sign that she saw the flowers. "Oh, August," and my name on her lips in a sigh was my second sign that I made the right choice. I fist pumped in the air before following her into the house. She turned around and looked at me sweetly with big puppy dog eyes. "What's all this?"

"Roses." I smirked. I was good. She smiled mischievously at me.

"Feeling pretty proud of yourself there, aren't ya?" Busted. I laughed and took a tentative step towards her.

She liked the roses, but I still didn't want to push it. "I may have heard you were on your way over, and I may or may not have confiscated a few roses from the bushes at work." That was the first place I had thought of to get some flowers this late at night, and it was perfect since I picked her first rose there.

I wasn't a fool. Girls loved that sentimental stuff, but Kensie was the first girl I ever wanted to do that kind of thing for. The joy it brought her, literally brought joy to me. Nothing felt better than doing something thoughtful for your girl and hearing the smile in her voice. Knowing I put it there was worth it every time.

"It's perfect." She smiled hesitantly up at me and took a few careful steps towards me. "How did I ever find you? How could I have not known somewhere in this mess of a world, you were there waiting to make it perfect for me?" Oh hell, she had my insides somersaulting. I loved this girl so much.

"I haven't made anything perfect," I admitted the truth first, "but I'm hoping you'll let me keep trying." That was all I could do. I'd try till the day I died to give Kensie perfect. "I love you," she took another step toward me and placed her hand over my heart.

"I love..." I started, but she cut me off with a quick chaste kiss to the lips.

"Let me say this first." She insisted.

She placed her hand back over my heart and I covered it with my own holding it tightly. "I'm sorry I walked away from you so quickly over Bree. I should have given you the opportunity to make the decision for yourself and I made it for you. I never even waited to see if you would work on separating yourself from her because I was too afraid of hearing you say you couldn't."

I was still dumbfounded over her thinking I would ever choose anyone over her. It wasn't even a choice I could make. "Kensie, that was never a choice I could have even made." I reached up and held her cheek in my other hand, "You have my heart," I tapped out clasped hands over my chest, "that's the simple truth."

She grinned up at me. "Simple, huh?"

I smiled back at her. "Simple." I leaned down capturing her lips in mine.

I usually contained my need to rip Kensie's clothes off and fuck her six ways past Sunday, but the way she kissed me had me losing all control. There wasn't a hint of the usual cautious woman in this kiss. It was all tongue and passion. She slid her arms up over my shoulders and gripped her fingers onto me. I reached around with one arm and pulled her against me using the other hand to pull her leg up around my waist, giving me better access to just the right spot. I bent my legs and pressed myself against her capturing her moan in my mouth. I was so hard, though, that the friction was too much. *Easy killa*. I pulled back and she whined in protest.

I chuckled and nibbled on her bottom lip while at the same time pulling her sweater up and over her head. She didn't waste anytime with our brief parting and yanked mine over my head. Our lips crashed back together and a frenzied removal of our clothes began. Thank god for athletic pants, I ripped them off and stepped out of them at a world speed, all while sucking Kensie's tongue into my mouth. *I'm an Olympian.*

I ran my hands roughly up and down her back in daze when she gasped uncomfortably. "Did I hurt you?" Shit. I softened my grip and realized that my hand wasn't touching her skin directly, but a layer of plastic on her shoulder. "What is this?" I asked panting and very aware of my erection nudging into her hip. *Hang on, big guy.*

Kensie grinned nervously and peeled back the layer of plastic with a slight wince. "I paid a visit to Wes tonight. That's why I was so late getting here." She removed the covering completely and revealed a delicate tattoo of a dandelion on her shoulder. I inhaled deeply and moved behind her to gently trace the path of the seeds that floated up towards the base of her neck.

Then, I laughed. It was probably not the best response. The tattoo was amazing, though. I could tell it was Wes's work with the way it looked like a gray and black pencil sketch. He added soft wisps and lines that gave it a feminine feel, and it looked damn hot on that part of Kensie's body. Again though, I probably shouldn't have laughed.

The mixture of shock and pain in her face broke my heart and I had to quickly turn around to show her my back before she got upset. I heard her gasp loudly, "What the fuck," she said and I laughed even more. Kensie never cursed. She was laughing right along with me now. "When did he do this?" I felt her fingers trace over my own dandelion on the backside of my ribs. Mine was a much more masculine version with thick black lines and razor edges, but the meaning was all heart.

"This afternoon." I told her realizing she probably walked into the shop not long after I had left.

I felt her fingers brush my skin like tiny pinpricks across the spots where the seeds were scattered. "Why are they all over your scars." She placed a soft kiss on one of the bigger ones that held the majority of the chorus to the song. "Because you healed me." I felt her freeze behind me, but I kept talking. "When I met you, I felt alone and all out of hope, but you made me want to live again. You came and moved me in a new direction toward a life I've always wanted, but never thought I deserved."

I turned around and brushed my thumb across her trembling lip. "Me too." She said making us both laugh. "That story you told me on our first date, on the Ferris wheel, it was me. I was so afraid to live, to really let go and find my happiness, but you showed me how. You took away all my fears and in their place gave me love. You're my wind." She pointed at her tattoo where Wes had effectively inked swirls of wind.

"You're mine." I told her making her eyebrows scrunch up at me adorably in confusion. "You are right, that story I told you that night was about us, but you have it mixed up. I was the weed, and you were the wind."

She giggled at me her eyes sparkling, "It's a flower." I leaned in and kissed her nose, "If the dandelion is you, it's a flower." I agreed with her there.

My Kensie. She's my wildflower, finding me alone in a field and growing right along with me.

"So...we're soul mates." She stated, but had a questioning tone.

"We are soul mates." I kissed her lips now. My lower half was still poking her, getting impatient. "Now, where were we?" I asked her sliding my tongue in not waiting for an answer. She tilted her head and accepted my intrusion with a soft moan that had me hoisting her around my waist once again and carrying her to my bed.

***

I'm not sure how much longer I could lie here with Kensie laying on top of me and pretend I was asleep. I was up long before she was, and found myself watching her sleep peacefully. She had the adorable little snore noise that sounded like whistled puffs of air, like a little mouse. I still couldn't believe she was mine. She knew everything there was to know about me, and she still let me have her. In fact, by my calculations, she let me have her three times last night and was aiming for number four right now.

When her eyes fluttered open, I snapped mine shut.

I'd managed to keep them shut and fake sleep the entire time she explored my exposed chest with her soft hands and even softer lips. Now those wet kisses were trailing further and further down my torso making my arousal impossible to hide. When it twitched spontaneously against her thigh I felt her sit up and grunt questioningly. "Yeah, pretty girl, it even works when I'm asleep." I chuckled when she jumped backed in surprise.

She hit me over the face with her pillow and laughed, "How long have you been awake?"

I pushed the pillow aside and looked at her above me. Kensie was beautiful no doubt, but when she woke up first thing in the morning, she was stunning. Her face reflected the newness of the day, full of anticipation and promise. Maybe that's what had me riveted by the soft glow that seemed to surround her while she slept. It was something I wanted to wake up to every morning. "Long enough to know you snore." I boldly declared and flinched anticipating another pillow to face.

"Do not." She said and crossed her arms over her chest stubbornly.

"It's okay, it's adorable." I assured her winning me a soft smile. "Did you want to investigate me any further?" I cocked my eyebrow at her. "I seem to remember you were in this general vicinity." I motioned towards my erection making her giggle.

"No, I think I'm done here." She teased me and began to climb off.

I sat up and wrapped my arms around her waist pulling her back on top of me, "Well, I was just getting started." I whispered in her ear and got the shiver out of her I had wanted. I rolled her off of me and followed until I was on top of her. She spread her legs so I could fit myself in between them and against her heat. "You're already wet." I whispered hoarsely planting kisses along her neck. Number one best reason for having Kensie in my bed, waking up with her naked.

She whimpered out her response digging her fingers into my back and raising her hips up to meet me. I reached over to my nightstand and grabbed a condom from my drawer. I tore it open with my teeth and rolled it on before getting back to my task at hand. I slid down to graze her on the outside, but didn't push in yet. I had been so desperate for her last night that I gave her anything and everything. This morning, I wanted to tease Kensie a bit.

I rubbed my length against her lightly making myself twitch. While I sucked on the spot just below her ear that made her mew, I chanted to myself *Siegfried and Roy, Siegfried and Roy, Siegfried and Roy.* Out of nowhere, she raised her hips and thrust me into her to the hilt with my new favorite sound. Kensie's sex moan.

"Shit, Kensie," I grunted out, "You did it now. I'm not going to be able to last long."

She swiveled her hips causing my eyes to roll back momentarily. "Me either." She panted.

I sucked in a breath through my teeth maintaining some semblance of control. I pumped slowly in and out of her, torturously so. This was my new favorite feeling. Kensie, all hot and wet around me.

"Go faster." She urged me on. *Don't mind if I do.*

I grabbed her knees and pulled them up around me, hanging on to them while increasing my tempo. As I picked up speed, I made sure to nail her right in the spot that caused her to gasp every time. Over and over and over again until I felt her heat begin to constrict around me. She screamed my name as she exploded around me. Her pulsating grasp on me caused my own release, and I spilled myself into her. I collapsed on top of her tiny body, but made sure my arms were resting on either side of her now, holding most of my weight.

I peppered her moist skin with kisses and rolled off to lie beside her while she still panted, sprawled out across my bed. That was my new favorite sight. Kensie freshly fucked by none other than me. I mentally patted myself on the back. She sighed pleasantly and rolled to her side to face me. Those big brown eyes twinkled at me, for me, and my heart sucker punched my chest. "Move in with me."

I watched as her smile fall, but not in disappointment. In something else, shock maybe. It was probably too soon to ask someone to move in with you, but Kensie wasn't someone. She was *the one*, and from what life had cruelly taught me, when you are sure of something you don't wait. I was sure I wanted to wake up just like this every morning with her. I wanted to come home from work to our house, have our friends over to our house, and spend every single damn day with her in *our* house.

"Really?" She asked me softly, but I wasn't worried about her hesitation. If Kensie didn't like an idea, she'd let me know. She was worried that I wasn't sure.

"I'm positive." I smiled at her. "I want to hear you snore every morning forever." I laughed out and earned another pillow to the face. "No, really," I pushed the pillow aside again and leaned over her so I could look her directly in the eyes, "I want to live with you. I want you near me, always."

She blinked a few times and a huge smile spread across her gorgeous face. "I want to live with you, too." She said to me so positively that I didn't even question it as the truth.

CHAPTER 31

August

"I love you, but that's hideous." I told her affectionately.

"Thanks." Kensie's face lit up. I suggested we have Christmas dinner here at our place this year. She thought it was a great idea, and took it a step further by making it an Ugly Sweater Party. I doubted this brilliant idea of hers, until I found my perfect sweater that read *Happy Holladays,* complete with a fake gold chain. Kensie's sweater was more, well... it just might win the ugliest sweater prize tonight.

I sent her off to a girls' night with a bag of craft supplies and wine, and the next thing I knew I had to go pick her up along with the puff ball covered monstrosity of a sweater.

"I'm glad you suggested we have everyone over tonight." She leaned in and kissed me quickly. She learned right away that anything more than a peck made me want pin her to the bed.

"Me too," I muffled while slipping my sweater on over my head. "It's the perfect way to celebrate our new life together."

Kensie moved in the very day I asked her to. Wes helped me move all of her stuff from her dorm to my house, and we were officially living together. Wes harped on me the entire time about giving my domain over to a female. He said there would be twenty pillows on my bed and fruity smelling candles everywhere before I could even blink. He was right about the candles, but I didn't mind. Other than that, all Kensie suggested we change was the bare walls. That weekend, she helped me frame and hang pictures of Ella and all of our family and friends. That was when my house became our place, our home.

A knock sounded from the front door. One accidental viewing of my ass running naked down the hallway, and our friends learned not to waltz in unannounced anymore. "I got it." I kissed Kensie on the cheek and left her to finish getting ready.

I opened the door and Capri came in. "Merry Christmas!" She beamed at me and checked around my shoulder for Kensie.

"She's still getting dressed." I hugged her to me. "Merry Christmas, sis." She handed me the small box I was waiting for. I didn't want Kensie to see it, so I had it sent to my parent's house. "Thank you." I took the small box that held so much power it felt much heavier in my hand than it really was.

"You're welcome. She's going to love it." She assured me, but I already knew that. What I was most nervous about was what came after the gift.

Kensie

Christmas in our home had just become the best Christmas yet, much like Thanksgiving last month. There was a trend beginning with everything involving August being the best. Being here surrounded by our favorite people was the perfect way to spend the holiday.

I tidied up the kitchen while everyone else gathered in the living room. We decided not the exchange gifts this year, but to instead donate one to the youth center for the kids. August and I personally hand delivered every gift card our friends and family had purchased. I'd like to call them slackers, but really what do you get a teenager. Gabby was especially thrilled with the prospect of shopping with her girlfriends.

"Ready for the ornaments?" August poked his head into the kitchen. After Wes complained over not having anything to open tonight, Capri suggested an ornament exchange. August had been nagging me all night about that damn exchange.

"Yes," I said smiling through my irritation, "now it's time for the ornaments." He smiled wide at me and disappeared back into the living room. I peered in watching him take his seat on the couch in the room filled with my family.

Lennon sat perched on the arm of the chair that Wes sat in. She flicked his ear and I laughed to myself imagining what could have come out of his mouth. Capri sat on the floor just to the right of Wes's chair, and I didn't miss the way his leg kept brushing against her shoulder. She glanced up at him and smiled shyly when he grinned down at her adoringly. Just a harmless crush my ass. I hoped those two would figure it out soon.

"You coming out soon to exchange ornaments, honey?" My mom came through the kitchen with an empty cookie platter. What was it with these people and the ornaments?

"Yes, all ready." I leaned into her when she wrapped her arm around me. My mom and John were still dating. Well, I guess they actually defined themselves as dating after I walked in on them in her living room. I shuddered at the image. Some things can never be unseen.

I get that now.

I couldn't be happier for her. After years of putting herself last to make sure I was adjusting as best I could, she had finally made a life for herself. I couldn't have picked a better guy than John for my mom either. Over the last few months he had taken on a role in my life that my own father couldn't seem to do in years.

That's was part of why he was not here tonight. My dad made a decent effort at calling me throughout the last weeks to say hello and see how I was. That was far more than he had ever done, so I had to give him that. He called last week and invited me to the house for Christmas, but I declined. August and I already had plans here with everyone, and even if we didn't I wasn't really interested in spending the holidays with my dad, not yet anyway.

I took my place on the couch snuggled up

next to August and he leaned in to give me a kiss. "This one's from mom and dad." He said unwrapping a small box Capri had brought over. His parents had wanted to be here, but his dad woke up that morning with a terrible case of the flu. I made sure to make a plate of leftovers for Capri to take to his mom.

I met them for the first time as August's girlfriend a few weeks ago just after August and I reconciled. They embraced me into their family immediately, and it was clear to me how August and Capri had become such warm living people.

August's eyes grew wide when he pulled out the tiny ornament with a snowman couple toasting with champagne flutes. "What's it say?" I asked leaning over him to get a better look. "Congratulations?" I asked.

The room was silent except for Wes, who coughed out a laugh, "Way to go Steve and Donna." Lennon and Capri simultaneously assaulted Wes, Lennon with an elbow to his temple, and Capri with a pinch to his leg.

"It's for moving in together." Capri spoke up, "To mark the year you guys got together." Oh. Well, that was a sweet idea.

Capri reached under the tree and pulled out another box. "This one is for you, Lennon." She tossed the box up behind her. Lennon grinned and opened the gift.

"Badass!" She yelled when she held up the silver mocking jay ornament. "Thanks Capri."

Capri picked up another box under the tree when both Wes and August yelled, "No!" I jumped into my mom.

"What the heck?" I asked my heart still

pounding in my chest.

"Sorry," August spoke more calmly." Not that one, Capri." She laughed at him.

"Relax, I was setting it aside and grabbing a different one." She smiled knowingly back at him and then at me. Okay, something was definitely going on here.

"Here, Capri," Wes reached down across her rigid body, "This one is yours." Yeah, before we had all exchanged names, Wes came to me and asked specifically for Capri's. He said something about getting a free ornament with the gift he ordered his mom, but I wasn't buying it.

Capri sat frozen and a bit shocked staring at the box Wes had placed in her hand. "Well, open it." He urged her excitedly. She shook herself out of her shock and opened up the box. She pulled out a tiny crystal ornament in the shape of a paintbrush. She placed her hand over her heart and held the ornament up to the light where it caught the shades of the colorful tree reflecting back onto the room. "It's beautiful." She said in awe more to herself than any of us.

Wes was fidgeting in his chair nervously, but calmed some when Lennon patted him on the shoulder and nodded her approval. Capri turned to look up at Wes. "It's perfect, thank you." Wes smiled so hard I swear his dimples were going to pop right out. That was definitely not a free ornament. That was something he put a lot of thought into, and I was proud of him.

August

I completely panicked when Capri picked up Kensie's gift. She had specific instructions to wait until the end of the exchange to give it to her. As grueling and not so riveting the whole thing was, it had worked out to be the perfect opportunity. Next year, though, I'd have to suggest a different type of exchange to liven things up a bit. Maybe a beer exchange? That's genius.

The room suddenly started to buzz with anticipation.

Kensie's mom fidgeted where she sat pressed against John's side, who laughed loudly for no apparent reason other than what he was about to witness. The guy had always been pretty happy, but now that he was seeing Kensie's mom, he was downright jovial.

Across the room, Lennon bounced up and down on the arm of the chair with cell phone in hand. I had asked her to take some pictures, and she squealed her reply. Piercingly, squealed her reply. I looked across the room to my best friend who gave me an encouraging wink, who had been there for me through every horror and now every triumph in my life. He could have walked away. He could have left me in my misery to go have some fun of his own, but he never did. He helped carry me to this point in my life. They all did.

"Alright Kensie, looks like this one is yours." Capri clenched her teeth in a smile and giggled, passing it to Kensie. She would make an awful actress. *What the hell?* Kensie mouthed to me, and all I could do was shrug my shoulders. Like my heart wasn't going all Jackie Chan in my chest. Like my body wasn't creating it's own sauna in my ugly sweater. Like I wasn't going to vomit all over her brand new mint green Chuck's I gave her this morning. *Open the damn box, Kensie.* "Open the box!"

Kensie

"Did you just yell at me?" I asked August, kind of amused. He was freaking out next to me. "No, well, yeah, but just, uh, I just really need to go to the bathroom." Wes roared in laughter across the room and Capri looked at August like he was a world-class idiot.

"So, go to the bathroom." I didn't see what the big deal was. I knew he wasn't completely excited about the ornament exchange, but he had been acting like it was the worst kind of torture, sighing and groaning each time someone else took a turn.

"Just open the box." He said awkwardly controlled. I shook my head and continued to unwrap the ornament. By process of elimination, I knew it was from him. It was probably against some sort of gift exchange rules that you couldn't receive a gift from your significant other, but I was glad our first ornament was one he had picked out for me.

I could feel the heat radiating off August when I peeled off the last piece of wrapping paper. I wish he'd just go to the bathroom already. I took off the lid to the tiny box and reached in pulling the ornament out by a delicate gold ribbon. I held it up in front of me and my mouth fell open in a surprised gasp.

He had gotten me an ornament with a quote from my favorite book Pride and Prejudice. He certainly had help with this one because only Capri and Lennon knew how much I loved Elizabeth Bennet. Don't even get me started on Mr. Darcy. That man is the epitome of book boyfriends, and in my hand, I held an ornament with his words on them. *"You must allow me to tell you how ardently I admire and love you."*

My heart warmed at the words. I had once read them and dreamt of having someone to love me that intensely. I smiled towards August. There he was. "I love it. I can't believe you even found this." He smiled at me, but I caught something different to it. That's when he slipped his lip into his teeth and bit on it. He was nervous.

"I know you love that book," he said, "but I wasn't sure if this was from a good part or not."

Was that a sniffle? I looked over to my mom quickly looked to the kitchen. Odd, I smiled back at August. "It's the best part of the whole story. It's when Mr. Darcy finally proposes to…" August fell onto both of his knees on the floor in front of me and I gasped in awareness.

"What part is it, Kensie?" He asked me again in a small smirk.

"It's *the* part." I was crying now, but I tried to talk through my tears, "It's when Darcy proposes to Elizabeth."

He held his hands up in front of me holding a tiny velvet box. I looked at him through my tears. "Truth or dare, Kensie?" I laughed then and heard the giggles and sniffles around the room reminding me that our family surrounded us.

"Dare." I said intentionally because I trusted him. I trusted him profoundly. He opened the box, but I could only tell by the movement and gasps in the room. My eyes were fixated on the beautiful soul behind his eyes. It was genuine, and it was kind. It was devoted and it was attentive. It was strong and steady, but above all, loved fiercely.

"Marry me?" He asked softly, and I lost it. I sobbed and hiccupped and fell to the floor on my knees with him.

He held me, and laughed into my hair, when I heard Wes yell from behind him, "You'd better answer or we'll make him serenade you."

I pulled away and looked into August's eyes. I wanted him to see into me when I answered him, just as I had seen into him when he asked me. "Yes."

August

Thank God. For a minute I was second-guessing how quickly I had done this. I'd known since the day I met her that she would be my wife, and I wasn't much for waiting on things you know to be true. Life wavered too often to hesitate. When she pulled back and looked me in the eyes, really looked into them, I knew my answer.

Cheers erupted in the room amidst the

sniffles and random clapping when she gave me our yes. I smashed my lips to hers and kissed into her salty tears and beautiful smile. I held her face in my hands and placed my nose to hers. "I love you." I whispered those three words that would never encompass the feelings I held for this woman, but yet said it all.

"I love you." She whispered back. That was all I needed in this life. The promise that when things were blurred and distorted, that there would be someone planted firmly beside me to simply be my truth.

Acknowledgments

My sincerest thanks go to my editor Autumn Hull at The Autumn Review. She not only helped in making this book ready for publishing, but she also aided me on this brand new experience of becoming a self-published author. For her guidance, expertise, and kindness I am truly grateful.

To my beta readers, especially Rebecca Jackson and Tiffany Pettijohn, thank you for your encouragement and your helpful thoughts and suggestions.

Thank you to the bloggers and editors that were there for me in the beginning of this journey, especially Amy R, Kelly F., and Amy K at 101 Ways to Make Love to a Spoon and Caryn Watson at Watz Books and Teasers for posting my first teasers. Thank you author B.L. Berry for your friendship, support, and guidance, and thank you to all of the authors at New Adult Authors Unite!.

To Victoria Routolo. Without her this book wouldn't exist. Thank you for reading everything, the good and the bad. Thank you for your late night texts and emails helping me to sort things out, and for helping me to create these characters and developing a story line that I am proud of. Thank you for your constant encouragement and friendship.

Thank you to my family, friends, and my wonderful husband. Thank you for the Mac Book you bought me for Christmas so that I could begin this journey. You offered me an endless amount of encouragement and support throughout the past year. I love you.

About the Author

Kimberly Rose is a self-proclaimed binge reader, devouring books one after another. She's creates characters and stories in the same way maintaining a notebook of thoughts and ideas. Truth in Wildflowers is the first time two characters have found a home in a full-length book.

Kim lives with her husband and daughter wherever the

Navy takes them. So far home has been San Diego,

California, Charleston, South Carolina, and next up Oahu, Hawaii. Yes, she's lucky and she knows it.

When she's not sitting on the couch with her laptop writing, Kim can be found with her nose stuck in her ereader or hidden under endless amounts of tulle and glitter with her daughter.

I'd love to hear from you!

Email: authorkrose@yahoo.com
Facebook: http://bit.ly/FBAuthorKimberlyRose
Goodreads: http://bit.ly/GRAuthorKimberlyRose
Blog: http://authorkimberlyrose.wordpress.com

Made in the USA
San Bernardino, CA
16 November 2014